INTRODUCTION BY DOROTHY CANFIELD FISHER

20 GrAND

SHORT STORIES

COVER/SHARON WAY

SCHOLASTIC BOOK SERVICES

NEW YORK • TORONTO • LONDON • AUCKLAND • SYDNEY • TOKYO

For reprint permission grateful acknowledgment is made to:

Thomas E. Adams for "Sled" by Thomas E. Adams from *The Sewanee Review*, copyright © 1961 by Thomas E. Adams.

Brandt & Brandt for "So Much Unfairness of Things" by C. D. B. Bryan, copyright © 1962 by The New Yorker Magazine, Inc.; "A Tooth for Paul Revere" from THE SELECTED WORKS OF STEPHEN VINCENT BENÉT, copyright 1937 by Stephen Vincent Benét, copyright renewed © 1965 by Thomas C. Benét, Stephanie B. Mahin and Rachel Benét Lewis.

Ernst, Cane, Berner & Gitlin for "Young Man Axelbrod" from SELECTED SHORT STORIES OF SINCLAIR LEWIS, copyright 1917 by Century Company, copyright 1945 by Sinclair Lewis.

Esquire, Inc., and Jesse Stuart for "Split Cherry Tree" by Jesse Stuart, copyright 1938 by Esquire, Inc.

Martha Foley for "One with Shakespeare" by Martha Foley from STORY Magazine, copyright 1930, 1957 by Martha Foley.

Albert Halper for "Prelude" by Albert Halper from *Harper's* Magazine, copyright 1938 by Harper's Magazine, Inc., copyright renewed 1966 by Albert Halper.

Harcourt, Brace & World, Inc., for "Rope" from FLOWERING JUDAS AND OTHER STORIES, copyright 1930, 1935, 1958, 1963 by Katherine Anne Porter.

Holt, Rinehart and Winston, Inc., for "The Heydey of the Blood" from HILLSBORO PEOPLE by Dorothy Canfield Fisher, copyright 1915 by Holt, Rinehart and Winston, Inc., copyright 1943 by Dorothy Canfield Fisher; "A Start in Life" from IOWA INTERIORS by Ruth Suckow, copyright 1926 by Alfred A. Knopf, Inc., copyright © 1954 by Ruth Suckow Nuhn.

Elliott Merrick for "Without Words" from FROST AND FIRE by Elliott Merrick.

Harold Ober Associates Inc., for "Fumble" by Katharine Brush, copyright 1928 by Katharine Brush.

Random House, Inc., for "After the Ball" from EMILY by Sally Benson, copyright 1938 and renewed 1966 by Sally Benson; "Strawberry Ice Cream Soda" from MIXED COMPANY by Irwin Shaw, copyright 1938 and renewed 1966 by Irwin Shaw.

Paul R. Reynolds, Inc., for "A Student in Economics" from NO MORE TRUMPETS by George Milburn, copyright 1933 by Harcourt, Brace and Company.

William Saroyan for "Romance" from PEACE, IT'S WONDERFUL by William Saroyan.

Scholastic Magazines, Inc., for "Sixteen" by Maureen Daly, copyright 1938 by Scholastic Corporation, copyright renewed 1966 by Maureen Daly.

Harry Sylvester for "Eight-Oared Crew" by Harry Sylvester from *Collier's*.

The Viking Press, Inc., for "The Chrysanthemums" from THE LONG VALLEY by John Steinbeck, copyright 1937, 1965 by John Steinbeck; "Clothe the Naked" from THE PORTABLE DOROTHY PARKER, copyright 1938, 1966 by Dorothy Parker.

ISBN: 0-590-08909-9

18 17 16 15 14 13 12 11 10 9

Printed in the U.S.A.

EDITOR'S NOTE

When this book was first published in 1941, it was described by Scholastic's editors as containing "twenty of the best stories that have appeared in *Scholastic Magazine* during the past twenty years." The astonishing thing about these stories is that they show no signs of age. They are readable, interesting, and relevant today — just as they were when they first appeared.

Only two stories have been dropped from the original twenty. These have been replaced by "Sled" and "So Much Unfairness of Things," two stories recently published in another Scholastic magazine, *Literary Cavalcade*. The reader can see for himself whether these two stories meet the high standards set by the original volume.

The essay by Dorothy Canfield Fisher which introduced the first edition of *Twenty Grand* is reprinted on the following pages. Mrs. Fisher described these stories as "living art, portraying the actual life of the present." While many of the stories are set in the "present" of the 1920s and 1930s, their characters are universal. Their thoughts and feelings and problems are part of the actual life of each new generation. The reader will find reflections of himself in *Twenty Grand*.

— THE EDITORS

INTRODUCTION

My gray hairs are honored by being asked to write an introduction for this volume of young stories for young people. The tales are by young authors too. Half, or almost, of the excellent stories in this volume were written by people in their twenties and thirties. Pushed far back under the eaves of the attic lie the photographs which hung on the classroom walls of my school days — the venerables, bald or bearded in white, who, to the young folks of that period, represented literature. That I am old enough to remember those photographs of Hawthorne, Longfellow, Whittier, and Lowell, makes me a better person to write this introduction than any of the brilliant younger people whose names are in the table of contents.

For it is only set in the perspective of time that the value of such a collection of fiction for high-school-age young people can be seen. One must be old enough to compare *Scholastic Magazine* with the magazine reading of adolescents forty years ago, to appreciate what it means. I'm not referring only to the fact that these are well-written tales of fine literary quality. It's not just a question of furnishing young folks with good, as well as readable, fiction. Something far more vital to our country's civilization is involved. This collection, and the five hundred tales as good as these, published in *Scholastic Magazine,* from which these were chosen, are a part of an epic change in the English teaching given to our teenage boys and girls. A sinister barrier is being broken down which, in earlier generations, cut young people off from any notion that literary art might be a factor in their own lives, might be part of the raw material of understanding themselves and their nation.

The "classics" were the only forms of fiction recognized as literature by the school authorities of my long-ago youth. By definition a classic is a production the value of which is proved by its having passed through the sieve of public opinion and taste during several generations. Hence the subject matter of classics is the life of a period left behind in the past. It is far away from the exciting new day to which every young person opens his eyes every morning.

Fifty and forty years ago, high-school-age young folks (I refer of course to the majority of them) read stories of good literary quality in order to pass their English examinations. When they read for fun or pleasure or to be moved, they expected as a matter of course, as an inevitable result of the nature of things, to read trash, or stories which would seem very mild, superficial, and childish to the mid-teens of today. The stories of college life which were written for my generation to read in the year or so before we expected to go to college would now to the keener ear of modern, pre-college-age boys and girls sound trivial, false, or idiotically romantic. The stories about college life in this collection are, comparatively speaking, as rawly realistic as Zola's novels to his contemporaries. They attempt to tell something of the truth

about college life. Compared to these portrayals of
real human beings, struggling in college as everywhere else with material difficulties and with the
complexities of human nature, the football-hero
and pretty-girl romance of my youth was a shiny-
paper, come-on prospectus, illustrated with posed
and much retouched photographs of actors and
actresses. Yet the enchantingly foolish romanticism
of Saroyan's story in this collection shows that
honesty in fiction does not exclude young love. We
young readers could have found a poignant por-
trayal of early adolescent emotion such as that in
"Sixteen" — and of course richer, deeper, and
more various — but only if we read *War and
Peace,* which, believe me, we did not at sixteen,
most of us. "Stories for young folks" always ended
cheerfully in those days, with everything coming
out all right for everybody. Not for us was the
harsh bite of reality as in Ruth Suckow's beautiful
story in this collection. This little masterpiece —
for I think it no less — paints a picture as startling
in its truth to each small detail of a familiar scene
as a Dutch genre painting. But unspoken, implied,
written between the lines with invisible ink which
leaps clear and black to the eye by the end of this
soberly realistic picture of a nice, everyday, ordinary, pleasant American home, is the beginning
of the process of turning a whole, natural human
being into a member of the "lower classes." In my
youth the idea that our American democracy was
not perfectly realized in every aspect was never
even mildly suggested to us in any story — let
alone one wringing the heart with remorseful sorrow like "A Start in Life." Publishers then expected authors to write cheerful stories with happy
endings for young folks. Yet young folks were then,
as now, as always, shaken to the heart by the fevers,

the exaltations, despairs, joys, aspiration of adolescence. They were perfectly aware that the fairy tales written for their consumption had no connection with their own inner, or outer, lives.

Now this separation of the material of art from the stuff of daily life is the basis of the philistine attitude toward art in the most poisonous and dangerous meaning of the word. It cuts the ordinary people of the general reading public off from living art, portraying the actual life of the present; and while this is rather hard on ordinary people, it is fatal to art, for only feeble tendrils can sprout from an art-stem not rooted in acceptance by humanity.

Such a collection as this is a door cut through a stone wall which used to separate ordinary reading Americans from contemporary writing of good literary quality. People who, in their teens, have acquired the habit of getting their reading pleasure not from sentimental or sensational hokum, but from honest, vivid, thoughtful interpretations of American life and American character, cannot but form a public vastly more favorable to the development of seriously practiced literary art than were preceding generations.

The stories in this book, moving, satiric, gay, sad, romantic, realistic, the constant presentation in *Scholastic* of fiction of this quality, and the work done in general by the best English teaching in our high schools — they are all milestones along a new road, undreamed of half a century ago. It leads ahead into a future, which, to my elderly eyes, looks remarkably like a golden age of writing.

And one reason I feel confident of such a golden age is that I know the kind of writing high school students themselves are capable of turning out. For years Scholastic has been conducting its Writing Awards — a remarkable and highly rewarding annual competition for the purpose of encouraging talent among high school students interested in creative writing. I have served as one of the judges in the short-story division of the Awards and, along with the other judges, have been amazed year after year at the quality of those stories. (If you have your doubts, turn to Maureen Daly's "Sixteen" in this volume. That story won first prize in its year — and Maureen was sixteen when she wrote it!) Today these young people are reading the best that's being written; tomorrow they will write the best that's being read.

DOROTHY CANFIELD FISHER

Arlington, Vermont, 1941

CONTENTS

1/PRELUDE

I was coming home from school, carrying my books by a strap, when I passed Gavin's poolroom and saw the big guys hanging around. They were standing in front near the windows, looking across the street. Gavin's has a kind of thick window curtain up to eye level, so all I saw was their heads. The guys were looking at Mrs. Oliver, who lately has started to get talked about. Standing in her window across the street, Mrs. Oliver was doing her nails. Her nice red hair was hanging loose down her back. She certainly is a nice-looking woman. She comes to my father's newspaper stand on the corner and buys five or six movie magazines a week, also the afternoon papers. Once she felt me under the chin, and laughed. My father laughed, too, stamping about in his old worn leather jacket to keep warm. My old man stamps a lot because he has leg pains and he's always complaining about a heavy cold in his head.

When I passed the poolroom one or two guys came out. "Hey, Ike, how's your good-looking sister?" they called, but I didn't turn around. The guys are eighteen or nineteen and haven't ever had a job in their life. "What they need is work," my father is always saying when they bother him too much. "They're not bad; they get that way because there's nothing to do," and he tries to explain the meanness of their ways. But I can't see it like my father. I hate those fellas and I hope every one of them dies under a truck. Every time I come home from school past Lake Street they jab me, and every time my sister Syl comes along they say things. So when one of them, Fred Gooley, calls, "Hey, Ike, how's your sister?" I don't answer. Besides, Ike isn't my name anyway. It's Harry.

I passed along the sidewalk, keeping close to the curb. Someone threw half an apple but it went over my head. When I went a little farther someone threw a stone. It hit me in the back of the leg and stung me, but it didn't hurt much. I kept a little toward the middle of the sidewalk because I saw a woman coming the other way and I knew they wouldn't throw.

When I reached the corner under the Elevated, two big news trucks were standing with their motors going, giving my father the latest editions. The drivers threw the papers onto the sidewalk with a nice easy roll so the papers wouldn't get hurt. The papers are bound with that heavy yellow cord which my father saves and sells to the junkyard when he fills up a bag. "All right, Silverstein," a driver calls out. "We'll give you a five-star at six," and both trucks drove off.

The drivers are nice fellas and when they take back the old papers they like to kid my old man. They say, "Hey, you old banker, when are you gonna retire?" or, "Let's roll him, boys, he's got bags of gold in his socks." Of course they know my old man isn't wealthy and that the bags in the inside of the newsstand hold only copper pennies. But they like to kid him and they know he likes it. Sometimes the guys from Gavin's pitch in, but the truck drivers would flatten them if they ever got rough with my old man.

I came up to the newsstand and put my school books inside. "Well, Pa," I said, "you can go to Florida now." So my Pa went to "Florida," that is, a chair near the radiator that Nick Pappas lets him use in his restaurant. He has to use Nick's place because our own flat is too far away, almost a quarter-mile off.

While my father was in Nick's place another truck came to a stop. They dropped off a big load of early sports editions and yelled. "Hey, there, Harry, how's the old man?" I checked off the papers, yelling back, "He's okay; he's in Nick's." Then the truck drove away and the two helpers waved.

I stood around, putting the papers on the stand and making a few sales. The first ten minutes after coming home from school and taking care of the newsstand always excites me. Maybe it's the traffic. The trucks and cars pound along like anything and of course there's the Elevated right up above you which thunders to beat the band. We have our newsstand right up against a big El post and the stand is a kind of cabin which you enter from the side. But we hardly use it, only in the late morning and around two p.m. when business isn't very rushing. Customers like to see you stand outside over the papers ready for business and not hidden inside where they can't get a look at you at all. Besides, you have to poke your head out and stretch your arm to get the pennies, and kids can swipe magazines from the sides if you don't watch. So we most always stand outside the newsstand, my father and me, and my sister. Anyhow, I like it. I like everything about selling papers for my father. The fresh air gets me and I like to talk to customers and see the rush when people are let

out from work. And the way the news trucks bring
all the new editions so we can see the latest headlines, like a bank got held up on the South Side
on Sixty-third Street, or the Cubs are winning
their tenth straight and have a good chance to cop
the pennant, is exciting.

The only thing I don't like is those guys from
Gavin's. But since my father went to the police
station to complain they don't come around so
often. My father went to the station a month ago
and said the gang was bothering him, and Mr.
Fenway, he's the desk sergeant there, said, "Don't
worry any more about it, Mr. Silverstein; we'll take
care of it. You're a respectable citizen and taxpayer
and you're entitled to protection. We'll take care
of it." And the next day they sent over a patrol-
man who stood around almost two hours. The
gang from Gavin's saw him and started to go
away, but the cop hollered, "Now listen, don't
bother this old fella. If you bother him any I'll
have to run some of you in."

And then one of the guys recognized that the
cop was Butch, Fred Gooley's cousin. "Listen
who's talkin'," he yells back. "Hey, Fred, they got
your cousin Butch takin' care of the Yid." They
said a lot of other things until the cop got mad
and started after them. They ran faster than
lightning, separating into alleys. The cop came
back empty-handed and said to my father, "It'll
blow over, Mr. Silverstein; they won't give you any
more trouble." Then he went up the street, turning into Steuben's bar.

Well, all this happened three or four weeks ago
and so far the gang has let us alone. They stopped
pulling my sixteen-year-old sister by her sweater
and when they pass the stand going home to supper all they give us is dirty looks. During the last
three or four days, however, they passed by and

kinda muttered, calling my father a Communist banker and me and my sister Reds. My father says they really don't mean it, it's hard times and bad feelings, and they got to put the blame on somebody, so they put the blame on us. It's certain speeches on the radio and the pieces in some of the papers, my father told us. "Something is happening to some of the people and we got to watch our step," he says.

I am standing there hearing the traffic and thinking it over when my little fat old man comes out from Nick's, looking like he liked the warm air in Nick's place. My old man's cheeks looked rosy, but his cheeks are that way from high blood pressure and not from good health. "Well, colonel," he says smiling, "I am back on the job." So we stand around, the two of us, taking care of the trade. I hand out change snappy and say thank you after each sale. My old man starts to stamp around in a little while and, though he says nothing, I know he's got pains in his legs again. I look at the weather forecast in all the papers and some of them say flurries of snow and the rest of them say just snow. "Well, Pa," I tell my old man, "maybe I can go skating tomorrow if it gets cold again."

Then I see my sister coming from high school carrying her brief case and heading this way. Why the heck doesn't she cross over so she won't have to pass the poolroom, I say to myself; why don't she walk on the other side of the street? But that's not like Sylvia; she's a girl with a hot temper, and when she thinks she is right you can't tell her a thing. I knew she wouldn't cross the street and then cross back, because according to her, why, that's giving in. That's telling those hoodlums that you're afraid of their guts. So she doesn't cross over but walks straight on. When she comes by the pool hall two guys come out and say something to her. She just holds herself tight and goes right on past them both. When she finally comes up she gives me a poke in the side. "Hello, you Mickey Mouse, what mark did you get in your algebra exam?" I told her I got A, but the truth is I got a C.

"I'll check up on you later," she says to me. "Pa, if he's lying to us we'll fine him ten years!"

My father started to smile and said, "No, Harry is a good boy, two years is enough."

So we stand around kidding and pretty soon, because the wind is coming so sharp up the street, my old man has to "go to Florida" for a while once more. He went into Nick's for some "sunshine," he said, but me and Syl could tell he had the pains again. Anyway, when he was gone we didn't say anything for a while. Then Hartman's furniture factory, which lately has been checking out early, let out and we were busy making sales to the men. They came up the sidewalk, a couple of hundred, all anxious to get home, so we had to work snappy. But Syl is a fast worker, faster than me, and we took care of the rush all right. Then we stood waiting for the next rush from the Hillman's cocoa factory up the block to start.

We were standing around when something hit me in the head, a half of a rotten apple. It hurt a little. I turned quick but didn't see anybody, but Syl started yelling. She was pointing to a big El post across the street behind which a guy was hiding.

"Come on, show your face," my sister was saying. "Come on, you hero, show your yellow face!" But the guy sneaked away, keeping the post between. Syl turned to me and her face was boiling. "The rats! It's not enough with all the trouble over in Europe; they have to start it here."

Just then our old man came out of Nick's and when he saw Syl's face he asked what was the matter.

"Nothing," she says. "Nothing. I'm just thinking."

But my old man saw the half of a rotten apple on the sidewalk, and at first he didn't say anything but I could see he was worried. "We just have to stand it," he said like he was speaking to himself, "we just have to stand it. If we give up the newsstand where else can we go?"

"Why do we have to stand it?" I exploded, almost yelling. "Why do we — "

But Mrs. Oliver just then came up to the stand, so I had to wait on her. Besides, she's a good customer and there's more profit on two or three magazines than from a dozen papers.

"I'll have a copy of *Film Fan*, a copy of *Breezy Stories*, and a copy of *Movie Stars on Parade*," she says. I go and reach for the copies.

"Harry is a nice boy," Mrs. Oliver told my father, patting my arm. "I'm very fond of him."

"Yes, he's not bad," my father answered smiling. "Only he has a hot temper once in a while."

But who wouldn't have one, that's what I wanted to say! Who wouldn't? Here we stand around minding our own business and the guys won't let us alone. I tell you sometimes it almost drives me crazy. We don't hurt anybody and we're trying to make a living, but they're always picking on us and won't let us alone. It's been going on for a couple of years now, and though my old man says it'll pass with the hard times, I know he's worried because he doesn't believe what he says. He reads the papers as soon as he gets them from the delivery trucks and lately the news about Europe is all headlines and I can see that it makes him sick. My old man has a soft heart and every time

he sees in the papers that something bad in Europe
has happened again he seems to grow older and he
stands near the papers kind of small and all
alone. I tell you, sometimes it almost drives me
crazy. My old man should be down in Florida,
where he can get healthy, not in Nick Pappas'
"Florida," but down in real Florida where you
have to go by train. That's where he should be.
Then maybe his legs would be all right and he
wouldn't have that funny color in his cheeks. Since
our mother died last year it seems the doctor's
treatments don't make him any better, and he has
to skip a treatment once in a while because he
says it costs too much. But when he stands there
with a customer chuckling you think he's healthy
and hasn't got any worries and you feel maybe he
has a couple thousand in the bank.

And another thing, what did he mean when he
said something two days ago when the fellas from
Gavin's passed by and threw a stone at the stand?
What did he mean, that's what I want to know.
Gooley had a paper rolled up with some headlines
about Europe on it and he wiggled it at us and
my father looked scared. When they were gone my
father said something to me, which I been thinking and thinking about. My pa said we got
to watch our step extra careful now because
there's no other place besides this country where
we can go. We've always been picked on, he said,
but we're up against the last wall now, he told me,
and we got to be calm because if they start going
after us here, there's no other place where we can
go. I been thinking and thinking about that, especially the part about the wall. When he said
that, his voice sounded funny and I felt like our
newsstand was a kind of island and if that went
we'd be under the waves.

"Harry, what are you thinking of?" Mrs. Oliver

asked me. "Don't I get any change?" She was laughing.

And then I came down from the clouds and found she had given me two quarters. I gave her a nickel change. She laughed again. "When he looks moody and kind of sore like that, Mr. Silverstein, I think he's cute."

My old man crinkled up his eyes and smiled. "Who can say, Mrs. Oliver. He should only grow up to be a nice young man and a good citizen and a credit to his country. That's all I want."

"I'm sure Harry will," Mrs. Oliver answered, then talked to Syl awhile and admired Syl's new sweater and was about to go away. But another half of a rotten apple came over and splashed against the stand. Some of it splashed against my old man's coat sleeve. Mrs. Oliver turned around and got mad.

"Now you boys leave Mr. Silverstein alone! You've been pestering him long enough! He's a good American citizen who doesn't hurt anybody! You leave him alone!"

"Yah!" yelled Gooley, who ducked behind an El post with two other guys. "Yah! Sez you!"

"You leave him alone!" hollered Mrs. Oliver.

"Aw, go peddle your papers," Gooley answered. "Go run up a rope."

"Don't pay any attention to them," Syl told Mrs. Oliver. "They think they're heroes, but to most people they're just yellow rats."

I could tell by my old man's eyes that he was nervous and wanted to smooth things over, but Syl didn't give him a chance. When she gets started and she knows she's in the right not even the Governor of the State could make her keep quiet.

"Don't pay attention to them," she said in a cutting voice while my old man looked anxious. "When men hide behind Elevated posts and

throw rotten apples at women you know they're
not men but just things that wear pants. In Europe they put brown shirts on them and call them
saviors of civilization. Here they haven't got the
shirts yet and hang around poolrooms."

Every word cut like a knife and the guys ducked
away. If I or my father would have said it we
would have been nailed with some rotten fruit,
but the way Syl has of getting back at those guys
makes them feel like yellow dogs. I guess that's
why they respect her even though they hate her,
and I guess that's why Gooley and one or two of
his friends are always trying to get next to her and
date her up.

Mrs. Oliver took Syl's side and was about to say
something more when Hillman's cocoa factory up
the block let out and the men started coming up
the street. The 4:45 rush was on and we didn't
have time for anything, so Mrs. Oliver left, saying
she'd be back when the blue-streak edition of the
News would arrive. Me and Syl were busy handing
out the papers and making change and our pa
helped us while the men took their papers and
hurried for the El. It started to get darker and
colder and the traffic grew heavier along the
street.

Then the *Times* truck, which was a little late,
roared up and dropped a load we were waiting
for. I cut the strings and stacked the papers and
when my father came over and read the first page
he suddenly looked scared. In his eyes there was
that hunted look I had noticed a couple of days
ago. I started to look at the first page of the paper
while my old man didn't say a word. Nick came to
the window and lit his new neon light and waved
to us. Then the light started flashing on and off,
flashing on the new headlines. It was all about
Austria and how people were fleeing toward the

borders and trying to get out of the country before it was too late. My old man grew sick and
looked kind of funny and just stood there. Sylvia,
who is active in the high-school social science club,
began to read the *Times* out loud and started an-
alyzing the news to us; but our pa didn't need her
analysis and kept standing there kind of small
with that hunted look on his face. He looked sick
all right. It almost drove me crazy.

"For Pete's sake," I yelled at Syl. "Shut up, shut
up!"

Then she saw our pa's face, looked at me, and
didn't say anything more.

In a little while it was after five and Syl had to
go home and make supper. "I'll be back in an
hour," she told me. "Then Pa can go home and
rest a bit and me and you can take care of the
stand." I said all right.

After she was gone it seemed kind of lonesome.
I couldn't stop thinking about what my father
had said about this being our last wall. It got me
feeling funny and I didn't want to read the papers
any more. I stood there feeling queer, like me and
my old man were standing on a little island and
the waves were coming up. There was still a lot of
traffic and a few people came up for papers, but
from my old man's face I could tell he felt the
same as me.

But pretty soon some more editions began coming and we had to check and stack them up. More
men came out from factories on Walnut Street and
we were busy making sales. It got colder than ever
and my old man began to stamp again. "Go into
Nick's, Pa," I told him. "I can handle it out here."
But he wouldn't do it because just then another
factory let out and we were swamped for a while.
"Hi, there, Silverstein," some of the men called to
him, "what's the latest news, you king of the

press?" They took the papers, kidding him, and hurried up the stairs to the Elevated, reading all about Austria and going home to eat. My father kept staring at the headlines and couldn't take his eyes off the print where it said that soldiers were pouring across the border and mobs were robbing people they hated and spitting on them and making them go down on their hands and knees to scrub the streets. My old man's eyes grew small, like he had the toothache and he shook his head like he was sick. "Pa, go into Nick's," I told him. He just stood there, sick over what he read.

Then the guys from Gavin's poolroom began passing the stand on their way home to supper after a day of just killing time. At first they looked as if they wouldn't bother us. One or two of them said something mean to me, but my old man and me didn't answer. If you don't answer hoodlums, my father once told me, sometimes they let you alone.

But then it started. The guys who passed by came back and one of them said, "Let's have a little fun with the Yids." That's how it began. A couple of them took some magazines from the rack and said they wanted to buy a copy and started reading.

In a flash I realized it was all planned out. My father looked kind of worried but stood quiet. There were about eight or nine of them, all big boys around eighteen and nineteen, and for the first time I got scared. It was just after six o'clock and they had picked a time when the newspaper trucks had delivered the five-star and when all the factories had let out their help and there weren't many people about. Finally one of them smiled at Gooley and said, "Well, this physical culture magazine is mighty instructive, but don't you think we ought to have some of the exercises demonstrated?" Gooley said, "Sure, why not?"

So the first fella pointed to some pictures in the magazine and wanted me to squat on the sidewalk and do the first exercises. I wouldn't do it. My father put his hand on the fella's arm and said, "Please, please." But the guy pushed my father's hand away.

"We're interested in your son, not you. Go on, squat."

"I won't," I told him.

"Go on," he said. "Do the first exercise so that the boys can learn how to keep fit."

"I won't," I said.

"Go on," he said, "do it."

"I won't."

Then he came over to me smiling, but his face looked nasty. "Do it. Do it if you know what's good for you."

"Please, boys," said my pa. "Please go home and eat and don't make trouble. I don't want to have to call a policeman — "

But before I knew it someone got behind me and tripped me so that I fell on one knee. Then another of them pushed me, trying to make me squat. I shoved someone and then someone hit me, and then I heard someone trying to make them stop. While they held me down on the sidewalk I wiggled and looked up. Mrs. Oliver, who had come for the blue-flash edition, was bawling them out.

"You let him alone! You tramps, you hoodlums, you let him alone!" She came over and tried to help me, but they pushed her away. Then Mrs. Oliver began to yell as two guys twisted my arm and told me to squat.

By this time a few people were passing and Mrs. Oliver called at them to interfere. But the gang

were big fellows and there were eight or nine of
them, and the people were afraid.

Then while they had me down on the sidewalk
Syl came running up the street. When she saw
what was happening she began kicking them and
yelling and trying to make them let me up. But
they didn't pay any attention to her, merely pushing her away.

"Please," my pa kept saying, "please let him up;
he didn't hurt you. I don't want to have to call
the police — "

Then Syl turned to the people who were watching and yelled at them, "Why don't you help us?
What are you standing there for?" But none of
them moved. Then Syl began to scream.

"Listen, why don't you help us? Why don't you
make them stop picking on us? We're human beings the same as you!"

But the people just stood there afraid to do a
thing. Then while a few guys held me, Gooley and
about four others went for the stand, turning it
over and mussing and stamping on all the newspapers they could find. Syl started to scratch them,
so they hit her, then I broke away to help her,
and then they started socking me too. My father
tried to reach me, but three guys kept him away.
Four guys got me down and started kicking me,
and all the time my father was begging them to
let me up and Syl was screaming at the people to
help. And while I was down, my face was squeezed
against some papers on the sidewalk telling all
about Austria and I guess I went nuts while they
kept hitting me, and I kept seeing the headlines
against my nose.

Then someone yelled, "Jiggers, the cops!" and
they got off me right away. Nick had looked out
the window and had called the station, and the
guys let me up and beat it away fast.

But when the cops came it was too late; the stand was a wreck. The newspapers and magazines were all over the sidewalk and the rack that holds the *Argosy* and *Western Aces* was all twisted up. My pa, who looked sicker than ever, stood there crying and pretty soon I began to bawl. People were standing looking at us like we were some kind of fish, and I just couldn't help it, I started to bawl.

Then the cops came through the crowd and began asking questions right and left. In the end they wanted to take us to the station to enter a complaint, but Syl wouldn't go. She looked at the crowd watching and she said, "What's the use? All those people standing around and none of them would help!"

They were standing all the way to the second El post, and when the cops asked for witnesses none of them except Mrs. Oliver offered to give their names. Then Syl looked at Pa and me and saw our faces and turned to the crowd and began to scream.

"In another few years, you wait! Some of you are working people and they'll be marching through the streets and going after you too! They pick on us Jews because we're weak and haven't any country, but after they get us down they'll go after you! And it'll be your fault; you're all cowards, you're afraid to fight back!"

"Listen," one of the cops told my sister, "are you coming to the station or not? We can't hang around here all evening."

Then Syl broke down and began to bawl as hard as me. "Oh, leave us alone," she told them and began wailing her heart out. "Leave us alone. What good would it do?"

By this time the crowd was bigger, so the cops started telling the people to break it up and move

on. Nick came out and took my father by the arm
into the lunchroom for a drink of hot tea. The
people went away slowly and then, as the crowd
began to dwindle, it started to snow. When she
saw that, Syl started bawling harder than ever and
turned her face to me. But I was down on my
hands and knees with Mrs. Oliver, trying to save
some of the magazines. There was no use going
after the newspapers, which were smeared up,
torn, and dirty from the gang's feet. But I
thought I could save a few, so I picked a couple
of them up.

"Oh, leave them be," Syl wept at me. "Leave
them be, leave them be!"

2/A START IN LIFE

The Switzers were scurrying around to get Daisy
ready by the time that Elmer Kruse should get
through in town. They had known all week that
Elmer might be in for her any day. But they
hadn't done a thing until he appeared. "Oh, it was
so rainy today, the roads were so muddy, they
hadn't thought he'd get in until maybe next
week." It would have been the same any other
day.

Mrs. Switzer was trying now at the last moment
to get all of Daisy's things into the battered telescope that lay on the bed. The bed had not "got
made" and just as soon as Daisy was gone, Mrs.
Switzer would have to hurry off to the Woodworths, where she was to wash today. Daisy's things
were scattered over the dark brown quilt and the
rumpled sheets that were dingy and clammy in this
damp weather. So was the whole bedroom, with its
sloping ceiling, and old-fashioned square-paned
windows, the commode that they used for a
dresser littered with pin trays, curlers, broken
combs, ribbons, smoky lamps, all mixed up together; the door of the closet open, showing the
confusion of clothes and shabby shoes. . . . They
all slept in this room — Mrs. Switzer and Dwight
in the bed, the two girls in the cot against the wall.

"Mama, I can't find the belt to that plaid dress."

"Oh, ain't it somewheres around? Well, I guess you'll have to let it go. If I come across it I can send it out to you. Someone'll be going past there."

She had meant to get Daisy all mended and "fixed up" before she went out to the country. But somehow . . . oh, there was always so much to see to when she came home. Gone all day, washing and cleaning for other people; it didn't leave her much time for her own home.

She was late now. The Woodworths liked to have her get the washing out early so that she could do some cleaning too before she left. But she couldn't help it. She would have to get Daisy off first. She already had on her wraps ready to go, when Elmer came — her cleaning cap, of a blue faded almost gray, and the ancient black coat with gathered sleeves that she wore over her work dress when she went out to wash.

"What's become of all your underclothes? They ain't all dirty, are they?"

"They are, too. You didn't wash for us last week, Mama."

"Well, you'll just have to take along what you've got. Maybe there'll be some way of getting the rest to you."

"Kruses come in every week, don't they?" Daisy demanded.

"Yes, but maybe they won't always be bringing you in."

She jammed what she could into the telescope, thinking with her helpless, anxious fatalism that it would have to do somehow.

"Daisy, you get yourself ready now."

"I am ready, Mama. I want to put on my other ribbon."

"Oh, that's way down in the telescope some-

where. You needn't be so anxious to fix yourself
up. This ain't like going visiting."

Daisy stood at the little mirror preening herself
— such a homely child, "all Switzer," skinny, with
pale sharp eyes set close together and thin, stringy
reddish hair. But she had never really learned yet
how homely she was. She was the oldest, and she
got the pick of what clothes were given to the Switzers. Goldie and Dwight envied her. She was important in her small world. She was proud of her blue
coat that had belonged to Alice Brooker, the town
lawyer's daughter. It hung unevenly above her
bony little knees, and the buttons came down too
far. Her mother had tried to make it over for her.

Mrs. Switzer looked at her, troubled, but not
knowing how she could tell her all the things she
ought to be told. Daisy had never been away before except to go to her Uncle Fred's at Lehigh. She
seemed to think that this would be the same.
She had so many things to learn. Well, she would
find them out soon enough — only too soon.
Working for other people — she would learn what
that meant. Elmer and Edna Kruse were nice
young people. They would mean well enough by
Daisy. It was a good chance for her to start in. But
it wasn't the same.

Daisy was so proud. She thought it was quite a
thing to be "starting in to earn." She thought she
could buy herself so much with her dollar and a
half a week. The other children stood back watching her, round-eyed and impressed. They wished
that they were going away, like Daisy.

They heard a car come splashing through the
mud on low. "There he is back! Have you got your
things on? Goldie — go out and tell him she's coming."

"No, me tell him, me!" Dwight shouted jeal-
ously.

"Well — both of you tell him. Land! . . ."

She tried hastily to put on the cover of the bulging telescope and to fasten the straps. One of them broke.

"Well, you'll have to take it the way it is."

It was an old thing, hadn't been used since her husband Mert had "left off canvassing" before he died. And he had worn it all to pieces.

"Well, I guess you'll have to go now. He won't want to wait. I'll try and send you out what you ain't got with you." She turned to Daisy. Her face was working. There was nothing else to do, as everyone said. Daisy would have to help, and she might as well learn it now. Only, she hated to see Daisy go off, to have her starting in. She knew what it meant. "Well — you try and work good this summer, so they'll want you to stay. I hope they'll bring you in sometimes."

Daisy's homely little face grew pale with awe, suddenly, at the sight of her mother crying, at something that she dimly sensed in the pressure of her mother's thin strong arm. Her vanity in her new importance was somehow shamed and dampened.

Elmer's big new Buick, mud-splashed but imposing, stood tilted on the uneven road. Mud was thick on the wheels. It was a bad day for driving, with the roads a yellow mass, water lying in all the wheel ruts. The little road that led past these few houses on the outskirts in town, and up over the hill, had a cold, rainy loneliness. Elmer sat in the front seat of the Buick, and in the back was a big box of groceries.

"Got any room to sit in there?" he asked genially. "I didn't get out, it's so muddy here."

"No, don't get out," Mrs. Switzer said hastily. "She can put this right on the floor there in the back." She added, with a timid attempt at courtesy, "Ain't the roads bad out that way?"

"Yes, but farmers get so they don't think so much about the roads."

"I s'pose that's so."

He saw the signs of tears on Mrs. Switzer's face, and they made him anxious to get away. She embraced Daisy hastily again. Daisy climbed over the grocery box and scrunched herself into the seat.

"I guess you'll bring her in with you sometime when you're coming," Mrs. Switzer hinted.

"Sure. We'll bring her."

He started the engine. It roared, half died down as the wheels of the car spun in the thick wet mud.

In that moment, Daisy had a startled view of home — the small house standing on a rough rise of land, weathered to a dim color that showed dark streaks from the rain; the narrow sloping front porch whose edge had a soaked, gnawed look; the chickens, grayish-black, pecking at the wet ground; their playthings, stones, a wagon, some old pail covers littered about; a soaked, discolored piece of underwear hanging on the line in the back yard. The yard was tussocky and overhung the road with shaggy long grass where the yellow bank was caved in under it. Goldie and Dwight were gazing at her solemnly. She saw her mother's face — a thin, weak, loving face, drawn with neglected weeping, with its reddened eyes and poor teeth . . . in the old coat and heavy shoes and cleaning cap, her work-worn hand with its big knuckles clutching at her coat. She saw the playthings they had used yesterday, and the old swing that hung from one of the trees, the ropes sodden, the seat in crooked. . . .

The car went off, slipping on the wet clay. She waved frantically, suddenly understanding that she was leaving them. They waved at her.

Mrs. Switzer stood there a little while. Then came the harsh rasp of the old black iron pump that stood out under the box elder tree. She was pumping water to leave for the children before she went off to work.

Daisy held on as the car skidded going down the short clay hill. Elmer didn't bother with chains. He was too used to the roads. But her eyes brightened with scared excitement. When they were down, and Elmer slowed up going along the tracks in the deep wet grass that led to the main road, she looked back, holding on her hat with her small scrawny hand.

Just down this little hill — and home was gone. The big car, the feel of her telescope on the floor under her feet, the fact that she was going out to the country, changed the looks of everything. She saw it all now.

Dunkels' house stood on one side of the road. A closed-up white house. The windows stared blank and cold between the cold shutters. There was a chair with a broken straw seat under the fruit trees. The Dunkels were old Catholic people who seldom went anywhere. In the front yard was a clump of tall pines, the rough brown trunks wet, the green branches dark and shining, heavy with rain, the ground underneath mournfully sodden and black.

The pasture on the other side. The green grass, lush, wet and cold, and the outcroppings of limestone that held little pools of rain water in all the tiny holes. Beyond, the low hills gloomy with timber against the lowering sky.

They slid out onto the main road. They bumped over the small wooden bridge above the swollen creek that came from the pasture. Daisy looked down. She saw the little swirls of foam, the long grass that swished with the water, the old rusted tin cans lodged between the rocks.

She sat up straight and important, her thin, homely little face strained with excitement, her sharp eyes taking in everything. The watery mud holes in the road, the little thickets of plum trees, low and wet, in dark interlacings. She held on fiercely, but made no sound when the car skidded.

She felt the grandeur of having a ride. One wet Sunday, Mr. Brooker had driven them all home from church, she and Goldie and Dwight packed tightly into the back seat of the car, shut in by the side curtains, against which the rain lashed, catching the muddy scent of the roads. Sometimes they could plan to go to town just when Mr. Pattey was going to work in his Ford. Then they would run out and shout eagerly, "Mr. Pattey! Are you going through town?" Sometimes he said, with curt good nature, "Well, pile in," and they all hopped into the truck back. "He says we can go along with him."

She looked at the black wet fields through which little leaves of bright green corn grew in rows, at showery bushels of sumac along the roadside. A gasoline engine pumping water made a loud desolate sound. There were somber-looking cattle in the wet grass, and lonely, thick-foliaged trees growing here and there in the pastures. She felt her telescope on the floor of the car, the box of groceries beside her. She eyed these with a sharp curiosity. There was a fresh pineapple — something the Switzers didn't often get at home. She wondered if Edna would have it for dinner. Maybe she could hint a little to Edna.

She was out in the country. She could no longer see her house even if she wanted to — standing dingy, streaked with rain, in its rough grass on the little hill. A lump came into her throat. She had

looked forward to playing with Edna's children.
But Goldie and Dwight would play all morning
without her. She was still proud of being the oldest, of going out with Elmer and Edna; but now
there was a forlornness in the pride.

She wished she were in the front seat with Elmer. She didn't see why he hadn't put her there.
She would have liked to know who all the people
were who lived on these farms; how old Elmer's
babies were; and if he and Edna always went to the
movies when they went into town on Saturday
nights. Elmer must have lots of money to buy a
car like this. He had a new house on his farm too,
and Mrs. Metzinger had said that it had plumb-
ing. Maybe they would take her to the movies too.
She might hint about that.

When she had gone to visit Uncle Fred, she had
had to go on the train. She liked this better. She
hoped they had a long way to go. She called out
to Elmer:

"Say, how much farther is your place?"

"What's that?" He turned around. "Oh, just
down the road a ways. Scared to drive in the mud?"

"No, I ain't scared. I like to drive most any
way."

She looked at Elmer's back, the old felt hat
crammed down carelessly on his head, the back of
his neck with the golden hair on the sunburned
skin above the blue of his shirt collar. Strong and
easy and slouched a little over the steering wheel
that he handled so masterly. Elmer and Edna
were just young folks; but Mrs. Metzinger said
that they had more to start with than most young
farmers did, and that they were hustlers. Daisy felt
that the pride of this belonged to her too, now.

"Here we are!"

"Oh, is this where you folks live?" Daisy cried
eagerly.

The house stood back from the road, beyond a space of bare yard with a little scattering of grass just starting — small, modern, painted a bright new white and yellow. The barn was new, too, a big splendid barn of frescoed brick, with a silo of the same. There were no trees. A raw, desolate wind blew across the back yard as they drove up beside the back door.

Edna had come out on the step. Elmer grinned at her as he took out the box of groceries, and she slightly raised her eyebrows. She said kindly enough:

"Well, you brought Daisy. Hello, Daisy, are you going to stay with us this summer?"

"I guess so," Daisy said importantly. But she suddenly felt a little shy and forlorn as she got out of the car and stood on the bare ground in the chilly wind.

"Yes, I brought her along," Elmer said.

"Are the roads very bad?"

"Kind of bad. Why?"

"Well, I'd like to get over to Mama's some time today."

"Oh, I guess they aren't too bad for that."

Daisy pricked up her sharp little ears. Another ride. That cheered her.

"Look in the door," Edna said in a low fond voice, motioning with her head.

Two little round, blond heads were pressed tightly against the screen door. There was a clamor of "Daddy, Daddy!" Elmer grinned with a bashful pride as he stood with the box of groceries, raising his eyebrows with mock surprise and demanding, "Who's this? What you shoutin' 'Daddy' for? You don't think Daddy's got anything for you, do you?" He and Edna were going into the kitchen together, until Edna remembered and called back hastily:

"Oh, come in, Daisy!"

Daisy stood, a little left out and solitary, there in the kitchen, as Billy, the older of the babies, climbed frantically over Elmer, demanding candy, and the little one toddled smilingly about. Her eyes took in all of it. She was impressed by the shining blue-and-white linoleum, the range with its nickel and enamel, the bright new woodwork. Edna was laughing and scolding at Elmer and the baby. Billy had made his father produce the candy. Daisy's sharp little eyes looked hungrily at the lemon drops and Edna remembered her.

"Give Daisy a piece of your candy," she said.

He would not go up to Daisy. She had to come forward and take one of the lemon drops herself. She saw where Edna put the sack, in a dish high in the cupboard. She hoped they would get some more before long.

"My telescope's out there in the car," she reminded them.

"Oh! Elmer, you go and get it and take it up for her," Edna said.

"What?"

"Her valise — or whatever it is — out in the car."

"Oh, sure," Elmer said with a cheerful grin.

"It's kind of an old telescope," Daisy said conversationally. "I guess it's been used a lot. My papa used to have it. The strap broke when Mama was fastening it this morning. We ain't got any suitcase. I had to take this because it was all there was in the house, and Mama didn't want to get me a new one."

Edna raised her eyebrows politely. She leaned over and pretended to swat the baby as he came toddling up to her, then rubbed her cheek against his round head with its funny fuzz of hair.

Daisy watched solemnly. "I didn't know both of

your children was boys. I thought one of 'em was a girl. That's what there is at home now — one boy and one girl."

"Um-hm," Edna replied absently. "You can come down and help me in the kitchen. You know we got you to help me," she reminded.

Daisy, subdued, followed Elmer up the bright new stairs. In the upper hall, two strips of very clean rag rug were laid over the shining yellow of the floor. Elmer had put her telescope in one of the bedrooms.

"There you are!"

She heard him go clattering down the stairs, and then a kind of murmuring and laughing in the kitchen. The back door slammed. She hurried to the window in time to see Elmer striding off toward the barn.

She looked about her room with intense curiosity. It, too, had a bright varnished floor. She had a bed all her own — a small, old-fashioned bed, left from some old furnishings, that had been put in this room that had the pipes and the hot water tank. She had to see everything, but she had a stealthy look as she tiptoed about, started to open the drawers of the dresser, looked out of the window. She put her coat and hat on the bed. She would rather be down in the kitchen with Edna than unpack her telescope now.

She guessed she would go down where the rest of them were.

Elmer came into the house for dinner. He brought in a cold, muddy outdoor breath with him. The range was going, but the bright little kitchen seemed chilly, with the white oilcloth on the table, the baby's varnished high chair and his little, fat mottled hands.

Edna made a significant little face at Elmer.

Daisy did not see. She was standing back from the stove, where Edna was at work, looking at the baby.

"He can talk pretty good, can't he? Dwight couldn't say anything but 'Mama' when he was that little."

Edna's back was turned. She said meaningly:

"Now, Elmer's come in for dinner, Daisy, we'll have to hurry. You must help me get on the dinner. You can cut bread and get things on the table. You must help, you know. That's what you are supposed to do."

Daisy looked startled, a little scared and resentful.

"Well, I don't know where you keep your bread."

"Don't you remember where I told you to put it this morning? Right over in the cabinet, in that big box. You must watch, Daisy, and learn where things are."

Elmer, a little embarrassed at the look that Edna gave him, whistled as he began to wash his hands at the sink.

"How's Daddy's old boy?" he said loudly, giving a poke at the baby's chin.

As Edna passed him, she shook her head and her lips just formed, "Been like that all morning!"

He grinned comprehendingly. Then both their faces became expressionless.

Daisy had not exactly heard, but she looked from one to the other, silent and dimly wondering. The queer ache that had kept starting all through the morning, under her interest in Edna's things and doings, came over her again. She sensed something different in the atmosphere than she had ever known before — some queer difference between the position of herself and of the two

babies, a faint notion of what Mama had meant
when she had said that this would not be visiting.

"I guess I'm going to have the toothache again,"
she said faintly.

No one seemed to hear her.

Edna whisked off the potatoes, drained the water. . . . "You might bring me a dish, Daisy."
Daisy searched a long time while Edna turned impatiently and pointed. Edna put the rest of the
things on the table herself. Her young, fresh, capable mouth was tightly closed, and she was making certain resolutions.

Daisy stood hesitating in the middle of the
room, a scrawny, unappealing little figure. Billy
— fat, blond, in funny, dark-blue union-alls —
was trotting busily about the kitchen. Daisy
swooped down upon him and tried to bring him
to the table. He set up a howl. Edna turned,
looked astonished, severe.

"You scared him. He isn't used to you. He
doesn't like it. Don't cry, Billy. The girl didn't
mean anything."

"Here, Daddy'll put him in his place," Elmer
said hastily.

Billy looked over his father's shoulder at Daisy
with suffused, resentful blue eyes. She did not understand it, and felt strangely at a loss. She had
been left with Goldie and Dwight so often. She
had always made Dwight go to the table. She had
been the boss.

Edna said in a cool, held-in voice, "Put these
things on the table, Daisy."

They sat down. Daisy and the other children
had always felt it a great treat to eat away from
home instead of at their own scanty, hastily set
table. They had hung around Mrs. Metzinger's
house at noon, hoping to be asked to stay, not of-
fended when told that "it was time for them to

run off now." Her pinched little face had a hungry
look as she stared at the potatoes and fried ham
and pie. But they did not watch and urge her to
have more, as Mrs. Metzinger did, and Mrs.
Brooker when she took pity on the Switzers and
had them there. Daisy wanted more pie. But none
of them seemed to be taking more, and so she said
nothing. She remembered when her mother had
said, with now a faint comprehension, "You must
remember you're out working for other folks,
and it won't be like it is at home."

After dinner, Edna said, "Now you can wash
the dishes, Daisy."

She went into the next room with the children.
Daisy, as she went hesitatingly about the kitchen
alone, could hear Edna's low contented humming
as she sat in there rocking, the baby in her lap.
The bright kitchen was empty and lonely now.
Through the window, Daisy could see the great
barn looming up against the rainy sky. She hoped
that they would drive to Edna's mother's soon.

She finished as soon as she could and went into
the dining room where Edna was sewing on the
baby's rompers. Edna went on sewing. Daisy sat
down disconsolately. That queer low ache went
all through her. She said in a small, dismal voice:

"I guess I got the toothache again."

Edna bit off a thread.

"I had it awful hard a while ago. Mama come
pretty near taking me to the dentist."

"That's too bad," Edna murmured politely. But
she offered no other condolence. She gave a little
secret smile at the baby asleep on a blanket and a
pillow in one corner of the shiny leather daven-
port.

"Is Elmer going to drive into town tomorrow?"

"Tomorrow? I don't suppose so."

"Mama couldn't find the belt of my plaid dress

and I thought if he was, maybe I could go along and get it. I'd like to have it."

Daisy's homely mouth drooped at the corners. Her toothache did not seem to matter to anyone. Edna did not seem to want to see that anything was wrong with her. She had expected Edna to be concerned, to mention remedies. But it wasn't a toothache, that strange lonesome ache all over her. Maybe she was going to be terribly sick. Mama wouldn't come home for supper to be told about it.

She saw Mama's face as in that last glimpse of it — drawn with crying, and yet trying to smile, under the old cleaning cap, her hand holding her coat together. . . .

Edna glanced quickly at her. The child was so mortally unattractive, unappealing even in her forlornness. Edna frowned a little, but said kindly:

"Now you might take Billy into the kitchen out of my way, Daisy, and amuse him."

"Well, he cries when I pick him up," Daisy said faintly.

"He won't cry this time. Take him out and help him play with his blocks. You must help me with the children, you know."

"Well, if he'll go with me."

"He'll go with you, won't he, Billy boy? Won't you go with Daisy, sweetheart?"

Billy stared and nodded. Daisy felt a thrill of comfort as Billy put his fat little hand in hers and trotted into the kitchen beside her. He had the fattest hands, she thought. Edna brought the blocks and put the box down on the floor beside Daisy.

"Now, see if you can amuse him so that I can get my sewing done."

"Shall you and me play blocks, Billy?" Daisy murmured.

He nodded. Then he got hold of the box with one hand, tipped out all the blocks on the floor with a bang and a rattle, and looked at her with a pleased, proud smile.

"Oh, no, Billy. You mustn't spill out the blocks. Look, you're too little to play with them. No, now — now wait! Let Daisy show you, Daisy'll build you something real nice — shall she?"

He gave a solemn nod of consent.

Daisy set out the blocks on the bright linoleum. She had never had such blocks as these to handle before. Dwight's were only a few old, unmatched, broken ones. Her spirit of leadership came back, and she firmly put away the fat hand of Billy's whenever he meddled with her building. She could make something really wonderful with these blocks.

"No, Billy, you mustn't. See, when Daisy's got it all done, then you can see what the lovely building is."

She put the blocks together with great interest. She knew what she was going to make — it was going to be a new house; no, a new church. Just as she got the walls up, in came that little hand again, and then with a delighted grunt Billy swept the blocks pell-mell about the floor. At the clatter, he sat back, pursing his mouth to give an ecstatic "Ooh!"

"Oh, Billy — you mustn't, the building wasn't done! Look, you've spoiled it. Now, you've got to sit way off here while I try to build it over again."

Billy's look of triumph turned to surprise and then to vociferous protest as Daisy picked him up and firmly transplanted him to another corner of the room. He set up a tremendous howl. He had never been set aside like that before. Edna came hurrying out. Daisy looked at Edna for justification, but instinctively on the defensive.

"Billy knocked over the blocks. He spoiled the building."

"Wah! Wah!" Billy gave loud heartbroken sobs. The tears ran down his fat cheeks and he held out his arms piteously toward his mother.

"I didn't hurt him," Daisy said, scared.

"Never mind, lover," Edna was crooning. "Of course he can play with his blocks. They're Billy's blocks, Daisy," she said. "He doesn't like to sit and see you put up buildings. He wants to play too. See, you've made him cry now."

"Do' wanna stay here," Billy wailed.

"Well, come in with Mother then." She picked him up, wiping his tears.

"I didn't hurt him," Daisy protested.

"Well, never mind now. You can pick up the blocks and then sweep up the floor, Daisy. You didn't do that when you finished the dishes. Never mind," she was saying to Billy. "Pretty soon Daddy'll come in and we'll have a nice ride."

Daisy soberly picked up the blocks and got the broom. What had she done to Billy? He had tried to spoil her building. She had always made Dwight keep back until she had finished. Of course it was Daisy, the oldest, who should lead and manage. There had been no one to hear her side. Everything was different. She winked back her tears as she swept, poorly and carelessly.

Then she brightened up as Elmer came tramping up on the back porch and then through the kitchen.

"Edna!"

"She's in there," Daisy offered.

"Want to go now? What? Is the baby asleep?" he asked blankly.

Edna gave him a warning look and the door was closed.

Daisy listened hard. She swept very softly. She

could catch only a little of what they said — "Kind
of hate to go off. . . . I know, but if we once start
. . . not a thing all day . . . what we got her
for. . . ." She had no real comprehension of it.
She hurried and put away the broom. She wanted
to be sure and be ready to go.

Elmer tramped out, straight past her. She saw
from the window that he was backing the car out
from the shed. She could hear Edna and Billy upstairs, could hear the baby cry a little as he was
awakened. Maybe she ought to go up and get on
her wraps too.

Elmer honked the horn. A moment later Edna
came hurrying downstairs, in her hat and coat,
and Billy in a knitted cap and red sweater
crammed over his union-alls, so that he looked
like a little brownie. The baby had on his little
coat too.

Edna called out, "Come and get this boy,
Daddy." She did not look at Daisy, but said hurriedly, "We're going out for a little ride, Daisy.
Have you finished the sweeping? Well, then, you
can pick up those pieces in the dining room. We
won't be gone very long. When it's a quarter past
five, you start the fire, like I showed you this noon,
and slice the potatoes that were left, and the
meat. And set the table."

The horn was honked again.

"Yes! Well, we'll be back, Daisy. Come, lover,
Daddy's in a hurry."

Daisy stood looking after them. Billy clamored
to sit beside his daddy. Edna took the baby from
Elmer and put him beside her on the back seat.
There was room — half of the big back seat.
There wasn't anything, really, to be done at home.
That was the worst of it. They just didn't want to
take her. They all belonged together. They didn't
want to take anyone else along. She was an out-

sider. They all — even the baby — had a freshened look of expectancy.

The engine roared — they had started; slipping on the mud of the drive, then forging straight ahead, around the turn, out of sight.

She went forlornly into the dining room. The light from the windows was dim now in the rainy, late afternoon. The pink pieces from the baby's rompers were scattered over the gray rug. She got down on her hands and knees, slowly picking them up, sniffing a little. She heard the Big Ben clock in the kitchen ticking loudly.

That dreadful ache submerged her. No one would ask about it, no one would try to comfort her. Before, there had always been Mama coming home, anxious, scolding sometimes, but worried over them if they didn't feel right, caring about them. Mama and Goldie and Dwight cared about her — but she was away out in the country, and they were at home. She didn't want to stay here, where she didn't belong. But Mama had told her that she must begin helping this summer.

Her ugly little mouth contorted into a grimace of weeping. But silent weeping, without any tears; because she already had the cold knowledge that no one would notice or comfort it.

3/WITHOUT WORDS

Jan McKenzie came over a knoll and stopped, head back, his rifle in one mitten, his axe in the other. Below him spread the river, ice-locked between the hills. A mile across, the birch bluffs were turning blue in the twilight.

He was not given to poetic fancies, but it touched him always, coming out to the river after days and nights in the spruces to the west, following brooks and isolated chains of lakes that didn't lead anywhere, plowing through willow tangles and up and down the wooded hills. It gave him a feeling of spaciousness, like stepping out of doors to see the broad river again, sweeping out of sight between the hills.

That country behind him, his east trap line where he had been for ten days, was just a cut-up jumble of wilderness, lost, nameless, known only to himself. But the river was the river. This was the road to home, this was the known thread that joined him to other men.

This water that was flowing under the ice would slide past the village sometime, in a month maybe. "It'll get there 'fore I do, anyways," he said aloud. It was nine weeks now since the day the crowd had waved from the wharf, and the double-barrel shotguns split the air in the old-time farewell, "Boomboom" . . . and a pause to load . . . "Boom," saying "Good-bye . . . Luck"; nine weeks since the trappers fired their one answering shot, "Luck." It gave a fellow something to remember way off here where you didn't hear anything much except your own voice.

It would be pretty near three months yet before he'd be home and maybe see Luce, he was thinking as he scrambled down the bank and legged it along the ice for the house. *This* cabin had a window, and a door with hinges, a good tight roof of birch bark, and within such luxuries as a sleeping bag, which his tiny log tilts back in the woods had not.

It was nearly dark when he got there, but not too dark to see in the cove the print of strange snowshoes. And by the point where the current flowed fast and the ice was thin, somebody had been chopping a water hole. "Hello!" he called to the cabin.

From the ridge that rose up behind the cabin came a silvery, mocking "Hello," and faintly, seconds later, a distant hello from across the river, the echo of the echo. Jan crossed the cove, bent double, studying the tracks. There were three of them, a big pair of snowshoes and two smaller pairs. The smaller snowshoes had been dragging in a stick of firewood from alongshore — the women.

Jan threw off his bag and hurried into the cabin. Nobody made snowshoes of that pattern but Mathieu Su-saka-shish, the Seven Islands Indian. Nobody but Mathieu knew this cabin was here. He and his wife and daughter had come last year and begged a little tea and sugar. Now they were here again with their Indian idea that food belongs to anybody who is hungry. The dirty dogs!

Where three fifty-pound bags of flour had been hanging, only two hung now. They had dripped candle grease onto his bunk and left his big meat kettle unwashed. He dove under the bunk and pulled out his food boxes. They'd made off with some of his split peas and a few of his beans, a handful of candles too. They had sliced a big chunk of salt pork neatly down the middle.

In a frenzy of rage he ripped open his fur bag. Every skin was there, and in addition, a black and shining otter skin lay crosswise on his bundles of mink and marten, fox and ermine. He held it up and blew the hair and felt its thickness and its length, stroking its blue-black luster. It was a prize. It would bring forty dollars, perhaps. But the sight of it made him angrier than before.

"So!" he muttered. "Mathieu thinks one miserable skin of fur pays me for my grub, eh?" He lit a candle, and his hand was trembling with rage. From now on he'd be half-hungry all the time, and hunting meat when he ought to be tending the trap line. This was his whole year's earnings, these five months in the bush. And Mathieu thought he could steal the grub that made it possible, did he? He thought he could come every year and fit himself out, likely.

Jan took his rifle and emptied the magazine. It was only one bag of flour — but still, there were men way off here in the country who'd died for lack of a cupful, yes, a spoonful. Slowly he reloaded with the soft-nosed cartridges he had always kept for caribou, heretofore. Would he ever tell anybody, Luce for instance, would he ever be able to forget that somewhere back in the ridges, by some secret little lake that no one knew, he had shot three Indians and stuffed them through the ice? Didn't the Bible say, an eye for an eye and a tooth for a tooth?

Jan had already walked twenty miles today. And he was tired with the piled-up weariness of weeks and weeks of that, traveling, traveling to cover and recover his two hundred miles of fur paths. With a sigh he set to work; wood to chop, water from the river, a partridge to be stewed and ten cakes of bannock bread to bake in the frying pan. While the bread was baking, he skinned two mink, a marten, four weasels, humming as he did so a song that he was very fond of:

"Oh, we've sailed the seven seas from pole to
     pole,
And we've conquered stormy gale and stinging
     foam,
And we've seen the strangest sights of far-off
     lands,
But the best is to see the cheery lights of home."

It called up visions of a light in the window, if he should ever have a real home, if, perhaps, he married Luce.

It was too bad he couldn't just shoot Mathieu, but it would be no use to leave the women to wander around and starve. At the thought of actually squeezing the trigger and seeing them drop, he shuddered.

It was nearly midnight when he stoked up the stove and rolled in on the bunk for the last good sleep he expected to know for a while. At five o'clock, in the starlight, he was out on the river shore with a candle lantern made of a baking-powder can, examining tracks. The polished, shallow trench that their two toboggans had left was so plain a child could have followed it. Mathieu was ahead, taking long steps, hurrying. The two women were behind, hauling their toboggan in double harness, tandem fashion. One of them fell and left the print of her knee going down the bank. Jan smiled as though he had seen it and heard her mutter.

He followed their track across the river to the top of a draw between two bare hills. There in the sunrise he turned and looked back at the ice, sparkling with frost in the soft golden light, spotted with long blue shadows of the hills. As he plunged downhill into the thick country to the north he had an ominous feeling that he was leaving something. Maybe Mathieu would ambush him; it would be an easy thing to do on a track like this. Would Mathieu guess that he was being tracked?

Jan studied the track, unconsciously noting every detail. Here in this book of the snow he might perhaps read Matheiu's thoughts, even a warning of an ambush. Ah, but Indians were smart in the woods. Did he really think he could out-track an Indian hunter?

"By the Lord Harry, I can have a try," he whispered to himself.

Two mornings ago, he decided it was, they had passed through here under the firs, across that little brook. Two days were not much of a start for them. They had sleds and he had none. Mathieu had to break trail, while he had their hard, frozen track to walk on. They had all their winter gear, their blankets and kettles, their tin stove and tent, traps, trout nets, probably. He had nothing but the game bag on his back, nine cakes of bread, tea and sugar, his rifle and axe, a single blanket. The chances were he could travel twice as fast as they.

He passed their first fire, where they had stopped to boil tea and thrown the leaves on the embers. The tea leaves were frozen stiff.

All day he swung on, parting the boughs where the spruces were thick, slipping through them as effortlessly as a weasel, trotting down all the hills with a tireless shuffle, trotting again where the way was level and open. Once he stopped for ten minutes to sit on a log and munch dry bread, then lit his pipe and swung on. It was frosty, and the edges of his fur cap grew white with his breathing.

Before sunset he had long passed their first night's camp. Through the semidarkness of early twilight he pressed on, following the hardness of their track more by touch than by sight. In the starlight he made his fire and boiled tea in a ravine by a brook. Here and there a tree snapped with the frost. The brook murmured under the ice. On the western hill a horn owl was hooting.

Every hour he woke with the cold, threw on more wood, turned over and slept again. Once, around three o'clock, he woke and could not sleep. He sat hunched in the blanket looking into the fire thinking what a fool he was. He should be on the trap line, not here. He had not come up the river so far away to waste time chasing Indians around the hills. Already he was hungry and wished he had brought more food.

The wind had risen and was blowing hard. That was bad. He could not feel it here, but the treetops were rocking, and branches now and then rubbed together and spoke with weird, childlike voices.

By half-past four he had boiled his tea and eaten, and was picking his way along the track again. He should have rested another hour, he knew. But he could not rest, though he was tired. He wanted to get it over with. Probably they would not bleed much, it was so cold.

The Indians were still heading northwest. Likely they were bound for the headwaters of streams that flowed into Hudson's Bay. Mathieu would feel safe there. And he would be too. It

was much farther than Jan could track him with
only three days' grub in the bag.

In the morning he passed their second night's
camp. By noontime he had come to the edge of a
big, oval marsh that was about six miles wide at
its narrowest. On its barren floor were occasional
clumps of dead sticks, juniper and fir, no higher
than a man's head, the firs rotten and falling, the
junipers gaunt and wind-carved. Compared to its
bleak, dead savagery the greenwoods' borders
seemed sociable and friendly and snug. As the
merciless northwest wind had stunted and killed
the trees, so it could shrivel and kill a man if it
caught him out here in a blizzard.

The trail was dim and wind-scoured on the
marsh. A mile out and there was nothing but the
dully shining spots the sleds had polished; two
miles out and Mathieu was veering off to the
east, deviating for the first time from his northwest course.

The marks petered out entirely, heading at the
last straight east. Jan stopped and rubbed his forehead. "Mathieu, you're a cute fox, eh?"

If Mathieu was heading northwest the blue
notch was the obvious way for him. Then why, in
the middle of the marsh, did he swing off for the
steep ridges?

Jan trotted about in a circle, slapping his mittens together and pounding the toes that were
aching in his moccasins. The drifting snow slid by
like sand, rising in little eddies as the wind rose.

He stopped and stood with his back to the wind,
leaning against it. "Now look. Mathieu wants to
go through the blue notch, but it's too plain. He
knows I'd pick up his track there first thing. So he
cuts off in the middle of the marsh, thinkin'
there'll be no sign of it when I gets yere, and he
makes a big half a circle. When I gets to the blue

draw I can't find ere a sign of him, and I don't know where he's gone.

"I don't, eh? Well, I know he's got to strike the valley of the notch-stream somewheres. Him and his women haulin' sleds can't get along in the hills no faster than a fox with a trap on his foot."

Jan picked up his game bag and trotted off toward the now-invisible notch. If he'd guessed right, all right; if he'd guessed wrong, all right too. What odds! Lord Harry, he was hungry. In all this time he hadn't seen a partridge, though he'd seen plenty of feathers where that devil Mathieu'd shot all there was.

He began to sing a song to rival the sweep of the strong wind. In the wind it was good to sing, the wind drowned sound, sang a song of its own, saved a man from feeling that miles of quiet woods were listening. He roared in a strong baritone:

"Oh, we've sailed the seven seas from pole to
    pole,
And we've conquered stormy gale and stinging
    foam,
And we've seen the strangest sights of far-off
    lands,
But the be-e-e-est is to see the chee-eery lights of
    ho-o-me."

The drift had obscured the shores now and he was as though alone in the middle of a white sea, snow above, below, and on all sides. But he did not think of it. The wind was compass enough for him and had been since boyhood.

He clasped his gun and axe in the crook of one elbow, put his curled mitts up around his mouth and imitated a mouth organ, hunching his shoulders and swinging his body, dancing on his snowshoes in the gale. When he got home and the fiddle was squeaking in the schoolhouse and old Si

Willetts was callin' out the figures, oh he'd swing
his girl like this — and he whirled around with
his gun and axe, holding them high in the air and
shaking them.

"You! You got no more sense than a porcupine," he said.

At dusk, miles beyond the blue notch, he picked
up the Indians' track again. He glowed with the
warmth of a hunter's pride, his nostrils quivered
and his jaw clenched. Lord Harry, how they had
traveled. But he had them now. They'd never get
away, they were doomed, unless it snowed.

A mile farther on they had camped, and there
he camped too. A few split chunks of wood that
they hadn't burned he used. There was still a
faint warmth in the depths of their ashes. But
something in the low branches of a spruce made
him pause. Lashed there, rolled up in a hairy caribou skin were a big trout net and a heavyish iron
Dutch oven. So, they were lightening loads were
they? They knew they were being tracked then.
How did they know?

Jan sat on the fir brush of their tent site and
thought about it. They didn't know, they couldn't
know. Mathieu was just playing safe, that was all,
announcing, if he should be followed, that he was
still a-drivin' 'er for all he was worth, bluffing a
pursuer, trying to say, "I know I am being followed" — just in case he should be followed. Mathieu would go on for a week, get his women set
in a good camp, then circle back, hunting, setting
traps in likely places, looking for beaver houses,
back to this very tree. Here he'd pick up his stuff,
have a look around, and mosey along westward.

"That's what you think, Mathieu."

That night he ate another half of a bannock,
only half when he could easily have eaten three
whole ones. What a fool he was to have traveled

so light. If by some mischance he didn't catch them now, he'd be stranded off here with nothing to eat.

Rolled in his blanket and their caribou robe, he had the best sleep yet. It was risky. He had his gun beside him. For why couldn't Mathieu come back tonight as well as in a week? All about was the ring of darkness. Here was the firelight. What a perfect mark to shoot at. Yes, but Mathieu wouldn't shoot him. Why, Mathieu's father used to camp on the shore at Turner's Harbor years ago. Mathieu's cousin used to wrestle with Jan by the hour, and Mathieu himself had been in the foot races they ran on the beach summer afternoons long ago by the blue cool bay. Mathieu knew him all to pieces, even if they didn't meet but once in years and years way off in the country. Mathieu'd steal a little grub, but Mathieu'd never shoot him.

He sat looking into the fire. "Mathieu wouldn't shoot you," he said, "but you'd shoot Mathieu. You wouldn't steal Mathieu's grub, but he'd steal yours." He rocked his head in his hands, bewildered and hating this mental tangle. Life was simple. You went up the river in winter, and you were home by the bay in summer. You had good luck furring, or you didn't. You were hungry once in a while, and you froze your chin, or a cheek or a toe odd times, but what was that? You fell through the thin ice, or you didn't. You lived or you died, and that was all there was to it.

Yes, but it wasn't so simple when people stole your grub. Oh, if only Mathieu hadn't taken a whole bag of flour, he would be so glad for Mathieu. He settled it this way: if Mathieu wants to come along and shoot me tonight, let him, that's good luck for Mathieu; but if Mathieu doesn't,

maybe Mathieu will get shot himself tomorrow
night.

The stars paled and the east grayed the same
as on other mornings. Jan did not set out until
there was a little light. It would be so easy for Mathieu to wait hidden by the track.

He walked with his cap on the side, exposing
one ear, and when that ear began to freeze he
tilted the cap and uncovered the other. Every
mile he stopped and listened, mouth open, holding his breath. Late in the forenoon he came to a
small valley thick with willows and boulders. As
he examined it he was conscious from the corner
of his eye that a tuft of snow was slipping down
the face of a gray boulder on his left. Was somebody behind there? He turned and ran, dodging
through the trees. Skirting the end of the willows
he stealthily approached the trail farther on. No,
no one had been there. It must have been a willow
twig brushing the rock in the breeze. Here were
the three prints, just the three prints, Mathieu's
almost indistinguishable under the women's and
the sled's. The women had given up hauling tandem. They took turns single, and when they
changed places Mathieu didn't wait for them.
They had to run a little to catch up, poor things.
Luce could never have hauled like that.

As he tramped he got to thinking of the otter
skin Mathieu had left. It was funny the way Indian hunters would take food. They'd been hunters for so many ages they thought a bag of flour,
like a caribou, was for anybody who needed it.
But they wouldn't steal fur. Indians! They were
like a necessary evil, they were like children. It
would be better if they *did* steal fur and left the
grub alone. They could pack food into this height-
of-land country as well as anybody else if they
wanted to. But they were too lazy. They let the

trappers wear themselves to skin and bone struggling up the river in canoes loaded to the gunnels, risking their lives for it in the white rapids, lugging their loads up the Great Bank, a mile long and steeper than the bridge of Satan's own nose, breaking their backs for it across twelve miles of swamps and brooks and slippery rocks on the Grand Portage where the tump lines pulled their hair out by the roots and they carried till their eyes turned black and their trembling knees sagged under them. And then — then the Indians came along and helped themselves as though flour was worth no more up here than down on the bay shore.

"They won't help themselves to my grub," said Jan grimly. "Some day I'll come back to my house maybe, and find it cleaned right out. And then what about me, livin' on jays' legs and moss till I fall in the snow and die?"

The sky was growing deeper gray, darkness coming early. The air was chill with a suspicion of dampness. Come a big batch of snow to cover their track and make the walkin' back heavy, right to the knees, no food, he'd be in a fine fix, wouldn't he? He smelled the wind and it smelled like snow. Before dark it began to fall, and at dark he still had not caught them. Must be gettin' weak, he thought ruefully. He'd set some rabbit snares tonight. Or maybe he'd get a partridge. And maybe he wouldn't.

He stood on the shore of a little lake and leaned against a tree, uncertain. What with the new snow and the dark, there was only the barest sign of the track now. By morning it would be gone. What was that sharp smell?

He threw back his head and sniffed. Wood smoke! He had caught them. Let the snow pelt down. Let it snow six feet in the night, he had caught them and they couldn't get away.

Strange, though, that they should camp before the snow got thick. An hour more and they would have been safe. Well, Mathieu had made his last mistake this time.

Over a knoll in a thick clump of firs he built a small fire to boil the kettle. He was ravenous, and weary to the bone. They were camped, they would keep till he got ready for them. And they couldn't smell his smoke with the wind this way.

He ate the last of his bannock, drank four cups of tea, and smoked his pipe to the last dregs. Then he left his bag and axe, took his rifle and stole out across the dark lake. It was black as ink, and the new snow was like cotton wool to muffle his steps. Just back from the far shore he saw their dome-shaped *meetchwop* glimmering. They were burning a candle in there, one of his own probably.

He crept up closer, on his belly, foot by foot. The two sleds were stuck up against a tree, there was the chopping block, the axe, the chips. Snowshoes were hanging from a limb, the two small pairs. The women inside were baking bread. He could hear the frying pan scrape on the tin stove. They were talking in their soft musical voices, more like a brook under the ice than like human talk. They weren't hardly human anyway. But he could not bring himself to walk into the tent and shoot the women in cold blood. Better get Mathieu first. But where were the big snowshoes? Where was Mathieu? Behind that black tree there with his rifle cocked?

Jan lay silent, scarcely breathing, ears stretched for the slightest sound. But there were only the wind and the falling snow and the women's voices and the scraping pan.

Fifteen minutes, half an hour, he lay thus.

He was freezing, he couldn't lie there all night. Inch by inch he crawled away. Silent as a shadow he went back across the lake. There was danger everywhere now, every time he moved a muscle. He could feel it all around him, feel a prickling in his scalp and a supernatural certainty that as he was stalking Mathieu, Mathieu was stalking him. Cautiously, with long waits, he approached his camp. The fire was out. His fingers touched the game bag and drew back. Something was there, something that shouldn't be! *Something was wrong.* Chills went up and down his spine. He whirled toward a deeper patch of shadow, knowing with the certainty of panic that gunfire would belch from that shadow and blind him. His eyes roamed round in his head in the darkness and he waited, turned to stone.

There was no sound. Nothing but the soft hiss of the snowflakes drifting down.

Then he smelled it. Bread, new-baked bread, sweet as life to his nostrils. He drew off his mitten and touched the game bag again. His finger counted them — seven crusty bannock cakes, still warm.

"Mathieu," he whispered to the engulfing darkness. There was no answer. He struck a match and looked at the cakes. He bit one, and shook his head, ashamed. All his muscles sagged, and he slumped into the snow as though it were a bed.

Everything was different now. Noisily he crashed down a big tree for his night's fire. He was sticking up a lean-to by the fireplace, chilled by the night's cold, not by the cold horror of that other unthinkable job. Lord, he'd rather Mathieu plugged him full of holes than to take a sight on Mathieu. It was like waking up from a nightmare. He had half a mind to go across the lake now and ask Mathieu's woman to sew up the tear in his britches and have a good sleep in the Indians' warm tent. How they'd giggle and talk, with their black eyes!

But he was too ashamed. Mathieu was a better man than he was, that was all; more forgiving, smarter in the woods. "I wouldn't forgive him for taking a bag of flour, but he forgives me for tryin' to kill him. All the time the snow's comin' down and he only had to go on a little piece farther tonight to lose me altogether. He knows that and he knows I was going to shoot him. But he takes a chance and sneaks back to feed me, me that's chasin' him to kill him. Mathieu don't want I should starve goin' back to the river. Mathieu — he don't want us to part unfriendly."

Lord, it beat all. If ever he told this to Luce, she'd say he was the head liar of all the liars on the whole river.

He finished one of the fragrant, tender bread cakes and lay down with his back to the fire. It was a long time since he'd felt so happy. Wonderful strange too, how much he and Mathieu had said to each other without words, way off here, never meeting, eating each other's grub.

Toward morning the snow stopped. Just after sunrise the Indian family broke camp and climbed the hill up from the shore. Jan, watching from the opposite hill across the lake, saw them silhouetted, three dark figures on the bare ridge. He pointed his gun at a treetop and let go greeting. Boomboom. . . . Boom. He saw the two women, startled, duck behind their sled.

But Mathieu stood erect against the brightening sky. He raised his rifle and fired one answering shot.

So they stood for a moment, on opposite hills, with upraised hand. *Good-bye. Luck.*

MAUREEN DALY

4 / SIXTEEN

Now don't get me wrong. I mean, I want you to understand from the beginning that I'm not really so dumb. I know what a girl should do and what she shouldn't. I get around. I read. I listen to the radio. And I have two older sisters. So you see, I know what the score is. I know it's smart to wear tweedish skirts and shaggy sweaters with sleeves pushed up and pearls and ankle socks and saddle shoes that look as if they've seen the world. And I know that your hair should be long, almost to your shoulders, and sleek as a wet seal, just a little fluffed on the ends and you should wear a campus hat or a dink or else a peasant hankie if you've that sort of face. Properly, a peasant hankie should make you think of edelweiss, mist and sunny mountains, yodeling and Swiss cheese. You know, that kind of peasant. Now, me, I never wear a hankie. It makes my face seem wide and Slavic and I look like a picture always in one of those magazine articles that run — "And Stalin says the future of Russia lies in its women. In its women who have tilled its soil, raised its children — " Well, anyway. I'm not exactly too small-town either. I read Winchell's column. You get to know what New York boy is that way about some pine-

61

apple princess on the West Coast and what Paradise pretty is currently the prettiest and why someone, eventually, will play Scarlett O'Hara. It gives you that cosmopolitan feeling. And I know that anyone who orders a strawberry sundae in a drugstore instead of a lemon Coke would probably be dumb enough to wear colored ankle socks with high-heeled pumps or use Evening in Paris with a tweed suit. But I'm sort of drifting. This isn't what I wanted to tell you. I just wanted to give you the general idea of how I'm not so dumb. It's important that you understand that.

You see, it was funny how I met him. It was a winter night like any other winter night. And I didn't have my Latin done either. But the way the moon tinseled the twigs and silver-plated the snowdrifts, I just couldn't stay inside. The skating rink isn't far from our house — you can make it in five minutes if the sidewalks aren't slippery — so I went skating. I remember it took me a long time to get ready that night because I had to darn my skating socks first. I don't know why they always wear out so fast — just in the toes too. Maybe it's because I have metal protectors on the toes of my skates. That probably is why. And then I brushed my hair — hard, so hard it clung to my hand and stood up around my head in a hazy halo.

My skates were hanging by the back door all nice and shiny for I'd just gotten them for Christmas and they smelled so queer — just like fresh smoked ham. My dog walked with me as far as the corner. She's a red chow, very polite and well-mannered, and she kept pretending it was me she liked when all the time I knew it was the ham smell. She panted along beside me and her hot breath made a frosty little balloon balancing on the end of her nose. My skates thumped me good-naturedly on my back as I walked and the night was breathlessly quiet and the stars winked down like a million flirting eyes. It was all so lovely.

It was all so lovely I ran most of the way and it was lucky the sidewalks had ashes on them or I'd have slipped surely. The ashes crunched like Cracker Jacks and I could feel their cindery shape through the thinness of my shoes. I always wear old shoes when I go skating.

I had to cut across someone's back garden to get to the rink and last summer's grass stuck through the thin ice, brown and discouraged. Not many people came through this way and the crusted snow broke through the little hollows between corn stubbles frozen hard in the ground. I was out of breath when I got to the shanty — out of breath with running and with the loveliness of the night. Shanties are always such friendly places. The floor all hacked to wet splinters from skate runners and the wooden wall frescoed with symbols of dead romance. There was a smell of singed wool as someone got too near the glowing isinglass grin of the iron stove. Girls burst through the door laughing with snow on their hair and tripped over shoes scattered on the floor. A pimply faced boy grabbed the hat from the frizzled head of an eighth-grade blonde and stuffed it into an empty galosh to prove his love and then hastily bent to examine his skate strap with innocent unconcern.

It didn't take me long to get my own skates on and I stuck my shoes under the bench — far back where they wouldn't get knocked around and would be easy to find when I wanted to go home. I walked out on my toes and the shiny runners of my new skates dug deep into the sodden floor.

It was snowing a little outside — quick, eager little Luxlike flakes that melted as soon as they touched your hand. I don't know where the snow came from for there were stars out. Or maybe the stars were in my eyes and I just kept seeing them every time I looked up into the darkness. I waited a moment. You know, to start to skate at a crowded rink is like jumping on a moving merry-go-round. The skaters go skimming round in a colored blur like gaudy painted horses and the shrill musical jabber re-echoes in the night from a hundred human calliopes. Once in, I went all right. At least after I found out exactly where that rough ice was. It was "Round, round, jump the rut, round, round, round, jump the rut, round, round — "

And then he came. All of a sudden his arm was around my waist so warm and tight and he said very casually, "Mind if I skate with you?" and then he took my other hand. That's all there was to it. Just that and then we were skating. It wasn't that I'd never skated with a boy before. Don't be silly. I told you before I get around. But this was different. He was a smoothie! He was a big shot up at school and he went to all the big dances and he was the best dancer in town except Harold Wright who didn't count because he'd been to college in New York for two years! Don't you see? This was different.

At first I can't remember what we talked about, I can't even remember if we talked at all. We just skated and skated and laughed every time we came to that rough spot and pretty soon we were laughing all the time at nothing at all. It was all so lovely.

Then we sat on the big snowbank at the edge of the rink and just watched. It was cold at first even with my skating pants on, sitting on that hard heap of snow but pretty soon I got warm all over. He threw a handful of snow at me and it fell in a little white shower on my hair and he leaned over to brush it off. I held my breath. The night stood still.

The moon hung just over the warming shanty like a big quarter slice of muskmelon and the smoke from the pipe chimney floated up in a sooty fog. One by one the houses around the rink twinked out their lights and somebody's hound wailed a mournful apology to a star as he curled up for the night. It was all so lovely.

Then he sat up straight and said, "We'd better start home." Not "Shall I take you home?" or "Do you live far?" but "We'd better start home." See, that's how I know he wanted to take me home. Not because he *had* to but because he *wanted* to. He went to the shanty to get my shoes. "Black ones," I told him. "Same size as Garbo's." And he laughed again. He was still smiling when he came back and took off my skates and tied the wet skate strings in a soggy knot and put them over his shoulder. Then he held out his hand and I slid off the snowbank and brushed off the seat of my pants and we were ready.

It was snowing harder now. Big, quiet flakes that clung to twiggy bushes and snuggled in little drifts against the tree trunks. The night was an etching in black and white. It was all so lovely, I was sorry I lived only a few blocks away. He talked softly as we walked as if every little word were a secret. "Did I like Wayne King, and did I plan to go to college next year, and had I a cousin who lived in Appleton and knew his brother?" A very respectable Emily Post sort of conversation and then finally — "How nice I looked with snow in my hair, and had I ever seen the moon so — close?" For the moon was following us as we walked and ducking playfully behind a chimney every time I turned to look at it. And then we were home.

The porch light was on. My mother always puts the porch light on when I go away at night. And we stood there a moment by the front steps and the snow turned pinkish in the glow of the colored light and a few feathery flakes settled on his hair. Then he took my skates and put them over my shoulder and said, "Good night now, I'll call you."

I went inside then and in a moment he was gone. I watched him from my window as he went down the street. He was whistling softly and I waited until the sound faded away so I couldn't tell if it was he or my heart whistling out there in the night. And then he was gone, completely gone.

I shivered. Somehow the darkness seemed changed. The stars were little hard chips of light far up in the sky and the moon stared down with a sullen yellow glare. The air was tense with sudden cold and a gust of wind swirled his footprints into white oblivion. Everything was quiet.

But he'd said, "I'll call you." That's what he said, "I'll call you." I couldn't sleep all night.

And that was last Thursday. Tonight is Tuesday. Tonight is Tuesday and my homework's, done, and I darned some stockings that didn't really need it, and I worked a crossword puzzle, and I listened to the radio, and now I'm just sitting. I'm just sitting because I can't think of anything else to do. I can't think of anything, anything but snowflakes and ice skates and yellow moons and Thursday night. The telephone is sitting on the corner table with its old black face turned to the wall so I can't see its leer. I don't even jump when it rings any more. My heart still prays but my mind just laughs. Outside the night is still, so still I think I'll go crazy and the white snow's all dirtied and smoked into grayness and the wind is blowing the arc light so it throws

weird, waving shadows from the trees onto the
lawn — like thin, starved arms begging for I don't
know what. And so I'm just sitting here and I'm
not feeling anything, I'm not even sad because
all of a sudden I know. All of a sudden I know. I
can sit here now forever and laugh and laugh and
laugh while the tears run salty in the corners of
my mouth. For all of a sudden I know, I know
what the stars knew all the time — he'll never,
never call — never.

5/SPLIT CHERRY TREE

"I don't mind staying after school," I says to Professor Herbert, "but I'd rather you'd whip me with a switch and let me go home early. Pa will whip me anyway for getting home two hours late."

"You are too big to whip," says Professor Herbert, "and I have to punish you for climbing up in that cherry tree. You boys knew better than that! The other five boys have paid their dollar each. You have been the only one who has not helped pay for the tree. Can't you borrow a dollar?"

"I can't," I says. "I'll have to take the punishment. I wish it would be quicker punishment. I wouldn't mind."

Professor Herbert stood and looked at me. He was a big man. He wore a gray suit of clothes. The suit matched his gray hair.

"You don't know my father," I says to Professor Herbert. "He might be called a little old-fashioned. He makes us mind him until we're twenty-one years old. He believes: 'If you spare the rod you spoil the child.' I'll never be able to make him understand about the cherry tree. I'm the first of my people to go to high school."

"You must take the punishment," says Professor Herbert. "You must stay two hours after school today and two hours after school tomorrow. I am allowing you twenty-five cents an hour. That is good money for a high school student. You can sweep the schoolhouse floor, wash the blackboards and clean windows. I'll pay the dollar for you."

I couldn't ask Professor Herbert to loan me a dollar. He never offered to loan it to me. I had to stay and help the janitor and work out my fine at a quarter an hour.

I thought as I swept the floor: "What will Pa do to me? What lie can I tell him when I go home? Why did we ever climb that cherry tree and break it down for anyway? Why did we run crazy over the hills away from the crowd? Why did we do all of this? Six of us climbed up in a little cherry tree after one little lizard! Why did the tree split and fall with us? It should have been a stronger tree! Why did Eif Crabtree just happen to be below us plowing and catch us in his cherry tree? Why wasn't he a better man than to charge us six dollars for the tree?"

It was six o'clock when I left the schoolhouse. I had six miles to walk home. It would be after seven when I got home. I had all my work to do when I got home. It took Pa and me both to do the work. Seven cows to milk. Nineteen head of cattle to feed, four mules, twenty-five hogs. Firewood and stovewood to cut and water to draw from the well. He would be doing it when I got home. He would be mad and wondering what was keeping me!

I hurried home. I would run under the dark leafless trees. I would walk fast uphill. I would run down the hill. The ground was freezing. I had to hurry. I had to run. I reached the long ridge that led to our cow pasture. I ran along this

ridge. The wind dried the sweat on my face. I ran
across the pasture to the house.

I threw down my books in the chipyard. I ran
to the barn to spread fodder on the ground for the
cattle. I didn't take time to change my clean
school clothes for my old work clothes. I ran out
to the barn. I saw Pa spreading fodder on the
ground for the cattle. That was my job. I ran up
to the fence. I says: "Leave that for me, Pa. I'll do
it. I'm just a little late."

"I see you are," says Pa. He turned and looked
at me. His eyes danced fire. "What in th' world
has kept you so? Why ain't you been here to help
me with this work? Make a gentleman out'n one
boy in th' family and this is what you get. Send
you to high school and you get too ornery fer th'
buzzards to smell!"

I never said anything. I didn't want to tell why
I was late from school. Pa stopped scattering the
bundles of fodder. He looked at me. He says:
"Why are you gettin' in here this time o' night?
You tell me or I'll take a hickory withe to you
right here on th' spot!"

I says: "I had to stay after school." I couldn't
lie to Pa. He'd go to school and find out why I had
to stay. If I lied to him it would be too bad for me.

"Why did you haf to stay atter school?" says Pa.

I says: "Our biology class went on a field trip
today. Six of us boys broke down a cherry tree. We
had to give a dollar apiece to pay for the tree. I
didn't have the dollar. Professor Herbert is
making me work out my dollar. He gives me
twenty-five cents an hour. I had to stay in this afternoon. I'll have to stay in tomorrow afternoon!"

"Are you telling me th' truth?" says Pa.

"I'm telling you the truth," I says. "Go and see
for yourself."

"That's just what I'll do in th' mornin'," says

Pa. "Jist whose cherry tree did you break down?"

"Eif Crabtree's cherry tree!"

"What was you doin' clear out in Eif Crabtree's place?" says Pa. "He lives four miles from th' County High School. Don't they teach you no books at that high school? Do they jist let you get out and gad over th' hillsides? If that's all they do I'll keep you at home, Dave. I've got work here fer you to do!"

"Pa," I says, "spring is just getting here. We take a subject in school where we have to have bugs, snakes, flowers, lizards, frogs, and plants. It is biology. It was a pretty day today. We went out to find a few of these. Six of us boys saw a lizard at the same time sunning on a cherry tree. We all went up the tree to get it. We broke the tree down. It split at the forks. Eif Crabtree was plowing down below us. He ran up the hill and got our names. The other boys gave their dollar apiece. I didn't have mine. Professor Herbert put mine in for me. I have to work it out at school."

"Poor man's son, huh," says Pa. "I'll attend to that myself in th' mornin'. I'll take keer o' 'im. He ain't from this county nohow. I'll go down there in th' mornin' and see 'im. Lettin' you leave your books and galavant all over th' hills. What kind of a school is it nohow! Didn't do that, my son, when I's a little shaver in school. All fared alike too."

"Pa, please don't go down there," I says. "Just let me have fifty cents and pay the rest of my fine. I don't want you to go down there! I don't want you to start anything with Professor Herbert!"

"Ashamed of your old pap, are you, Dave," says Pa, "atter the way I've worked to raise you! Tryin' to send you to school so you can make a better livin' than I've made."

I thought once I'd run through the woods

above the barn just as hard as I could go. I
thought I'd leave high school and home forever!
Pa could not catch me! I'd get away! I couldn't go
back to school with him. He'd have a gun and
maybe he'd shoot Professor Herbert. It was hard
to tell what he would do. I could tell Pa that
school had changed in the hills from the way it
was when he was a boy, but he wouldn't understand. I could tell him we studied frogs, birds,
snakes, lizards, flowers, insects. But Pa wouldn't
understand. If I did run away from home it
wouldn't matter to Pa. He would see Professor
Herbert anyway. He would think that high school
and Professor Herbert had run me away from
home. There was no need to run away. I'd just
have to stay, finish foddering the cattle, and go to
school with Pa the next morning.

The moon shone bright in the cold March sky.
I finished my work by moonlight. Professor Herbert really didn't know how much work I had to
do at home. If he had known he would not have
kept me after school. He would have loaned me a
dollar to have paid my part on the cherry tree. He
had never lived in the hills. He didn't know the
way the hill boys had to work so that they could
go to school. Now he was teaching in a County
High School where all the boys who attended were
from hill farms.

After I'd finished doing my work I went to the
house and ate my supper. Pa and Mom had eaten.
My supper was getting cold. I heard Pa and Mom
talking in the front room. Pa was telling Ma about
me staying in after school.

"I had to do all th' milkin' tonight, chop th'
wood myself. It's too hard on me atter I've turned
ground all day. I'm goin' to take a day off tomorrow and see if I can't remedy things a little. I'll go
down to that high school tomorrow. I won't be a

very good scholar fer Professor Herbert nohow. He won't keep me in atter school. I'll take a different kind of lesson down there and make 'im acquainted with it."

"Now, Luster," says Mom, "you jist stay away from there. Don't cause a lot o' trouble. You can be jailed fer a trick like that. You'll get th' Law atter you. You'll jist go down there and show off and plague your own boy Dave to death in front o' all th' scholars!"

"Plague or no plague," says Pa, "he don't take into consideration what all I haf to do here, does he? I'll show 'im it ain't right to keep one boy in and let the rest go scot-free. My boy is good as th' rest, ain't he? A bullet will make a hole in a schoolteacher same as it will anybody else. He can't do me that way and get by with it. I'll plug 'im first. I aim to go down there bright and early in the mornin' and get all this straight! I aim to see about bug larnin' and this runnin' all over God's creation huntin' snakes, lizards, and frogs. Ransackin' th' country and goin' through cherry orchards and breakin' th' trees down atter lizards! Old Eif Crabtree ought to a-poured th' hot lead into 'em instead o' chargin' six dollars fer th' tree! He ought to a-got old Herbert the first one!"

I ate my supper. I slipped upstairs and lit the lamp. I tried to forget the whole thing. I studied plane geometry. Then I studied my biology lesson. I could hardly study for thinking about Pa. "He'll go to school with me in the morning. He'll take a gun for Professor Herbert! What will Professor Herbert think of me! I'll tell him when Pa leaves that I couldn't help it. But Pa might shoot him. I hate to go with Pa. Maybe he'll cool off about it tonight and not go in the morning."

Pa got up at four o'clock. He built a fire in the stove. Then he built a fire in the fireplace. He got

Mom up to get breakfast. Then he got me up to help feed and milk. By the time we had our work done at the barn, Mom had breakfast ready for us. We ate our breakfast. Daylight came and we could see the bare oak trees covered white with frost. The hills were white with frost.

"Now, Dave," says Pa, "let's get ready fer school. I aim to go with you this mornin' and look into bug larnin', frog larnin', lizard and snake larnin', and breakin' down cherry trees! I don't like no sicha foolish way o' larnin' myself!"

Pa hadn't forgot. I'd have to take him to school with me. He would take me to school with him. I was glad we were going early. If Pa pulled a gun on Professor Herbert there wouldn't be so many of my classmates there to see him.

I knew that Pa wouldn't be at home in the high school. He wore overalls, big boots, a blue shirt and a sheepskin coat and a slouched black hat gone to seed at the top. He put his gun in its holster. We started trudging toward the high school across the hill.

It was early when we got to the County High School. Professor Herbert had just got there. I just thought as we walked up the steps into the schoolhouse: "Maybe Pa will find out Professor Herbert is a good man. He just doesn't know him. Just like I felt toward the Lambert boys across the hill. I didn't like them until I'd seen them and talked to them, then I liked them and we were friends. It's a lot in knowing the other fellow."

"You're th' Professor here, ain't you?" says Pa.

"Yes," says Professor Herbert, "and you are Dave's father?"

"Yes," says Pa, pulling out his gun and laying it on the seat in Professor Herbert's office. Professor Herbert's eyes got big behind his black-rimmed glasses when he saw Pa's gun. Color came into his pale cheeks.

"Jist a few things about this school I want to know," says Pa. "I'm tryin' to make a scholar out'n Dave. He's the only one out'n eleven youngins I've sent to high school. Here he comes in late and leaves me all th' work to do! He said you's all out bug huntin' yesterday and broke a cherry tree down. He had to stay two hours atter school yesterday and work out money to pay on that cherry tree! Is that right?"

"W-w-why," says Professor Herbert, "I guess it is."

He looked at Pa's gun.

"Well," says Pa, "this ain't no high school. It's a damn bug school, a lizard school, a snake school! It ain't no damn school nohow!"

"Why did you bring that gun?" says Professor Herbert to Pa.

"You see that little hole," says Pa as he picked up the long blue .44 and put his finger on the end of the barrel. "A bullet can come out'n that hole that will kill a schoolteacher same as it will any other man. It will kill a rich man same as a poor man. It will kill a man. But atter I come in and saw you, I know'd I wouldn't need it. This maul o'mine could do you up in a few minutes."

Pa stood there, big, hard, brown-skinned, and mighty beside of Professor Herbert. I didn't know Pa was so much bigger and harder. I'd never seen Pa in a schoolhouse before. I'd seen Professor Herbert. He always looked big before to me. He didn't look big standing beside of Pa.

"I was only doing my duty," says Professor Herbert, "Mr. Sexton, and following the course of study the state provided us with."

"Course o' study!" says Pa. "What study? Bug study? Varmint study? Takin' youngins to th' woods. Boys and girls all out there together a-galavantin' in the brush and kickin' up their heels and their poor old ma's and pa's at home a-slavin' to keep 'em in school and give 'em a education!"

Students are coming into the schoolhouse now. Professor Herbert says: "Close the door, Dave, so others won't hear."

I walked over and closed the door. I was shaking like a leaf in the wind. I thought Pa was going to hit Professor Herbert every minute. He was doing all the talking. His face was getting red. The red color was coming through the brown, weather-beaten skin on Pa's face.

"It jist don't look good to me," says Pa, "a-takin' all this whole swarm of youngins out to pillage th' whole deestrict. Breakin' down cherry trees. Keepin' boys in atter school."

"What else could I have done with Dave, Mr. Sexton?" says Professor Herbert. "The boys didn't have any business all climbing that cherry tree after one lizard. One boy could have gone up the tree and got it. The farmer charged us six dollars. It was a little steep, I think, but we had it to pay. Must I make five boys pay and let your boy off? He said he didn't have the dollar and couldn't get it. So I put it in for him. I'm letting him work it out. He's not working for me. He's working for the school!"

"I jist don't know what you could a-done with 'im," says Pa, "only a-larruped 'im with a withe! That's what he needed!"

"He's too big to whip," says Professor Herbert, pointing to me. "He's a man in size."

"He's not too big for me to whip," says Pa. "They ain't too big until they're over twenty-one! It jist didn't look fair to me! Work one and let th' rest out because they got th' money. I don't see

what bugs has got to do with a high school!
It don't look good to me nohow!"

Pa picked up his gun and put it back in its holster. The red color left Professor Herbert's face.
He talked more to Pa. Pa softened a little. It
looked funny to see Pa in the high school building.
It was the first time he'd ever been there.

"We're not only hunting snakes, toads, flowers,
butterflies, lizards," says Professor Herbert, "but,
Mr. Sexton, I was hunting dry timothy grass to
put in an incubator and raise some protozoa."

"I don't know what that is," says Pa. "Th' incubator is th' new-fangled way o' cheatin' th' hens
and raisin' chickens. I ain't so sure about th' breed
o' chickens you mentioned."

"You've heard of germs, Mr. Sexton, haven't
you?" says Professor Herbert.

"Jist call me Luster if you don't mind," says Pa,
very casual like.

"All right, Luster, you've heard of germs,
haven't you?"

"Yes," says Pa, "but I don't believe in germs. I'm
sixty-five years old and I ain't seen one yet!"

"You can't see them with your naked eye," says
Professor Herbert. "Just keep that gun in the holster and stay with me in the high school today. I
have a few things I want to show you. That scum
on your teeth has germs in it."

"What," says Pa, "you mean to tell me I've got
germs on my teeth!"

"Yes," says Professor Herbert. "The same kind
as we might be able to find in a living black snake
if we dissect it!"

"I don't mean to dispute your word," says Pa,
"but damned if I believe it. I don't believe I have
germs on my teeth!"

"Stay with me today and I'll show you. I want
to take you through the school anyway. School has

changed a lot in the hills since you went to school. I don't guess we had high schools in this county when you went to school."

"No," says Pa, "jist readin', writin', and cipherin'. We didn't have all this bug larnin' and findin' germs on your teeth and in the middle o' black snakes! Th' world's changin'."

"It is," says Professor Herbert, "and we hope all for the better. Boys like your own there are going to help change it. He's your boy. He knows all of what I've told you. You stay with me today."

"I'll shore stay with you," says Pa. "I want to see th' germs off'n my teeth. I jist want to see a germ. I've never seen one in my life. 'Seein' is believin', Pap allus told me."

Pa walks out of the office with Professor Herbert. I just hoped Professor Herbert didn't have Pa arrested for pulling his gun. Pa's gun has always been a friend to him when he goes to settle disputes.

The bell rang. School took up. I saw the students when they marched in the schoolhouse look at Pa. They would grin and punch each other. Pa just stood and watched them pass in at the schoolhouse door. Two long lines marched in the house. The boys and girls were clean and well-dressed. Pa stood over in the schoolyard under a leafless elm, in his sheepskin coat, his big boots laced in front with buckskin and his heavy socks stuck above his boot tops. Pa's overalls' legs were baggy and wrinkled between his coat and boot tops. His blue work shirt showed at the collar. His big black hat showed his gray-streaked black hair. His face was hard and weather-tanned to the color of ripe fodder blade. His hands were big and gnarled like the roots of the elm tree he stood beside.

When I went to my first class I saw Pa and Professor Herbert going around over the school-

house. I was in my geometry class when Pa and
Professor Herbert came in the room. We were explaining our propositions on the blackboard. Professor Herbert and Pa just quietly came in and sat
down for a while. I heard Fred Wurts whisper to
Glenn Armstrong: "Who is that old man? Lord,
he's a rough-looking scamp." Glenn whispered
back: "I think he's Dave's pap." The students in
geometry looked at Pa. They must have wondered
what he was doing in school. Before the class was
over, Pa and Professor Herbert got up and went
out. I saw them together down on the playground.
Professor Herbert was explaining to Pa. I could see
the outline of Pa's gun under his coat when he'd
walk around.

At noon in the high school cafeteria Pa and Professor Herbert sat together at the little table where
Professor Herbert always ate by himself. They ate
together. The students watched the way Pa ate.
He ate with his knife instead of his fork. A lot of
the students felt sorry for me after they found out
he was my father. They didn't have to feel sorry
for me. I wasn't ashamed of Pa after I found out
he wasn't going to shoot Professor Herbert. I was
glad they had made friends. I wasn't ashamed of
Pa. I wouldn't be as long as he behaved.

In the afternoon when we went to biology Pa
was in the class. He was sitting on one of the high
stools beside the microscope. We went ahead with
our work just as if Pa wasn't in the class. I saw Pa
take his knife and scrape tartar from one of his
teeth. Professor Herbert put it on the lens and adjusted the microscope for Pa. He adjusted it and
worked awhile. Then he says: "Now, Luster,
look! Put your eye right down to the light. Squint
the other eye!"

Pa put his head down and did as Professor Herbert said: "I see 'em," says Pa. "Who'd a-ever

thought that? Right on a body's teeth! Right in a body's mouth! You're right certain they ain't no fake to this, Professor Herbert?"

"No, Luster," says Professor Herbert. "It's there. That's the germ. Germs live in a world we cannot see with the naked eye. We must use the microscope. There are millions of them in our bodies. Some are harmful. Others are helpful."

Pa holds his face down and looks through the microscope. We stop and watch Pa. He sits upon the tall stool. His knees are against the table. His legs are long. His coat slips up behind when he bends over. The handle of his gun shows. Professor Herbert quickly pulls his coat down.

"Oh, yes," says Pa. He gets up and pulls his coat down. Pa's face gets a little red. He knows about his gun and he knows he doesn't have any use for it in high school.

"We have a big black snake over here we caught yesterday," says Professor Herbert. "We'll chloroform him and dissect him and show you he has germs in his body too."

"Don't do it," says Pa. "I believe you. I jist don't want to see you kill the black snake. I never kill one. They are good mousers and a lot o' help to us on the farm. I like black snakes. I jist hate to see people kill 'em. I don't allow 'em killed on my place."

The students look at Pa. They seem to like him better after he said that. Pa with a gun in his pocket but a tender heart beneath his ribs for snakes, but not for man! Pa won't whip a mule at home. He won't whip his cattle.

Professor Herbert took Pa through the laboratory. He showed him the different kinds of work we were doing. He showed him our equipment. They stood and talked while we worked. Then they walked out together. They talked louder when they got out in the hall.

When our biology class was over I walked out of the room. It was our last class for the day. I would have to take my broom and sweep two hours to finish paying for the split cherry tree. I just wondered if Pa would want me to stay. He was standing in the hallway watching the students march out. He looked lost among us. He looked like a leaf turned brown on the tree among the treetops filled with growing leaves.

I got my broom and started to sweep. Professor Herbert walked up and says: "I'm going to let you do that some other time. You can go home with your father. He is waiting out there."

I laid my broom down, got my books, and went down the steps.

Pa says: "Ain't you got two hours o' sweepin' yet to do?"

I says: "Professor Herbert said I could do it some other time. He said for me to go home with you."

"No," says Pa. "You are goin' to do as he says. He's a good man. School has changed from my day and time. I'm a dead leaf, Dave. I'm behind. I don't belong here. If he'll let me I'll get a broom and we'll both sweep one hour. That pays your debt. I'll hep you pay it. I'll ast 'im and see if he won't let me hep you."

"I'm going to cancel the debt," says Professor Herbert. "I just wanted you to understand, Luster."

"I understand," says Pa, "and since I understand, he must pay his debt fer th' tree and I'm goin' to hep 'im."

"Don't do that," says Professor Herbert. "It's all on me."

"We don't do things like that," says Pa; "we're just and honest people. We don't want somethin' fer nothin'. Professor Herbert, you're wrong now and I'm right. You'll haf to listen to me. I've larned a lot from you. My boy must go on. Th' world has left me. It changed while I've raised my family and plowed th' hills. I'm a just and honest man. I don't skip debts. I ain't larned 'em to do that. I ain't got much larnin' myself but I do know right from wrong atter I see through a thing."

Professor Herbert went home. Pa and I stayed and swept one hour. It looked funny to see Pa use a broom. He never used one at home. Mom used the broom. Pa used the plow. Pa did hard work. Pa says: "I can't sweep. Durned if I can. Look at th' streaks o' dirt I leave on th' floor! Seems like no work a-tall fer me. Brooms is too light 'r somethin'. I'll jist do th' best I can, Dave. I've been wrong about th' school."

I says: "Did you know Professor Herbert can get a warrant out for you for bringing your pistol to school and showing it in his office! They can railroad you for that!"

"That's all made right," says Pa. "I've made that right. Professor Herbert ain't goin' to take it to court. He likes me. I like 'im. We jist had to get together. He had the remedies. He showed me. You must go on to school. I am as strong a man as ever come out'n th' hills fer my years and th' hard work I've done. But I'm behind, Dave. I'm a little man. Your hands will be softer than mine. Your clothes will be better. You'll allus look cleaner than your old pap. Jist remember, Dave, to pay your debts and be honest. Jist be kind to animals and don't bother th' snakes. That's all I got agin th' school. Puttin' black snakes to sleep and cuttin' 'em open."

It was late when we got home. Stars were in the
sky. The moon was up. The ground was frozen.
Pa took his time going home. I couldn't run like I
did the night before. It was ten o'clock before
we got the work finished, our suppers eaten. Pa
sat before the fire and told Mom he was going to
take her and show her a germ some time. Mom
hadn't seen one either. Pa told her about the high
school and the fine man Professor Herbert was. He
told Mom about the strange school across the hill
and how different it was from the school in their
day and time.

SALLY BENSON

6/AFTER THE BALL

No one could have guessed her age seeing her
drive around town in the cream-colored convert-
ible coupé, its top down. She drove carelessly, a
cigarette in one hand, her other hand resting casually on the wheel. Her lipstick matched her nails
and blended with the color of her dress; rust polish with green, red with white or brown, rose with
pastel shades. She was perfect from her smart well-
fitting sandals to her seemingly endless supply of
small felts. Her manner was perfect too. She spoke
in a tired, low-pitched voice, and she looked at the
person she was addressing as though he were very,
very far away. Every morning when she strolled
in Osborne's Market, she created something of a
sensation. The two boys who sold fruits and vege-
tables simply stared and even old Mr. Osborne
who had, as he put it, "seen hundreds of them
come and go," was impressed and suggested filet
mignon or a nice rib roast, feeling vaguely that
chopped round steak or shoulder lamb for stew-
ing was out of the question.

She might have been Joan Crawford, Myrna
Loy, or the pampered daughter of a millionaire,
home from a winter on the Riviera. She might
have been anyone romantic and exciting. But her

name was Norma Martin and she was sixteen years old. In her smart little bag with her lipstick, compact, and cigarette case, was her first driver's license.

She was not the same Norma Martin who had recently been graduated from Saint Catherine's School for Girls. Her hockey stick had been left to warp in the hall closet at home; her plain white underthings with their name tapes lay packed in a trunk in the attic; her school books had been sold to a child who still believed that being a senior at Saint Catherine's was all that Life could hold. For the Norma Martin summering at Pine Bluffs, Saint Catherine's was gone forever. School days were in the dim past of a month ago. Pine Bluffs was the Present. It was Life.

The idea of going someplace new, someplace different, had come to her in the Easter vacation. She had caught her mother in the very act of writing old Mrs. Hillis to say that they would take her Spoondrift Cottage at Monroe, Connecticut, as they had done for the last fourteen years, and she realized that never again could she stand Monroe. In the first place, there was Annie with whom she had played every summer for as long as she could remember. Annie was nice, she thought, she was a good kid, but Annie was fifteen. When you were only fifteen, you were as good as dead. She knew what it was like to be only fifteen in Monroe. She could see herself as she had been last summer, being a little noisy on the beach to attract the attention of the older crowd — the smooth crowd; pretending to think it fun when loathsome little boys threw you off the raft; dancing with other girls at the Tuesday night dances at the Yacht Club, being bumped into by rowdy ten-year-olds who thought a dance floor was meant to slide on;

trying to keep time to the foul four-piece orchestra when your feet twitched to step to the tropical beat of Hap Harvey's Hey-Makers who played for the real dances on Saturday nights. Last summer she and Annie would sit on the fence around the parking space and look in the windows, content with the sound of the music and the cool deliciousness of their ice-cream cones, content with the soft summer nights and glimpses of the world that revolved before them. But this summer, she knew, she could never bring herself merely to look on. She was sixteen. Pretty soon she would be seventeen, eighteen, nineteen, and then twenty. She would be married at twenty. Twenty would be the end.

So in a panic she begged her mother not to write for Spoondrift Cottage. In desperation she fished a name from her memory — Pine Bluffs. A girl from school had been there once. It was awfully smart, the girl said, there were loads of people, the casino was perfect, there were beach umbrellas and even cabanas on the beach — just like Europe. And no one would know how old she was. She would have her driver's license, and as far as anyone could tell, she would be as good as eighteen.

Norma didn't paint this picture for her mother. She told her that there was practically no traffic on the roads, which would be awfully good since her mother was so nervous in a car; that it was *much* cooler, being farther north; that the cottages were lovely and had gas stoves; that there were beautiful drives, free lectures about wild flowers, no undertow, and any number of bridge clubs that met once or twice a week, to say nothing of the duplicate tournaments at the casino.

Mrs. Martin was won over. "I don't know but

what I'd like a change myself," she told her husband. "I feel as though I know every cameo pin on every bosom in Monroe. And you know the bridge I get with Peggy Blake — one spade, two spades, six spades. Goodness! I don't think I could face it again. Besides," she added in her innocence, "it sounds quite different."

Mrs. Martin was a little disappointed when she saw the cottage. They had rented The Breakers, a bare, wind-swept cottage with a view of the ocean from the bathroom, and it was dishearteningly like Spoondrift Cottage in Monroe. It had the same walnut stain on its walls, the same sort of wicker furniture, an identical bridge lamp, similar faded chintz at the windows. But there was a gas stove, the fireplace was large and drew well, and the breeze from the ocean was salty and fresh. Besides, Norma was delighted. She pronounced the cottage perfect, the bathing marvelous, the summer visitors *really* attractive. And she underwent a great change.

She began to fuss over her appearance, spending hours in the tub, hours over her nails, hours pressing her clothes and getting dressed. It seemed to Mrs. Martin that Norma was always underfoot, fussing with the electric iron, fussing with her hair. It was nice, she thought, that the child was beginning to take an interest in her appearance, but it had been nice, too, in the days when she was up, out of the house, and out of the way. She remonstrated with her about it. "I don't see why wearing a dress twice, just twice, without pressing it is going to make you or break you."

Norma answered patiently. "You've got to be well-groomed. Now, you always look all right and sweet, really. But no one could say you were well-groomed. It's a matter of detail."

"Well-groomed!" Mrs. Martin sniffed. "You've

been reading the advertisements in the magazines. If you ask me, young lady, I shouldn't say you had much to be well-groomed *for!*"

The minute she said this, she was sorry. Because, although they had been at Pine Bluffs ten days, Norma knew no one. Every morning, after patient hours in front of her mirror, she went to the car, immaculately put together, and drove to the village to do the marketing. This was an innovation, but she was so proud of her driving and there were so few places to drive to that Mrs. Martin had agreed to let her go, a little relieved to be spared a tiresome chore, quite staggered at the amount of stuff Norma sent home. By the time the marketing was done, it was time for lunch — a salad for Norma, a glass of orange juice, a glass of buttermilk. "You've got to eat!" Mrs. Martin cried in desperation over this starvation diet.

"First you tell me I'm too fat, and then you tell me I'm too thin," Norma answered, smoothing her hands over her hips, pulling her stomach in.

Though she did nothing, she seemed strangely contented, during the daytime, anyway. She drove around town every spare moment, remembering small errands that had to be done; she dressed and undressed and dressed again; she was practically the girl her mother had hoped she'd be. But somehow it was not quite right. There were the evenings, for instance, when they sat on the porch until dark, and then went in and sat in the wicker chairs in the living room. They talked a little, or read. At ten they went to bed. Mrs. Martin felt she was living with a beautifully dressed, horribly aloof stranger. Outside in the dark, young people passed the cottage, walking or in cars, talking, laughing, singing, but none of them stopped for Norma. She sat sedately in her wicker chair, determinedly reading, looking pale and very young.

The moths beat against the screen door, the wicker furniture creaked, and nothing happened.

Then one day Mrs. Martin came back from the beach, flushed and happy, bearing pleasant news. "Norma!" she called. "What do you think? I met the nicest woman on the beach, and she has a daughter — Jerry, I think they call her. Anyway, she is having a beach picnic tonight and they want you to come."

For a second there was a brief flicker of excitement in Norma's face. But almost immediately she assumed the curiously set expression that lately had been habitual with her. "How old is she?" she asked.

"Oh, I don't know," her mother said. "About your age, I'd say. Fifteen or sixteen."

"Oh, Mother!" Norma exclaimed. "A kid! A perfect child!"

"She's no more a child than you are," Mrs. Martin argued. "What's gotten into you?"

"You haven't found out as much about this place as I have," Norma told her. "There are two sets, not counting the actual *babies*. There are the kids, fourteen or fifteen, and then there's the older crowd. And if you once go around with the kids, you're absolutely *cooked* with the older crowd. You might as well be dead."

"Well, those kids, as you call them, look anything but dead. They don't look half as dead as you do. They look to me as though they were having a very fine time."

But Norma would not budge. And Mrs. Martin, to teach her a lesson, left her alone and went to the beach picnic herself. To help out, she said. She returned about ten, conscience-stricken and uneasy, to find Norma patting cold cream on her smooth, young cheeks.

"It was fun!" Mrs. Martin told her brightly.

"Loads of fun! Those young people are lovely,
really nicer than the crowd at Monroe, I think.
They have more get up and go to them."

"Oh, they're all right, I suppose," Norma
agreed in her new, tired voice. "But they're dreadfully silly. They never say a thing really interesting, though. They just fool all the time."

So things went on as they had been, until
Norma met Bill James. He was a blond young
man who looked like a composite picture of all the
young men in the cigarette advertisements. He
had talked to her at the garage where she was having a tire changed, and later that day he had
stopped by their cottage with the casual informal-
ity, Mrs. Martin thought disapprovingly, of a
much older acquaintance.

He was almost as immaculately gotten up as
Norma. His gray slacks were spotless, his blond
hair was wet and smooth. And he talked unceas-
ingly.

"So this is your first summer here," he said
kindly to Mrs. Martin. "Well, you're going to love
it. There's a great crowd and the first thing you
know you'll be in a whirl. Wait till things get going!" He laughed reminiscently. "The clans
haven't gathered yet. Things don't really get
started until Scotty MacFarlane and his wife get
here. And Ham Brown! He's a great guy! Say, he
doesn't have his eyes open, not really open, from
the day he comes to the day we pour him on the
boat."

"You mean he's — ?" Mrs. Martin asked,
startled and shocked.

But Bill James knew mothers and how to handle them. "Oh, he acts all right," he assured her.
"He knows how to handle it. But he's a riot. Why,
one day Mrs. Grossmith — she's one of the old-

timers here and very much the dowager — gave a cocktail party. Everyone was seeing that Ham got his share, because he's a circus when he's slightly high. Well, I guess we all went to work on him too well, and when he went to say good-bye to Mrs. Grossmith, he kind of stood weaving, and then he said, 'Don't think it hasn't been charming, Mrs. Grossmith.' And fell flat on his nose!''

"Goodness!" Mrs. Martin exclaimed. She looked nervously at Norma.

Norma was sitting forward in her chair watching Bill James.

"Yes, it's a great crowd," he went on. "There are the Harrises, the Waites, Dizzy Thomas, the Smith girls — " He reeled off names.

"It's a tight corporation," he told them. But he looked at Norma and his eyes seemed to say, "Don't worry. I'll get you in."

Later, he arose. "We'll call on some of them. They mostly live on the Point."

Mrs. Martin was about to speak when she caught Norma's pleading look. "Well, if you're going to walk to the Point," she said reluctantly, "you'd better change your shoes."

"Oh, nobody walks here," Bill James told her. "You weren't going to use your car, were you, Mrs. Martin?"

For the first time his voice lost some of its brashness.

That night Mrs. Martin wrote her husband. "It's awful here," she wrote. "I don't know what to do. If I put my foot down, Norma will hate me." She went on to tell him about Bill James. "Although I must admit, from what Norma told me, those people don't sound as bad as I'd pictured them. They gave her tea, and I gather all they talk about is the fine time they had *last* summer. I don't know what they'll find to talk about next summer because, heaven knows, they don't seem to be doing much now."

To Norma she said, "They sound very dull. I should think you'd be bored. Why, they're older people. Some of them are married, and some are engaged to be married. That Bill James is twenty-six. Ten years older than you. The idea!"

But Norma, it seemed, was not bored. She was impressed and flattered. She allowed Bill James to take her out in her mother's car. She waited in town in the hot sun while he did his errands. He rented, every summer, a small shack near the beach and it was lots of fun there, Norma explained. He kept beer on ice and everyone dropped in.

"Well, don't you drink his beer, young lady," Mrs. Martin said.

"I don't like beer."

Every evening about half-past nine, Bill James dropped by. Sometimes he stayed and talked and Mrs. Martin went tactfully to her room. He smoked their cigarettes, lounged with his feet on their couch, and occasionally took Norma places in their car. "I don't want him driving the car," Mrs. Martin protested.

"Oh, Mother, he's a good driver," Norma said impatiently. "He's been driving for years."

"There's to be a dance at the casino this Saturday," Norma announced one day. "It's the first one."

She went to her closet and took out her three evening dresses; the one old one from last winter and the two new ones.

"Which one would you wear?" she asked.

"Well, I always loved that blue net on you," Mrs. Martin said. "It's a sweet dress."

"It's too sweet. It makes me look about twelve."

She laid the blue net aside and studied the others; a flame-colored lace one and a trim black one with a white poplin mess jacket. "The black one's awfully smart," she said vaguely, and hung them up again.

"Are you going with Bill?"

"Oh, I imagine so," Norma answered confidently. "He hasn't said yet. Of course, the tickets are two dollars apiece and he hasn't a lot of money."

"He has enough money to keep himself in beer," Mrs. Martin said acidly.

"He has to keep up his share," Norma explained.

Two nights before the dance, she said unexpectedly to her mother, "Let's go to the movies, the early show."

"What about Bill?"

"Oh, I'm not going to sit here and wait for him to stop by every night. He needn't think I'm just sitting here *waiting*. Come on, let's go."

They went early and sat in the crowded, hot movie theatre a half hour waiting for the pictures to begin. Groups of young girls came in; three or four girls with one young man; couples, young, obviously married. Norma explained them to her mother. "That's Scotty and his wife with the Harrises. Those are the Smith girls and that's Ham Brown with them."

Mrs. Martin looked curiously at Ham Brown, the riot. He was what she called a fat boy, sleepy, dull-looking. He sat with the Smith girls, slouched in his chair, and although Mrs. Martin watched him for quite a while, he never said a word.

"He doesn't look like a ball of fire to me," she said.

"He's awfully funny sometimes," Norma told her.

As people came in, Norma sat forward in her chair and looked eagerly around. She called to people in the rows ahead. "Hello, Diz! Hello, Patty!"

A few negligent heads were turned in their direction, a few casual voices answered, "Oh, hello, Norma."

It was a relief when the house grew dark and the newsreel started. Mrs. Martin was unable to concentrate on the pictures. "What horrid young people," she thought. "How noisy and rude they are."

Afterward, it was even worse. Norma pulled at sleeves as she wormed her way up the aisle. She was demanding attention. Mrs. Martin's heart sank for her.

When they got home, Bill James was waiting for them. He was lying on the couch reading a magazine. "Well, where have *you* been?" he wanted to know.

Norma was animated with him. "To the movies. It was packed. Everybody was there — Ham, and Diz, and Patty, and all the crowd."

Bill James seemed interested. He asked questions about who had been with whom with an almost feminine curiosity. Mrs. Martin went to her room feeling baffled. They were still talking when she went to sleep.

The day before the dance, Norma came home from the beach, white and tearful. She came alone and she began talking before she was in the house. "Oh, Mother! The most terrible thing happened! We were sitting around at Bill's, having the grandest time, and Diz got fooling with my bag. She wanted to borrow my lipstick, she said. But I think she was just snooping, because all the girls looked at one another as though they'd put her up to it. And she found my driver's license! And read it!"

"Well, what about it?" Mrs. Martin asked. "There's nothing incriminating on your driver's license as far as I know. You've never been arrested for anything."

"But now they know!" Norma cried. "And they acted so funny!"

"Know what?" Mrs. Martin was puzzled.

"How old I am! They know how old I am!"

"Do you mean to tell me that no one knew how old you are?" Mrs. Martin was aghast.

"Of course not! You don't think for one minute that Bill or any of them would have paid any attention to me for one minute if they'd known I was sixteen, do you? They thought I was about eighteen. I sort of let them think I was."

"Well!" Mrs. Martin exclaimed.

"I'm through," Norma said. "They'll drop me like a hot cake. You ought to hear how they joke about the kids. You ought to have seen how they acted. They said, 'You old cradle-snatcher, you,' to Bill. And he didn't like it, let me tell you!"

"Now, now," her mother said. "Bill likes you. Goodness knows he comes around here enough. I *know* he's too old for you. I told you he was. But he seemed to like you, and you got along together. I mean, why shouldn't he still come around? If he likes you. After all, it wasn't anything serious. It was never any life or death matter. I don't see what all the fuss is about. Maybe the girls did act a little catty. Girls often do. Especially when there aren't enough boys to go around."

"You don't understand," Norma said. "It is a matter of life or death. The summer's just begun and I'm through!"

The rest of the day was awful. Mrs. Martin found herself listening eagerly for Bill James to call at the front door. She watched Norma, no longer busy with nail polish and cold cream, slink about the house, the banner of her lovely youth pulled down as though she wished to hide it. As though, indeed, she would like to kill her youth. In the evening, Mrs. Martin suggested the movies again, but Norma shook her head. "I couldn't," she said.

Bill James did not come that day, nor did he come the next. "Well, now you know what *he's* like," Mrs. Martin said scornfully.

Norma's look was stricken, but her voice was old with understanding. "He can't help it. He couldn't stand the kidding. He hasn't much money or anything, and all those people have. And they just kind of let him hang around because he's funny and fits in with the crowd. He wouldn't *dare* get them down on him."

About nine, when the cars began to go by the house and the music at the casino started, Mrs. Martin pulled down the shades of the front windows. "Those moths," she said brightly. "I can't stand hearing them beat their wings off on the screen. Let's have a fire."

They lit the fire and the room looked more cheerful. Mrs. Martin tried not to think of the flame-colored dress and the awfully smart black one hanging in the closet. There was no shutting out the noise of the cars passing, the laughing, the sound of the music, the perfectly smooth sax, the gay drum.

At ten she suggested a walk and, surprisingly, Norma agreed. The night was cool but soft, and the stars were brilliant. They walked along the shore looking at them. "That's Venus," Mrs. Martin pointed out. "And that's Mars. I wonder if there are people on Mars."

They walked on, looking at the stars, talking about them, ignoring the deserted look the cot-

tages wore, pretending not to see the cars that
passed them. They walked until after eleven.

"I'm going to sit up a while," Norma said. "I'm
going to write some letters. I'm going to write
Annie."

Mrs. Martin brought in a glass of milk and some
cookies.

"I was thinking," she said, "that we might hire
a sailboat tomorrow and ask that little Jerry to
go with us. Or, maybe, you two would rather go
alone."

"Mmm, that would be swell," Norma said. She
started her letter.

It was about twelve when there was a knock at
the door, and Mrs. Martin heard Bill James' voice.
He was feeling fine, she heard him say, not tight
but just high. The party was going like a forest
fire, and he had come to take Norma to the dance.

"Hop into your things," he said.

Mrs. Martin waited sickeningly for Norma's
answer. "If she is grateful, I'll die," she thought.

Then Norma's voice came to her, cool and fresh.
"I couldn't, not possibly. It's late."

"Late!" Bill James laughed. "It's only twelve!
We've got three hours! It's the crest of the evening and I'm on the crest of the wave!"

"No, really," Norma said in a prim, schoolgirl's
voice. "Thanks just the same."

"Oh, be a sport," Bill James urged. "The whole
gang is there — Scotty, Mrs. Scotty, Ham, and all
the crowd."

"And I suppose Mrs. Scotty is singing with the
orchestra the way she sings to that little piano of
theirs?"

"She hasn't started yet," Bill James said happily.
"But it won't be long now."

"Well, the orchestra will have to go back about

six years to play any of the songs *she* knows. All
that old stuff she sings! Why doesn't she get something new for a change?"

"She's all right," Bill James said, surprised.
"She's a darn good sport."

There was venom in Norma's voice. "Frankly,
she bores me."

There was silence in the living room. "Well, if
you won't come — " Bill James said, no longer
sounding high.

"No. No, thank you," Norma answered. "I
don't feel like it, really. Thanks for dropping by
for me."

Mrs. Martin heard the screen door close as Bill
James took himself away. "I hope he's miserable,"
she thought meanly. "I honestly think he liked
her. Quite a lot."

Her door opened suddenly and Norma's head
looked in. "Did you hear that?" she asked. "Coming around this time of night! Who does he think
he is? What does he think I am?"

She smiled suddenly and gaily at her mother.
"The old stiff," she said. And added as an afterthought, "The old *cripple!*"

HARRY SYLVESTER

7 / EIGHT-OARED CREW

Dusk lay on the river, making all things its own color. Lights had begun to appear in the other boathouses but where Al Leyden — at 38, the "Old Man" — stood on the landing, there was only the growing shadow, quick-deepening now that the sun had gone out of sight behind the west bank of the Hudson. The shell, moving leisurely toward the landing, was only a darker shadow when it docked. Leyden stood apart from the crew, the mood of the evening heavy in him.

The crew swung the shell out of the water at Kip Grant's command and marched it past Leyden. In the blue light they looked like some giant insect, the shell held over their heads. Kip Grant walked by them, silent now and no longer harrying the crew. Too silent, Leyden thought, but he felt no better for knowing the reason for that silence toward the crew of sophomores.

He touched Kip on the arm and the coxswain turned to him. "How was it?" Leyden said.

In the dusk he could barely see the slight shrug of the other's shoulders. "I don't know. Their form is still good — when they don't have to turn on the heat." He paused and said again:

"What they'll do in the race, I don't know. They learned too quickly. . . ."

Leyden nodded.

"My brothers and some friends are in town for the race," Kip said. "Mind if I run into town for an hour or so?"

"Go ahead," Leyden said. He almost added: "Don't make your going too obvious," but with Grant that wasn't necessary, Leyden knew. These boys from the school's traditional families were mentally precocious. . . .

Leyden watched Kip Grant go into the coaches' room to dress. Grant had begun to do this after Leyden had made the change in the crews. It was not a good thing, Leyden knew, for crew and coxswain to be so sharply divided as they were. Regret stirred in him again at having made that change, but in his mind he knew that he had done the right thing. He came from poor people himself. Even if the university was or had been a "rich man's school," Leyden felt that he himself must be just. His sense of justice lay on him now like a weight. He went wearily up the wooden stairs to his own room.

Two years ago the university had gone out and got some scholarship men to bolster up the football team, which had been bad for three years in a row. They were good boys, the new scholarship men, intelligent enough to get by the stiff entrance exams, but hailing from mine and mill and with names new to the school: Kowalik, Leary, and Pivarnik; Granski, Lisbon, and Guttman; the Slavs already replacing the Irish among the athletes.

None of them had ever seen a shell; some of them had never seen a river before coming to the school. They came out for crew in the winter of their freshman year and Leyden had watched them that first day in the barge, with the ice still on the river; watched them with pride and with foreboding.

Leyden had two freshman crews that year and the football coach complained that he was keeping the scholarship men from spring practice. So Leyden let them go for spring football practice and they had returned to him after it and said that they still wanted to row. So Leyden had let them row. . . . It was too late to mold them, or some of them, into the freshman crew that would compete at Poughkeepsie that year. So Leyden had let the scholarship men row alone, as a unit . . . and Leyden saw then the thing that might happen.

Leyden had been an athlete and a coach long enough to know that any great team, whether it be a crew or a football eleven, is more than half accident. The unbelievable and precise coordination that made a team great, as a team, was largely beyond the ability of any coach to create. He could develop it once the accident had occurred but he could not create it.

What Leyden had seen was that eight of the scholarship men had or were part of that curious accident of coordination that might make a great crew. He knew, guiltily, that they, for all their crudeness, could beat the freshman crew already formed. And even when that crew was a close second at Poughkeepsie, Leyden still felt that he had been less than just. Rowing was the traditional sport at the university and, partly by accident, partly by design, the crew was almost always composed of names old in the school's history. Leyden wondered just how much this had affected his judgment.

The next spring he had left the scholarship men together as a unit, as the junior varsity, and

he had gone about the always difficult business of
making a new crew of some of last year's varsity
and some of the freshmen. It was not better than
an average crew although it had a great coxswain,
the senior, Kip Grant. It was a traditional crew
in that it had the old names, Carteret, Grant, Mor-
gan, Fairlee. It won one sprint race, was second in
two others, and last in a longer race.

That spring it took Leyden a long time to do
the thing he felt compelled to do. In May, for
the first time, he had the varsity and junior varsity meet in a brush along the river. The junior
varsity, the scholarship men, won by a little. They
won by a bow a week later, despite having lost
their form in the middle of the race. Then, they
won by two lengths in a three-mile race with
the varsity.

Leyden did then the thing he had to do. He
called the varsity together. "The junior varsity,"
he told them, "has beaten you, decisively. If you
want to row at Poughkeepsie as the varsity, go
ahead. . . . Knowing you as I do, I don't think
you'll want to go to Poughkeepsie that way. The
better way is to race the junior varsity the Poughkeepsie distance, four miles . . . and if they beat
you, let them go — as the varsity. Tell me tomorrow how you want to go to Poughkeepsie."

So their captain, Jim Fairlee, had come and told
Leyden quite gravely that they would go to Poughkeepsie only if they could beat the junior varsity.
And they had raced and the junior varsity, stroked
by Kowalik, had won by three lengths.

They needed a coxswain and Leyden had asked
Kip Grant to go into their boat. And Kip had con-
sented to but he hadn't liked it or them. And so
Leyden's varsity was the eight scholarship men
and Kip Grant, third generation of his family to
sit in one of the university shells.

His dislike for the men he handled the tiller grips for was not unreasonable. They had displaced his friends, had broken a long tradition of which he was a part. Alumni had protested privately and Kip's brothers had even urged him not to sit in the varsity shell. They had done so half humorously, but Kip knew how they felt. He knew, too, how Leyden felt and the weight of the justice that lay heavy on Leyden. . . .

His brothers were waiting for him now in the private dining room they always had the evening before the race. When he opened the door of the room they were yelling at him:

"The kid himself!"

"Say, Kip, is it really true you had to learn to speak Polish?"

In a way he didn't hear them. For he had seen her face. Among the other women there, among the tall Old Blues, it stood out quietly, as Kip expected that it always might. He greeted the others and sat beside her — Mary Adams, his friend since childhood, now the girl he was going to marry. She took his hand under the table and was silent until the others had stopped shouting at Kip.

"Sure," he kept telling them, "we'll win in a breeze."

"They'll blow up in your face under the bridge," Ad Grant said. "I was watching them from the bank this afternoon through glasses."

"They'll row those other crews into the river," Kip said. Their antagonism, however friendly, did something to him. For the first time, and in surprise, he felt as though he were really part of his crew. . . .

They let him alone after a while and he was able to slip out with Mary Adams. The side streets of the town were quiet under the old trees, the wind from the river rich with spring.

"You seem quiet," Mary Adams said. "I had thought you'd be more nervous with the race so close."

"As I get older I suppose I conceal things better," he said. "If the race has made me nervous, something else has made me quiet. Something else besides you." His hand tightened on her arm. "You can always make me quiet. Just being near you."

"It makes me very happy, Kip," she said.

"The other thing," he went on gravely, "is that I've suddenly realized I've been dishonest. I've snooted those men on the crew when I should have tried to know them better. Why I did, I don't know. They're good men."

"I understand," she said quietly. "I suppose it would have been more honest for you to have resigned from the squad or stroked your — own people on the junior varsity."

"My own people," Kip said. There was an edge to his tone. "They rode me tonight. And they're apt to go haywire and fire Al Leyden after the race."

"I think not," she said. "Coming down in the train, they agreed they'd just let him know that they wanted him not to do anything like it again."

"Even if they win," Kip said.

"None of them expect you to win tomorrow," she said.

An old car squeaked to a stop near them. It had Pennsylvania license plates. A head with a battered hat on it poked out one window and spoke unintelligibly to them. Kip went closer to the car and Mary stood on the curb.

"You know where this faller, Pete Kowalik, he stay at? Faller what row in front in bast crew on here?"

From the curb Mary saw Kip straighten. "I imagine it's a bit late to see him. All the crew men are in bed."

"All day long, most last night, we drive this flivver," the voice went on in a singsong. "Stop every garage on road, by damn. Pete Kowalik, he be worried about us. Couldn't phone him eider, I bet."

"They wouldn't call him to the phone at this time of night," Kip said. He moved back to the curb. Mary touched his arm. "These people — " she hesitated. "They've come a long way. You could take a message to Kowalik. He's your stroke, isn't he?"

"I suppose," he said, "I'll be a snob until I die." He walked back to the old car, which was refusing to start. "I'll see Kowalik — if not tonight, first thing in the morning. I can take a message to him."

"You just tell him that his brother Joe got here all hokay and that Malie Stefansik, he come too, and we both be there tomorrow, yalling like hell! Say, who are you, mister? Your face, it — "

"I'm one of the managers," Kip said. He turned away.

"I feel better at your having done that," Mary Adams said.

"I feel better myself." They walked a while in silence.

"Something still bothers you," Mary said.

"I know. I don't think we'll win tomorrow. I had to say it in front of the others, but the men are still green for all their power and natural ability."

"No," she said. "It's just the night that makes you think so." She turned to him in the shadow and he kissed her, feeling some old tension in him become lost in another one, renewed. He broke from her. "I have to get back," he said. At the hotel she pressed his hand. "Until after the race," she said.

The boathouse was in darkness when Kip got there. Going up the wooden stairs to the dormitory where the crews slept, the only light he could see was from the crack under the door of Al Leyden's room. Kip was a long time getting to sleep.

After breakfast, Kip said to Kowalik: "I'd like to speak to you on the float." The tall boy looked surprised but followed Kip outside.

"I ran into your brother last night in town," Kip said. "He had trouble getting here, but he wanted to let you know that he had arrived."

Kowalik looked at once grateful and amused. "Thanks a lot, Grant. I'm glad to hear about my brother getting here all right. But when you called me over here I thought you had something important to say about the race."

"No," Kip said. He turned away, flushing a little. Was he at fault or they? he thought. Was he a snob or were they crude? He had not wanted the others to know that he had spoken even that intimately to Kowalik. Strangely, though, he felt once more his new kinship with the crew, a relation delayed and now hastened by the attitude of his brothers, by Mary Adams' quiet words.

A manager came and told Kip that Leyden would like to see him. He found the coach in his room with the crossed oars on the wall. One of them, Kip knew, had been used by Ad Grant six years ago. "Close the door," Leyden said. "Sit down."

"Guess you didn't sleep much," Kip said. "Saw your light on when I came in."

"I never do the night before a race. The crew did, though."

"They all look good," Kip said. His words fell

hollowly into a silence created by Leyden's looking away. When he turned to Kip again, Leyden's face showed his weariness.

"They might win," Leyden said, "but probably they won't."

Kip nodded once.

"They have stuff," Leyden said, "a lot of it. And guts. They just haven't rowed long enough. They'll try too hard and go to pieces."

"It's a touch late to substitute the jayvee for them," Kip said. "I don't mean to be a wise guy," he added quickly.

"I know," Leyden said. "I made my decision and I'm going to stand by it. About the job I don't have to worry. Your brothers and old man Calder of the crew committee phoned me last night while you were away and said that no matter what happened my job was safe. So it's not me. It's those kids. You don't like them. I can see your point even though I come from the same kind of people they do. But I let them win their place, didn't I?"

"You don't have to talk me into anything," Kip said. "I've changed some. It would be hard to tell you why. But I'll do all I can for them. And I want to win myself. It's my last chance. I'm the only one in the family that never sat in a winning boat at least once at Poughkeepsie."

Leyden nodded. "It's not their last chance," he said. "That's why I called you in here. They have two more big years. What I ask you is this. If they win, all right. If they lose, that's all right, too, in a way, although none of us likes to lose. But bring them in a crew — an eight-oared varsity crew." He paused and the two men looked at each other. "You know what I mean," Leyden said. "If they go to pieces today they may never get together again, this year or any other. I don't know what you may have to do . . . but bring them in right — for their sake and the school's . . . if not for anyone else's."

The river was like glass, the stake boats hardly moving in it. Kip's crew had the outside lane, the fastest but also the roughest if the river kicked up. Also the nearest to the line of yachts at the finish.

The referee called: "Ready all?" and the California cox raised his hand. Kowalik and Guttman cursed at the delay. "Steady," Kip said. It was the first word he had spoken outside of commands since leaving the boathouse. He looked down the line of them and pride in them and what was left of his vanity of class fought in him. They stared at him and formed a curious foreshortened design of white on bronze: the sweatbands sharp against their dark faces, the adhesive tape strapped to their bellies, the heavy wool socks.

"Ready all?" the referee said again and no hand was raised. The little cannon boomed and Kip's "Row!" was lost in its echoes, in the sudden rush of water as the oars bent in the swift, tremendous beat of the racing start. Something had begun to flow in Kip like his blood, but swifter and more subtle, so that he let them come out of the racing start only gradually, his hands beating out the stroke with the tiller grips at forty before he consciously knew how high the beat was.

Already they had a quarter length on the others and the lead grew rapidly, was over a length before the mile mark.

"Bring it down! Down, you madmen!" Kip yelled. Something in their eyes dismayed him. They were trying too hard, almost as though they were trying to escape something. . . . He felt older than they . . . but kept shouting at them until they dropped their beat. Still open water showed between them and Navy and California, leading the others.

"Leary — you're shooting your slide!" Kip yelled. Under the excitement, he could marvel at the power they were getting in spite of their form, worse than usual. He saw that Navy was coming up and, with the edge of his eyes, caught the flash of orange-tipped oars, Syracuse making an early bid. We're not getting much run, he thought, and that's where the bad form counts.

"Get together!" he barked. There was blood on the lips of Lisbon and Guttman. They're trying too hard, he thought. If I yell too much they'll blow up.

The beat was up again, he realized, and wondered vaguely whether he was taking the stroke from Kowalik or Kowalik from him. This annoyed him as did their passing the two-mile mark without his knowing it.

"Down, down, you lugs!" he yelled. His voice had risen higher than usual. They eyed him fearfully. They still led, but in dropping the beat they lost ground and Navy's bow was almost even with them, and Syracuse and California less than a length behind.

Kip knew that this crew was in no mood for subtleties, whether of thought or action. He saw the bridge ahead and that decided him. "All right," he called. "Bring it up." He felt the thrill of their tremendous power move through the frail boat and he saw, with pride, the lead begin to grow again. They liked that, he saw, letting them go all out.

"Give it to them!" he called. "Give it to them! Break their damned hearts!"

They liked to hear him talk that way. They had never heard him do it before. Some of them were even grinning. They led by open water again. Something like a coldness dropped on Kip and was gone, and the noise of many voices. They had passed the bridge and the third mile.

Kip turned a little. They had over a length on Syracuse. The others were strung out, Navy and California at Syracuse's bow.

Leary was shooting his slide again, Guttman getting his oar out of the water too fast. "Steady," Kip called, afraid to say more. Still the cedar shell fled like a thing alive, still the long oars bit deeply into the river, shoveling the water back.

Seven bombs had gone off on the bridge when they went under it to tell those at the finish that the crew in the seventh lane was leading. So they would be ready for him, Kip knew, on the yacht. And he would be ready for them. He would bring his crew aboard with him and see how his brothers liked that!

Exultation beat up in him. Half a mile now. The crew's bodies, sheeted in sweat, gleamed strangely in the twilight. The line of yachts was opening on either side. They were in, Kip thought. "Pick it up," he called. "Pick it up!"

They drove the blades deep, the great bodies bent. "We're in!" he kept thinking in time with the beat of his tiller grips. "We're in! We're in!" The shell trembled as it tore through the water.

Then they blew. Guttman had taken his oar out of the water too soon, had bothered the No. 6 in front of him and made him catch a crab. Leary, shooting his slide, losing power, almost caught one. What he screamed at them, Kip never knew. But when he saw that the bow oar was catching when Kowalik, the stroke, was taking his blade from the water, he knew that it was all over. What boat first slid by them, he did not know. He saw only the strained faces, the terrible confusion in

the waist of the shell, and Kowalik's efforts to keep
rowing, to pass the rhythm back to the others. The
other shells slipped by like ghosts in the deepening twilight.

"Get together," he said, mechanically. Pathetically, they were trying to. The shell had almost
lost headway.

People were yelling on the yachts but one voice,
out of a megaphone, pierced to Kip's ears. "Leave
those punks by themselves," Ad Grant was yelling
from the bow of the yacht. Kip turned. They were
abreast his brother's yacht, *Cormorant*. He could
see them in the bow, yelling and gesturing to him.
"Jump in and swim over here," Ad said.

The full meaning of it all came to Kip in a rush.
He should abandon these men before him as a
last, contemptuous gesture and sign that they did
not belong or deserve to belong to that long tradition of which he and his brothers were a part.
In doing so, he would appease his brothers and
take some of the edge off their sarcasm tonight.
His anger at and scorn of the crew returned to him,
strong, and Kip half rose to ease himself over the
side of the shell. He remembered what Leyden
had asked, with curious foresight, of himself — to
bring them in an eight-oared crew, so that they
would be fully such in the coming years. To hell
with them, he thought, and to hell with Leyden.
All of them had humiliated him.

Pathetically, they were still rowing, their oars
clashing under the sound of the whistles which
were already blowing for the winning crew. From
his half-crouch, Kip turned to go over the side. He
saw them in the bow of the *Cormorant* again . . .
this time saw Mary Adams, a little apart from the
others as he always liked to think of her. She was
shaking her head, almost sadly. When he turned
she waved her hand — for him to go on.

He had sat in the shell again before he knew he had done so. Why? he thought and felt stupid. This is silly, he tried to tell himself, but he saw the years that were to come, for them, and some strong, nameless excitement passed over him and left him weak and clearheaded. Sarcasm could never hurt him as much as he had the power to hurt these men before him.

"Way enough!" he called. They looked at him, startled. "Way enough!" His voice bit. The oars came out of the water, hung poised for his command. He made his voice as casual, as even, as he could. "Now get together," he said, as though they were just out for a practice paddle. "You've been going like a bunch of washwomen.

"Ready — " he said. Their faces had grown almost composed. He felt pleasantly the sense of his own power, heard Ad Grant's voice through the megaphone, but did not hear Ad's words. . . . "Row!" Kip said. The eight oars took the water like a machine.

Ahead the whistles were screaming for a Navy crew that had come up in the dusk to beat Syracuse and California. And that dusk filled the river, turning the shells into shadows. But those who happened to be looking saw a curious sight — last by almost an eighth of a mile, but moving with a rhythm precise and sure, with unbelievable power; last now, but rich with great promise, an eight-oared varsity shell come home.

8/SLED

All the adventure of the night and snow lay before him: if only he could get out of the house.

"You can't go out," his mother said, "until you learn how to act like a gentleman. Now apologize to your sister."

He stared across the table at his sister.

"Go on," his mother said.

His sister was watching her plate. He could detect the trace of a smile at the corners of her mouth.

"I won't! She's laughing at me!" He saw the smile grow more pronounced. "Besides, she *is* a liar!"

His sister did not even bother to look up, and he felt from looking at her that he had said exactly what she had wanted him to say. He grew irritated at his stupidity.

"That settles it," his mother said calmly, without turning from the stove. "No outs for you."

He stared at his hands, his mind in a panic. He could feel the smile on his sister's face. His hand fumbled with the fork on his plate. "No," he said meekly, prodding a piece of meat with the fork. "I'll apologize."

His sister looked up at him innocently.

113

"Well?" said his mother. "Go on."

He took a deep breath. "I'm . . ." He met his
sister's gaze. "I'm sorry!" But it came out too
loudly, he knew.

"He is not," his sister said.

He clenched his teeth and pinched his legs with
his fingers. "I am too," he said. It sounded good,
he knew; and it was half over. He had control
now, and he relaxed a bit and even said further:
"I'm sorry I called you a liar."

"That's better," his mother said. "You two
should love each other. Not always be fighting."

He paused strategically for a long moment.

"Can I go out now?"

"Yes," his mother said.

He rose from the table glaring at his sister with
a broad grin, calling her a liar with his eyes.

His hand plucked his jacket from the couch and
swirled it around his back. The buttons refused to
fit through the holes, so he let them go in despair.
He sat down just long enough to pull on his shiny
black rubbers. Finally he put on his gloves. Then
with four proud strides he arrived at the door and
reached for the knob.

"Put your hat on," his mother said without looking at him.

His face toward the door, screwed and tightened
with disgust. "Aw, Ma."

"Put it on."

"Aw, Ma, it's not that cold."

"Put it on."

"Honest, Ma, it's not that cold out."

"Are you going to put your hat on, or are you
going to stay and help with the dishes?"

He sighed. "All right," he said. "I'll put it on."

The door to the kitchen closed on his back and
he was alone in the cold gloom of the shed. Pale
light streamed through the frosted window and

fell against the wall where the sled stood. The
dark cold room was silent, and he was free. He
moved into the shaft of light and stopped, when
from the kitchen he heard the muffled murmur of
his mother's voice, as if she were far away. He
listened. The murmuring hushed and he was alone
again.

The sled. It was leaning against the wall, its
varnished wood glistening in the moonlight. He
moved closer to it and saw his shadow block the
light, and he heard the cold cracking of the loose
linoleum beneath his feet.

He picked it up. He felt the smooth wood slippery in his gloved hands. The thin steel runners
shone blue in the light, as he moved one finger
along the polished surface to erase any dust. He
shifted the sled in his hands and stood getting the
feel of its weight the way he had seen his brother
hold a rifle. He gripped the sled tightly, aware of
the strength in his arms; and he felt proud to be
strong and alone and far away with the sled in the
dark cold silent room.

The sled was small and light. But strong. And
when he ran with it, he ran very quickly, quicker
than anyone, because it was very light and small
and not bulky like other sleds. And when he ran
with it, he carried it as if it were part of him, as if
he carried nothing in his arms. He set the rear end
on the floor, now, and let the sled lean against
him, his hands on the steering bar. He pushed
down on the bar and the thin runners curved
gracefully because they were made of shiny blue
flexible steel; and with them he could turn sharply
in the snow, sharper than anyone. It was the best
sled. It was his.

He felt a slight chill in the cold room, and in the
moonlight he saw his breath in vapor rising like
cigarette smoke before his eyes. His body shivered

with excitement as he moved hurriedly but noise-
lessly to the door. He flung it open; and the snow
blue and sparkling, and the shadows deep and
mysterious, the air silent and cold; all awaited
him.

"Joey!" From the kitchen came his mother's
voice. He turned toward the kitchen door and refused to answer.

"Joseph!"

"What!" His tone was arrogant, and a chill of
fear rushed through his mind.

There was a long awful silence.

"Don't you forget to be home by seven o'clock."
She hadn't noticed, and his fear was gone.

"All right!" he answered, ashamed of his fear.
He stepped across the threshold and closed the
door. Then he removed the hat and dropped it
in the snow beside the porch.

He plodded down the alley, thrilling in the
cold white silence — the snow was thick. The gate
creaked as he pushed it open, holding and guiding
the sled through the portal. The street was white,
and shiny were the icy tracks of automobiles in the
lamplight above, while between him and the light
the black branches of trees ticked softly, in the
slight wind. In the gutters stood enormous heaps
of snow, pale and dark in the shadows, stretching away from him like a string of mountains. He
moved out of the shadows, between two piles of
snow, and into the center of the street where he
stood for a moment gazing down the white road
that gradually grew darker until it melted into the
gloom at the far end.

Then he started to trot slowly down the street.
Slowly, slowly gaining speed without losing balance. Faster he went now, watching the snow
glide beneath his shiny black rubbers. Faster and

faster, but stiffly, don't slip. Don't fall, don't fall:
now! And his body plunged downward and the
sled whacked in the quiet and the white close to
his eyes was flying beneath him as he felt the thrill
of gliding alone along a shadowy street, with only
the ski-sound of the sled in the packed snow. Then
before his eyes the moving snow gradually
slowed. And stopped. And he heard only the low
sound of the wind and his breath.

Up again and start the trot. He moved to the
beating sound of his feet along the ground. His
breath came heavily and quickly, and matched the
rhythm of his pumping legs, straining to carry the
weight of his body without the balance of his
arms. He reached a wild dangerous breakneck
speed, and his leg muscles swelled and ached from
the tension, and the fear of falling too early filled
his mind; and down he let his body go. The white
road rushed to meet him; he was off again, guiding the sled obliquely across the street toward a
huge pile of snow near a driveway.

Squinting his eyes into the biting wind, he cal-
culated when he would turn to avoid crashing.
The pile, framed against the darkness of the sky,
glistened white and shiny. It loomed larger and
larger before him. He steered the sled sharply,
bending the bar; and the snow flew as the sled
churned sideways, and he heard suddenly a cold
metallic snap. He and the sled went tumbling over
in the hard wet snow. He rolled with it and the
steering bar jarred his forehead. Then the dark
sky and snow stopped turning, and all he felt was
the cold air stinging the bump on his forehead.

The runner had snapped; the sled was broken.
He stared at the shiny smooth runner and touched
the jagged edge with his fingers. He sat in the
middle of the driveway, the sled cradled in his lap,

running his fingers up and down the thin runner until he came to the jagged edge where it had broken.

With his fingers he took the two broken edges and fitted them back into place. They stuck together with only a thin crooked line to indicate the split. But it was like putting a broken cup together. He stared at it, and wished it would be all right and felt like crying.

He got up and walked slowly back down to the street to his house. He sat down between the back bumper of a parked car and a pile of snow. Cradling the sled across his legs, he put the two edges together again and stared at them. He felt a thickness in his throat, and he swallowed hard to remove it, but it did not go away.

He leaned back, resting his head against the snowpile. Through his wet eyelids he saw the lamplight shimmering brightly against the sky. He closed his eyes and saw again the shiny graceful curve of the runner. But it was broken now. He had bent it too far; too far. With his hand he rubbed his neck, then his eyes, then his neck again. He felt the snow coming wet through his pants. As he shifted to a new position, he heard the creaking of a gate. He turned toward the sound.

His sister was walking away from his house. He watched her move slowly across the street and into the grocery store. Through the plate-glass window he saw her talking with the storekeeper. He stared down at the runner. With his gloves off, he ran his fingers along the cold smooth surface and felt the thin breakline. He got up, brushed the snow off the seat of his pants, and walked to the gate to wait for his sister.

He saw her take a package from the man and come out of the store. She walked carefully on the smooth white, her figure dark in its own shadow as she passed beneath the streetlight, the package in her arm. When she reached the curb of his side, he rested his arms on the nose of the sled and exhaled a deep breath nervously. He pretended to be staring in the opposite direction.

When he heard her feet crunching softly in the snow, he turned: "Hi," he said.

"Hi," she said and she paused for a moment. "Good sledding?"

"Uh-huh," he said. "Just right. Snow's packed nice and hard. Hardly any slush at all." He paused. "I'm just resting a bit now."

She nodded. "I just went for some milk."

His fingers moved slowly down the runner and touched the joined edges.

"Well . . ." she said, about to leave.

His fingers trembled slightly, and he felt his heart begin to beat rapidly: "Do you want to take a flop?" In the still night air he heard with surprise the calm sound of his voice.

Her face came suddenly alive. "Can I? I mean, will you let me? Really?"

"Sure," he said. "Go ahead." And he handed her the sled very carefully. She gave him the package.

He put the bag under his arm and watched her move out of the shadows of the trees and into the light. She started to trot slowly, awkwardly, bearing the sled. She passed directly beneath the light and then she slipped and slowed to regain her balance. The sled looked large and heavy in her arms, and seeing her awkwardness, he realized, she would be hurt badly in the fall. She was moving away again, out of the reach of the streetlight, and into the gray haze farther down the road.

He moved to the curb, holding the bag tightly under his arm, hearing his heart pounding in his ears. He wanted to stop her, and he opened his mouth as if to call to her; but no sound came. It was too late; her dark figure was already starting the fall, putting the sled beneath her. Whack! And her head dipped with the front end jutting the ground, and the back of the sled and her legs rose like a seesaw and down they came with another muffled sound. The street was quiet, except for a low whimper that filled his ears.

He saw her figure rise slowly and move toward him. He walked out to meet her beneath the light. She held the sled loosely in one hand, the broken runner dangling, reflecting light as she moved.

She sobbed and looking up he saw bright tears falling down her cheeks, and a thin line of blood trickling down her chin. In the corner of her mouth near the red swelling of her lip, a little bubble of spit shone with the blood in the light.

He felt that he should say something but he did not speak.

"I'm . . . I'm sorry," she said and the bubble broke. "I'm sorry I . . . your sled." She looked down at the sled. "It'll never be the same."

"It'll be all right," he said. He felt that he ought to do something but he did not move. "I can get it soldered. Don't worry about it." But he saw from her expression that she thought he was only trying to make her feel better.

"No," she said, shaking her head emphatically. "No, it won't! It'll always have that weak spot now." She began to cry very hard. "I'm sorry."

He made an awkward gesture of forgiveness with his hand. "Don't cry," he said.

She kept crying.

"It wasn't your fault," he said.

"Yes, it was," she said. "Oh, yes, it was."

"No!" he said. "No, it wasn't!" But she didn't seem to hear him, and he felt his words were useless. He sighed wearily with defeat, not knowing what to say next. He saw her glance up at him as if to see whether he was still watching her, then she quickly lowered her gaze and said with despair and anguish: "Oh . . . girls are so stupid!"

There was no sound. She was no longer crying. She was looking at the ground: waiting. His ears heard nothing; they felt only the cold silent air.

"No, they aren't," he said half-heartedly. And he heard her breathing again. He felt he had been forced to say that. In her shining eyes he saw an expression he did not understand. He wished she would go in the house. But seeing the tears on her cheeks and the blood on her chin, he immediately regretted the thought.

She wiped her chin with her sleeve, and he winced, feeling rough cloth on an open cut. "Don't do that." His hand moved to his back pocket. "Use my handkerchief."

She waited.

The pocket was empty. "I haven't got one," he said.

Staring directly at him, she patted gingerly the swollen part of her lip with the tips of her fingers.

He moved closer to her. "Let me see," he said. With his hands he grasped her head and tilted it so that the light fell directly on the cut.

"It's not too bad," she said calmly. And as she said it she looked straight into his eyes, and he felt she was perfectly at ease; while standing that close to her, he felt clumsy and out of place.

In his hands her head was small and fragile, and her hair was soft and warm; he felt the rapid pulsing of the vein in her temple: his ears grew hot with shame.

"Maybe I better go inside and wash it off?" she asked.

With his finger he wiped the blood from her

chin. "Yes," he said, feeling relieved. "You go inside and wash it off." He took the sled and gave her the package.

He stared at the ground as they walked to the gate in silence. When they reached the curb he became aware that she was watching him.

"You've got a nasty bump on your forehead," she said.

"Yes," he said. "I fell."

"Let me put some snow on it," she said reaching to the ground.

He caught her wrist and held it gently. "No," he said.

He saw her about to object: "It's all right. You go inside and take care of your lip." He said it softly but with his grip and his eyes he told her more firmly.

"All right," she said after a moment, and he released his hold. "But don't forget to put your hat on."

He stared at her.

"I mean, *before* you go back in the house."

They both smiled.

"Thanks for reminding me," he said, and he dropped the sled in the snow and hurried to hold the gate open for her.

She hesitated, then smiled proudly as he beckoned her into the alley.

He watched her walk from him down the dark alley in the gray snow. Her small figure swayed awkwardly as she stepped carefully in the deep snow, so as not to get her feet too wet. Her head was bowed and her shoulders hunched and he humbly felt her weakness. And he felt her cold. And he felt the snow running cold down her boots around her ankles. And though she wasn't crying now, he could still hear her low sobbing, and he saw her shining eyes and the tears falling and she trying to stop them and they fell even faster. And he wished he had never gone sledding. He wished that he had never even come out of the house tonight.

The back door closed. He turned and moved about nervously kicking at the ground. At the edge of the curb he dug his hands deep into the cold wet snow. He came up with a handful and absently began shaping and smoothing it. He stopped abruptly and dropped it at his feet.

He did not hear it fall. He was looking up at the dark sky but he did not see it. He put his cold hands in his back pockets but he did not feel them. He was wishing that he were some time a long time away from now and somewhere a long way away from here.

In the corner of his eye something suddenly dimmed. Across the street in the grocery store the light was out: it was seven o'clock.

GEORGE MILBURN

9/A STUDENT IN ECONOMICS

All of the boys on the third floor of Mrs. Gooch's approved rooms for men had been posted to get Charlie Wingate up that aftenoon. He had to go to see the Dean. Two or three of them forgot all about it and two or three of them had other things to do, but Eddie Barbour liked waking people up. Eddie stuck his weasel face in at Charlie's door just as the alarm clock was giving one last feeble tap. The clock stood on the bottom of a tin washpan that was set upside down on a wooden chair beside the bed. The alarm had made a terrific din. Eddie had heard it far down the hall. The hands showed two o'clock. Pale needles from a December sun were piercing the limp green window shade in a hundred places.

Eddie Barbour yelled, "Aw right, Charlie! Snap out of it!" He came into the chilly room and stood for a moment staring vaguely at the ridge of quilts on the sagging iron bed. The only sound was the long, regular sigh of Charlie Wingate's breathing. He hadn't heard a thing. Eddie made a sudden grab for the top of the covers, stripped them back, and began jouncing the sleeper by the shoulders. Charlie grunted every time the bed springs creaked, but he nuzzled his pillow and went on sleeping. Eddie went over to the study table where a large, white-enameled water pitcher stood and he came back to the bed with the water, breathing giggles. He tipped the water pitcher a little and a few drops fell on the back of Charlie's neck without waking him. Eddie sloshed the icy water up over the pitcher's mouth. A whole cupful splashed on Charlie's head. Charlie sat up quickly, batting his arms about, and Eddie Barbour whinnied with laughter.

"Arise, my lord, for the day is here," he said, going across and ceremoniously raising the crooked window shade. Charlie sat straight up among the rumpled quilts with his head cocked on one side, staring dully. He had slept with his clothes on. He sat up in bed all dressed, in a soldier's brown uniform, all but his shoes and roll puttees.

"You got army today?" asked Eddie, putting the pitcher down.

Charlie looked at him for a moment and blinked. Then he said in a voice stuffy with sleep, "Naw. I had army yesterday. I got army make-up today." He worked his mouth, making clopping noises.

"What time you got army make-up, Charlie? When you come in from class you said get you up because you had to go see the Dean at two-thirty."

"Yeah, I do have to go see the Dean at two-thirty. But I got army make-up too. I got to make up drill cuts from three till six." All at once he flopped back down on the bed, sound asleep again.

"Hey!" Eddie cried, jumping forward. "Come out of that! Wake up there, Charlie! You can't sleep no more if you got to see the Dean at two-thirty. You just about got time to make it." He jerked him back up in bed.

"Two hours' sleep ain't enough," Charlie said.

"Is two hours all the sleep you got last night?"

"Where you get the 'last night'? I worked all night last night. I had classes till noon today. Two hours' sleep was all I got today. And darn little more yesterday or the day before. When is Sunday? Sunday's the first day I'm due to get any real sleep. Two hours' sleep is not enough sleep for a man to get."

Charlie Wingate loped up the steps of the Administration Building, hurried through the revolving doors, and walked past hissing steam radiators down the long hall to the Dean of Men's office. He was ten minutes late. Before he opened the frosted-glass door he took out a pair of amber-colored spectacles and put them on. Then he went in and handed his summons to the secretary.

"The Dean will see you in a moment," she said. "Please take a chair."

Charlie sat down and gave an amber-hued glance about the outer office. Three dejected freshmen, holding their green caps, were waiting with him. He recognized none of them, so he picked up a week-old copy of the *Christian Science Monitor* and started to read it. But the room was warm and he immediately went to sleep. He had his head propped back against the wall. The newspaper slipped down into his lap. His amber-colored glasses hid his eyes and no one could see that they were closed. He was awakened by the secretary shaking him. She was smiling and the freshmen were all snickering.

"Wake up and pay for your bed, fella!" one of the freshmen called, and everyone laughed heartily.

"I sort of drowsed off. It's so nice and warm in here," Charlie said, apologizing to the pretty secretary.

The Dean of Men got up as he entered and, with his eyes on the slip bearing Charlie's name, said, "Ah, this is Charles Wingate, isn't it?" He grasped Charlie's hand as if it were an honor and pressed a button under the edge of his desk with his other hand. The secretary appeared at the door. "Miss Dunn, will you bring in Wingate's folder — Charles W-i-n-g-a-t-e. How do you like college by now, Wingate? Eyes troubling you?"

"Pretty well, sir. Yes, sir, a little. I wear these glasses."

The secretary came back with the folder and the Dean looked through it briefly. "Well, Wingate, I suppose you're anxious to know why I sent for you. The unpleasant truth is, Wingate, you don't seem to be doing so well in your college work. Your freshman advisor conferred with you twice about this, and this week he turned your case over to me. My purpose, of course, is to help you. Now, to be quite frank, Wingate, you're on the verge of flunking out. Less than a third of the semester remains, and you have a failing grade in English 101, conditional grades in Psychology 51 and Military Training; three hours of F and four hours of D, almost half your total number of hours. On the other hand, you have an A average in Spanish 1 and a B in Economics 150. Wingate, how do you account for your failing English when you are an A student in Spanish?"

"To tell you the truth, sir, I got behind on my written work in English, and I've never been able to catch up. And I don't really have to study Spanish. My father is a railway section foreman in my home town, and he's always had a gang of Mexicans working for him. I've been speaking Mexican ever since I was a kid. It's not the pure, what they call Castilian, Spanish, but I probably know almost as much Spanish as my professor."

"How about this B in economics? That's a fairly high grade."

"Yes, sir. Doctor Kenshaw — he's my ec professor — doesn't give exams. Instead he gives every one a B until he calls for our term papers. We don't recite in his class. We just listen to him lecture. And the grade you get on your term paper is your semester grade."

"Ah! What you students term a pipe course, eh, Wingate?"

"Not exactly, sir. We have to do a lot of outside reading for the term paper. But I'm counting on keeping that B in ec."

"That's fine, Wingate. But it appears to me that it's high time you were getting busy on some of these other grades too. Why can't you dig in and pull these D's up to B's, and this F up to at least a C? You've got it in you. You made an unusually high grade on your entrance exams, your record shows. Graduated from high school with honors. What's the trouble, Wingate? Tell me!"

"I don't know, sir, except I work at night and — "

"Oh, I see it here on your enrollment card. Where do you work?"

"I work nights for Nick Pappas, down at The Wigwam."

"How many hours do you work?"

"Ten hours, sir. From nine till seven. The Wigwam stays open all night. I eat and go to eight o'clock class when I get off."

"Very interesting, Wingate. But don't you suppose that it would be advisable to cut down a bit on this outside work and attend a little more closely to your college work? After all, that's what you're here for, primarily — to go to college, not work in a café."

"I couldn't work fewer hours and stay in school, sir. I just barely get by as it is. I get my board at The Wigwam, and I pay my room rent, and I've been paying out on a suit of clothes. That leaves only about a dollar a week for all the other things I have to have."

"Wingate, shouldn't you earn more than that, working ten hours?"

"I get the regular, first-year-man rate, sir. Twenty-five cents an hour. It's set by the university. Nick takes out for board."

"Can't you arrange for a little financial support from home?"

"No, sir, I'm afraid I couldn't. I have two brothers and two sisters at home younger than I am. It wouldn't be right for me to ask my father to send money out of what he makes."

"But surely you could get out and land something a little more lucrative than this all-night restaurant job, Wingate."

"No, sir. Twenty-five cents is the standard rate for working students, and I haven't found anything better. Nick says he has at least twenty men on the waiting list for this job I have."

"Well, there's this about it, Wingate. The university is here, supported by the taxpayers of this state, for the purpose of giving the young men and women of this state educational opportunities. The university is not here for the purpose of training young men to be waiters in all-night restaurants. And, so far as I can see, that's about all you are deriving from your university career. So it occurs to me that you should make a choice: either find some way to devote more attention to your college work or drop out of school altogether. We are very loath to encourage students who are *entirely* self-supporting. And yet, I will admit that I know any number of first-rate students who are entirely self-supporting. There's Aubery Carson, for example. Quarterback on the football team, delegate to the Olympics, president of the Student Senate, and he's a straight A student. Aubery Carson was telling me only last week that he hasn't had any financial assistance from home since he enrolled as a freshman. Aubery is a fine example of the working student."

"Yes, sir; but look at the job Carson has. He works for a big tobacco company, and all he has to do is hand out Treasure Trove cigarettes to other students. The tobacco company pays him a good salary for passing out samples of their cigarettes."

"Why, Wingate, you surely must be mistaken about that. I don't believe Aubery Carson smokes. In fact, I know he doesn't smoke. He's one of the finest all-round athletes in this country."

"No, sir; I don't say he smokes either. But that's the straight stuff about his job with the cigarette company. They figure it's a good advertisement to have a popular guy like Aubery Carson passing out Treasure Troves. Sort of an endorsement."

"All the same, Wingate, it doesn't reflect a very good attitude on your part, criticizing the way one of your fellow students earns his college expenses."

"Oh, I didn't mean to criticize him, sir. I was only saying — "

"Yes, yes, I know; but all this is beside the point. We're here to discuss the state of your grades, Wingate. The fact is, you are on probation right now. As you must know, any student who is passing in less than half his work is automatically suspended from the university and must return to his home. Now one F more and out you'll go, Wingate. That's just being frank with you."

"I'd hate to have to go back home like that, sir."

"Well, you'd have to. If you flunk out, the university authorities are obliged to see that you return to your home immediately."

"I'd hate that, sir. I'd hate to go back home and have to live off my family, and that's probably what I'd have to do. I had a letter from my mother yesterday, and she says that nearly all the boys who graduated from high school with me are still there, loafing on the streets and living off their old folks. I don't like that idea. Mother's proud of me because I'm working my way through college. You know there are not many jobs to be had nowadays, sir, and I'd hate to have to go back home and loaf."

"It is a problem, I'll confess, Wingate. But what's the point in your coming to the university and working all night in a café and then flunking your class work? Moreover, your freshman advisor reports that you make a practice of sleeping in class. Is that true?"

"Well, yes, sir. I suppose I do drop off sometimes."

"Pretty impossible situation, isn't it, Wingate? Well, I've given you the best advice I can. Unless you can alter your circumstances I suggest that you withdraw from the university at once. We have six thousand other students here who need our attention, and the university has to be impartial and impersonal in dealing with these problems. Unless you can find some means to avoid flunking out I suggest withdrawing beforehand."

"Withdrawal would be a disgrace to me, sir. If I withdrew and went back home now, everyone at home would say that I had been expelled. You know how small towns are."

"Ah, now, Wingate, when you begin dealing

with small-town gossip, I fear you're really getting outside my province. But I should think you'd prefer honorable withdrawal to flunking out."

"I believe I'll try to stick it through, sir. I'll try to remove the conditional grades, and maybe I can luck through on my finals."

"I hope you can, Wingate. As long as you feel that way about it, good luck to you." The Dean of Men stood up. Charlie stood up too. The Dean put out his hand and showed his teeth in a jovial smile and bore down hard on Charlie's knuckles. "I'm counting on you strong, old man," he said, encircling Charlie's shoulders with his left arm. "I know you have the stuff and that you'll come through with flying colors one of these days."

"Thank you, sir," Charlie said, grinning tearfully while the Dean gave his shoulder little pats. He edged toward the door as soon as the Dean released him, but when he reached it he hesitated and pulled the postal card out of his pocket. "Oh, pardon me, sir, but there's something I forgot to ask you. I got this in the mail today. I've been a little bothered about what to make of it."

The Dean of Men took the mimeographed card and read it quickly. "Why, I should say that you ought to go see what they want, Wingate. You shouldn't ignore things of this sort, you know. It's all a part of the normal activities of college life. No reason for antagonizing your fellow students."

"All right, sir; I'll go see them."

"Why, to be sure, go see them! Always keep in mind that the university is a social as well as an educational institution, Wingate."

Room 204, Student Union Building, was a newly finished, rather barren office that smelled dankly of lime in the fresh plaster. It was fitted with a metal desk painted to imitate walnut, a large brass spittoon, a square metal wastepaper basket, a green metal filing cabinet, a large bank calendar, a huge pasteboard shipping case, and J. Aubery Carson, who had the freshman cap concession.

Charlie Wingate hesitantly opened the door and saw J. Aubery Carson tilted back in a chair, his feet on the metal walnut desk, reading a copy of *Life*.

"Co-ome in! Co-ome in!" J. Aubery Carson called loudly without putting down his magazine. "All right, old-timer. What's on your mind?"

Charlie held out the mimeographed card. Carson held his magazine a moment longer before accepting the card. He shoved his hat down over one eye, turning the card, looking first at the back, then at the name on the front. "Um-m-m," he grunted. He reached over to a drawer in the filing cabinet without taking his feet down and flipped through the cards. He looked at the name on the postal card again, pulled his thick lips up into a rosette. He looked at the file card in silence.

"Wingate," he said at last in a severe tone, "you have been dilatory. Indeed, Wingate, I might even go so far as to say you have been remiss. At the beginning of this semester you applied for and received a refund on your student ticket fee. That signifies that you have not attended a single football game this season, and that you have no intention of honoring any of the university's athletic spectacles with your presence this season. Also, the record discloses that you did not register at the Y.M.C.A. freshman mixer. Neither did you respond to polite solicitation for a trifling monetary pledge to the Memorial Stadium Fund.

"And, furthermore, your most heinous offense of all, Wingate, we find that you have yet to pay in

one dollar for your freshman cap, prescribed by
your seniors and purveyed to you on a nonprofit
basis by the Student Committee on Freshman Activities. And yet, Wingate, I find you duly enrolled
and attending classes in this here now university.
Wingate, what possible excuse do you have for
such gross neglect of university tradition? Speak
up!"

Charlie said meekly, "Well, I work nights and
it's hard for me to get here in the daytime, and I
can't afford to buy a cap."

"What's this!" Carson exclaimed, jerking his
legs down from the desk top and banging the desk
with two flat hands. "Why, boy, this is treason!
You mean you can't afford *not* to buy a freshman
cap."

"No, I just came to tell you that a dollar has to
go a long way with me and that I need every cent
I earn to stay in school. So I wish you'd please excuse me from buying a freshman cap."

Carson's lean, florid face suddenly became rigid
and he stuck his jaw out with his lower teeth showing and, in spite of his marcelled taffy pompadour
and his creased tailored suit, he again looked very
much as he did in all the sporting section photographs. "See here, Wingate," he said, hard-
lipped, "you're still a freshman at this university.
You'll have to wait another year before you can
start saying what you will do and won't do, see?
Now we've been patient with you. You've been in
school here three months without putting on a
freshman cap. Do you realize that over eighty-five
per cent of the freshman class came in here and
bought their caps before the first week of school
ended? Now who do you think you are, Wingate?
You're going to get you a cap, and you're going
to wear it. See? No ifs, ands, or buts about it. And

if you don't leave this office with a green cap on your head then I don't mind telling you that we've got ways of getting one on you before another day passes."

"Well, if I buy one it's going to put me in a bad hole. All the money I've got is what I saved out to pay my room rent this week."

"Listen, fella, if we let horse feathers like that go here, half the freshman class wouldn't be wearing freshman caps right now. Now I've said all I'm going to to you. Do you want your green cap now or will you wait till later? That's all I want to know. I don't aim to give you any high-pressure sales talk on something that's already been decided for you. Take it or leave it."

Carson reached over into the large pasteboard box, groped far down in it, and brought forth a small green monkey cap. He tossed it on the desk. Charlie Wingate stuck his forefinger in his watch pocket and pulled out a small pad of three carefully folded dollar bills. He unfolded them and laid one on the desk and picked up the cap. Carson put the dollar in his pocket and stood up.

Charlie stood holding his cap. He scuffed the cement floor with his shoe toe and began doggedly, "The only thing is — "

"Aw, that's okay, Wingate, old man," Carson said suavely. "No hard feelings whatsoever." He held out a freshly opened pack of cigarettes. "Here, have a Treasure Trove on me before you go."

That night all the stools along the counter at The Wigwam were filled when Charlie Wingate came in, still dusty from the drill field. He got himself a setup back of the counter and went into the kitchen. He moved about the steam table, dishing up his dinner. He dragged a stool over to a zinc-

covered kitchen table and sat down to eat. The
kitchen was warm and steamy and the air was
thick with the odors of sour chili grease and yellow soap melting in hot dishwater. Charlie's fork
slipped through his fingers and he began nodding
over his plate.

Fat Kruger, the night dishwasher and short-
order cook, yelled, "Hey, there, wake up and pay
for your bed!" Charlie jerked his head up and
looked at the ponderous, good-humored cook with
half-lidded eyes. "Why'n't you try sleeping in bed
once in a while, Charlie?" Fat said in friendly tone.
"You're going to kill yourself if you don't watch
out, trying to go without sleep."

"Don't worry, Fat. I can take it," Charlie said.

Almost two hours had to pass before it would
be the hour for him to come on, but not time
enough for him to walk back to his room and catch
a nap, so he took the book on which he had to
make an outside reading report in Economics 150
and went up to the last booth to study until nine
o'clock. He fell asleep and he did not wake up
until Red Hibbert, going off, shook him and told
him that it was almost time for him to come on.
He took down his apron and tied it on over his
army breeches. Then he slipped into a white coat.

At one o'clock Charlie finished cleaning off the
last of the tables. The Wigwam was empty, so he
opened the book he must read for Ec 150. He had
read a few lines when a bunch of girls from the
Theta house down the street came charging in,
giggling and talking in gasps and screams, their fur
coats clutched over their sleeping pajamas. It was
long after the closing hour, and they told Charlie
to keep an eye out for the university night watch-
man. They took up the two back booths and they
consulted The Wigwam's printed menu card

without failing to read aloud the lines "Nick
(Pericles) Pappas," "We Employ Student Help
Exclusively," and "Please Do Not Tip, A Smile Is
Our Reward" with the customary shrieks. Nearly
all ordered filet mignon and French fries, which
were not on the menu, but two or three ordered
pecan waffles and coffee, which were. When he
had served their orders Charlie went back to his
book again, but the low buzz of their talk and
their sudden spurts of laughter disturbed him and
he could not read. At a quarter of two they began
peering round the corners of their booths. They
asked Charlie in stage whispers if the coast was
clear.

Charlie went to the door and looked out on the
street and beckoned widely with his arm. They
trooped out with their fur coats pulled tight, their
fur-trimmed silken mules slapping their bare
heels. Charlie went on back to clear away their
dishes. They had left about thirty cents as a tip, all
in cents and nickels. The coins were carefully im-
bedded in the cold steak grease and gluey syrup
and putty-colored cigarette leavings on their
plates. Charlie began stacking the plates without
touching the money. He carried the dirty dishes
back and set them through the opening in the
kitchen wall. Fat Kruger came to the opening and
Charlie went back to his book. Fat called, "Hey,
Charlie, you leavin' this tip again?"

"You're right, I'm leaving it!" Charlie said.
"I can get along without their tips. They leave it
that way every time. I guess they think I'll grabble
on their filthy plates to get a lousy thirty cents.
It takes a woman to think up something like that."

"Charlie, you're too proud. I don't see where
you can afford to be so proud. The way I figure
it, thirty cents is thirty cents."

"I'm not proud, Fat. I just try to keep my self-respect. When those sorority girls come in and plant their tips in the dirt and grease of their plates, damn' if I'll lower myself to grub it out."

He sat down on a counter stool with the economics book before him, trying to fix his mind on it. He read a page. The print became thin, blurred parallels of black on the page. His eyelids kept drooping shut and he propped them up with his palms at his temples, trying to keep his eyes open. His head jerked forward and he caught it and began reading again. Soon his face lowered slowly through his hands and came to rest on the open book.

Fat Kruger came through the kitchen swinging door and tiptoed up front. Fat stood grinning, watching Charlie sleep. Cramped over with his head on the counter, Charlie snored softly. Fat gave his head a gentle shove, and Charlie started up to catch his balance.

"For gosh sakes, guy, you're *dead!*" Fat howled. "Don't you never get no sleep except like that?"

"What time is it?" Charlie said, yawning and arching his back.

"Half-past two."

"Is that all?"

"Charlie, I wouldn't put my eyes out over that book if I was you, when you're dyin' for sleep," Fat said.

"I've got to get it read, Fat. It's my outside reading in economics and the whole semester grade depends on it. It's the hardest book to keep your mind on you ever saw. I've been reading on it for over a month and I'm only half through, and he's going to call for these reports any day now. If I flunk ec I flunk out of school."

"Why mess with reading it? I know a guy over at the Masonic dorm who'll read it and write your report for two bucks. He writes all my English themes for me, and I'm making a straight A in English. He only charges fifty cents for short themes and two bucks for term papers. You ought to try him."

"Well, Fat, you get five dollars a week from home. Where am I going to get two dollars for hiring a guy to read this book?"

"Charlie, I just can't figure you out. You never do get any real sleep. You sure must want a college education bad. It don't look to me like you would figure it's worth it."

"Oh, it's worth it! It's a big satisfaction to my folks to have me in college. And where can a man without a college degree get nowadays? But I'll tell you the truth, I didn't know it was going to be like this when I came down here last fall. I used to read *College Humor* in high school, and when fellows came home from university for the holidays, all dressed up in snappy clothes, talking about dates and football and dances, and using college slang — well, I had a notion I'd be like that when I got down here. The university publicity department sent me a little booklet showing how it was easy to work your way through college. So here I am. I haven't had a date or been to a dance or seen a football game since I enrolled. And there are plenty of others just like me. I guess I'm getting a college education, all right — but the only collegiate thing I've been able to do is go to sleep in class."

"How you get by with sleeping in class, Charlie?"

"I wear those colored spectacles and prop myself, and the profs can't see I've got my eyes closed."

Fat waggled his heavy face mournfully. "Boy, it sure is tough when a man don't get his sleep."

"Yeah, it is," Charlie said, looking down at his

book again. "I'll get a break pretty soon, though. I'd rather chop off a hand than to flunk out of university before I'd even finished one semester."

The tardiest of the hundred students enrolled in Dr. Sylvester C. O. Kenshaw's Economics 150 straggled into the lecture room and made their way to alphabetically assigned chairs with much scuffling and trampling of toes and mumbled apologies. Ec 150, renowned as a pipe course, was always crowded. The only students who ever flunked Ec 150 were those who gave affront to Doctor Kenshaw by neglecting to buy his textbooks or by not laughing at his wit or by being outrageously inattentive to his lectures.

Doctor Kenshaw was late that morning. Charlie Wingate sat in his chair on the back row in an agony of waiting. He had on his amber glasses and he could fall asleep as soon as Doctor Kenshaw opened his lecture. But he had to stay awake until then. There was a slow ache in the small of his back. The rest of his body was numb. He had not taken off his army shoes for twenty hours, and his feet were moist and swollen. Every time he shifted position his arms and legs were bathed in prickling fire. He kept his eyes open behind the amber lenses, watching the clock. Small noises of the classroom came to him as a low, far-off humming.

When the clock on the front wall showed nine after eleven the seated class began stirring as if it were mounted on some eccentric amusement-park device. Excited whispers eddied out on the warm air of the steam-heated lecture room. "He's giving us another cut!" "He's not meeting this class today!" "He's got one more minute to make it!" "Naw; six more! You have to wait fifteen minutes on department heads."

There was a seething argument on this point, but when the clock showed fourteen minutes after eleven a bold leader sprang up and said, "Come on, everybody!" All but five or six especially conscientious students rose and milled after him toward the door. Charlie Wingate followed, thoroughly awakened by the chance of getting to bed so soon. The leader yanked the door open and Doctor Kenshaw stumbled in, all out of breath, his eyeglasses steamed, his pointed gray beard quivering, a vain little man in a greenish-black overcoat.

"Go back to your seats!" Doctor Kenshaw commanded sternly as soon as he could get his breath. He marched over to his lecture table and planked down his leather brief case. He took off his overcoat and began wiping the steam from his eyeglasses while the students hurried back to their chairs. "It does seem to me," he said, his voice quavering with anger, "that it would be no more than courteous for this class to await my arrival on those rare occasions when I am delayed."

A few students exchanged meaning glances. They meant, "Now we're in for it. The old boy has on one of his famous mads."

"Today, I believe I shall forego delivering my prepared lecture," Doctor Kenshaw went on in a more even voice, but with elaborate sarcasm, "and let you do the talking. Perhaps it would be moot to hear a few outside reading reports this morning. All of you doubtless are aware that these reports were due last week, although I had not expected to call for them at once. I trust that I have impressed you sufficiently with the importance of these reports. They represent to me the final result of your semester's work in this course. The grades you receive on these reports will be your grades for the semester. Let us begin forthwith.

When your name is called, you will rise and read your report to the class."

"Mr. Abbot!" he called. Mr. Abbot stammered an excuse. Doctor Kenshaw passed coldly on to Miss Adams, making no comment. All through the A's it was the same. But with the B's an ashen, spectacled Miss Ballentyne stood up and began reading in a droning voice her report on "The Economic Consequences of the Peace." Obviously Doctor Kenshaw was not listening to her. His hard little eyes under craggy brows were moving up one row and down the other, eager for a victim. In the back row, Charlie Wingate's propped legs had given way and he had slipped far down into his seat, fast asleep. When Doctor Kenshaw's preying eyes reached Charlie they stopped moving. Someone tittered nervously and then was silent as Doctor Kenshaw jerked his head round in the direction of the noise. Miss Ballentyne droned on.

When she had finished, Doctor Kenshaw said dryly, "Very good, Miss Ballentyne, very good indeed. Er — ah — would someone be kind enough to arouse the recumbent young gentleman in the last row?"

There was a murmur of laughter while everyone turned to look at Milton Weismann nudging Charlie Wingate. Doctor Kenshaw was running down the list of names in his small record book. Milton Weismann gave Charlie another stiff poke in the ribs, and Charlie sprang up quickly. Everyone laughed loudly at that.

"Mr. — ah — *Wingate*, isn't it? Mr. Wingate, your report."

"Pardon me, sir?"

"Mr. Wingate, what was the title of the book assigned to you for report in this class?"

"*Theory of the Leisure Class* by Veblen, sir."

"Ah, then that's the explanation. So you were

assiduously engaged in evolving your own theory
of the leisure class. Is that right, Mr. Wingate? You
have evidently concluded that Economics 150 is
the leisure class."

The class rocked with laughter. Doctor Kenshaw, pleased with his pun and flattered by the
response to it, found it hard to keep his face
straight. Suddenly he was back in good humor.
"Mr. Wingate's theory is quite apparently one to
which the majority of this class subscribes. Now I
try to be lenient with students in this class. Surely
no one could describe me as a hard taskmaster.
But I resent your implication that I have been too
easygoing. Now these reading reports were assigned to you last September, and you have had
ample time to prepare them. I'll not call for any
more of them today, but at the next session of
this class I expect every one of these papers in. As
for you, Mr. Wingate, if you'll see me directly
after class, I'll be glad to hear any explanation or
apology that you may wish to make. I want most
of all to be fair. I have always given every student
the benefit of the doubt until a student deliber-
ately flouts me with his indifference. But I am
capable of being quite ruthless, I assure you."

"Thank you, sir," Charlie mumbled. He entered
a slow torture, trying to keep awake until the class
bell rang. He rolled his hot, red-veined eyes up
with drunken precision to see the clock. Fifteen
minutes had to pass before the bell would ring.

When the bell rang the class arose quickly and
began clumping out. Several co-eds and men,
politickers and apple-polishers wangling for A's,
crowded about the lecture table. Doctor Kenshaw
always remained behind after each class to accept
their homage. But today he looked up over the
heads of the eager group. He silenced their inane
questions and flagrant compliments by placing his

right forefinger against his thin, unsmiling lips. "Sh-h-h!" he said. The apple-polishers turned their heads in the direction of his gaze and then, giggling softly, tiptoed away. When the last had gone out, Doctor Kenshaw unscrewed his fountain pen and opened his roll book. He ran his finger down the list until he came to "Wingate, C." and in the space opposite under "Smstr Grd" he marked a precise little F.

A whiffling snore escaped Charlie Wingate in the back of the room. Doctor Kenshaw looked back across the varnished chair rows with a frown of annoyance. He took his overcoat from its hanger, slipped into it, and strapped up his brief case. He jammed on his hat and strode out of the lecture room, slamming the door. The noise made a hollow echo in the empty room, but it did not disturb Charlie Wingate. He slept on behind his amber glasses.

WILLIAM SAROYAN

10 / ROMANCE

Would you rather sit on this side or would you rather sit on the other side? the redcap said.

Hmm? the young man said.

This side is all right? the redcap said.

Oh, the young man said. Sure.

He gave the redcap a dime. The redcap accepted the small thin coin and folded the young man's coat and placed it on the seat.

Some people like one side, he said, and some like the other.

What? the young man said.

The redcap didn't know if he ought to go into detail, about some people being used to and preferring certain things in the landscape looking out of the tran from one side, and others wanting, to get both sides of the landscape all the way down and back, preferring one side going down, usually the shady side, but in some cases the opposite, where a lady liked sunlight or had read it was healthy, and the other side coming up, but he imagined it would take too long to explain everything, especially in view of the fact that he wasn't feeling real well and all morning hadn't been able to give that impression of being on excellent terms with everybody which pleased him so much.

145

I mean, he said, it's no more than what any-body wants, I guess.

The redcap figured the young man was a clerk who was going to have a little Sunday holiday, riding in a train from a big city to a little one, go-ing and coming the same day, but what he didn't understand was why the young man seemed so lost, or, as the saying is, dead to the world. The boy was young, not perhaps a college graduate, more likely a boy who'd gone through high school and gotten a job in an office somewhere, maybe twenty-three years old, and perhaps in love. Any-how, the redcap thought, the young man looked to be somebody who might at any moment fall in love, without much urging. He had that sad or dreamy look of the potential adorer of something in soft and colorful cloth with long hair and smooth skin.

The young man came to an almost violent awakening which very nearly upset the redcap.

Oh, he said, I've been sort of daydreaming.

He wiggled the fingers of his right hand near his head, or where people imagined one daydreamed.

Have I given you a tip? he said.

The redcap felt embarrassed.

Yes, sir, he said.

The young man wiggled the fingers of his left hand before his face.

I very often forget what I'm doing, he said, until long afterwards — sometimes years. May I ask how much I gave you?

The redcap couldn't figure it out at all. If the young man was being funny or trying to work some sort of racket, it was just too bad because the redcap wasn't born yesterday. The young man had given him a dime and if the young man came out with the argument that he had given the red-

cap some such ridiculous coin as a five-dollar gold
piece the redcap would simply hold his ground
and say, this is all you gave me — this dime.

You gave me a dime, he said.

I'm sorry, the young man said, here.

He gave the redcap another dime.

Thank you, sir, the redcap said.

Were you saying something while we were
coming down the aisle? the young man said.

Nothing important, the redcap said. I was only
saying how some folks liked to sit on one side and
others on the other.

Oh, the young man said. Is this side all right?

Yes, it is, the redcap said. Unless of course you
prefer not getting the sunshine.

No, the young man said, I kind of like the sunshine.

It's a fine day too, the redcap said.

The young man looked out the window as if at
the day. There was nothing but trains to see, but
he looked out the window as if he were looking to
see how fine a day it was.

The sun don't get in here where it's covered
up, the redcap said, but no sooner than you get
out of here into the open you'll be running into
a lot of sunshine. Most California folks get tired
of it and get over on the other side. You from
New York?

There was nothing about the young man to suggest that he was from New York or for that matter
from anywhere else either, but the redcap wondered where the young man was from, so he asked.

No, the young man said, I've never been out of
California.

The redcap was in no hurry, although there
was considerable activity everywhere, people pil-
ing into the car, other redcaps rushing about,

helping with bags, and hurrying away. Nevertheless, he lingered and carried on a conversation. There was a girl across the aisle who was listening to the conversation and the redcap fancied he and the young man were cutting quite a figure with her, one way or another. It was charming conversation, in the best of spirits, and, although between men in different stations of life, full of that fraternal feeling which is characteristic of westerners and Americans.

I've never been out of California myself, the redcap said.

You'd think you'd be the sort of man to travel a good deal, the young man said.

Yes, you would at that, the redcap said. Working on trains, or least-ways near them, on and off most of my life since I was eighteen, which was thirty years ago, but it's true, I haven't set foot outside the boundary lines of this state. I've met a lot of travelers though, he added.

I wouldn't mind getting to New York some day, the young man said.

I don't blame a young man like you for wanting to get to New York, the redcap said. New York sure must be an interesting place down around in there.

Biggest city in the world, the young man said.

It sure is, the redcap said, and then he made as if to go, dragging himself away as it were, going away with tremendous regret.

Well, he said, have a pleasant journey.

Thanks, the young man said.

The redcap left the car. The young man looked out the window and then turned just in time to notice that the girl across the aisle was looking at him and was swiftly turning her head away, and he himself, so as not to embarrass her, swiftly continued turning his head so that something almost happened to his neck. Almost instantly he brought his head all the way back to where it had been, near the window, looking out, and felt an awful eagerness to look at the girl again and at the same time a wonderful sense of at last beginning to go places, in more ways than one, such as meeting people like her and marrying one of them and settling down in a house somewhere.

He didn't look at the girl again, though, for some time but kept wanting to very eagerly, so that finally when he did look at her he was embarrassed and blushed and gulped and tried very hard to smile but just couldn't quite make it. The girl just couldn't make it either.

That happened after they'd been moving along for more than ten minutes, the train rolling out among the hills and rattling pleasantly and making everything everywhere seem pleasant and full of wonderful potentialities, such as romance and a good deal of good humor and easygoing naturalness, especially insofar as meeting her and being friendly and pleasant and little by little getting to know her and falling in love.

They saw one another again after about seven minutes more, and then again after four minutes, and then they saw one another more steadily by pretending to be looking at the landscape on the other side, and finally they just kept seeing one another steadily for a long time, watching the landscape.

At last the young man said, are you from New York?

He didn't know what he was saying. He felt foolish and unlike young men in movies who do such things on trains.

Yes, I am, the girl said.

What? the young man said.

Didn't you ask if I was from New York? the girl said.

Oh, the young man said. Yes, I did.

Well, the girl said, I am.

I didn't know you were from New York, the young man said.

I know you didn't, the girl said.

The young man tried very hard to smile the way they smiled in pictures.

How did you know? he said.

Oh, I don't know, the girl said. Are you going to Sacramento?

Yes, I am, the young man said. Are you?

Yes, I am, the girl said.

What are you doing so far from home? the young man said.

New York isn't my home, the girl said. I was born there, but I've been living in San Francisco most of my life.

So have I most of mine, the young man said. In fact all of it.

I've lived in San Francisco practically all of my life too, the girl said, with the possible exception of them few months in New York.

Is that all the time you lived in New York? the young man said.

Yes, the girl said, only them first five months right after I was born in New York.

I was born in San Francisco, the young man said. There's lots of room on these two seats, he said with great effort. Wouldn't you like to sit over here and get the sun?

All right, the girl said.

She stepped across the aisle and sat across from the young man.

I just thought I'd go down to Sacramento on the special Sunday rate, the young man said.

I've been to Sacramento three times, the girl said.

The young man began to feel very happy. The sun was strong and warm and the girl was wonderful. Unless he was badly mistaken, or unless he got fired Monday morning, or unless America got into a war and he had to become a soldier and go away and get himself killed for no good reason, he had a hunch some day he would go to work and get acquainted with the girl and marry her and settle down.

He sat back in the sunlight while the train rattled along and smiled romantically at the girl, getting ready for the romance.

DOROTHY PARKER

11/CLOTHE THE NAKED

Big Lannie went out by the day to the houses of secure and leisured ladies, to wash their silks and their linens. She did her work perfectly; some of the ladies even told her so. She was a great, slow mass of a woman, colored a sound brown-black save for her palms and the flat of her fingers that were like gutta-percha from steam and hot suds. She was slow because of her size, and because the big veins in her legs hurt her, and her back ached much of the time. She neither cursed her ills nor sought remedies for them. They had happened to her; there they were.

Many things had happened to her. She had had children, and the children had died. So had her husband, who was a kind man, cheerful with the little luck he found. None of their children had died at birth. They had lived to be four or seven or ten, so that they had had their ways and their traits and their means of causing love; and Big Lannie's heart was always wide for love. One child had been killed in a street accident and two others had died of illnesses that might have been no more than tedious, had there been fresh food and clear spaces and clean air behind them. Only Arlene, the youngest, lived to grow up.

Arlene was a tall girl, not so dark as her mother

but with the same firm flatness of color. She was so
thin that her bones seemed to march in advance
of her body. Her little pipes of legs and her broad
feet with jutting heels were like things a child
draws with crayons. She carried her head low, her
shoulders scooped around her chest, and her stomach slanted forward. From the time that she was
tiny, there were men after her.

Arlene was a bad girl always; that was one of
the things that had happened to Big Lannie.
There it was, and Big Lannie could only keep
bringing her presents, surprises, so that the girl
would love her mother and would want to stay at
home. She brought little bottles of sharp perfume,
and pale stockings of tinny silk, and rings set with
bits of green and red glass; she tried to choose
what Arlene would like. But each time Arlene
came home she had bigger rings and softer stockings and stronger perfume than her mother could
buy for her. Sometimes she would stay with her
mother over a night, and sometimes more than a
week; and then Big Lannie would come back from
work one evening, and the girl would be gone,
and no word of her. Big Lannie would go on
bringing surprises, and setting them out along
Arlene's bed to wait a return.

Big Lannie did not know it, when Arlene was
going to have a baby. Arlene had not been home
in nearly half a year; big Lannie told the time
in days. There was no news at all of the girl until
the people at the hospital sent for Big Lannie to
come to her daughter and grandson. She was
there to hear Arlene say the baby must be named
Raymond, and to see the girl die. For whom Raymond was called, or if for anyone, Big Lannie
never knew.

He was a long, light-colored baby, with big,
milky eyes that looked right back at his grand-

mother. It was several days before the people at
the hospital told her he was blind.

Big Lannie went to each of the ladies who employed her and explained that she could not work
for some while; she must take care of her grandson. The ladies were sharply discommoded, after
her steady years, but they dressed their outrage
in shrugs and cool tones. Each arrived, separately,
at the conclusion that she had been too good to
Big Lannie, and had been imposed upon, therefore. "Honestly, those people!" each said to her
friends. "They're all alike."

Big Lannie sold most of the things she lived
with, and took one room with a stove in it.
There, as soon as the people at the hospital would
let her, she brought Raymond and tended him.
He was all her children to her.

She had always been a saving woman, with few
needs and no cravings, and she had been long
alone. Even after Arlene's burial, there was
enough left for Raymond and Big Lannie to go on
for a time. Big Lannie was slow to be afraid of
what must come; fear did not visit her at all, at
first, and then it slid in only when she waked,
when the night hung motionless before another
day.

Raymond was a good baby, a quiet, patient
baby, lying in his wooden box and stretching out
his delicate hands to the sounds that were light
and color to him. It seemed but a little while, so
short to Big Lannie, before he was walking about
the room, his hands held out, his feet quick and
sure. Those of Big Lannie's friends who saw him
for the first time had to be told that he could not
see.

Then, and it seemed again such a little while,
he could dress himself, and open the door for his
granny, and unlace the shoes from her tired feet,

and talk to her in his soft voice. She had occasional employment — now and then a neighbor would hear of a day's scrubbing she could do, or sometimes she might work in the stead of a friend who was sick — infrequent, and not to be planned on. She went to the ladies for whom she had worked, to ask if they might not want her back again; but there was little hope in her, after she had visited the first one. Well, now, really, said the ladies; well, really, now.

The neighbors across the hall watched over Raymond while Big Lannie looked for work. He was no trouble to them, nor to himself. He sat and crooned at his chosen task. He had been given a wooden spool around the top of which were driven little brads, and over these with a straightened hairpin he looped bright worsted, working faster than sight until a long tube of woven wool fell through the hole in the spool. The neighbors threaded big, blunt needles for him, and he coiled the woolen tubes and sewed them into mats. Big Lannie called them beautiful, and it made Raymond proud to have her tell him how readily she sold them. It was hard for her, when he was asleep at night, to unravel the mats and wash the worsted and stretch it so straight that even Raymond's shrewd fingers could not tell, when he worked with it next day, that it was not new.

Fear stormed in Big Lannie and took her days and nights. She might not go to any organization dispensing relief, for dread that Raymond would be taken from her and put in — she would not say the word to herself, and she and her neighbors lowered their voices when they said it to one another — an institution. The neighbors wove lingering tales of what happened inside certain neat, square buildings on the cindery skirts of the town and, if they must go near them, hurried as if passing graveyards, and came home heroes. When they got you in one of those places, whispered the neighbors, they laid your spine open with whips, and then when you dropped, they kicked your head in. Had anyone come into Big Lannie's room to take Raymond away to an asylum for the blind, the neighbors would have fought for him with stones and rails and boiling water.

Raymond did not know about anything but good. When he grew big enough to go alone down the stairs and into the street, he was certain of delight each day. He held his head high, as he came out into the little yard in front of the flimsy wooden house, and slowly turned his face from side to side, as if the air were soft liquid in which he bathed it. Trucks and wagons did not visit the street, which ended in a dump for rusted bedsprings and broken boilers and staved-in kettles; children played over its cobbles, and men and women sat talking in open windows and called across to one another in gay, rich voices. There was always laughter for Raymond to hear, and he would laugh back, and hold out his hands to it.

At first, the children stopped their play when he came out, and gathered quietly about him, and watched him, fascinated. They had been told of his affliction, and they had a sort of sickened pity for him. Some of them spoke to him, in soft, careful tones. Raymond would laugh with pleasure, and stretch his hands, the curious smooth, flat hands of the blind, to their voices. They would draw sharply back, afraid that his strange hands might touch them. Then, somehow ashamed because they had shrunk from him and he could not see that they had done so, they said gentle good-byes to him, and backed away into the street again, watching him steadily.

When they were gone, Raymond would start on his walk to the end of the street. He guided himself by lightly touching the broken fences along the dirt sidewalk, and as he walked he crooned little songs with no words to them. Some of the men and women at the windows would call hello to him, and he would call back and wave and smile. When the children, forgetting him, laughed again at their games, he stopped and turned to the sound as if it were the sun.

In the evening, he would tell Big Lannie about his walk, slapping his knee and chuckling at the memory of the laughter he had heard. When the weather was too hard for him to go out in the street, he would sit at his worsted work, and talk of going out the next day.

The neighbors did what they could for Raymond and Big Lannie. They gave Raymond clothes their own children had not yet worn out, and they brought food when they had enough to spare, and other times Big Lannie would get through a week, and would pray to get through the next one; and so the months went. Then the days on which she could find work fell farther and farther apart, and she could not pray about the time to come because she did not dare to think of it.

It was Mrs. Ewing who saved Raymond's and Big Lannie's lives, and let them continue together. Big Lannie said that then and ever after; daily she blessed Mrs. Ewing, and nightly she would have prayed for her, had she not known, in some dimmed way, that any intercession for Mrs. Delabarre Ewing must be impudence.

Mrs. Ewing was a personage in the town. When she went to Richmond for a visit, or when she returned from viewing the azalea gardens in Charleston, the newspaper always printed the fact.

She was a woman rigorously conscious of her noble obligation; she was prominent on the Community Chest committee, and it was she who planned and engineered the annual Bridge Drive to raise funds for planting salvia around the cannon in front of the D.A.R. headquarters. These and many others were her public activities, and she was no less exacting of herself in her private life. She kept a model, though childless, house for her husband and herself, relegating the supervision of details to no domestic lieutenant, no matter how seemingly trustworthy.

Back before Raymond was born, Big Lannie had worked as laundress for Mrs. Ewing. Since those days, the Ewing washtubs had witnessed many changes, none for the better. Mrs. Ewing took Big Lannie back into her employment. She apologized for this step to her friends by the always winning method of self-deprecation. She knew she was a fool, she said, after all that time, and after the way that Big Lannie had treated her. But still, she said — and she laughed a little at her own ways — anyone she felt kind of sorry for could always get around her, she said. She knew it was awful foolish, but that, she said, was the way she was. Mr. Ewing, she said behind her husband's hearing, always called her just a regular little old easy mark.

Big Lannie had no words in which to thank Mrs. Ewing, nor to tell her what two days' assured employment every week could mean. At least, it was fairly assured. Big Lannie, as Mrs. Ewing pointed out to her, had got no younger, and she had always been slow. Mrs. Ewing kept her in a state of stimulating insecurity by referring, with perfect truth, to the numbers of stronger, quicker women who were also in need of work.

Two days' work in the week meant money for

rent and stovewood and almost enough food for
Raymond and Big Lannie. She must depend, for
anything further, on whatever odd jobs she could
find, and she must not stop seeking them. Pressed
on by fear and gratitude, she worked so well for
Mrs. Ewing that there was sometimes expressed
satisfaction at the condition of the lady's house-
hold linen and her own and her husband's cloth-
ing. Big Lannie had a glimpse of Mr. Ewing occasionally, leaving the house as she came, or enter-
ing it as she was leaving. He was a bit of a man,
not much bigger than Raymond.

Raymond grew so fast that he seemed to be
taller each morning. Each day he had his walk
in the street to look forward to and experience,
and tell Big Lannie about at night. He had ceased
to be a sight of the street; the children were so
used to him that they did not even look at him,
and the men and women at the windows no longer
noticed him enough to hail him. He did not know.
He would wave to any gay cry he heard, and go on
his way, singing his little songs and turning toward the sound of laughter.

Then his lovely list of days ended as sharply
as if ripped from some bright calendar. A winter
came, so sudden and savage as to find no comparison in the town's memories, and Raymond had
no clothes to wear out in the street. Big Lannie
mended his outgrown garments as long as she
could, but the stuff had so rotted with wear that it
split in new places when she tried to sew together
the ragged edges of rents.

The neighbors could give no longer; all they
had they must keep for their own. A demented
colored man in a nearby town had killed the
woman who employed him, and terror had spread
like brush fire. There was a sort of panic of re-
prisal; colored employees were dismissed from

their positions, and there was no new work for
them. But Mrs. Ewing, admittedly soft-hearted
certainly to a fault and possibly to a peril, kept her
black laundress on. More than ever Big Lannie
had reason to call her blessed.

All winter, Raymond stayed indoors. He sat at
his spool and worsted, with Big Lannie's old
sweater about his shoulders and, when his tattered
knickerbockers would no longer hold together, a
calico skirt of hers lapped around his waist. He
lived, at his age, in the past; in the days when he
had walked, proud and glad, in the street, with
laughter in his ears. Always, when he talked of it,
he must laugh back at that laughter.

Since he could remember, he had not been allowed to go out when Big Lannie thought the
weather unfit. This he had accepted without question, and so he accepted his incarceration through
the mean weeks of the winter. But then one
day it was spring, so surely that he could tell it
even in the smoky stinking rooms of the house,
and he cried out with joy because now he might
walk in the street again. Big Lannie had to explain to him that his rags were too thin to shield
him, and that there were no odd jobs for her, and
so no clothes and shoes for him.

Raymond did not talk about the street any more,
and his fingers were slow at his spool.

Big Lannie did something she had never done
before; she begged of her employer. She asked
Mrs. Ewing to give her some of Mr. Ewing's old
clothes for Raymond. She looked at the floor and
mumbled so that Mrs. Ewing requested her to talk
up. When Mrs. Ewing understood, she was, she
said, surprised. She had, she said, a great, great
many demands on her charity, and she would
have supposed that Big Lannie, of all people,
might have known that she did everything she

could, and, in fact, a good deal more. She spoke of inches and ells. She said that if she found she could spare anything, Big Lannie was kindly to remember it was to be just for this once.

When Big Lannie was leaving at the end of her day's work, Mrs. Ewing brought her a package with her own hands. There, she said, was a suit and a pair of shoes; beautiful, grand things that people would think she was just a crazy to go giving away like that. She simply didn't know, she said, what Mr. Ewing would say to her for being such a crazy. She explained that that was the way she was when anyone got around her, all the while Big Lannie was trying to thank her.

Big Lannie had never before seen Raymond behave as he did when she brought him home the package. He jumped and danced and clapped his hands, he tried to speak and squealed instead, he tore off the paper himself, and ran his fingers over the close-woven cloth and held it to his face and kissed it. He put on the shoes and clattered about in them, digging with his toes and heels to keep them on; he made Big Lannie pin the trousers around his waist and roll them up over his shins. He babbled of the morrow when he would walk in the street, and could not say his words for laughing.

Big Lannie must work for Mrs. Ewing the next day, and she had thought to bid Raymond wait until she could stay at home and dress him herself in his new garments. But she heard him laugh again; she could not tell him he must wait. He might go out at noon next day, she said, when the sun was so warm that he would not take cold at his first outing; one of the neighbors across the hall would help him with the clothes. Raymond chuckled and sang his little songs until he went to sleep.

After Big Lannie left in the morning, the neighbor came in to Raymond, bringing a pan of cold
pork and corn bread for his lunch. She had a call
for a half-day's work, and she could not stay to see
him start out for his walk. She helped him put on
the trousers and pinned and rolled them for him,
and she laced the shoes as snug as they would go
on his feet. Then she told him not to go out till
the noon whistles blew, and kissed him, and left.

Raymond was too happy to be impatient. He
sat and thought of the street and smiled and sang.
Not until he heard the whistles did he go to the
drawer where Big Lannie had laid the coat, and
take it out and put it on. He felt it soft on his
bare back, he twisted his shoulders to let it fall
warm and loose from them. As he folded the
sleeves back over his thin arms, his heart beat
so that the cloth above it fluttered.

The stairs were difficult for him to manage, in
the big shoes, but the very slowness of the descent
was delicious to him. His anticipation was like
honey in his mouth.

Then he came out into the yard, and turned his
face in the gentle air. It was all good again; it was
all given back again. As quickly as he could, he
gained the walk and set forth, guiding himself by
the fence. He could not wait; he called out, so that
he would hear gay calls in return, he laughed so
that laughter would answer him.

He heard it. He was so glad that he took his
hand from the fence and turned and stretched out
his arms and held up his smiling face to welcome
it. He stood there, and his smile died on his face,
and his welcoming arms stiffened and shook.

It was not the laughter he had known; it was
not the laughter he had lived on. It was like great
flails beating him flat, great prongs tearing his flesh
from his bones. It was coming at him, to kill him.

It drew slyly back, and then it smashed against him. It swirled around and over him, and he could not breathe. He screamed and tried to run out through it, and fell, and it licked over him, howling higher. His clothes unrolled, and his shoes flapped on his feet. Each time he could rise, he fell again. It was as if the street were perpendicular before him, and the laughter leaping at his back. He could not find the fence, he did not know which way he was turned. He lay screaming, in blood and dust and darkness.

When Big Lannie came home, she found him on the floor in a corner of the room, moaning and whimpering. He still wore his new clothes, cut and torn and dusty, and there was dried blood on his mouth and his palms. Her heart had leapt in alarm when he had not opened the door at her footstep, and she cried out so frantically to ask what had happened that she frightened him into wild weeping. She could not understand what he said; it was something about the street, and laughing at him, and make them go away, and don't let him go in the street no more, never in the street no more. She did not try to make him explain. She took him in her arms and rocked him, and told him, over and over, never mind, don't care, everything's all right. Neither he nor she believed her words.

But her voice was soft and her arms warm. Raymond's sobs softened, and trembled away. She held him, rocking silently and rhythmically, a long time. Then gently she set him on his feet, and took from his shoulders Mr. Ewing's old full-dress coat.

DOROTHY CANFIELD FISHER

12/THE HEYDAY OF THE BLOOD

The older professor looked sharply at his assistant, fumbling with a pile of papers. "Farrar, what's the *matter* with you lately?" he asked, brusquely.

The younger man started, "Why — why — " his face twitched. He went on desperately, "I've lost my nerve, Professor Mallory, that's what's the matter with me."

"What do you mean — nerve?" asked Mallory, challenging impatience in his tone.

The younger man started. "Why — why — " His face twitched. He was trembling so that the papers he held fell on the floor. "I worry — I forget things — I take no interest in life. The psychiatrists tell me to relax, to rest. I try to but it's no good. I never go out — every evening I'm in bed by nine o'clock. I take no part in college life beyond my own work. I turned down that chance to organize a summer seminar in New York, you know — I'll never have such a splendid professional opportunity again! If I could only sleep! Heavens, what nights I have! Yet I never do anything exciting in the evening. I keep seeing myself in a sanitarium, dependent on my brother — why, I'm in hell — that's what's the matter — "

164

Professor Mallory interrupted him, patiently now, as if he were quieting a frightened saddle horse. "But don't your psychiatrists do more than just advise you to take it easy? What do they tell you about your case?"

The young man's face drew together in a spasm. "That's just it," he cried. "They won't tell me the truth. Not one. They won't speak right out. They pretend to believe that a little rest and quiet is all I need. But I've read enough case histories to know I'm doomed by the craving for defeat. I've heard about the 'will to — ' " He choked and stopped.

The older man looked at him speculatively. When he spoke again his voice was neither challenging nor patient. It had a relaxed, offhand quality. "Well, well," he said, "let's leave it at that. I can't advise you. All this is no field of mine. I don't know anything about psychiatry except what I read in the papers. I do know from there that psychiatrists pay a lot of attention to childhood impressions, and I should say they show their good sense in that. I've had childhood experiences of my own." He paused, hesitated, swung around in his swivel chair from his desk, and said as if on an impulse, "I'd sort of like to tell you about one. You're not too busy?"

"Busy! I've forgotten the meaning of the word! I don't dare to put any pressure on myself."

"Very well, then; I mean to carry you back to the stony little farm in the Green Mountains, where I had the good luck to be born and raised. You've heard me speak of Hillsboro. The story is all about my great-grandfather, who came to live with us when I was a little boy."

"Your great-grandfather?" protested the other. "People don't remember their great-grandfathers!"

"Oh, yes, they do, in Vermont. There was my
father on one farm, and my grandfather on another, without a thought that he was no longer
young, and there was 'Gran'ther' as we called him,
eighty-eight years old and just persuaded to settle back, let his descendants take care of him. He
had been in the War of 1812 — think of that, you
mushroom! — and had lost an arm and a good
deal of his health there. He had lately begun to
get a pension of twelve dollars a month. For an
old man he was quite independent financially,
as poor Vermont farmers look at things; and he
was a most extraordinary character. His arrival in
our family was an event.

"He took precedence at once over the oldest
man in the township, who was only eighty-four
and not very bright. I can remember bragging at
school about Gran'ther Pendleton, who'd be
eighty-nine come next Woodchuck Day, and could
see to read without glasses. He had been ailing all
his life, ever since the fever he took in the war.
He used to remark triumphantly that he had now
outlived six doctors who had each given him but
a year to live, 'and the seventh is going downhill
fast, so I hear!' This last was his never-failing answer to the attempts of my conscientious mother
and anxious, dutiful father to check the old man's
reckless indifference to any of the rules of hygiene.

"Our parents had never been stern or harsh
with us, but we children never dreamed of ques-
tioning their firm decisions. Neither did Gran'-
ther Pendleton question them. He ignored them,
this naughty old man, who would give his weak
stomach frightful attacks of indigestion by steal-
ing out to the pantry and devouring a whole
mince pie because he had been refused two pieces
at the table — this rebellious, unreasonable,
whimsical old madcap brought a high-voltage elec-

tric element into our quiet, orderly life. He insisted on going to every picnic and church sociable, where he ate all the indigestible dainties he could lay his hands on, stood in drafts, tired himself to the verge of fainting away by playing games with the children, and returned home, exhausted, animated, and quite ready to pay the price of a day in bed, groaning and screaming out with pain as heartily and unaffectedly as he had laughed with the pretty girls the evening before.

"The climax came, however, in the middle of August, when he announced his desire to go to the county fair, held some fourteen miles down the valley from our farm. Father never dared let Gran'ther go anywhere without going with the old man himself, but he was perfectly sincere in saying that it was not because he could not spare a day from the haying that he refused point-blank to consider it. The doctor who had been taking care of Gran'ther since he came to live with us said that it would be crazy to think of such a thing. He added that the wonder was that Gran'ther lived at all, for his heart was all wrong, his asthma was enough to kill a young man, and he had no digestion; in short, if Father wished to kill his old grandfather, there was no surer way than to drive fourteen miles in the heat of August to the noisy excitement of a county fair.

"So Father for once said 'No,' in the tone that we children had come to recognize as final. Gran'ther grimly tied a knot in his empty sleeve — a curious way he took to express strong emotion — put his one hand on his cane, and his chin on his hand, and withdrew himself into that incalculable distance from the life about him where very old people spend so many hours.

"He did not emerge from this until one morning toward the middle of fair week, when all the rest of the family were away — Father and the bigger boys on the far-off upland meadows haying, and Mother and the girls blackberrying in the burnt-over lot, across the valley. I was too little to be of any help, so I had been left to wait on Gran'ther, and to set out our lunch of bread and milk and huckleberries. We had not been alone half an hour when Gran'ther sent me to extract, from under the mattress of his bed, the wallet in which he kept his pension money. He counted it over carefully, sticking out his tongue like a schoolboy doing a sum. 'Six dollars and forty-three cents!' he cried. He began to laugh and snap his fingers and sing out in his high, cracked old voice:

" 'We're goin' to go a skylarkin'! Little Jo Mallory is going to the county fair with his Gran'ther Pendleton, an' he's goin' to have more fun than ever was in the world, and he — '

" 'But, Gran'ther, Father said we mustn't!' I protested, horrified.

" 'But I say we *shall!* I was your gre't-gran'ther long before he was your feyther, and anyway I'm here and he's not — so, *march!* Out to the barn!'

"He took me by the collar and pushed me ahead of him to the stable, where old white Peggy, the only horse left at home, looked at us amazed.

" 'But it'll be twenty-eight miles, and Peg's never driven over eight!' I cried, my established world of rules and orders reeling.

" 'Eight — and — twenty-eight
But I — am — *eighty*-eight!'

"Gran'ther improvised a sort of whooping chant of scorn as he pulled the harness from the peg. 'It'll do her good to drink some pink lemonade —

old Peggy! An' if she gits tired comin' home, I'll git out and carry her part way myself!'

"I thought this the funniest idea I'd ever heard and laughed loudly as together we hitched up, I standing on a chair to slip the checkrein in place, Gran'ther doing wonders with his one hand. Then, just as we were — Gran'ther in a hickory shirt not very clean, an old hat flapping over his wizened face, I barelegged, in my faded everyday old clothes — we drove out of the grassy yard, down the steep, stony hill that led to the main valley road. Along the hot, white turnpike, deep with dust, we joined the farm teams on their way to the fair. Gran'ther exchanged hilarious greetings with the people who constantly overtook old Peg's jogging trot. Between times he regaled me with spicy stories of the hundreds of thousands — they seemed no less numerous to me then — of county fairs he had attended in his youth. He was horrified to find that I had never been even to one.

" 'Why, Joey, how old be ye? 'Most eight, ain't it? When I was your age I had run away and been to two fairs an' a hangin'.'

" 'But didn't they lick you when you got home?' I asked shudderingly.

" 'You *bet* they did!' cried Gran'ther with gusto.

"I felt the world expanding into an infinitely larger place with every word he said.

" 'Now, this is somethin' *like!*' he exclaimed, as we drew near to Granville and fell into a procession of wagons all filled with country people in their best clothes, who looked with friendly curiosity at the ancient, shriveled cripple, his face shining with sweat and animation, and at the small boy beside him, his bare feet dangling high above the floor of the battered buckboard, overcome with the responsibility of driving a horse for the

first time in his life, and filled with such a flood of
new emotions and ideas that he must have been
quite pale."

Professor Mallory leaned back and laughed
aloud at the vision he had been evoking —
laughed with so joyous an abandon and relish in
his reminiscences that the face of his listener relaxed a little.

"Oh, that was a day!" went on the professor,
still laughing and wiping his eyes. "Never will I
have another like it! At the entrance to the
grounds Gran'ther stopped me while he solemnly
untied the knot in his empty sleeve. I don't know
what kind of harebrained vow he had tied up in
it, but with the little ceremony disappeared every
last trace of restraint, and we plunged head over
ears into the saturnalia of delights that was an
old-time county fair.

"People had little cash in those days, and Gran'-
ther's six dollars and forty-three cents lasted like
the widow's cruse of oil. We went to see the fat
lady, who, if she was really as big as she looked to
me then, must have weighed at least a ton. My ad-
miration for gran'ther's daredevil qualities rose to
infinity when he entered into free-and-easy talk
with her, about how much she ate, and could she
raise her arms enough to do up her own hair, and
how many yards of velvet it took to make her gorgeous, gold-trimmed robe. She laughed a great
deal at us, but she was evidently touched by his
human interest, for she confided to him that it
was not velvet at all, but furniture covering; and
when we went away she pressed on us a bag of
peanuts. She said she had more peanuts than she
could eat — a state of unbridled opulence which
fitted in for me with all the other superlatives of
that day.

"We saw the dog-faced boy, whom we did not like at all; Gran'ther expressing, with a candidly outspoken cynicism, his belief that 'them whiskers was glued to him.' We wandered about the stock exhibit, gazing at monstrous oxen, and hanging over the railings where the prize pigs lived to scratch their backs. In order to miss nothing, we even conscientiously passed through the Woman's Building, where we were very much bored by the serried ranks of preserve jars.

" 'Sufferin' Hezekiah!' cried Gran'ther irritably. 'Who cares how gooseberry jell *looks*. If they'd give a felly a taste, now — '

"This reminded him that we were hungry, and we went to a restaurant tent, where, after taking stock of the wealth that yet remained of Gran'-ther's hoard, he ordered the most expensive things on the bill of fare."

Professor Mallory suddenly laughed out again. "Perhaps in heaven, but certainly not until then, shall I ever taste anything so ambrosial as that fried chicken and coffee ice cream! I have not lived in vain that I have such a memory back of me!"

This time the younger man laughed with the narrator, settling back in his chair as the professor went on:

"After lunch we rode on the merry-go-round, both of us, Gran'ther clinging desperately with his one hand to his red camel's wooden hump, and crying out shrilly to me to be sure and not lose his cane. The merry-go-round had just come in at that time, and Gran'ther had never experienced it before. After the first giddy flight we retired to a lemonade stand to exchange impressions, and finding that we both alike had fallen completely under the spell of the new sensation, Gran'ther said that we 'sh'd keep on a-ridin' till we'd had enough! Nobody could tell when we'd ever git a chance again!' So we returned to the charge, and rode and rode and rode, through blinding clouds of happy excitement, so it seems to me now, such as I was never to know again. The sweat was pouring off from us, and we had tried all the different animals on the machine before we could tear ourselves away to follow the crowd to the race track.

"We took reserved seats, which cost a quarter apiece, instead of the unshaded ten-cent benches, and Gran'ther began at once to pour out to me a flood of horse talk and knowing race track aphorisms, which finally made a young fellow sitting next to us laugh superciliously. Gran'ther turned on him heatedly.

" 'I bet-che fifty cents I pick the winner in the next race!' he said sportily.

" 'Done!' said the other, still laughing.

"Gran'ther picked a big black mare, who came in almost last, but he did not flinch. As he paid over the half-dollar he said: 'Everybody's likely to make mistakes about *some* things; King Solomon was a fool in the head about womenfolks. I bet-che a dollar I pick the winner in *this* race!' and 'Done!' said the disagreeable young man, still laughing. I gasped, for I knew we had only eighty-seven cents left, but Gran'ther shot me a command to silence out of the corner of his eyes, and announced that he bet on the sorrel gelding.

"If I live to be a hundred and break the bank at Monte Carlo three times a week," said Mallory, shaking his head reminiscently, "I could not know a tenth part of the frantic excitement of that race or of the mad triumph when our horse won. Gran'-ther cast his hat upon the ground, screaming like a steam calliope with exultation as the sorrel swept past the judges' stand ahead of all the others, and

I jumped up and down in an agony of delight which was almost more than my little body could hold.

"After that we went away, feeling that the world could hold nothing more glorious. It was five o'clock, and we decided to start back. We paid for Peggy's dinner out of the dollar we had won on the race — I say 'we,' for by that time we were welded into one organism — and we still had a dollar and thirty-seven cents left. 'While ye're about it, always go the whole hog!' said Gran'ther, and we spent twenty minutes in laying out that money in trinkets for all the folks at home. Then, dusty, penniless, laden with bundles, we stowed our exhausted bodies and our uplifted hearts into the old buckboard, and turned Peg's head toward the mountains. We did not talk much during that drive, and though I thought at the time only of the carnival of joy we had left, I can now recall every detail of the trip — how the sun sank behind Indian Mountain, a peak I had known before only through distant views; then, as we journeyed on, how the stars came out above Hemlock Mountain — our own home mountain behind our house, and later, how the fireflies filled the darkening meadows along the river below us, so that we seemed to be floating between the steady stars of heaven and their dancing, twinkling reflection in the valley.

"Gran'ther's dauntless spirit still upheld me. I put out of mind doubts of our reception at home, and lost myself in delightful ruminatings on the splendors of the day. At first, every once in a while, Gran'ther made a brief remark, such as, ' 'Twas the hindquarters of the sorrel I bet on. He was the only one in the hull kit and bilin' of 'em that his quarters didn't fall away'; or, 'You needn't tell *me*

that them Siamese twins ain't unpinned every
night as separate as you and me!' But later on, as
the damp evening air began to bring on his
asthma, he subsided into silence, only broken by
great gasping coughs.

"These were heard by the anxious, heartsick
watchers at home, and, as old Peg stumbled wearily up the hill, Father came running down to meet
us. 'Where you be'n?' he demanded, his face pale
and stern in the light of his lantern. 'We be'n to
the county fair!' croaked Gran'ther with a last
flare of triumph, and fell over sideways against
me. Old Peg stopped short, hanging her head as
if she, too, were at the limit of her strength. I
was frightfully tired myself, and frozen with terror
of what Father would say. Gran'ther's collapse
was the last straw. I began to cry loudly, but Father ignored my distress with an indifference
which cut me to the heart. He lifted Gran'ther out
of the buckboard, carrying the unconscious little
old body into the house without a glance backward at me. But when I crawled down to the
ground, sobbing and digging my fists into my eyes,
I felt Mother's arms close around me.

" 'Oh, poor, naughty little Joey!' she said.
'Mother's bad, dear little boy!' "

Professor Mallory stopped short.

"Perhaps that's something else I'll know again
in heaven," he said soberly, and waited a moment
before he went on: "Well, that was the end of our
day. I was so worn out that I fell asleep over my
supper, in spite of the excitement in the house
about sending for a doctor for Gran'ther, who
was, so one of my awestruck sisters told me, having some kind of 'fits.' Mother must have put me
to bed, for the next thing I remember, she was
shaking me by the shoulder and saying, 'Wake

up, Joey. Your great-grandfather wants to speak to you. He's been suffering terribly all night, and the doctor thinks he's dying.'

"I followed her into Gran'ther's room, where the family was assembled about the bed. Gran'ther lay drawn up in a ball, groaning so dreadfully that I felt a chill like cold water at the roots of my hair; but a moment or two after I came in, all at once he gave a great sigh and relaxed, stretching out his legs, laying his one good arm down on the coverlet. He looked at me and attempted a smile.

" 'Well, it was wuth it, warn't it, Joey?' he said, and closed his eyes peacefully to sleep."

"Did he die?" asked the young professor, leaning forward.

"Die? Gran'ther Pendleton? Not much! He came tottering down to breakfast the next morning, as white as an old ghost, with no voice left, his legs trembling under him, but he kept the whole family an hour and a half at the table, telling them in a loud whisper all about the fair, until Father said really he would have to take us to the one next year. Afterward he sat out on the porch watching old Peg graze around the yard. I thought he was in one of his absent-minded fits, but when I came out, he called me to him, and, setting his lips to my ear, he whispered:

" 'An' the seventh is a-goin' downhill fast, so I hear!' He chuckled to himself for some time over his familiar battle cry, wagging his head feebly, and then he said: 'I tell ye, Joey, I've lived a long time, and I've larned a lot about the way folks is made. The trouble with most of 'em is, they're 'fraid-cats! As Jeroboam Warner used to say — he was in the same regiment with me in 1812 — the only way to manage this business of livin' is to give a whoop and let her rip! If ye just about half-live, ye just the same as half-die; and if ye spend yer time half-dyin', someday, ye turn in and die all over, without rightly meanin' to at all — just a kind o' bad habit ye've got yerself inter.' Gran'ther fell into a meditative silence for a moment. 'Jeroboam, he said that the evenin'- before the battle of Lundy's Lane, and he got killed the next day. Some live, and some die; but folks that live all over die happy, anyhow! Now I tell you what's my motto, an' what I've lived to be eighty-eight on — ' "

Professor Mallory stood up and, laying a hand on the younger man's shoulder, said: "This was the motto he told me: 'Live while you live, and then die and be done with it!' "

13/ROPE

On the third day after they moved to the country he came walking back from the village carrying a basket of groceries and a twenty-four-yard coil of rope. She came out to meet him, wiping her hands on her green smock. Her hair was tumbled, her nose was scarlet with sunburn; he told her that already she looked like a born country woman. His gray flannel shirt stuck to him, his heavy shoes were dusty. She assured him he looked like a rural character in a play.

Had he brought the coffee? She had been waiting all day long for coffee. They had forgot it when they ordered at the store the first day.

Gosh, no, he hadn't. Lord, now he'd have to go back. Yes, he would if it killed him. He thought, though, he had everything else. She reminded him it was only because he didn't drink coffee himself. If he did he would remember it quick enough. Suppose they ran out of cigarettes? Then she saw the rope. What was that for? Well, he thought it might do to hang clothes on, or something. Naturally she asked him if he thought they were going to run a laundry? They already had a fifty-foot line hanging right before his eyes. Why, hadn't he noticed it, really? It was a blot on the landscape to her.

177

He thought there were a lot of things a rope might come in handy for. She wanted to know what, for instance. He thought a few seconds, but nothing occurred. They could wait and see, couldn't they? You need all sorts of strange odds and ends around a place in the country. She said, yes, that was so; but she thought just at that time when every penny counted, it seemed funny to buy more rope. That was all. She hadn't meant anything else. She hadn't just seen, not at first, why he felt it was necessary.

Well, thunder, he had bought it because he wanted to, and that was all there was to it. She thought that was reason enough, and couldn't understand why he hadn't said so, at first. Undoubtedly it would be useful, twenty-four yards of rope, there were hundreds of things, she couldn't think of any at the moment, but it would come in handy. Of course. As he had said, things always did in the country.

But she was a little disappointed about the coffee, and oh, look, look, look at the eggs! Oh, my, they're all running! What had he put on top of them? Hadn't he known eggs mustn't be squeezed? Squeezed, who had squeezed them, he wanted to know. What a silly thing to say. He had simply brought them along in the basket with the other things. If they got broke it was the grocer's fault. He should know better than to put heavy things on top of eggs.

She believed it was the rope. That was the heaviest thing in the pack, she saw him plainly when he came in from the road, the rope was a big package on top of everything. He desired the whole wide world to witness that this was not a fact. He had carried the rope in one hand and the basket in the other, and what was the use of her having eyes if that was the best they could do for her?

Well, anyhow, she could see one thing plain: no eggs for breakfast. They'd have to scramble them now, for supper. It was too bad. She had planned to have steak for supper. No ice, meat wouldn't keep. He wanted to know why she couldn't finish breaking the eggs in a bowl and set them in a cool place.

Cool place! If he could find one for her, she'd be glad to set them there. Well, then, it seemed to him they might very well cook the meat at the same time they cooked the eggs and then warm up the meat for tomorrow. The idea simply choked her. Warmed-over meat, when they might as well have had it fresh. Second best and scraps and makeshifts, even to the meat! He rubbed her shoulder a little. It doesn't really matter so much, does it, darling? Sometimes when they were playful, he would rub her shoulder and she would arch and purr. This time she hissed and almost clawed. He was getting ready to say that they could surely manage somehow when she turned on him and said, if he told her they could manage somehow she would certainly slap his face.

He swallowed the words red hot, his face burned. He picked up the rope and started to put it on the top shelf. She would not have it on the top shelf, the jars and tins belonged there; positively she would not have the top shelf cluttered up with a lot of rope. She had borne all the clutter she meant to bear in the flat in town, there was space here at least and she meant to keep things in order.

Well, in that case, he wanted to know what the hammer and nails were doing up there? And why had she put them there when she knew very well he needed that hammer and those nails upstiars to fix the window sashes? She simply slowed down everything and made double work on the place

with her insane habit of changing things around
and hiding them.

She was sure she begged his pardon, and if she
had had any reason to believe he was going to fix
the sashes this summer she would have left the
hammer and nails right where he put them; in
the middle of the bedroom floor where they could
step on them in the dark. And now if he didn't
clear the whole mess out of there she would throw
them down the well.

Oh, all right, all right — could he put them in
the closet? Naturally not, there were brooms and
mops and dustpans in the closet, and why couldn't
he find a place for his rope outside her kitchen?
Had he stopped to consider there were seven rooms
in the house, and only one kitchen?

He wanted to know what of it? And did she realize she was making a complete fool of herself? And
what did she take him for, a three-year-old idiot?
The whole trouble with her was she needed something weaker than she was to heckle and tyrannize
over. He wished now they had a couple of children she could take it out on. Maybe he'd get some
rest.

Her face changed at this, she reminded him he
had forgot the coffee and had bought a worthless
piece of rope. And when she thought of all the
things they actually needed to make the place
even decently fit to live in, well, she could cry,
that was all. She looked so forlorn, so lost and de-
spairing he couldn't believe it was only a piece of
rope that was causing all the racket. What *was* the
matter?

Oh, would he please hush and go away, and
stay away, if he could, for five minutes? By all
means, yes, he would. He'd stay away indefinitely
if she wished. Lord yes, there was nothing he'd like
better than to clear out and never come back. She

couldn't for the life of her see what was holding
him, then. It was a swell time. Here she was, stuck,
miles from a railroad, with a half-empty house on
her hands, and not a penny in her pocket, and
everything on earth to do; it seemed the God-sent
moment for him to get out from under. She was
surprised he hadn't stayed in town until she had
come out and done the work and got things
straightened out. It was his usual trick.

It appeared to him that this was going a little
far. Just a touch out of bounds, if she didn't mind
his saying so. Why had he stayed in town the summer before? To do a half-dozen extra jobs to get
the money he had sent her. That was it. She knew
perfectly well they couldn't have done it otherwise. She had agreed with him at the time. And
that was the only time so help him he had ever
left her to do anything by herself.

Oh, he could tell that to his great-grand-
mother. She had her notion of what had kept him
in town. Considerably more than a notion, if he
wanted to know. So, she was going to bring all that
up again, was she? Well, she could just think what
she pleased. He was tired of explaining. It may
have looked funny but he had simply got hooked
in, and what could he do? It was impossible to
believe that she was going to take it seriously. Yes,
yes, she knew how it was with a man: if he was left
by himself a minute, some woman was certain to
kidnap him. And naturally he couldn't hurt her
feelings by refusing!

Well, what was she raving about? Did she forget
she had told him those two weeks alone in the
country were the happiest she had known for four
years? And how long had they been married when
she said that? All right, shut up! If she thought
that hadn't stuck in his craw.

She hadn't meant she was happy because she

was away from him. She meant she was happy getting the devilish house nice and ready for him. That was what she had meant, and now look! Bringing up something she had said a year ago simply to justify himself for forgetting her coffee and breaking the eggs and buying a wretched piece of rope they couldn't afford. She really thought it was time to drop the subject, and now she wanted only two things in the world. She wanted him to get that rope from underfoot, and go back to the village and get her coffee, and if he could remember it, he might bring a metal mitt for the skillets, and two more curtain rods, and if there were any rubber gloves in the village, her hands were simply raw, and a bottle of milk of magnesia from the drugstore.

He looked out at the dark blue afternoon sweltering on the slopes, and mopped his forehead and sighed heavily and said, if only she would wait a minute for *anything*, he was going back. He had said so, hadn't he, the very instant they found he had overlooked it?

Oh, yes, well . . . run along. She was going to wash windows. The country was so beautiful! She doubted they'd have a moment to enjoy it. He meant to go, but he could not until he had said that if she wasn't such a hopeless melancholiac she might see that this was only for a few days. Couldn't she remember anything pleasant about the other summers? Hadn't they ever had any fun? She hadn't time to talk about it, and now would he please not leave that rope lying around for her to trip on? He picked it up, somehow it had toppled off the table, and walked out with it under his arm.

Was he going this minute? He certainly was. She thought so. Sometimes it seemed to her he had second sight about the precisely perfect moment to leave her ditched. She had meant to put the mattresses out to sun, if they put them out this minute they would get at least three hours, he must have heard her say that morning she meant to put them out. So of course he would walk off and leave her to do it. She supposed he thought the exercise would do her good.

Well, he was merely going to get her coffee. A four-mile walk for two pounds of coffee was ridiculous, but he was perfectly willing to do it. The habit was making a wreck of her, but if she wanted to wreck herself there was nothing he could do about it. If he thought it was coffee that was making a wreck of her, she congratulated him: he must have an easy conscience.

Conscience or no conscience, he didn't see why the mattresses couldn't very well wait until tomorrow. And anyhow, were they living *in* the house, or were they going to let the house ride them to death? She paled at this, her face grew livid about the mouth, she looked quite dangerous, and reminded him that housekeeping was no more her work than it was his: she had other work to do as well, and when did he think she was going to find time to do it at this rate?

Was she going to start on that again? She knew as well as he did that his work brought in the regular money, hers was only occasional, if they depended on what *she* made — and she might as well get straight on this question once for all!

That was positively not the point. The question was, when both of them were working on their own time, was there going to be a division of the housework, or wasn't there? She merely wanted to know, she had to make her plans. Why, he thought that was all arranged. It was understood that he was to help. Hadn't he always, in summers?

Hadn't he, though? Oh, just hadn't he? And when, and where, and doing what? Lord, what an uproarious joke!

It was such a very uproarious joke that her face turned slightly purple, and she screamed with laughter. She laughed so hard she had to sit down, and finally a rush of tears spurted from her eyes and poured down into the lifted corners of her mouth. He dashed toward her and dragged her up to her feet and tried to pour water on her head. The dipper hung by a string on a nail and he broke it loose. Then he tried to pump water with one hand while she struggled in the other. So he gave it up and shook her instead.

She wrenched away, crying out for him to take his rope and get out, she had simply given him up: and ran. He heard her high-heeled bedroom slippers clattering and stumbling on the stairs.

He went out around the house and into the lane; he suddenly realized he had a blister on his heel and his shirt felt as if it were on fire. Things broke so suddenly you didn't know where you were. She could work herself into a fury about simply nothing. She was terrible, damn it: not an ounce of reason. You might as well talk to a sieve as that woman when she got going. Damned if he'd spend his life humoring her! Well, what to do now? He would take back the rope and exchange it for something else. Things accumulated, things were mountainous, you couldn't move them or sort them out or get rid of them. They just lay and rotted around. He'd take it back. But why should he? He wanted it. What was it anyhow? A piece of rope. Imagine anybody caring more about a piece of rope than about a man's feelings. What earthly right had she to say a word about it? He remembered all the useless, meaningless things she bought for herself. Why? because I wanted it, that's why! He stopped and selected a large stone by the road. He would put the rope behind it. He would put it in the toolbox when he got back. He'd heard enough about it to last him a lifetime.

When he came back she was leaning against the post box beside the road waiting. It was pretty late, the smell of broiled steak floated nose high in the cooling air. Her face was young and smooth and fresh-looking. Her unmanageable funny black hair was all on end. She waved to him from a distance, and he speeded up. She called out that supper was ready and waiting, was he starved?

You bet he was starved. Here was the coffee. He waved it at her. She looked at his other hand. What was that he had there?

Well, it was the rope again. He stopped short. He had meant to exchange it but forgot. She wanted to know why he should exchange it, if it was something he really wanted. Wasn't the air sweet now, and wasn't it fine to be here?

She walked beside him with one hand hooked into his leather belt. She pulled and jostled him a little as he walked, and leaned against him. He put his arm clear around her and patted her stomach. They exchanged wary smiles. Coffee, coffee for the Ootsum-Wootsums! He felt as if he were bringing her a beautiful present.

He was a love, she firmly believed, and if she had had her coffee in the morning, she wouldn't have behaved so funny. . . . There was a whippoorwill still coming back, imagine, clear out of season, sitting in the crab-apple tree calling all by himself. Maybe his girl stood him up. Maybe she did. She hoped to hear him once more, she loved whippoorwills. . . . He knew how she was, didn't he?

Sure, he knew how she was.

STEPHEN VINCENT BENÉT

14/A TOOTH FOR PAUL REVERE

Some say it all happened because of Hancock and
Adams (said the old man, pulling at his pipe), and
some put it back to the Stamp Act and before.
Then, there's some hold out for Paul Revere and
his little silver box. But the way I heard it, it
broke loose because of Lige Butterwick and his
tooth.

What's that? Why, the American Revolution, of
course. What else would I be talking about? Well,
your story about the land down South that they
had to plough with alligators reminded me.

No, this is a true story — or at least that's how
I heard it told. My great-aunt was a Butterwick
and I heard it from her. And, every now and then,
she'd write it out and want to get it put in the history books. But they'd always put her off with
some trifling sort of excuse. Till, finally, she got
her dander up and wrote direct to the President
of the United States. Well, no, he didn't answer
himself exactly — the President's apt to be a
pretty busy man. But the letter said he'd received her interesting communication and thanked
her for it, so that shows you. We've got it framed,
in the trailer — the ink's a little faded, but you
can make out the man's name who signed it. It's
either Bowers or Thorpe and he wrote a very nice
hand.

You see, my great-aunt, she wasn't very respectful to the kind of history that does get into the books. What she liked was the queer corners of it and the tales that get handed down in families. Take Paul Revere, for instance — all most folks think about, with him, is his riding a horse. But when she talked about Paul Revere — why, you could just see him in his shop, brewing the American Revolution in a silver teapot and waiting for it to settle. Oh yes, he was a silversmith by trade — but she claimed he was something more. She claimed there was a kind of magic in that quick, skillful hand of his — and that he was one of the kind of folks that can see just a little bit farther into a millstone than most. But it was when she got to Lige Butterwick that she really turned herself loose.

For she claimed that it took all sorts to make a country — and that meant the dumb ones too. I don't mean ijits or nincompoops — just the ordinary folks that live along from day to day. And that day may be a notable day in history — but it's just Tuesday to them, till they read all about it in the papers. Oh, the heroes and the great men — they can plan and contrive and see ahead. But it isn't till the Lige Butterwicks get stirred up that things really start to happen. Or so she claimed. And the way that they do get stirred up is often curious, as she'd tell this story to prove.

For, now you take Lige Butterwick — and, before his tooth started aching, he was just like you and me. He lived on a farm about eight miles from Lexington, Massachusetts, and he was a peaceable man. It was troubled times in the American colonies, what with British warships in Boston Harbor and British soldiers in Boston and Sons of Liberty hooting the British soldiers — not to speak of Boston tea parties and such. But Lige

Butterwick, he worked his farm and didn't pay much attention. There's lots of people like that, even in troubled times.

When he went into town, to be sure, there was high talk at the tavern. But he bought his goods and came home again — he had ideas about politics, but he didn't talk about them much. He had a good farm and it kept him busy — he had a wife and five children and they kept him bumping. The young folks could argue about King George and Sam Adams — he wondered how the corn was going to stand that year. Now and then, if somebody said that this and that was a burning shame, he'd allow as how it might be, just to be neighborly. But, inside, he was wondering whether next year he mightn't make an experiment and plant the west field in rye.

Well, everything went along for him the way that it does for most folks with good years and bad years, till one April morning, in 1775, he woke up with a toothache. Being the kind of man he was, he didn't pay much attention to it at first. But he mentioned it that evening, at supper, and his wife got a bag of hot salt for him He held it to his face and it seemed to ease him, but he couldn't hold it there all night, and next morning, the tooth hurt worse than ever.

Well, he stood it the next day and the next, but it didn't improve any. He tried tansy tea and other remedies — he tried tying a string to it and having his wife slam the door. But, when it came to the pinch, he couldn't quite do it. So, finally, he took the horse and rode into Lexington town to have it seen to. Mrs. Butterwick made him — she said it might be an expense, but anything was better than having him act as if he wanted to kick the cat across the room every time she put her feet down hard.

When he got into Lexington, he noticed that
folks there seemed kind of excited. There was a
lot of talk about muskets and powder and a couple of men called Hancock and Adams who were
staying at Parson Clarke's. But Lige Butterwick
had his own business to attend to — and, besides,
his tooth was jumping so he wasn't in any mood
for conversation. He set off for the local barber's,
as being the likeliest man he knew to pull a tooth.

The barber took one look at it and shook his
head.

"I can pull her, Lige," he said. "Oh, I can pull
her, all right. But she's got long roots and strong
roots and she's going to leave an awful gap when
she's gone. Now, what you really need," he said,
kind of excited, for he was one of those perky little men who's always interested in the latest notion, "what you really need — though it's taking
away my business — is one of these-here artificial
teeth to go in the hole."

"Artificial teeth!" said Lige. "It's flying in the
face of Nature!"

The barber shook his head. "No, Lige," he said,
"that's where you're wrong. Artificial teeth is all
the go these days, and Lexington ought to keep
up with the times. It would do me good to see
you with an artificial tooth — it would so."

"Well, it might do *you* good," said Lige, rather
crossly, for his tooth was jumping, "but, suppos-
ing I did want one — how in tunket will I get one
in Lexington?"

"Now you just leave that to me," said the barber, all excited, and he started to rummage
around. "You'll have to go to Boston for it, but I
know just the man." He was one of those men
who can always tell you where to go and it's usually wrong. "See here," he went on. "There's a
fellow called Revere in Boston that fixes them

and they say he's a boss workman. Just take a look
at this prospectus" — and he started to read from a
paper: " 'Whereas many persons are so unfortu-
nate as to lose their foreteeth' — that's you, Lige
— 'to their great detriment, not only in looks but
in speaking, both in public and private, this is to
inform all such that they may have them replaced
by artificial ones' — see? — 'that look as well as
the natural and answer the end of speaking to all
intents' — and then he's got his name — Paul Revere, goldsmith, near the head of Dr. Clarke's
wharf, Boston."

"Sounds well enough," said Lige, "but what's
it going to cost?"

"Oh, I know Revere," said the barber, swelling
up like a robin. "Comes through here pretty often,
as a matter of fact. And he's a decent fellow, if he
is a pretty big bug in the Sons of Liberty. You
just mention my name."

"Well, it's something I hadn't thought of," said
Lige, as his tooth gave another red-hot jounce,
"but in for a penny, in for a pound. I've missed
a day's work already and that tooth's got to come
out before I go stark, staring mad But what sort
of a man is this Revere, anyway?"

"Oh, he's a regular wizard!" said the barber. "A
regular wizard with his tools."

"Wizard!" said Lige. "Well, I don't know about
wizards. But if he can fix my tooth I'll call him
one."

"You'll never regret it," said the barber — and
that's the way folks always talk when they're sending someone else to the dentist. So Lige Butterwick
got on his horse again and started out for Boston. A couple of people shouted at him as he rode
down the street, but he didn't pay any attention.
And, going by Parson Clarke's, he caught a glimpse

of two men talking in the Parson's front room. One was a tallish, handsomish man in pretty fine clothes and the other was shorter and untidy, with a kind of bulldog face. But they were strangers to him and he didn't really notice them — just rode ahead.

II

But as soon as he got into Boston he started to feel queer — and it wasn't only his tooth. He hadn't been there in four years and he'd expected to find it changed, but it wasn't that. It was a clear enough day and yet he kept feeling there was thunder in the air. There'd be knots of people, talking and arguing, on street corners, and then, when you got closer to them, they'd kind of melt away. Or, if they stayed, they'd look at you, out of the corners of their eyes. And there, in the Port of Boston, were the British warships, black and grim. He'd known they'd be there, of course, but it was different, seeing them. It made him feel queer to see their guns pointed at the town. He'd known there was trouble and dispute, in Boston, but the knowledge had passed over him like rain and hail. But now here he was in the middle of it — and it smelt like earthquake weather. He couldn't make head or tail of it, but he wanted to be home.

All the same, he'd come to get his tooth fixed, and, being New England, he was bound to do it. But first he stopped at a tavern for a bite and a sup, for it was long past his dinnertime. And there, it seemed to him, things got even more curious.

"Nice weather we're having, these days," he said, in a friendly way, to the barkeep.

"It's bitter weather for Boston," said the barkeep, in an unfriendly voice, and a sort of low growl went up from the boys at the back of the room and every eye fixed on Lige.

Well, that didn't help the toothache any, but, being a sociable person, Lige kept on.

"May be, for Boston," he said, "but out in the country we'd call it good planting weather."

The barkeep stared at him hard.

"I guess I was mistaken in you," he said. "It *is* good planting weather — for some kinds of trees."

"And what kind of trees were you thinking of?" said a sharp-faced man at Lige's left and squeezed his shoulder.

"There's trees and trees, you know," said a red-faced man at Lige's right, and gave him a dig in the ribs.

"Well, now that you ask me — " said Lige, but he couldn't even finish before the red-faced man dug him hard in the ribs again.

"The liberty tree!" said the red-faced man. "And may it soon be watered in the blood of tyrants!"

"The royal oak of England!" said the sharp-faced man. "And God save King George and loyalty!"

Well, with that it seemed to Lige Butterwick as if the whole tavern kind of riz up at him. He was kicked and pummeled and mauled and thrown into a corner and yanked out of it again with the red-faced man and the sharp-faced man and all the rest of them dancing quadrilles over his prostrate form. Till, finally, he found himself out in the street with half his coat gone galley-west.

"Well," said Lige to himself, "I always heard city folks were crazy. But politics must be getting serious in these American colonies when they start fighting about trees!"

Then he saw the sharp-faced man was beside

him, trying to shake his hand. He noticed with
some pleasure that the sharp-faced man had the
beginnings of a beautiful black eye.

"Nobly done, friend," said the sharp-faced man,
"and I'm glad to find another true-hearted loyal-
ist in this pestilent, rebellious city."

"Well, I don't know as I quite agree with you
about that," said Lige. "But I came here to get my
tooth fixed, not to talk politics. And as long as
you've spoken so pleasant, I wonder if you could
help me out. You see, I'm from Lexington way —
and I'm looking for a fellow named Paul Revere — "

"Paul Revere!" said the sharp-faced man, as if
the name hit him like a bullet. Then he began to
smile again — not a pleasant smile.

"Oh, it's Paul Revere you want, my worthy and
ingenuous friend from the country," he said.
"Well, I'll tell you how to find him. You go up to
the first British soldier you see and ask the way.
But you better give the password first."

"Password?" said Lige Butterwick, scratching
his ear.

"Yes," said the sharp-faced man, and his smile
got wider. "You say to that British soldier, 'Any
lobsters for sale today?' Then you ask about Revere."

"But why do I talk about lobsters first?" said
Lige Butterwick, kind of stubborn.

"Well, you see," said the sharp-faced man, "the
British soldiers wear red coats. So they like being
asked about lobsters. Try it and see." And he went
away, with his shoulders shaking.

Well, that seemed queer to Lige Butterwick,
but no queerer than the other things that had happened that day. All the same, he didn't quite trust
the sharp-faced man, so he took care not to come
too close to the British patrol when he asked them

about the lobsters. And it was lucky he did, for no
sooner were the words out of his mouth than the
British soldiers took after him and chased him
clear down to the wharves before he could get
away. At that, he only managed it by hiding in an
empty tar barrel, and when he got out he was certainly a sight for sore eyes.

"Well, I guess that couldn't have been the right
password," he said to himself, kind of grimly, as
he tried to rub off some of the tar. "All the same,
I don't think soldiers ought to act like that when
you ask them a civil question. But, city folks or
soldiers, they can't make a fool out of me. I came
here to get my tooth fixed and get it fixed I will, if
I have to surprise the whole British Empire to do
it."

And just then he saw a sign on a shop at the
end of the wharf. And, according to my great-
aunt, this was what was on the sign. It said "PAUL
REVERE, SILVERSMITH" at the top, and then,
under it, in smaller letters, "Large and small bells
cast to order, engraving and printing done in job
lots, artificial teeth sculptured and copper boilers
mended, all branches of goldsmith and silversmith
work and revolutions put up to take out. Express
Service, Tuesdays and Fridays, to Lexington, Concord and Points West."

"Well," said Lige Butterwick, "kind of a Jack-
of-all-trades. Now maybe I can get my tooth fixed."
And he marched up to the door.

III

Paul Revere was behind the counter when Lige
came in, turning a silver bowl over and over in his
hands. A man of forty-odd he was, with a quick,
keen face and snapping eyes. He was wearing Boston clothes, but there was a French look about

him — for his father was Apollos Rivoire from the
island of Guernsey, and good French Huguenot
stock. They'd changed the name to Revere when
they crossed the water.

It wasn't such a big shop, but it had silver pieces
in it that people have paid thousands for, since.
And the silver pieces weren't all. There were
prints and engravings of the Port of Boston and
caricatures of the British and all sorts of goldsmith
work, more than you could put a name to. It was
a crowded place, but shipshape. And Paul Revere moved about it, quick and keen, with his
eyes full of life and hot temper — the kind of man
who knows what he wants to do and does it the
next minute.

There were quite a few customers there when
Lige Butterwick first came in — so he sort of
scrooged back in a corner and waited his chance.
For one thing, after the queer sign and the barber's calling him a wizard, he wanted to be sure
about this fellow Revere and see what kind of customers came to his shop.

Well, there was a woman who wanted a chris-
tening mug for a baby and a man who wanted a
print of the Boston Massacre. And then there was a
fellow who passed Revere some sort of message,
under cover — Lige caught the whisper "powder"
and "Sons of Liberty," though he couldn't make
out the rest. And, finally, there was a very fine silk-
dressed lady who seemed to be giving Revere considerable trouble. Lige peeked at her round the
corner of his chair, and somehow or other, she reminded him of a turkey-gobbler, especially the
strut.

She was complaining about some silver that
Paul Revere had made for her — expensive silver
it must have been. And "Oh, Master Revere, I'm
so disappointed!" she was saying. "When I took

the things from the box, I could just have
cried!"

Revere drew himself up a little at that, Lige noticed, but his voice was pleasant.

"It is I who am disappointed, madam," he said,
with a little bow. "But what was the trouble? It
must have been carelessly packed. Was it badly
dented? I'll speak to my boy."

"Oh no, it wasn't dented," said the turkey-gobbler lady. "But I wanted a really impressive silver
service — something I can use when the Governor comes to dinner with us. I certainly *paid* for
the best. And what have you given me?"

Lige waited to hear what Paul Revere would
say. When he spoke, his voice was stiff.

"I have given you the best work of which I am
capable, madam," he said. "It was in my hands
for six months — and I think they are skillful
hands."

"Oh," said the woman, and rustled her skirts.
"I know you're a competent artisan, Master Revere — "

"Silversmith, if you please — " said Paul Revere, and the woman rustled again.

"Well, I don't care what you call it," she said,
and then you could see her fine accent was put on
like her fine clothes. "But I know I wanted a real
service — something I could show my friends. And
what have you given me? Oh, it's silver, if you
choose. But it's just as plain and simple as a picket
fence!"

Revere looked at her for a moment and Lige
Butterwick thought he'd explode.

"Simple?" he said. "And plain? You pay me
high compliments, madam!"

"Compliments indeed!" said the woman, and
now she was getting furious. "I'm sending it back
tomorrow! Why, there isn't as much as a lion or a

unicorn on the cream jug. And I told you I wanted the sugar bowl covered with silver grapes! But you've given me something as bare as the hills of New England! And I won't stand it, I tell you! I'll send to England instead."

Revere puffed his cheeks and blew, but his eyes were dangerous.

"Send away, madam," he said. "We're making new things in this country — new men — new silver — perhaps, who knows, a new nation. Plain, simple, bare as the hills and rocks of New England — graceful as the boughs of her elm trees — if my silver were only like that indeed! But that is what I wish to make it. And, as for you, madam," — he stepped toward her like a cat — "with your lions and unicorns and grape leaves and your nonsense of bad ornament done by bad silversmiths — your imported bad taste and your imported British manners — puff!" And he blew at her, just the way you blow at a turkey-gobbler, till she fairly picked up her fine silk skirts and ran. Revere watched her out of the door and turned back, shaking his head.

"William!" he called to the boy who helped him in the shop. "Put up the shutters — we're closing for the day. And William — no word yet from Dr. Warren?"

"Not yet, sir," said the boy, and started to put up the shutters. Then Lige Butterwick thought it was about time to make his presence known.

So he coughed, and Paul Revere whirled and Lige Butterwick felt those quick, keen eyes boring into his. He wasn't exactly afraid of them, for he was stubborn himself, but he knew this was an unexpected kind of man.

"Well, my friend," said Revere impatiently, "and who in the world are you?"

"Well, Mr. Revere," said Lige Butterwick. "It is

Mr. Revere, isn't it? It's kind of a long story. But, closing or not, you've got to listen to me. The barber told me so."

"The barber!" said Revere, kind of dumbfounded.

"Uh-huh," said Lige, and opened his mouth. "You see, it's my tooth."

"Tooth!" said Revere, and stared at him as if they were both crazy. "You'd better begin at the beginning. But wait a minute. You don't talk like a Boston man. Where do you come from?"

"Oh, around Lexington way," said Lige. "And, you see — "

But the mention of Lexington seemed to throw Revere into a regular excitement. He fairly shook Lige by the shoulders.

"Lexington!" he said. "Were you there this morning?"

"Of course I was," said Lige. "That's where the barber I told you about — "

"Never mind the barber!" said Revere. "Were Mr. Hancock and Mr. Adams still at Parson Clarke's?"

"Well, they might have been, for all I know," said Lige. "But I couldn't say."

"Great heaven!" said Revere. "Is there a man in the American colonies who doesn't know Mr. Hancock and Mr. Adams?"

"There seems to be me," said Lige. "But, speaking of strangers — there *was* two of them staying at the parsonage, when I rode past. One was a handsomish man and the other looked more like a bulldog — "

"Hancock and Adams!" said Revere. "So they are still there." He took a turn or two up and down the room. "And the British ready to march!" he muttered to himself. "Did you see many soldiers as you came to my shop, Mr. Butterwick?"

"See them?" said Lige. "They chased me into a tar barrel. And there was a whole passel of them up by the Common with guns and flags. Looked as if they meant business."

Revere took his hand and pumped it up and down.

"Thank you, Mr. Butterwick," he said. "You're a shrewd observer. And you have done me — and the colonies — an invaluable service."

"Well, that's nice to know," said Lige. "But speaking about this tooth of mine — "

Revere looked at him and laughed, while his eyes crinkled.

"You're a stubborn man, Mr. Butterwick," he said. "All the better. I like stubborn men. I wish we had more of them. Well, one good turn deserves another — you've helped me and I'll do my best to help you. I've made artificial teeth — but drawing them is hardly my trade. All the same, I'll do what I can for you."

So Lige sat down in a chair and opened his mouth.

"Whew!" said Revere, with his eyes dancing. His voice grew solemn. "Mr. Butterwick," he said, "it seems to be a compound, agglutinated infraction of the upper molar. I'm afraid I can't do anything about it tonight."

"But — " said Lige.

"But here's a draught — that will ease the pain for a while," said Revere, and poured some medicine into a cup. "Drink!" he said, and Lige drank. The draught was red and spicy, with a queer, sleepy taste, but pungent. It wasn't like anything Lige had ever tasted before, but he noticed it eased the pain.

"There," said Revere. "And now you go to a tavern and get a good night's rest. Come back to see me in the morning — I'll find a tooth-drawer for you, if I'm here. And — oh yes — you'd better have some liniment."

He started to rummage in a big cupboard at the back of the shop. It was dark now, with the end of day and the shutters up, and whether it was the tooth, or the tiredness, or the draught Paul Revere had given him, Lige began to feel a little queer. There was a humming in his head and a lightness in his feet. He got up and stood looking over Paul Revere's shoulder, and it seemed to him that things moved and scampered in that cupboard in a curious way, as Revere's quick fingers took down this box and that. And the shop was full of shadows and murmurings.

"It's a queer kind of a shop you've got here, Mr. Revere," he said, glad to hear the sound of his own voice.

"Well, some people think so," said Revere — and that time Lige was almost sure he saw something move in the cupboard. He coughed. "Say — what's in that little bottle?" he said, to keep his mind steady.

"That?" said Paul Revere, with a smile, and held the bottle up. "Oh, that's a little chemical experiment of mine. I call it Essence of Boston. But there's a good deal of East Wind in it."

"Essence of Boston," said Lige, with his eyes bulging. "Well, they did say you was a wizard. It's gen-u-wine magic, I suppose?"

"Genuine magic, of course," said Revere, with a chuckle. "And here's the box with your liniment. And here — " He took down two little boxes — a silver and a pewter one — and placed them on the counter. But Lige's eyes went to the silver one — they were drawn to it, though he couldn't have told you why.

"Pick it up," said Paul Revere, and Lige did so

and turned it in his hands. It was a handsome box. He could make out a growing tree and an eagle fighting a lion. "It's mighty pretty work," he said.

"It's my own design," said Paul Revere. "See the stars around the edge — thirteen of them? You could make a very pretty design with stars — for a new country, say — if you wanted to — I've sometimes thought of it."

"But what's in it?" said Lige.

"What's in it?" said Paul Revere, and his voice was light but steely. "Why, what's in the air around us? Gunpowder and war and the making of a new nation. But the time isn't quite ripe yet — not quite ripe."

"You mean," said Lige, and he looked at the box very respectful, "that this here revolution folks keep talking about — "

"Yes," said Paul Revere, and he was about to go on. But just then his boy ran in, with a letter in his hand.

"Master!" he said. "A message from Dr. Warren!"

IV

Well, with that Revere started moving, and when he started to move, he moved fast. He was calling for his riding boots in one breath and telling Lige Butterwick to come back tomorrow in another — and, what with all the bustle and confusion, Lige Butterwick nearly went off without his liniment after all. But he grabbed up a box from the counter, just as Revere was practically shoving him out of the door — and it wasn't till he'd got to his tavern and gone to bed for the night that he found out he'd taken the wrong box.

He found it out then, because, when he went

to bed, he couldn't get to sleep. It wasn't his tooth
that bothered him — that had settled to a kind of
dull ache and he could have slept through that.
But his mind kept going over all the events of the
day — the two folks he'd seen at Parson Clarke's
and being chased by the British and what Revere
had said to the turkey-gobbler woman — till he
couldn't get any peace. He could feel something
stirring in him, though he didn't know what it
was.

"'Tain't right to have soldiers chase a fellow
down the street," he said to himself. "And 'tain't
right to have people like that woman run down
New England. No, it ain't. Oh me — I better look
for that liniment of Mr. Revere's."

So he got up from his bed and went over and
found his coat. Then he reached his hand in the
pocket and pulled out the silver box.

Well, at first he was so frustrated that he didn't
know rightly what to do. For here, as well as he
could remember it, was gunpowder and war and
the makings of a new nation — the revolution itself — shut up in a silver box by Paul Revere. He
mightn't have believed there could be such things
before he came to Boston. But now he did.

The draught was still humming in his head, and
his legs felt a mite wobbly. But being human, he
was curious. "Now, I wonder what *is* inside that
box," he said.

He shook the box and handled it, but that
seemed to make it warmer, as if there was something alive inside it, so he stopped that mighty
quick. Then he looked all over it for a keyhole,
but there wasn't any keyhole, and, if there had
been, he didn't have a key. Then he put his ear to
the box and listened hard. And it seemed to him
that he heard, very tiny and far away, inside the

box, the rolling fire of thousands of tiny muskets and the tiny, faraway cheers of many men. "Hold your fire!" he heard a voice say. "Don't fire till you're fired on — but, if they want a war, let it begin here!" And then there was a rolling of drums and a squeal of fifes. It was small, still, and far away, but it made him shake all over, for he knew he was listening to something in the future — and something that he didn't have a right to hear. He sat down on the edge of his bed, with the box in his hands.

"Now, what am I going to do with this?" he said. "It's too big a job for one man."

Well, he thought, kind of scared, of going down to the river and throwing the box in, but, when he thought of doing it, he knew he couldn't. Then he thought of his farm near Lexington and the peaceful days. Once the revolution was out of the box, there'd be an end to that. But then he remembered what Revere had said when he was talking with the woman about the silver — the thing about building a new country and building it clean and plain.

"Why, I'm not a Britisher," he thought. "I'm a New Englander. And maybe there's something beyond that — something people like Hancock and Adams know about. And, if it has to come with a revolution — well, I guess it has to come. We can't stay Britishers forever, here in this country."

He listened to the box again, and now there wasn't any shooting in it — just a queer tune played on a fife. He didn't know the name of the tune, but it lifted his heart.

He got up, sort of slow and heavy. "I guess I'll have to take this back to Paul Revere," he said.

Well, the first place he went was Dr. Warren's, having heard Revere mention it, but he didn't get much satisfaction there. It took quite a while to convince them that he wasn't a spy, and, when he did, all they'd tell him was that Revere had gone over the river to Charlestown. So he went down to the waterfront to look for a boat. And the first person he met was a very angry woman.

"No," she said, "you don't get any boats from me. There was a crazy man along here an hour ago and he wanted a boat, too, and my husband was crazy enough to take him. And then, do you know what he did?"

"No, ma'am," said Lige Butterwick.

"He made my husband take my best petticoat to muffle the oars so they wouldn't make a splash when they went past that Britisher ship," she said, pointing out where the man-of-war *Somerset* lay at anchor. "My best petticoat, I tell you! And when my husband comes back he'll get a piece of my mind!"

"Was his name Revere?" said Lige Butterwick. "Was he a man of forty-odd, keen-looking, and kind of Frenchy?"

"I don't know what his right name is," said the woman, "but his name's mud with me. My best petticoat tore into strips and swimming in that nasty river!" And that was all he could get out of her.

All the same, he managed to get a boat at last — the story doesn't say how — and row across the river. The tide was at young flood and the moonlight bright on the water, and he passed under the shadow of the *Somerset*, right where Revere had passed. When he got to the Charlestown side, he could see the lanterns in North Church, though he didn't know what they signified. Then he told the folks at Charlestown he had news for Revere and they got him a horse and so he started to ride.

And, all the while, the silver box was burning his pocket.

Well, he lost his way more or less, as you well might in the darkness, and it was dawn when he came into Lexington by a side road. The dawn in that country's pretty, with the dew still on the grass. But he wasn't looking at the dawn. He was feeling the box burn his pocket and thinking hard.

Then, all of a sudden, he reined up his tired horse. For there, on the side road, were two men carrying a trunk — and one of them was Paul Revere.

They looked at each other and Lige began to grin. For Revere was just as dirty and mud-splashed as he was — he'd warned Hancock and Adams all right, but then, on his way to Concord, he'd got caught by the British and turned loose again. So he'd gone back to Lexington to see how things were there — and now he and the other fellow were saving a trunk of papers that Hancock had left behind, so they wouldn't fall into the hands of the British.

Lige swung off his horse. "Well, Mr. Revere," he said, "you see, I'm on time for that little appointment about my tooth. And, by the way, I've got something for you." He took the box from his pocket. And then he looked over toward Lexington Green and caught his breath. For, on the Green, there was a little line of Minute Men — neighbors of his, as he knew — and, in front of them, the British regulars. And, even as he looked, there was the sound of a gunshot, and, suddenly, smoke wrapped the front of the British line and he heard them shout as they ran forward.

Lige Butterwick took the silver box and stamped on it with his heel. And with that the box broke open — and there was a dazzle in his eyes for a moment and a noise of men shouting — and then it was gone.

"Do you know what you've done?" said Revere. "You've let out the American Revolution!"

"Well," said Lige Butterwick, "I guess it was about time. And I guess I'd better be going home, now. I've got a gun on the wall there. And I'll need it."

"But what about your tooth?" said Paul Revere.

"Oh, a tooth's a tooth," said Lige Butterwick. "But a country's a country. And, anyhow, it's stopped aching."

All the same, they say Paul Revere made a silver tooth for him, after the war. But my great-aunt wasn't quite sure of it, so I won't vouch for that.

15/FUMBLE

The lamps were not lighted in the room; but light from the street, falling through the double casement windows, cascading over the cushioned window seat to a wide white pool on the floor, illumined it faintly. You could tell that it was a college room, a careless and a gay room. There were Morris chairs. There were smoking stands. There were photographs of girls. On the couch in the corner a large young man lay. Face downward. Motionless.

That day, in the concrete horseshoe that loomed at the edge of the town, a game had been played; and eighty-five thousand people had watched it. They were trying to go home now. "Let us out," smarled their horns. "Out of this town! We're cold! We're tired! Let us o-o-o-u-u-ut!" Whole carloads went by, singing and shouting. Carloads of the conquerors. Triumphant. Pitiless. Howling defiance to the campus of the conquered. "Team! Team! Team!" Bawling the score: "Nine to seven! Y-a-a-ay! Nine to seven!"

A tea dance was going on in the Beta house next door. The throb of the jazz came, muffled by walls, like a beaten jungle tom-tom miles away. Nearer were the sounds of sociability downstairs. Collegians and their girls, grads and their wives, warming themselves before the fire in the living room. Discussing the game.

The young man above heard only their voices; but he knew. He knew what they said. It was the thing they were saying tonight all over the campus, all over the town. It was the thing that, in the basement of the telegraph office on High Street, the newspaper men from the cities were saying, rattling it out on their portable typewriters, handing it page by yellow page to the telegraph operators, so that, tomorrow morning, headlines wide and black might cry it to the world at large: "Evans' Fumble Loses to the Scarlet in Final Minutes of Gridiron Classic. . . ."

He stirred, and dug his face deeper in the damp, warm curve of the pillow. He was back at the field. The dusk of two hours earlier was graying all around him, the ceaseless raucous roar of just two hours ago was crashing on his heedless ears. The game was almost over. It was almost their game, seven to three. All they had to do was hold 'em, hold 'em. Seated on a bench in a dark blue blanket, hunched like a crippled thing, he was holding 'em, from the sidelines. His cleated shoes were clawing the sod beneath him, his fists were flaying wildly, pounding his knees; his breath was short. Every muscle of him, every sinew and nerve, was fighting with the team. . . . Now he was darting out onto the field, carrying his right arm high, feeling on his jerseyed back the sting of the coach's hand. His heart bursting, bursting. Now he was there. He was saying two quick choked words to the referee, and Andrews was pulling off his headguard. Andrews, mud-streaked, bloody, going to the bench — so that Jeffry Evans, substitute, might win his letter before it was forever too late.

You had to play in this game, or the Army game, to win a letter. Lesser games didn't count. Jeffry Evans was a senior, and in three aching years he had only played in the games that didn't count. Or none at all.

Three minutes more. They were huddled for signals again. Bending very low, heads together, quick breaths mingling white in the tight little circle they made. Le Marr coughing and Caprou dashing the perspiration from his eyes. Himself pulling at a dislocated thumb with his other hand. The thirty-five-yard line. First down. "Formation left! Evans! Off tackle!"

He had leaped into place, he had received the ball, he had carried it — how far? A couple of yards maybe, three, four. Then he had fallen, struggling, sobbing for breath, under three men. And the ball —

This was his zero hour. In all his life to come (he was twenty-two) he would never quite again know such despair. He always failed. Not pettily and inconspicuously, at the very start; but terribly, later, when it mattered. As now. How much, how infinitely better never to have made the football squad than to have made it and toiled on and on — to this!

"Fumble." Butterfingered word. Thick and slow and stupid word. It had branded him at last, stamped itself upon him. Now all men should know him for the sorry thing he was, the almost good, the near-do-well. . . .

His mind was momentarily diverted from himself by a sudden commotion at the door. Someone was trying to get in. He had forgotten that the door was locked.

"Hey, Jeff! Lemme in, will you, Jeff? It's Weary."

The identification was necessary. Jeffry's roommate, "Weary" Haynes — so called because of his
habit of napping in classes, in chapel, and else-
where where the world was rather dull — had led
cheers from two until half-past five that afternoon. His voice was now not a voice but a gutteral
wheeze, quite unrecognizable.

Jeffry rose from the couch. He had an impulse
to tell Weary to go away and stay away and let him
alone. This impulse was babyish. He drew a quick
sleeve across his eyes, humiliated at the gesture
even though there was none but himself to witness
it.

"Hullo," he said.

"Hullo," said Weary hoarsely. "Why the bolts
and bars?"

"No special reason. I — just thought I'd lock
it."

This was lame, and Weary's eyes upon him were
wise and rather uncomfortably sympathetic. Weary
shut the door and dropped into a chair.

"Hey! Hey! I'm done up."

"I'll bet. It sounded great, though," said Jeffry,
who had not really heard a single rah of it.

"Fair," Weary nodded, "fair."

Constraint between them, born of the things
that had not been said but must be said, was in-
creasing. "Well, say it," thought Jeffry ahead. "Go
on, let's get it over with."

He stole a glance at his roommate, and felt an
abrupt new pang. Here was a man who was all the
things that he himself was not. Here was a man
who never fumbled. His progress through the university had been strewn with laurels, attended
with hysterical hosannas. He was not athletic, but
it came to Jeffry now that if he had been — if
Weary had been the substitute put into today's

game in the last five minutes — he would have made a touchdown, like the substitutes of fiction, and emerged trailing clouds of glory. "But," thought Jeffry, "he wouldn't have been a substitute. . . ."

Weary broadcast a small cough into the silence — a sort of preparatory "Stand by!"

"I think it's fine, Jeff, getting your letter."

Jeffry was silent.

"If ever a guy deserved one," Weary continued warmly, "you deserved one. Every day for three years, all through the fall, working out there like a horse — Lord! I'll say you deserved it! They should've given it to you years ago."

"I wish they had," said Jeffry. "If I'd copped it before, they wouldn't have put me in the game today, and we'd have won."

"Bilge!" exploded Weary promptly, loyally. "That's no way to look at it, Jeff."

"How else can I look at it?" Jeffry turned from the window, presenting a tragic face. "I threw the game away. I know it and you know it." He turned back. "Everybody knows it."

"Everybody doesn't know it!" Weary cried out, sitting erect in his earnestness. "In the first place, it isn't *so!* That is — well, a fumble — that might happen to anybody, mightn't it? Sure it might! Happens all the time!"

Weary cleared his throat hurriedly, risking no interruption. "And in the second place, Jeff, you haven't any idea how — how anonymous the players are on a football field! Why, I'll bet you money that out of those eighty or ninety thousand people in the stadium this afternoon, only a few knew who it was who — fumbled. I'll bet you!"

"They'll know tomorrow," Jeffry said in the same low voice. "Leave it to the sports writers!

They never heard of Jeff Evans till this afternoon
— but they found out. And so will everybody. Anyway, what difference does it make whether everybody knows or doesn't? I know. I knew beforehand."

"What?"

"I mean," explained Jeffry patiently, quietly,
"I might've. I ought to have known. It was like
me, what I did, I *would* do something like that.
I'm one of those people."

"Oh, listen!" Weary was dismayed. "Don't talk
like that, Jeff! Forget it!"

Jeffry smiled a twisted smile. He looked
straight at Weary and said, "Yes, you know how
soon I'll forget it, don't you?"

And Weary was silenced.

He didn't forget it. Other people did, as other
people do; but Jeffry forgot it never at all, nor did
he comprehend that others had forgotten. He had
always been a sensitive boy; now he was hypersen-
sitive, almost quite truly mad with brooding and
grieving. He went looking for wounds, and
thought he found in the eyes of his fellows dag-
gers of unforgiveness, and in their casual tongues
lashes of scorn.

The night of the football banquet, when they
gave his letter — with careful words anent his
three-year service to the team — he died a little.
The applause which was generous seemed merciless; hands slapping him on the raw — and so in-
terminably! Perspiration was chill on his face, his
fingers nagged and worried his napkin; he could
not look up.

"Fellows," he said, "you — all know whose
fault — " He couldn't go on. They were very kind
to him afterward, they shook his hand and mumbled things about not being an ass. But he was not

comforted. Pity — he felt it was nothing else —
is never comforting to strong men.

He tried to wear the letter; not to wear it
seemed absurd when all the campus knew he had
it. But wearing it meant minutes of screwing up his
courage, meant agonies of sharp self-conscious-
ness. Everybody eyed it. Freshmen, classmates,
townspeople. That their eyes were envious, impressed or interested, according to their several stations, he never dreamed. To him the glances lev-
eled at his chest were jeering glances, "Look-at-
that-you've-got-a-nerve" glances. . . . He took to
wearing the sweater with a buttoned coat above
it, and finally he stopped wearing it altogether.

There was one good result of all this. Because
he was so much alone in his room, avoiding com-
panionship, he studied; and his grades achieved
unprecedented heights. He had never been a brilliant student; he was not now; but he had become
a diligent one, and it told. He passed his examinations in June, his final finals, easily; though not
as easily as Weary Haynes, who seldom, in the ver-
nacular, "cracked" a book.

It was a relief to graduate, to go away from
there, even though the pall of that ruined year
went with him. It was a relief to leave Weary,
whom he loved.

The first of July found him in New York, which,
because of its cruelty, its colossal carelessness, its
myriads who are cleverer, stronger, richer, higher
up — no matter how high or rich or strong or
clever one may be — was the very worst place in
the world for him.

He had an uncle in New York, his mother's
brother, Peter Lambert, of Lambert and Company, publishers. For years it had been casually
understood that when Jeffry finished college he

would go to work for his uncle; and lately they had
had some definite correspondence on the matter.
"The job," Peter Lambert had written, a month
before commencement, "awaits you. That's all it
is, Jeff — a 'job.' Whether or not it becomes in due
time a 'position' depends on you, precisely as if
you and I were strangers."

This was strategic, but not altogether true. Peter
Lambert was a bachelor, and owner of the business. Jeffry, fatherless since childhood, was his favorite among several nephews. He thought of him
paternally, with fondness and with faith. He
planned, as he had always planned, to bring Jeffry
up and up, until he was of the firm; until, indeed,
Jeffry *was* the firm, carrying on after him.

Unfortunately, Jeffry divined these things, aided
by hints from his mother; and in his new frame
of mind they distressed and frightened him. He
pondered them long. And in the end, deciding
that he could not disappoint his uncle by falling
down on the job, he hurt him sorely by declining
to try it at all, on the ground that he didn't believe
the publishing game appealed to him.

He took a very small apartment, and went hunting for work. He thought he would sell bonds. Everybody did. Almost anybody, apparently, could.
Accordingly, every morning for many successive
mornings, he subwayed down to Wall Street and
lower Broadway, and knocked at various and sun-
dry doors. Sometimes he gained admittance,
oftener he did not. Two things militated against
him. One was that summer's bumper campus crop
of would-be bond salesmen; a supply far in excess
of the demand. The other was his manner of ap-
proach. He always entered thinking, "I suppose I
won't get this," "Not a chance here, of course," and
this showed in his bearing, which was timid, even

apologetic, so that office boys dared to bully him
and stenographers to say at once, "No. Sorry.
They're not taking anybody now." Feeling, as he
felt, the worthlessness of the commodity, he could
not even sell Jeffry Evans.

At the end of several weeks his uncle, who had
watched from afar, repeated his offer, albeit this
time rather gruffly. This time Jeffry accepted. He
had to accept. He was down to his last ten dollars.

The thing was too bad all around. Jeffry now
firmly believed that nobody but a relative would
employ him. And Peter Lambert was now convinced that this pet nephew of his would have
gone to work for almost anyone rather than for
him. So neither was content.

Futile as he had come to believe himself, Jeffry
found that the work was fascinating, and often it
absorbed him so he quite forgot to watch the chip
on his shoulder. He was very busy. In line with
Peter Lambert's plan to teach him the business
from every angle, from the ground up, he belonged to no set department, but labored in them
all by turns.

Sometimes he read manuscript, sometimes proof.
Sometimes he wrote advertisements. He spent
whole days at the printing plant in Brooklyn, seeing books made; he packed books for shipment,
delivered copies to spectacled reviewers in newspaper offices, sold novels across the counter at one
or another of the several little shops maintained
and managed by the firm. Once he accompanied
the firm's star salesman on a trip through the Middle West, listening and learning, and lugging the
sample case.

His salary to start was forty dollars a week. At
the end of six months it was forty dollars a week.

At the end of a year it still was. He was doing well, he deserved more, and his uncle was aware that he did. But Peter Lambert had got everything he had by asking for it, not by keeping quiet and waiting for it. He believed in demand — provided, of course, there was justice to back it up. Jeffry had not approached him on the subject of a raise.

"And," vowed Jeffry's uncle to himself, "he won't get one till he does."

This was a matter of discipline, a lesson. Lambert did not guess that to Jeffry it was simply another proof of his hopeless inefficiency. A whole year — and he was worth no more than when he started! Not even worth that, probably. Had you encountered him about this time, you would have seen a serious, unsmiling big fellow, young except for the slight, beaten droop of his splendid shoulders. Had you met him, shaken his hand, you would have found him polite, but unresponsive; either preoccupied, or — or what?

Then he fell in love. It happened without preamble, without warning; and that was the worst of it. Afterward, Jeffry told himself that if he had only seen it coming, he could have headed it off — and would have. But he didn't see it.

On a morning in September he was called on the telephone by a half-forgotten classmate named Caruthers, who, it appeared, had written a book. Caruthers was in from his home town, which Jeffry's mind dimly identified as Johnstown, or possibly Williamsburg, for the purpose of placing his book with a New York publishing house; and he wanted to know whether if he submitted the manuscript to Jeffry's uncle's firm, Jeffry would personally guarantee that somebody — preferably his uncle, but failing that, "somebody who means something" — read it.

"All I ask," Caruthers said, "is a reading. That's all. Just a reading. You see, I know this publishing racket. If I simply send it in without a word it won't be read. They never are. Don't tell me!"

Jeffry promised that *Clinging Vines,* by Rodney H. Caruthers, would be read, thoroughly and discerningly; and he also agreed, albeit without undue enthusiasm, to be taken to luncheon that day by the grateful author. They met in the lobby of the Cherokee, where Caruthers (having heard that it was literary) was staying, and exchanged the feverish "Well — well — wells" of two who never knew one another well at all, but are striving to overlook the fact.

Toward the end of a meal, which seemed to Jeffry doomed to endlessness, Caruthers interrupted himself long enough to inquire what his old classmate was going to do that evening. Jeffry said, after only a tiny pause, "Why — nothing." He heard himself saying it with astonishment. It, of course, committed him to the further society of this merciless egotist; he could have fibbed out of it with ease and he was at a loss to understand why he had not. The truth was that Caruthers was flattering Jeffry. He felt that Jeffry was important to him, and he treated him with deference and respect. Jeffry in his sore heart wanted more of this — much more, at whatever cost.

"I know a little girl," observed Caruthers now (and Jeffry had a quick, bleak picture of the kind of little girl Caruthers would know), "from my home town. Barbara Kincaid, her name is. Awfully nice kid. She has an apartment down in Greenwich Village — she's here designing, or something. I'm going to take her to dinner tonight. Like to have you join us."

"Thanks," said Jeffry. "I — I'd like to."

Her apartment was the first shock. Huge studio room, rough-walled, high-ceilinged, tasteful, and beautiful. Lamps under odd-shaped parchment shades, diffusing low soft gold. Dark things, velvet things to sit on and lie on, and sudden flaming gorgeous splashes of color. Books in long cases, unglassed.

Her voice was the second shock. Soft and laughing — cool, and just a trifle breathless, as if she feared she might be interrupted before the end of each sentence. "Hello, ol' Rod Caruthers!" she said. And then, "Oh! How nice. You've brought someone — "

The third shock was dizzying. Not the studio, the setting, not even the voice had prepared him properly. Blonde she was, slim, wrapped tight with cloth-of-silver, tinted like a gay bouquet in which an artist-florist had blended yellow, scarlet, pink, and gray, exquisitely. A glamorous person. At first glance a light and frivolous person, belonging to the world of shine and bubbles and string bands. Then you saw her eyes. And her peaked, firm chin. And the eyebrows, dark and straight and rather heavy. And the hands, intelligent, restless, pale. Hands with temperament.

"I should think," observed Barbara at the first break in Caruthers' monologue, "that the publishing business would be awfully interesting. Isn't it?"

"It certainly is," Jeffry said.

"Tell me about it."

He told her. He described, he explained, he gesticulated. Encouraged and drawn out of himself by Barbara's eyes, her intentness, her questions, he talked glibly and well, without diffidence. At least he knew that nothing he said was as idiotic as anything and everything said by Caruthers.

"You really ought to see for yourself," he wound up. "You ought to let me take you through our plant, and show you."

During dinner he was reminded, by a chance remark of Barbara's about her shop, that Caruthers had told him she did designing. This suddenly became exceedingly important. Just what did she do? What sort of designing? Where was the shop? How long had she had it?

"The shop," replied Barbara, "is on Madison Avenue, between Fifty-second and Fifty-third. It's the very littlest shop in New York, and the cutest, if I do say so as I shouldn't. I've had it three years, and it's called Bal Masqué, and we make fancy-dress costumes."

"Who's we?"

"I am we," Barbara said. "Then I've three girls who sew. I design, and they manufacture."

"Fancy-dress costumes," mused Jeffry aloud.

Barbara nodded. "And original ones. I have never in my life," she added, buttering a roll, "turned out a Pierrette, and so help me, I never shall."

They went from dinner to a play, and from the theatre to a supper club, and from that to another, and thence to a third. This was known as "giving Rod a whirl," and was done by Barbara and Jeffry with the customary relentlessness of New Yorkers entertaining out-of-towners.

"See here!" said Jeffry, sitting bolt upright excitedly, turning to her, "maybe you don't have to go home yet, hmm? You haven't had a thing to eat since dinner, and now it's — "

"Four a.m.," Barbara laughed. "I'd love to, Jeff. But — ask me again. I'm a business woman, you know. With an alarm clock."

It was plain that she was not to be persuaded. By forcing Barbara to repeat her refusal twice, thrice, more and more firmly, he reminded himself that she probably didn't like him, really; he had been merely the lesser of two evils, after all.

There was a moment at the door of her apartment house when he thought he might have been mistaken. Her lifted gray eyes were so seemingly sincere, her voice when she said, "I'll see you soon, Jeff?" sounded so as if she wanted to, that his breath came short, his pulses pounded, and he hoped again.

"But tonight's tonight!" he cried desperately. "How do I know I'll ever — " He broke off. Stared at her. Flung down her hands. He picked up his hat from the parquet floor where it had fallen, and rammed it on. "I'm sorry you were bored," he said bitterly and strode to his cab and slammed himself in.

An absurd performance. Two seconds afterward he knew that it had been; and shame boiled in him, and he writhed. What must she think of him now? Oh, fool! Fathead!

He decided to forget her. He said to himself naïvely that there wasn't any use getting interested in her. A girl like that who counted her income in five figures and her suitors in three. He would put her out of his mind. And for all time.

Having settled this, and emphasized it with a blow of his fist on the desk, he telephoned her and asked her to dine with him that evening. She couldn't, or wouldn't. She had, she said, a previous engagement. She was terribly sorry; and would Jeffry surely try her again very soon?

The next day, however, the sun was shining and the air was tonic and brisk, and it came to Jeffry, returning from an errand downtown in midmorning, that maybe she really had had an engagement, after all. She would. She was the kind that of necessity kept a little gilt-edged date book: "Bill, tea, Friday, five." "Jimmy, luncheon, Monday, twelve." You couldn't expect to get her on two hours' notice — or on two days' notice, even.

In the office he sought a telephone behind a door that would lock and rang her at her place of business. He said, "This is Jeff Evans again," and she said, "Oh, hel-lo there!" as if she were delighted that it was.

"Listen," he said, "when can you go to dinner, hmmm?"

"We-ell," Barbara said, "let's see. How is Saturday?"

Saturday was not very good, because it was four days off; but Jeffry took it without argument. "Write me down," he directed, "in the little book."

Jeffry's party for two was a smooth and flawless and wonderful thing, even surpassing anticipation. One couldn't, of course, anticipate Barbara. She was lovelier than one's most bewitching visions of her, more gracious than one's fondest, brightest hopes.

It was dawn when he took her home. They had been, as Barbara said, "Pretty nearly everywhere." They had danced miles on rhythmic, obedient feet, called by the silver horns.

Barbara said, "I don't feel like talking."

"I don't either."

After a moment her hand pressed his. "You're so — comfortable, Jeff. It's as if I'd known you — almost always."

Their kiss was brief, unpremeditated. One instant they were smiling at one another, blue eyes into gray in the halflight. The next their lips were touching, softly, swiftly like children's lips. A kiss to remember the night, and to go with the dawn.

Afterward, they rode a little closer together, they held hands a little tighter. But there were no more kisses. Jeffry in that moment was wise with a wisdom that later he marveled at. Too very wise to lose a fragrance in a flame.

When he reached home, Weary's telegram was waiting:

Kill the fatted calf Stop Dress the Avenue in flags and wrestle down the Murphy bed for good Stop I arrive tomorrow Century to take charge promotion our New York office Stop Appointment very sudden but permanent and boy how swell Stop Meet me

(Signed) Weary

Jeffry met him. He had had no sleep to speak of, and perhaps this fact accounted for the barely perceptible listlessness of his welcome, the lack, in a degree or two, of the fervor that was fitting. Weary himself was looking very striking, very picturesque and brown and debonair. Jeff had forgotten that he looked like that.

They taxied to Jeffry's apartment, hemmed in by incredible baggage. Weary talked all the way, occasionally thumping and pummeling Jeffry, now and then uttering a war whoop of sheer young animal glee. They were going to have, he announced, the time of their lives. Parties? Hey! Hey! Jeffry would see. For a starter, they were going to give up Jeffry's apartment, and get a bigger and better one.

"How, by the way," said Weary as an afterthought, "are you fixed for women?"

"I don't know any," said Jeffry.

"Wh-at?"

"Fact. I don't."

"Not a one?" Weary was appalled and unbelieving. "Who were you out with last night, then?" he demanded.

Jeffry bent over the pile of luggage. "Just some fellows. Fellows from the office."

Early in the morning, Weary betook himself to his new office; and when they parted, Jeffry said, "If you get a chance during the day, drop over. I want you to meet my uncle, and see where I slave, and all."

Weary arrived about four in the afternoon. Jeffry, performing some duty in an outer office in which there were numbers of youthful feminine clerks, was apprised of his coming by the little flutter that began at the door and went through the room like a breeze, tilting faces, sending hands to coiffures in a hurry. Weary was radiant, buoyant. He had much to tell, and when he and Jeffry were shut into privacy, he told it joyously. Everything was great. Everybody had been fine to him, and he was to have a corking private office with his name on the door — "The fellow was lettering it when I blew in — and what a secretary! And really very little to do. Really a pipe job, absolutely."

He broke off and regarded the door, and Jeffry also regarded the door, saying, "Come in," because someone had knocked.

Barbara came in. Barbara in a tan dress and a small enchanting hat, with a pair of former foxes, the teeth of one sunk forever into the flank of the other, slanted around her shoulder.

"Am I — interrupting?" she asked hesitantly from the threshold.

"Not at all," said Weary before Jeffry could speak.

Barbara smiled at him, smiled at Jeffry; came all the way in; and closed the door. "I was going

by" — she addressed Jeffry — "and I thought I'd
stop. You know you said any time I wanted to see
the office — "

"Of course," agreed Jeffry, stiff-lipped. He
looked at Weary. "This is Weary Haynes. Miss
Kincaid."

"How-do-you-do?" said Barbara.

"I'm very happy to meet you," Weary said.

They looked so like a magazine cover, that
beautiful pair, shaking hands. . . .

"Take this chair," directed Weary. He had become master of ceremonies, naturally and at once.

"You're not interrupting," he repeated, beaming
down at her. "I should say not! This isn't a business conference — it's part of a reunion! To join
which," he assured her, "you are invited. Not to
say urged."

"A reunion?"

Weary nodded. "Jeff and I used to room together."

"Oh, really?"

"He hasn't told you about me," Weary deduced
mournfully. "But then he didn't tell me about
you either. In fact" —here Weary fixed Jeffry
with a stern accusing eye — "in fact I seem to recall his telling me, not twenty-four hours ago, that
he didn't know any girls in New York. How 'bout
that, Jeff?"

"He forgot me," Barbara proclaimed. She made
a little face. "Just a girl that men forget," she
sighed mock-tragically.

"Not men of sanity," Weary said. "Never. Never
in the world."

Jeffry showed them through the plant. He did
it mechanically, stalking in and out of elevators,
down long corridors ahead of them — pausing and
turning when occasion demanded, saying, "This is

the business office," "Proofreaders in this room"
— mere statements without elaboration.

Every time he spoke he interrupted something
amusing and bright that Weary was saying.
Weary would cease, he and Barbara would look in
and murmur appropriate comments; then they
would move on, Weary resuming, Barbara listening appreciatively. The inspection tour took
twenty minutes. Jeffry was glad it was over, and
felt that they were glad. It had been flat.

Then Barbara consulted a dot of a watch set in
diamonds and platinum, and said she must go.

"So must I," Weary echoed, rising instantly.
He took up his hat and confronted Jeffry. "Can'
you break off now, old man? Or will I see you
later?"

"Later," Jeffry said, because he could feel that
they wanted him to say that.

He gave them a ten-minute start. Then he, too,
left, and went home. Weary's trunks had been
delivered at the apartment and dumped in the living room. Two of them. Very big ones. He sat and
gazed at them.

Weary joined him. He was in high spirits.
"Hullo!" he said "What ho! And how is Lambert
and Company's pride?" He began ridding his
pockets of letters and change, his watch and his
wallet, laying them all on Jeffry's chiffonier. "I'm
late," he observed, "because I took the Glorious
Baby to tea."

"You did?" said Jeffry.

"Yeah. I did." Weary, in the act of unfastening
the fraternity pin from his vest, wheeled around.
"Say," he said, "what was the idea? Why didn't you
tell me about her?"

"I — didn't think," Jeffry answered with difficulty. "I don't know her very well — "

"Don't you like her?"

For a racking instant Jeffry thought he was going to make a fool of himself, going to throw himself on Weary's mercy, crying, "Like her? I love her! Oh, let her alone, will you, Weary? Give me a chance!" He had to fight himself to keep this back.

"She's all right," he said indifferently.

"She's marvelous!" Weary declared. "If you weren't such an old woman-hater — " He left the sentence there. He thought a minute, unbuttoning his vest with absent fingers. "Well," he said, "then there's no reason why I shouldn't press my suit, as they say in subtitles? . . . Much as it needs it," he added, holding out the corners of his vest, "I do not mean the suit you see before you."

"No reason," said Jeffry tonelessly, "as far as I'm concerned."

Then he was the onlooker. He was the confidant, the ear, for Weary's detailed reports of progress. He was the mutual friend to whom they said, "Come on along with us, Jeff. We'd love to have you!" He rarely went. The pain of staying at home alone and following them in his mind was tortuous; but the pain ᶜ watching them — so magnificent, so *right* together — was worse.

They were together constantly, tea-ing, dining, dancing. They went to football games away from town; they motored far in Weary's new machine. Once they attended a weekend party in Connecticut. It was during this weekend that Jeffry went one night and looked at the river. He did it because it seemed the thing for a man as wretched as he was to do; he was amazed to find when he got there that he had no real inclination to throw himself in.

Weary was always talking about her. Discussing, speculating, asking advice.

"She's the funniest girl," he assured Jeffry once. "No fooling now, she is. For instance — she won't let me kiss her. Can you imagine a girl like that?"

"No," said Jeffry.

Weary reddened. "Rats!" he said. "I didn't mean — I didn't mean *me,* for heaven's sake! I meant, can you imagine a girl that simply won't be kissed in this age of quick and easy osculation?" He grew reflective. "Sometimes," he remarked, "sometimes I think she must be in love with somebody."

"Who?"

"I haven't an idea. Have you?"

"No," said Jeffry. And he hadn't.

His lease expired on the first of November, and he and Weary moved. The new apartment was spacious and expensive — too expensive, Jeffry thought. Weary, however, was deaf to all protests.

"Pipe down," he said. "It's a short life. Why spend it where the plaster's dirty?"

They bought new furniture, carpets, and curtains, and the effect was good. But it didn't suit Weary. On the Sunday afternoon when they were finally settled, their last book tucked in place, their final picture hung, he paced around, hands in his trousers' pockets, scowling into corners and at the walls.

"It could be better," he said. "It needs something. I don't know just exactly what, but something — Barbara'll know," he concluded. "By the way, have we got cakes, and all that junk? She's coming to tea to look the place over."

Jeffry sat motionless for a moment. Then he shambled to his feet. "We've got cakes, I guess.

There's tea in that can marked 'Sugar,' and sugar around somewhere. Cream on the ice. If you want lemons, I'll stop at Luigi's on my way out and have some sent — "

"You're not going out?"

"Sure. Why not?"

"Oh, now, Jeff," said Weary earnestly, "stick around. You ought to be here. It's your place as well as mine, you know."

"But it's — your girl."

There was a slight pause. Then Jeffry strolled on into his bedroom, rolling down his sleeves as he went. He felt aimless. He had to tell himself, with words in his mind, just what to do. Snap cuff links. Comb hair. Tie tie. . . .

"Jeff!"

"What?"

Weary was sitting on the divan, looking solemn. Looking at Jeffry. "You ass," he said, "she's in love with you."

Jeffry merely stared at him.

"Heaven help me," said Weary, "for telling you. She made me swear I wouldn't — but you'll never wake up and hear the birdies sing unless I do. I'm convinced of that."

"What," asked Jeffry, "are you talking about?"

"I'm talking about Barbara. She's in love with you. *Love*." Weary repeated. "L-o-v-e. *Amo, amas, amat* — and all that sort of thing." He moaned abruptly, and seized his banjo from a neighboring chair, brandishing it aloft. "Gosh! Have I got to *beat* it in? What is that object you call your head? Just a parking place for teeth? Or does it work?"

"Say what you said again," said Jeffry.

"She's in love with you."

"What makes you think so?"

"She told me!" said Weary, his patience frayed.

"She told me the first — no, the second time I ever saw her. I tried to sell myself — and what happened? I got enlisted! Committee of one, to try to make you jealous — so you'd wake up." He made a wry face. "She picked me," he said, "because I'd be the most conspicuous — to you, d'you see? But *you!* — blind, dumb, and unconscious you — "

"Wait," begged Jeffry, "wait a minute." He was thinking hard; his lips were moving. "She — she could have had — "

He stopped, overcome; and in that dazzling split second, all his ideas about himself shifted as a backfield shifts, in one swift simultaneous leap. He was in place again, mentally. He had courage once more, and faith in himself. For the man whom Barbara preferred to Weary — *to Weary!* — well, that man could not be such a dud, after all.

He lifted his gleaming eyes and met Weary's eyes, which had watched him with affection from the divan.

"Eureka!" said Weary. "It penetrates. At last it penetrates! And" — his voice softened — "you're crazy about her, aren't you? I wasn't sure. She was pretty sure, but I wasn't absolutely. I see now." He stood up. "*This* baby," he declared, tapping his chest, "will get the lemons. He may even pick them, so don't expect him too soon."

For fully three minutes after the door banged shut, Jeffry stayed in his chair. He was seeing things he had not seen. He was understanding things he had misunderstood. He was steeping himself in heavenly realization. Then he thought of the time.

He bolted into his bedroom, changed his suit, borrowed a shirt of Weary's, shaved. He emerged

immaculate, rushed to the kitchenette, and there
wildly broke things and upset things. Presently
his jaw set hard, and he marched to the telephone.
He called up his uncle.

"Listen," he said, "I've just been thinking, and
— well, the fact is — I've got to have more money.
A whole lot more," he insisted stubbornly. "I — "
He swallowed. "I'll quit if I don't — "

"Now why," crowed his uncle, "why in tarna-
tion didn't you say so before?"

When his feet moved again, it was off at a tan-
gent into his bedroom. He dug into the depths of
his lowest bureau drawer, and by and by he
dragged out something. Something woolen and
blue. And lettered in white.

He bore this into the living room and arranged
it on a chair back. Carelessly, as if he had just
taken it off. Yet carefully, with the letter showing
. . . so that, in case no one had told her, she
would know that he had been a football player.

16/ONE WITH SHAKESPEARE

Yes, Miss Cox was there, sitting at her desk in the almost empty classroom. Elizabeth took in the theme she had written to make up for a class missed because of illness.

A description of people under changing circumstances was the assignment.

Elizabeth had chosen immigrants arriving at a Boston dock. She had got quite excited as she wrote about the black-eyed women and their red and blue dresses, the swarthy men and their earrings, and the brightness of a faraway Mediterranean land slipping off a rocking boat to be lost in the grayness of Boston streets.

Elizabeth had liked writing this theme better than anything she had done since the description of a sunset. Amethyst and rose with a silver ribbon of river. Elizabeth shivered. A silver ribbon — that was lovely. And so was "scarlet kerchief in the night of her hair" in this theme. Words were so beautiful.

Miss Cox read the new theme, a red pencil poised in her authoritative fingers. Miss Cox was so strong. She was strongest of all the teachers in the school. Stronger even than the two men teachers, Mr. Carpenter of physics and Mr. Cattell

of math. A beautiful strongness. Thought of Miss
Cox made Elizabeth feel as she did when two
bright shiny words suddenly sprang together to
make a beautiful, a perfect phrase.

Elizabeth was glad she had Miss Cox as an English teacher and not Miss Foster any more. Miss
Foster had made the class last year count the number of times certain words occurred in *Poor Rich-
ard's Almanack* to be sure they read the book right
through word for word. And the words were all so
ugly. Like the picture of Benjamin Franklin. But
Miss Cox made you feel the words. As when she
read from *A Tale of Two Cities* in her deep singing voice, "This is a far, far better thing than I
have ever done." Poor Sydney Carton.

Miss Cox had finished the second page of the
theme. She was looking up at Elizabeth, her small
dark blue eyes lighting up her glasses.

"Let me give you a pointer, my dear."

Elizabeth automatically looked toward the
blackboard ledge at the chalky pointer until the
words "my dear" bit into her mind. My dear! Miss
Cox had called her "my dear."

"You have a spark of the divine fire," Miss Cox
said. "You should make writing your vocation."

Elizabeth flamed. Miss Cox, "my dear," themes
about immigrants, blackboards, and desks whirled
and fused in the divine fire.

Miss Cox marked "A" in red pencil at the top
of the theme and Elizabeth said, "Thank you,"
and went away.

Elizabeth went back to her desk in the III A
classroom which was in the charge of Miss Perry.
Miss Perry was her Greek teacher as well as her
room teacher. Somehow Miss Perry made Elizabeth hate Greek. Elizabeth liked to think of
Greece. White and gold in a blue Aegean. I, Sap-

pho. Wailing Trojan women. Aristotle and Plato and Socrates. Grace and brains, said her father, of the men. But that was outside of Greek class. To Miss Perry, Greece was the aorist of *tithemi* and Xenophon's march in the *Anabasis*. Elizabeth always said to herself as she came into the III A room, "I hate Miss Perry, the aorist, and Xenophon. Oh, how I hate them!"

But this morning Elizabeth only pitied Miss Perry. She had no spark of the divine fire, poor thing.

Greek was the first class this morning. Elizabeth didn't care. She should make writing her vocation. That was something Miss Perry could never do. If she were called on for the list of irregular verbs this morning she would like to tell Miss Perry that. It would explain why she hadn't studied her Greek home lesson. Why should she be bothered with conjugations when she had to describe blue and red men arriving on an alien shore?

"Now, Miss Morris, will you please give me the principal parts of the verb *to give*."

That was *didomi*. But what was the perfect tense? Divine fire, divine fire.

"If you don't know, you may sit down. But I warn you that unless you do your home lessons better you are not going to pass this month."

Divine fire, divine fire.

The second hour was study class. Under Miss Pratt with the ugly bulb of a nose, splotchy face, and eternal smile. Miss Pratt taught something or other to the younger girls down in the sixth class. She always smiled at Elizabeth but Elizabeth seldom smiled back. Her smile never means anything, thought Elizabeth.

Elizabeth dumped her books down on her desk in Miss Pratt's room. She opened Virgil at the part

she liked — where Aeneas told Dido the story of
his wandering while the stars waned and drooped
in the sky. It was not her lesson. She had had that
months ago. But she liked going back over it, just
as she liked the beginning of the first book. Great
bearded Aeneas rang out in *arma virgumque cano*.
That was strong. She would write strong some day.
Strong like Virgil, and fine like Swinburne:

> I will go back to the great sweet mother,
> Mother and lover of men, the sea.

Swinburne had divine fire. Keats. Shelley: "Hail
to thee, blithe spirit." And Masefield, whose auto-
graph she had bought for five shillings not to help
the British but to have a bit of the man who wrote
The Widow in the Bye Street.

Elizabeth looked out into the school courtyard.
Fine green shoots. Yellow on the laburnum. Spring
was here. Divine fire, divine fire.

"Miss Morris, haven't you any work to do?"

Miss Pratt smiling. Nasty, nasty smiling. Didn't
she know whom she was talking to like that? A
great writer. A girl who would be famous. Let her
ask Miss Cox. Why, I have a spark of the divine
fire. I am one with Shakespeare and Keats,
Thackeray and Brontë, and all the other great
writers.

Elizabeth plumped her head in her hands and
stared at the Latin page. Opposite was an illustra-
tion of an old statue, supposed to be Dido. Further
on was a pen and ink sketch of Dido mounting the
funeral pyre. Further on was a sketch of Aeneas
nearing Rome. Further on was the vocabulary.
Then the end of the book. Elizabeth turned, page
by page. She could not study, and if she looked
out the window at spring again Miss Pratt would
be nasty.

"Please, Miss Pratt, may I go to the library?"

"Must you go to the library? What for?"

"I have a reference in my history lesson to look up in the encyclopedia."

"Very well."

The library was large and quiet — a whole floor above Miss Pratt and the study class. It was divided off into alcoves. History in one. Encyclopedias in another. Languages, sciences. Fiction and poetry were in the farthest end which opened out toward the Fenway. The Fenway with its river and wide sky where Elizabeth liked to walk alone.

Elizabeth had read all the fiction and all the poetry. All of Jane Austen and *The Sorrows of Werther* and lots of other books which had nothing to do with her classes. She was always afraid one of her teachers would come in some day during study class and ask her what she was reading that book for. But that had never happened. And the librarian never paid any attention to her.

Now she went into the fiction and poetry alcove and sat on a small shelf ladder. She looked out the window at the long line of poplars rimming the fens. What would she call them if she were writing about them? Black sentinels against the sky. Oh beautiful, oh beautiful! that was the divine fire.

There was ancient history with Miss Tudor, who had had the smallpox and it showed all over her face; and geometry with Mr. Cattell who had a gray beard and gray eyes and gray clothes and gray manner. Elizabeth liked that — gray manner. That was what the Advanced English Composition called penetrating analysis of character. She would do lots of penetrating analysis when she wrote in earnest.

She would write novels, the greatest, most moving novels ever written, like *Jean-Christophe,*

Elizabeth was deciding when the bell rang for the end of the history lesson. And in between the novels she would write fine medallions of short stories like Chekhov's, Elizabeth told herself when the bell rang for the end of the geometry lesson. And she would always write lovely poems in between the novels and the short stories, she was thinking when the bell rang for the end of the school day.

Elizabeth walked past Miss Cox's room on her way out of the building. She slowed down her steps as she came to the door. Miss Cox was putting away her things in the drawer of her desk. Elizabeth would dedicate her first book to Miss Cox. "To Miss Eleanor G. Cox this book is gratefully dedicated by the author."

Eileen and Ruth were waiting for Elizabeth at the entrance. Eileen was the cousin of a famous poet and her mother was an anarchist. Elizabeth liked the thought of anyone being an anarchist. It sounded so much more beautiful than being a Democrat or a Republican. And Ruth, who was a class ahead, had already had her poems printed in the *Transcript*. Four times. And one of the poems had been reprinted by William Stanley Braithwaite in his anthology. Oh, they were going to be great and famous, all three.

"Let's walk home and save our fares for fudge sundaes," said Eileen.

"All right, only I am going to have pineapple," said Ruth.

"I'll go with you but I won't have any sundae," Elizabeth said. "I'm going to save my fares this week to buy Miss Cox flowers."

"You have a crush on Miss Cox."

"Perhaps I have and perhaps I haven't. Anyway she said something wonderful to me this morning. She said I had a spark of the divine fire and should make writing my vocation."

"Oh, that is wonderful. She never told me that, not even after Mr. Braithwaite took one of my poems for his anthology."

"This is the happiest day of my life. Even when I have written many books and proved Miss Cox's faith in me, I shall always look back to this day. I never expected to be so wonderfully happy."

The three girls, arm in arm, walked through the Fenway.

"I tell you, let's not get sundaes. Since Elizabeth's saving her money, it isn't fair to go in and eat them right before her. Let's you, Ruth, and I buy some of those big frosted doughnuts and some bananas and eat them on the Charles River esplanade. Then Elizabeth can have some too."

"All right, and we can watch the sun set."

"Oh, but that's what isn't fair. To save my money and then eat up what you buy."

"Next time you can give us something."

Elizabeth loved the Charles River. It always hurt her to think that it was on a Charles River bridge that Longfellow should have made up "I stood on the bridge at midnight." Perhaps that wasn't so bad, but so many parodies of the poem had ridiculed the river. Once Elizabeth had written a "Letter to a River." Elizabeth pretended she was away off somewhere like in New York, and was writing to the river to tell how much she missed its beauty. She had put so many lovely phrases in it, she thought, and she couldn't understand why the editor of the *Atlantic Monthly* had sent it back to her. But great writers always had many rejections first. That Scottish writer in whose eyes Ruth said she saw his soul, had said in his lecture that to write greatly, one must first suffer greatly.

How she had suffered, thought Elizabeth. Her math and Greek teachers were so cruel to her. She who had a spark of divine fire to be treated as they treated her. Tears came to her eyes. And now, when she was tired, she was walking home instead of riding so she could buy Miss Cox flowers. Pink sweetheart roses. Little tight knots of flowers. That was suffering and sacrifice. But it was for love as well as for literature.

"I felt the rhythm of the universe last night," Ruth was saying, "I was sitting on the roof in the dark and I felt the night all around me."

"That makes me think of 'swiftly walk over the western wave, spirit of Night.' But it always bothers me that the wave is to the east in Boston," said Eileen. "Otherwise I like that poem very much."

"The rhythm of the universe? What do you mean?"

"Oh, you know. The way someone said the stars swing around in their courses. And that's why I never, never want to study astronomy. I want only to imagine the stars. That's so much more beautiful than any facts about them can ever be."

"I don't agree with you at all. Why when you think that the light of the nearest star started coming to you three years ago and what you were doing then and how this minute some star is starting to send you light, that may not get to you until far away and old and—"

"Stop! Don't give me facts about the stars! You can have those facts about your stars, if you want. But leave me my stars to love as I please."

"Oh, very well. There, now the sky is coloring. See that lovely clear green high up. Pretty soon the deep colors will come. My, these frosted doughnuts are good! Much better than any near where we live."

"There's the first light on the other bank. Over near the Tech building."

That was what it was to have a spark of divine fire. Elizabeth's thoughts flowed on with the darkening river. She could put all this, the river and the sky colors and the lights, into writing. People would feel the loveliness of the world as they had never felt it before. People would no longer walk with their heads bent to the street when there was a sunset to be seen. What have you done to her, masters of men, that her head should be bowed down thus, thus in the deepening twilight and golden angelus? Her father said Noyes wrote maudlin singsong. It was jingly sometimes but she did like it. And too many heads were bowed down, you masters of men.

"Mother'll scold me if I stay any later," said Eileen.

"And my mother said she wouldn't get me a new dress for the class party if I came home late again."

"Yes, we must all be going. But isn't it nice to think when you wake up at home in bed at night that the river is out here, creeping on and on under the stars?"

"No wonder Miss Cox said you had divine fire. Let's put our banana peels in here. This is Spring Clean-Up Week, you know."

"Good night."

"Good night."

"Good night."

Holding the thought of her own greatness close to her, Elizabeth went home. A sliver of moon curled in the sky. That is the moon Shelley, Shakespeare, Spenser, and yes, 'way back, Chaucer looked at. And now I am looking at it.

"Mother, Miss Cox says I have a spark of divine fire. I am to be a great writer some day."

"Isn't that nice? Did you remember not to wipe your pen point on your petticoat today?"

"Oh, Mother, you know that's not a question of remembering. I never do it when I'm thinking about it. But you didn't half listen to what Miss Cox said about me."

"Indeed I did. She said you had a divine spark of fire. That means you'll get another A in English this month on your report card."

"It means more than any old report card. It means my whole life. I'm to be a writer, a great writer."

"But first you must finish school and college. And that means you have to do your mathematics better. Remember how angry your father was about that E in geometry last month."

Elizabeth sighed. She went out on the back porch which looked across the city. Lights pricked the blackness. Like a necklace which had spilled over velvet. Oh, words were lovely.

The moon was still there, a more emphatic sliver now. "Moon of Shelley and Keats and Shakespeare, and my moon," said Elizabeth, and went in to dinner.

JOHN STEINBECK

17/THE CHRYSANTHEMUMS

The high gray-flannel fog of winter closed off the Salinas Valley from the sky and from all the rest of the world. On every side it sat like a lid on the mountains and made of the great valley a closed pot. On the broad, level land floor the gang plows bit deep and left the black earth shining like metal where the shares had cut. On the foothill ranches across the Salinas River, the yellow stubble fields seemed to be bathed in pale cold sunshine, but there was no sunshine in the valley now in December. The thick willow scrub along the river flamed with sharp and positive yellow leaves.

It was a time of quiet and of waiting. The air was cold and tender. A light wind blew up from the southwest so that the farmers were mildly hopeful of a good rain before long; but fog and rain do not go together.

Across the river, on Henry Allen's foothill ranch there was little work to be done, for the hay was cut and stored and the orchards were plowed up to receive the rain deeply when it should come. The cattle on the higher slopes were becoming shaggy and rough-coated.

Elisa Allen, working in her flower garden, looked down across the yard and saw Henry, her

husband, talking to two men in business suits.
The three of them stood by the tractor shed, each
man with one foot on the side of the little Ford-
son. They smoked cigarettes and studied the machine as they talked.

Elisa watched them for a moment and then went
back to her work. She was thirty-five. Her face was
lean and strong and her eyes were as clear as
water. Her figure looked blocked and heavy in her
gardening costume, a man's black hat pulled low
down over her eyes, clodhopper shoes, a figured
print dress almost completely covered by a big
corduroy apron with four big pockets to hold the
snips, the trowel and scratcher, the seeds, and the
knife she worked with. She wore heavy leather
gloves to protect her hands while she worked.

She was cutting down the old year's chrysanthemum stalks with a pair of short and powerful scissors. She looked down toward the men by the tractor shed now and then. Her face was eager and
mature and handsome; even her work with the
scissors was overeager, overpowerful. The chrysanthemum stems seemed too small and easy for
her energy.

She brushed a cloud of hair out of her eyes with
the back of her glove, and left a smudge of earth
on her cheek in doing it. Behind her stood the neat
white farm house with red geraniums close-banked
around it as high as the windows. It was a hard-
swept looking little house, with hard-polished
windows, and a clean mud-mat on the front steps.

Elisa cast another glance toward the tractor
shed. The strangers were getting into their Ford
coupé. She took off a glove and put her strong
fingers down into the forest of new green chrysanthemum sprouts that were growing around the
old roots. She spread the leaves and looked down

among the close-growing stems. No aphids were there, no sowbugs or snails or cutworms. Her terrier fingers destroyed such pests before they could get started.

Elisa started at the sound of her husband's voice. He had come near quietly, and he leaned over the wire fence that protected her flower garden from cattle and dogs and chickens.

"At it again," he said. "You've got a strong new crop coming."

Elisa straightened her back and pulled on the gardening glove again. "Yes. They'll be strong this coming year." In her tone and on her face there was a little smugness.

"You've got a gift with things," Henry observed. "Some of those yellow chrysanthemums you had this year were ten inches across. I wish you'd work out in the orchard and raise some apples that big."

Her eyes sharpened. "Maybe I could do it too. I've a gift with things, all right. My mother had it. She could stick anything in the ground and make it grow. She said it was having planters' hands that knew how to do it."

"Well, it sure works with flowers," he said.

"Henry, who were those men you were talking to?"

"Why, sure, that's what I came to tell you. They were from the Western Meat Company. I sold those thirty head of three-year-old steers. Got nearly my own price too."

"Good," she said. "Good for you."

"And I thought," he continued, "I thought how it's Saturday afternoon, and we might go into Salinas for dinner at a restaurant, and then to a picture show — to celebrate, you see."

"Good," she repeated. "Oh, yes. That will be good."

Henry put on his joking tone. "There's fights tonight. How'd you like to go to the fights?"

"Oh, no," she said breathlessly. "No, I wouldn't like fights."

"Just fooling, Elisa. We'll go to a movie. Let's see. It's two now. I'm going to take Scotty and bring down those steers from the hill. It'll take us maybe two hours. We'll go in town about five and have dinner at the Dominos Hotel. Like that?"

"Of course I'll like it. It's good to eat away from home."

"All right, then. I'll go get up a couple of horses."

She said, "I'll have plenty of time to transplant some of these sets, I guess."

She heard her husband calling Scotty down by the barn. And a little later she saw the two men ride up the pale yellow hillside in search of the steers.

There was a little square sandy bed kept for rooting the chrysanthemums. With her trowel she turned the soil over and over, and smoothed it and patted it firm. Then she dug ten parallel trenches to receive the sets. Back at the chrysanthemum bed she pulled out the little crisp shoots, trimmed off the leaves of each one with her scissors, and laid it on a small orderly pile.

A squeak of wheels and plod of hoofs came from the road. Elisa looked up. The country road ran along the dense bank of willows and cottonwoods that bordered the river, and up this road came a curious vehicle, curiously drawn. It was an old spring wagon, with a round canvas top on it like the cover of a prairie schooner. It was drawn by an old bay horse and a little gray-and-white burro. A big stubble-bearded man sat between the cover flaps and drove the crawling team.

Underneath the wagon, between the hind wheels, a lean and rangy mongrel dog walked sedately. Words were painted on the canvas, in clumsy, crooked letters. "Pots, pans, knives, sisors, lawn mores, Fixed." Two rows of articles, and the triumphantly definitive "Fixed" below. The black paint had run down in little sharp points beneath each letter.

Elisa, squatting on the ground, watched to see the crazy, loose-jointed wagon pass by. But it didn't pass. It turned into the farm road in front of her house, crooked old wheels skirling and squeaking. The rangy dog darted from between the wheels and ran ahead. Instantly the two ranch shepherds flew out at him. Then all three stopped and with stiff and quivering tails, with taut straight legs, with ambassadorial dignity, they slowly circled, sniffing daintily. The caravan pulled up to Elisa's wire fence and stopped. Now the newcomer dog, feeling outnumbered, lowered his tail and retired under the wagon with raised hackles and bared teeth.

The man on the wagon seat called out, "That's a bad dog in a fight when he gets started."

Elisa laughed. "I see he is. How soon does he generally get started?"

The man caught up her laughter and echoed it heartily. "Sometimes not for weeks and weeks," he said. He climbed stiffly down, over the wheel. The horse and the donkey dropped like unwatered flowers.

Elisa saw that he was a very big man. Although his hair and beard were graying, he did not look old. His worn black suit was wrinkled and spotted with grease. The laughter had disappeared from his face and eyes the moment his laughing voice ceased. His eyes were dark, and they were full of the brooding that gets in the eyes of teamsters and of sailors. The calloused hands he rested on the wire fence were cracked, and every crack was a black line. He took off his battered hat.

"I'm off my general road, ma'am," he said. "Does this dirt road cut over across the river to the Los Angeles highway?"

Elisa stood up and shoved the thick scissors in her apron pocket. "Well, yes, it does, but it winds around and then fords the river. I don't think your team could pull through the sand."

He replied with some asperity, "It might surprise you what them beasts can pull through."

"When they get started?" she asked.

He smiled for a second. "Yes. When they get started."

"Well," said Elisa, "I think you'll save time if you go back to the Salinas road and pick up the highway there."

He drew a big finger down the chicken wire and made it sing. "I ain't in any hurry, ma'am. I go from Seattle to San Diego and back every year. Takes all my time. About six months each way. I aim to follow nice weather."

Elisa took off her gloves and stuffed them in the apron pocket with the scissors. She touched the under edge of her man's hat, searching for fugitive hairs. "That sounds like a nice kind of a way to live," she said.

He leaned confidentially over the fence. "Maybe you noticed the writing on my wagon. I mend pots and sharpen knives and scissors. You got any of them things to do?"

"Oh, no," she said quickly. "Nothing like that." Her eyes hardened with resistance.

"Scissors is the worst thing," he explained. "Most people just ruin scissors trying to sharpen 'em, but I know how. I got a special tool. It's a little bobbit kind of thing, and patented. But it sure does the trick."

"No. My scissors are all sharp."

"All right, then. Take a pot," he continued earnestly, "a bent pot, or a pot with a hole. I can make it like new so you don't have to buy no new ones. That's a saving for you."

"No," she said shortly. "I tell you I have nothing like that for you to do."

His face fell to an exaggerated sadness. His voice took on a whining undertone. "I ain't had a thing to do today. Maybe I won't have no supper tonight. You see I'm off my regular road. I know folks on the highway clear from Seattle to San Diego. They save their things for me to sharpen up because they know I do it so good and save them money."

"I'm sorry," Elisa said irritably. "I haven't anything for you to do."

His eyes left her face and fell to searching the ground. They roamed about until they came to the chrysanthemum bed where she had been working. "What's them plants, ma'am?"

The irritation and resistance melted from Elisa's face. "Oh, those are chrysanthemums, giant whites and yellows. I raise them every year, bigger than anybody around here."

"Kind of a long-stemmed flower? Looks like a quick puff of colored smoke?" he asked.

"That's it. What a nice way to describe them."

"They smell kind of nasty till you get used to them," he said.

"It's a good bitter smell," she retorted, "not nasty at all."

He changed his tone quickly. "I like the smell myself."

"I had ten-inch blooms this year," she said.

The man leaned farther over the fence. "Look. I know a lady down the road a piece, has got the nicest garden you ever seen. Got nearly every kind of flower but no chrysanthemums. Last time I was mending a copper-bottom washtub for her (that's a hard job but I do it good), she said to me, 'If you ever run acrost some nice chrysanthemums I wish you'd try to get me a few seeds.' That's what she told me."

Elisa's eyes grew alert and eager. "She couldn't have known much about chrysanthemums. You *can* raise them from seed, but it's much easier to root the little sprouts you see there."

"Oh," he said. "I s'pose I can't take none to her, then."

"Why yes you can," Elisa cried. "I can put some in damp sand, and you can carry them right along with you. They'll take root in the pot if you keep them damp. And then she can transplant them."

"She'd sure like to have some, ma'am. You say they're nice ones?"

"Beautiful," she said. "Oh, beautiful." Her eyes shone. She tore off the battered hat and shook out her dark pretty hair. "I'll put them in a flower pot, and you can take them right with you. Come into the yard."

While the man came through the picket gate Elisa ran excitedly along the geranium-bordered path to the back of the house. And she returned carrying a big red flower pot. The gloves were forgotten now. She kneeled on the ground by the starting bed and dug up the sandy soil with her fingers and scooped it into the bright new flower pot. Then she picked up the little pile of shoots she had prepared. With her strong fingers she pressed them into the sand and tamped around them with her knuckles. The man stood over her.

"I'll tell you what to do," she said. "You remember so you can tell the lady."

"Yes, I'll try to remember."

"Well, look. These will take root in about a month. Then she must set them out, about a foot apart in good rich earth like this, see?" She lifted a handful of dark soil for him to look at. "They'll grow fast and tall. Now remember this: In July tell her to cut them down, about eight inches from the ground."

"Before they bloom?" he asked.

"Yes, before they bloom." Her face was tight with eagerness. "They'll grow right up again. About the last of September the buds will start."

She stopped and seemed perplexed. "It's the budding that takes the most care," she said hesitantly. "I don't know how to tell you." She looked deep into his eyes, searchingly. Her mouth opened a little, and she seemed to be listening. "I'll try to tell you," she said. "Did you ever hear of planting hands?"

"Can't say I have, ma'am."

"Well, I can only tell you what it feels like. It's when you're picking off the buds you don't want. Everything goes right down into your fingertips. You watch your fingers work. They do it themselves. You can feel how it is. They pick and pick the buds. They never make a mistake. They're with the plant. Do you see? Your fingers and the plant. You can feel that, right up your arm. They know. They never make a mistake. You can feel it. When you're like that you can't do anything wrong. Do you see that? Can you understand that?"

She was kneeling on the ground looking up at him. Her breast swelled passionately.

The man's eyes narrowed. He looked away self-consciously. "Maybe I know," he said. "Sometimes in the night in the wagon there — "

Elisa's voice grew husky. She broke in on him, "I've never lived as you do, but I know what you mean. When the night is dark — why, the stars are sharp-pointed, and there's quiet. Why, you rise up and up! Every pointed star gets driven into your body. It's like that. Hot and sharp and — lovely."

Kneeling there, her hand went out toward his legs in the greasy black trousers. Her hesitant fingers almost touched the cloth. Then her hand dropped to the ground. She crouched low like a fawning dog.

He said, "It's nice, just like you say. Only when you don't have no dinner, it ain't."

She stood up then, very straight, and her face was ashamed. She held the flower pot out to him and placed it gently in his arms. "Here. Put it in your wagon, on the seat, where you can watch it. Maybe I can find something for you to do."

At the back of the house she dug in the can pile and found two old and battered aluminum saucepans. She carried them back and gave them to him. "Here, maybe you can fix these."

His manner changed. He became professional. "Good as new I can fix them." At the back of his wagon he set a little anvil, and out of an oily toolbox dug a small machine hammer. Elisa came through the gate to watch him while he pounded out the dents in the kettles. His mouth grew sure and knowing. At a difficult part of the work he sucked his underlip.

"You sleep right in the wagon?" Elisa asked.

"Right in the wagon, ma'am. Rain or shine I'm dry as a cow in there."

"It must be nice," she said. "It must be very nice. I wish women could do such things."

"It ain't the right kind of a life for a woman."

Her upper lip raised a little, showing her teeth. "How do you know? How can you tell?" she said.

"I don't know, ma'am," he protested. "Of course I don't know. Now here's your kettles, done. You don't have to buy no new ones."

"How much?"

"Oh, fifty cents'll do. I keep my prices down and my work good. That's why I have all them satisfied customers up and down the highway."

Elisa brought him a fifty-cent piece from the house and dropped it in his hand. "You might be surprised to have a rival some time. I can sharpen scissors too. And I can beat the dents out of little pots. I could show you what a woman might do."

He put his hammer back in the oily box and shoved the little anvil out of sight. "It would be a lonely life for a woman, ma'am, and a scarey life, too, with animals creeping under the wagon all night." He climbed over the singletree, steadying himself with a hand on the burro's white rump. He settled himself in the seat, picked up the lines. "Thank you kindly, ma'am," he said. "I'll do like you told me; I'll go back and catch the Salinas road."

"Mind," she called, "if you're long in getting there, keep the sand damp."

"Sand, ma'am? . . . Sand? Oh, sure. You mean around the chrysanthemums. Sure I will." He clucked his tongue. The beasts leaned luxuriously into their collars. The mongrel dog took his place between the back wheels. The wagon turned and crawled out the entrance road and back the way it had come, along the river.

Elisa stood in front of her wire fence watching the slow progress of the caravan. Her shoulders were straight, her head thrown back, her eyes half-closed, so that the scene came vaguely into them.

Her lips moved silently, forming the words "Good-bye — good-bye." Then she whispered, "That's a bright direction. There's a glowing there." The sound of her whisper startled her. She shook herself free and looked about to see whether anyone had been listening. Only the dogs had heard. They lifted their heads toward her from their sleeping in the dust, and then stretched out their chins and settled asleep again. Elisa turned and ran hurriedly into the house.

In the kitchen she reached behind the stove and felt the water tank. It was full of hot water from the noonday cooking. In the bathroom she tore off her soiled clothes and flung them into the corner. And then she scrubbed herself with a little block of pumice, legs and thighs, loins and chest and arms, until her skin was scratched and red. When she had dried herself she stood in front of a mirror in her bedroom and looked at her body. She tightened her stomach and threw out her chest. She turned and looked over her shoulder at her back.

After a while she began to dress, slowly. She put on her newest underclothing and her nicest stockings and the dress which was the symbol of her prettiness. She worked carefully on her hair, penciled her eyebrows, and rouged her lips.

Before she was finished she heard the little thunder of hoofs and the shouts of Henry and his helper as they drove the red steers into the corral. She heard the gate bang shut and set herself for Henry's arrival.

His step sounded on the porch. He entered the house calling, "Elisa, where are you?"

"In my room, dressing. I'm not ready. There's hot water for your bath. Hurry up. It's getting late."

When she heard him splashing in the tub, Elisa laid his dark suit on the bed, and shirt and socks and tie beside it. She stood his polished shoes on the floor beside the bed. Then she went to the porch and sat primly and stiffly down. She looked toward the river road where the willow-line was still yellow with frosted leaves so that under the high gray fog they seemed a thin band of sunshine. This was the only color in the gray afternoon. She sat unmoving for a long time. Her eyes blinked rarely.

Henry came banging out of the door, shoving his tie inside his vest as he came. Elisa stiffened and her face grew tight. Henry stopped short and looked at her. "Why — why, Elisa. You look so nice!"

"Nice? You think I look nice? What do you mean by 'nice'?"

Henry blundered on. "I don't know. I mean you look different, strong and happy."

"I am strong? Yes, strong. What do you mean 'strong'?"

He looked bewildered. "You're playing some kind of a game," he said helplessly. "It's a kind of a play. You look strong enough to break a calf over your knee, happy enough to eat it like a watermelon."

For a second she lost her rigidity. "Henry! Don't talk like that. You didn't know what you said." She grew complete again. "I'm strong," she boasted. "I never knew before how strong."

Henry looked down toward the tractor shed, and when he brought his eyes back to her, they were his own again. "I'll get out the car. You can put on your coat while I'm starting."

Elisa went into the house. She heard him drive to the gate and idle down his motor, and then she took a long time to put on her hat. She pulled it here and pressed it there. When Henry turned the motor off she slipped into her coat and went out.

The little roadster bounced along the dirt road by the river, raising the birds and driving the rabbits into the brush. Two cranes flapped heavily over the willow-line and dropped into the river bed.

Far ahead on the road Elisa saw a dark speck. She knew.

She tried not to look as they passed it, but her eyes would not obey. She whispered to herself sadly, "He might have thrown them off the road. That wouldn't have been much trouble, not very much. But he kept the pot," she explained. "He had to keep the pot. That's why he couldn't get them off the road."

The roadster turned a bend and she saw the caravan ahead. She swung full around toward her husband so she could not see the little covered wagon and the mismatched team as the car passed them.

In a moment it was over. The thing was done. She did not look back.

She said loudly, to be heard above the motor, "It will be good, tonight, a good dinner."

"Now you're changed again," Henry complained. He took one hand from the wheel and patted her knee. "I ought to take you in to dinner oftener. It would be good for both of us. We get so heavy out on the ranch."

"Henry," she asked, "could we have wine at dinner?"

"Sure we could. Say! That will be fine."

She was silent for a while; then she said, "Henry, at those prize fights, do the men hurt each other very much?"

"Sometimes a little, not often. Why?"

"Well, I've read how they break noses, and blood runs down their chests. I've read how the fighting gloves get heavy and soggy with blood."

He looked around at her. "What's the matter, Elisa? I didn't know you read things like that." He brought the car to a stop, then turned to the right over the Salinas River bridge.

"Do any women ever go to the fights?" she asked.

"Oh, sure, some. What's the matter, Elisa? Do you want to go? I don't think you'd like it, but I'll take you if you really want to go."

She relaxed limply in the seat. "Oh, no. No. I don't want to go. I'm sure I don't." Her face was turned away from him. "It will be enough if we can have wine. It will be plenty." She turned up her coat collar so he could not see that she was crying weakly — like an old woman.

C. D. B. BRYAN

18/SO MUCH UNFAIRNESS OF THINGS

The Virginia Preparatory School lies just off the Shirley Highway between Washington, D.C., and Richmond. It is a small Southern school with dull red brick dormitories and classroom buildings, quiet old school buildings with quiet old Southern names — Page House, Stuart Hall, Randolph Hall, Reckinridge, Pickney, and Coulter. The high brick wall that surrounds the school is known as the Breastworks, and the shallow pond behind the football field is the Crater. V.P.S. is an old school, with an old school's traditions. A sign commemorates the use of the school by Union troops as a military hospital in 1861, and every October the school celebrates "Liberation Day," in honor of the day in 1866 when the school reopened.

Graduates of the Virginia Preparatory School who have not returned for some years are shocked by the glass-and-steel apartment houses and cinder-block ramblers that have sprung up around the school grounds, but once they have driven along the Breastworks and passed through the ornate wrought-iron East Gate, they see, with satisfaction, that the school has not changed. Neither have its customs. For example, new boys, or "toads," still must obey the Toad Code. They must be courteous to old boys and faculty. They must know the school song and cheers by the end of the second week. They must hold doors open for old boys and see that old boys are served first in the dining room. And they must "run relay" — meaning that they have to wake up the old boys in the morning when they wish to be awakened and see that they are not disturbed when they wish to sleep.

Philip Sadler Wilkinson was fourteen; he was an old boy. The new boy shook him lightly. "Mr. Wilkinson? Mr. Wilkinson? It's five-thirty, sir. You asked me to wake you up."

Next year the new boy would be permitted to call Philip Sadler Wilkinson "P.S.," like the others. He watched P.S. stretch, turn over, and go back to sleep. "Sir, Hey! Wake up!"

P.S. rolled out of his metal cot, rubbed his eyes, felt around the top of his desk for his glasses, put them on, and looked at the new boy.

"Toad?"

"Yes, sir?"

"What is the date?"

"Thursday, the seventh of June."

"How much longer do we have until the end of the school year?"

"Seven days, twenty-three hours, and" — the new boy looked at his wristwatch — "and thirteen minutes, sir."

P.S. smiled. "Are you sure?"

"No, sir."

"Ah — hah! Ah — HAH! Toad, assume the position!"

The new boy locked his knees and bent over and grabbed his ankles.

"What is a 'toad,' toad?" P.S. asked.

"Sir, a toad is a loathsome warty creature who eats insects and worms, sir. A toad is the lowest form of amphibian. A toad is despicable."

"Well, well, now, straighten those knees, toad." P.S. looked at the new boy and saw that his face was turning red with strain. "Toad, are you in pain?"

"No, sir," the new boy lied.

"Then you may straighten up."

The new boy massaged his calves. "Honest to Pete, P.S., you're a sadist."

"No, no, wait till next year. You'll be pulling the same thing on some toad yourself. I had it done to me, you had it done to you. And did I detect you calling me by my rightful name?"

The new boy smiled.

"Ah, you toads will never learn. Assume the position."

The new boy started to bend over again.

"Oh, go away," P.S. said. The new boy started out of the door and P.S. called him back. "Hey, toad? You gonna kill the Latin exam?"

"I hope so."

"How do you conjugate the verb 'to spit'?"

"*Exspuo, exspuere, exspui —* "

"Heck, no!" P.S. laughed. "It's *spitto, spittere, ach tui, splattus!*"

The new boy groaned and left the room.

P.S. looked at his watch. It was twenty minutes to six. He could hear the new boy waking up the boy in the next room. P.S. picked up his water glass and toothbrush and tiptoed down the corridor. He stopped at Charlie Merritt's room and knocked softly.

"Who is it?"

"It's me, Charlie."

"Oh, hey, P.S. Come on in."

P.S. pushed aside the curtain of the cubicle. Charlie was sitting at his desk studying.

"Morning," P.S. whispered.

"Morning."

"Studying the Latin?"

"Yep."

"You know how to conjugate the verb 'to spit'?"

"Yep," Charlie said. *"Spitto, spittere, ach —"*

"Okay, okay!" P.S. laughed. "You gonna kill the exam?"

"I hope so. You think you'll pass it?"

"Doubt it. I haven't passed one yet." P.S. looked over at Charlie's bureau. "Say, Charlie? Can I borrow your toothpaste? I'm out."

"Sure, but roll it from the bottom of the tube, will you?"

P.S. picked up the toothpaste and went down the hall to the bathroom. Mabrey, the head monitor, was shaving. P.S. watched him in the mirror.

"You must have a porcupine for a father," P.S. said. "You've got the heaviest beard in the school."

Mabrey began to shave the length of his neck. "Wilkinson, you're about as funny as a rubber crutch."

"Cut your throat! Cut your throat!" P.S. began to dance around behind Mabrey, sprinkling voodoo potions on the top of the older student's head. "Monkey dust! Monkey dust! Oh, black Pizoola! Great Kubla of the Ancient Curse! Make this bad man cut his throat!"

Mabrey cursed and a small red stain began to seep through the lather on his throat. "P.S., *will you get out of here!*"

P.S. stared, eyes wide open, at the broadening stain.

"Hey! Hey, it worked!"

Mabrey undid the towel from around his waist and snapped P.S.'s skinny behind. P.S. yelped and jumped away. "Hey, Mr. Mabrey, sir? Hey, Mabrey? I'm sorry, I really am. I didn't know it would work."

"What would work?"

"My voodoo curse. I didn't know it would make you cut yourself."

"For Pete's sake, P.S., what're you talking about? I cut a pimple. Will you leave me alone before I throw you out of a closed window?"

P.S. was quiet for a moment. Then he moved over to the washbasin next to Mabrey and looked at himself in the mirror. He ran his fingers through his light-brown hair and pushed his glasses higher on his nose. "Hey, Mabrey? Do you think I'm fresh? I mean, I have great respect for you — you being the head monitor and all. I mean it. Sometimes I worry. I mean, do you think I'm too fresh?"

Mabrey finished rinsing his face. "P.S., kid," he said as he dried himself, "you're all right. You're a nice guy. And I'm willing to bet that if you could only learn to throw a baseball from center field to second base overhand, you might turn out to be a pretty fair little baseball player."

"*Overhand!* Whaddya mean 'overhand'? They call me 'Deadeye Wilkinson.' " P.S. wound up with an imaginary baseball and threw it as hard as he could. Then he pantomimed being the second baseman. He crouched and caught the incoming ball at his knees and thrust his hand down to tag out the runner. "*Safe!*" he shouted. "I mean, out! Out! Out!"

"Too late," Mabrey said, and laughed. "An umpire never changes his decision."

"I meant *out*," P.S. said.

Mabrey disappeared down the hall.

P.S. brushed his teeth, being careful to squeeze the toothpaste from the bottom of the tube. He looked at himself in the mirror and chanted, *"Fuero, fueris, fuerit, fuerimus, fueritis, fuerint!"* He examined his upper lip and was disappointed. He wished that he didn't have such a young face. He wished he had a heavy beard, like Mabrey. He washed his face, wet his hair down, and walked back into Charlie's room. Charlie was P.S.'s best friend. He was very short. The other boys kidded him about being an engineer for Lionel trains. P.S. was very tall and thin, and he had not yet grown into his height. At fourteen he was already six feet tall, and he had a tendency to stoop to compensate. He and Charlie were known as Mutt and Jeff. When P.S. entered the room, Charlie was curled up on his bed studying his Latin notes. He didn't look up until P.S. dropped the toothpaste tube on his pillow.

"Rolled from the bottom," P.S. said.

"Hey, how do you expect to pass your Latin exam if you don't study? I heard you and Mabrey clowning around in the can."

"If I don't study!" P.S. said. "Do you know how long I've studied for this exam? If I flunk it again this year, I get to keep the trophy."

"What trophy?"

"For Pete's sake, I don't know what trophy. But I'll get something for sure. I've spent the last two weeks practically doing nothing but studying Latin. I recopied all my notes. I underlined practically the whole book. And I memorized all the irregular verbs. Come on, come on, ask me anything. If I don't pass it this year, I've had it. Come on, ask me anything."

"Okay, what's the word for 'ridge'?"

"The word for 'ridge'?" P.S. stalled.

"Yep."

P.S. thought for a moment. "Look, I don't know. Make it two for three."

"The word for 'ridge' is *'iugum.'*" Charlie looked at his notes. "Okay, two out of three. What's the word for 'crowd'? And 'troop,' as in 'a troop of cavalry'?"

"The word for 'crowd' is *'turba, turbae.'* . . . What was the other one?"

" 'Troop of cavalry.' "

" 'Cavalry' is *'equitatus.'* . . . I don't know. What is 'troop'?"

" 'Troop' is *'turma.'*" Charlie laughed. "Well, you got one out of three."

"Did I get partial credit for the 'cavalry'?"

"Nope."

"I hope Dr. Fairfax is more lenient than you are."

"He won't be," Charlie said.

"If I flunk the Latin exam again this year . . ."

"How come you flunked it last year?"

"How come anybody flunks an exam? I didn't know the answers. Boy, Charlie, I don't know what I'm going to do with you. If you weren't such a nice guy and lend me your toothpaste and things like that all the time, I'd probably feed you to the — to the what's-their-name fish. Those fish who eat people in South America all the time."

"Well, since you don't know what to do with me, as a start, why don't you let me study?"

"Sure. Sure, okay. . . . Okay, be a grind. See if I care."

P.S. walked back to his cubicle and pulled his Ullman and Henry "Latin II" from his unpainted bookcase. First he studied the irregular verbs in the back of the book. Then he went over his vocabulary list. He concentrated for as long as he

could; then he leaned out of his window to look
at the shadows of the trees directly below, dropped
a penny out of the window to see if a squir-
rel would pick it up, checked his window sill to see
if the cookie crumbs he had left for the mocking-
bird were still there.

He turned back to his Latin book and leafed
through the Forestier illustrations of Roman soldiers. He picked up the picture his father had
given him last Christmas. Within the frame were
four small round photographs of Wilkinsons in
uniform. There was his father as an infantry
major during the Second World War, his grandfather as a captain in the field artillery during the
First World War, his great-great-grandfather as a
corporal in a soft gray Confederate uniform and a
great-great-great-great something or other in a
dark uniform with a lot of bright buttons. P.S.
didn't know who the last picture was of. He imagined it to be somebody from the Revolutionary
War. P.S. had seen the oil portrait the photograph
had been taken from hanging in the hallway of
his grandfather's house. P.S. had the long, thin
nose of the other Wilkinsons in the pictures, but
he still had the round cheeks of youth and the perfect eyebrows. He was the fifteenth of his family
to attend the Virginia Preparatory School. Among
the buildings at V.P.S. there was a Wilkinson
Memorial Library and a Sadler Gymnasium.
When P.S. was packing to begin his first year at
the school, his father had said, "Son, when your
great-grandfather went off to V.P.S., his father
gave him a dozen silk handkerchiefs and a pair of
warm gloves. When I went off to V.P.S., your
grandfather gave me a dozen silk handkerchiefs
and a pair of warm gloves. And now here are a

dozen silk handkerchiefs and a pair of warm gloves for you."

P.S. looked at the brightly patterned Liberty-silk handkerchiefs and the fuzzy red mittens. No thirteen-year-old ever wore red mittens, except girls, and particularly not fuzzy red mittens. And P.S. knew he would never dare to wear the silk handkerchiefs.

"Well, thank you very much, Dad," he said.

"That's all right, son."

P.S. left the red mittens behind when he went away to V.P.S. He used two of the silk handkerchiefs to cover the top of his bureau and bookcase, gave one other away to a girl, and hid the rest beneath his underwear on the second shelf of his bureau. His father had done very well at the school; he had been a senior monitor, editor-in-chief of the yearbook, and a distance runner in winter and spring track. P.S. hoped he would do as well, but he knew he had disappointed his father so far. When he flunked the Latin examination last year and tried to explain to his father that he just could not do Latin, he could see the disbelief in his father's eyes. "Good Lord, son, you just didn't study. 'Can't do Latin,' what nonsense!" But P.S. knew that studying had nothing to do with it. His father said that no Wilkinson had ever flunked at V.P.S.; P.S. was the first. His father was not the kind to lose his temper. P.S. wished he were. When P.S. had done something wrong, his father would just look at him and smile sadly and shake his head.

The boy had never felt particularly close to his father. He had never been able to talk to or with his father. He had found the best means of getting along with his father was to keep out of his way. He had given up their ever sharing anything. He had no illusions about leading a calendar-picture life with his father — canoeing or hunting together. He could remember trying to get his father to play catch with him and how his father would always say, "Not now, son, not now." But there were certain occasions that his father felt should be shared with P.S. These were the proper father-son occasions that made P.S. feel like some sort of ornament. There would be Father's Day, or the big football game of the season. P.S. would be told to order two tickets, and the afternoon of the game he and his father would watch the first half together. His father remembered all of the cheers and was shocked when P.S. didn't remember some of the words to the school song. At the half, his father would disappear to talk to his friends and P.S. would be left alone to watch the overcoats or umbrellas.

After the game P.S. would wander back to the field house, where the alumni tables were set up. He would locate his father and stand next to him until his father introduced him to the persons he was talking to. Then his father would say, "Run along, son. I'll meet you back in your room." So, P.S. would go back to his room and wait for his father to come by. The boy would straighten up the bed, dust the bureau, and sweep the floor. And then after a long wait his father would come in and sit down. "Well, how are you, son?" the conversation would always start. And P.S. would answer, "Fine, thank you, sir." His father would look around the room and remark about its not being large enough to swing a cat in, then there would be two or three anecdotes about the times when he was a boy at V.P.S., and then he would look at his watch and say, "Well, I guess I'd better be pushing off." His father would ask him if there was anything he needed, and P.S. would say that he didn't think there was anything. His father would give him a five-dollar bill and drive away. And P.S., with enormous relief, would go look for Charlie. "Did you and your dad have a good time?" Charlie would ask. "Sure," P.S. would say. And that would end the conversation.

P.S. knew that his father loved him, but he also knew better than to expect any sign of affection. Affection always seemed to embarrass his father. P.S. remembered his first year at school, when his father had first come up to see him. He had been very happy to see his father, and when they were saying good-bye P.S. stepped forward as usual to kiss him and his father drew away. P.S. always made it a point now to shake hands with the father. And at fourteen respect and obedience had taken the place of love.

P.S. picked up his Latin notes and went over the translations he had completed. He wished he knew what questions would be asked. In last year's exam there were questions from all over the book, and it made the exam very difficult to study for, if they were going to do that. He pictured himself handing in the finished examination to Dr. Fairfax and saying, "Sir? Wilkinsons do not flunk. Please grade my exam accordingly."

P.S. looked at his wristwatch. The dining hall would begin serving breakfast in fifteen minutes. He made his bed and put on a clean pair of khakis and a button-down shirt. He slipped into his old white bucks and broke a lace tying them, and pulled out the shorter piece and threaded what was left through the next eyelet up, as the older boys did. He tidied up his room for inspection, picked up his notes, and went back to Charlie's room. Charlie was sweeping the halls and emptying all trash baskets. P.S. entered and sat down on the bed.

"Hey, P.S.! I just made the bed!"

"Okay, okay, I'll straighten it up when I leave." P.S. ran his fingers across the desk top. "Merritt, two demerits — dust. . . . Hey, you know what, Charlie?"

Charlie dusted the desk and then said, "What?"

"You're such a grump in the morning. I sure'd hate to be married to you."

"Well, I wouldn't worry about that. In the first place, my parents wouldn't approve."

"I'm not so sure that my family would want me to marry a Merritt, either. I think you'd have to take my family name. I mean, you know, you're just not our class."

"P.S., buddy, you're in a class all by yourself."

"Well, anyway, what I mean is that you're such a grump in the morning that I can see someday your wife coming in — if you ever find a girl who's foolish enough to marry you. But I mean, she might come in some morning and give you grapefruit juice instead of orange juice and you'll probably bite her hand off or something."

"Or *something*." Charlie laughed.

P.S. punched Charlie on the arm. "Garbage mind!"

"What do you mean? I didn't say anything. You've got the dirty mind. All I said was 'or something' and you say I've got a garbage mind."

"Well, you know what I meant."

"I don't know anything at all."

P.S. looked at Charlie for a moment, then he laughed. "I'm not going to take advantage of your last remark. I'm much too good a sport to rake you over the coals when you place your ample foot in your ample mouth."

"*Ample foot!*" Charlie held up his foot. "I've

got a very small foot. It's a sign of good breeding."

"Only in horses, Twinkletoes, only in horses."

"Horses, *horses!* What do horses have to do with it?"

"Ask me no questions and I'll tell you no lies." P.S. leafed through Charlie's notes. "Hey, the exam's at ten-thirty, isn't it?"

"Yep. If you flunk Latin again, will they make you go to summer school?"

"Probably. I really think it's archaic the way they make you pass Latin to get out of this place."

"Boy, I sure hope I pass it," Charlie said.

"You will. You will. You're the brain in the class."

"Come on, let's go to chow."

"That's what I've been waiting for, my good buddy, my good friend, old pal of mine." P.S. jumped off the bed, scooped up his notebook, and started out of the room.

"Hey!" Charlie said. "What about the bed?"

At eight o'clock chapel, P.S. knelt in the pew and prayed: "*Dear God, I pray that I pass my Latin exam this morning. . . . If I can pass this exam, then I'll do anything you want me to do. . . . God, please. If I don't pass this exam, I've really had it. . . .* They must have made these pews for midgets; I never fit in them right. . . . How am I ever going to get out to Colorado this summer unless I pass that exam? *. . . Please God, I don't want a high grade, all I want is to pass . . . and you don't have to help me on the others. . . . I don't want to pass this exam for myself only. I mean, it means a lot to my family. My father will be very disappointed if I flunk the exam. . . .* I wonder if Charlie will be able to go out to Colorado with me. *. . . God bless Mom, God bless*

*Dad, God Bless Grandpa Sadler and Grandma
Sadler, God bless Grandpa Wilkinson and Granny
Wilkinson, God bless all my relatives I haven't
mentioned. . . . Amen. And . . . and God?
Please, please help me to pass this exam."*

At ten-fifteen, P.S. and Charlie fell in step and
walked over to Randolph Hall, where the examination was to be held.

"Well, if we don't know it now, we never will,"
Charlie said.

"Even if I did know it now, I wouldn't know it
tomorrow." P.S. reached into his pants pocket and
pulled out his lucky exam tie. It was a stained and
unraveled blue knit. As they walked up the path,
he was careful to tie the tie backward, the wide
end next to his shirt, the seam facing out. Then he
checked his watch pocket to see that his lucky silver dollar was there.

"What's the Latin for 'then'?" Charlie asked.

" *'Tum,' "* P.S. answered. "Tums for *tummy."*

"What's the word for 'thence,' or 'from there'?"

" *'Inde.' "* P.S. began to sing: *"Inde* evening
byde moonlight you could *hearde* — "

"For Pete's sake, P.S.!" Charlie laughed.

"You don't like my singing?"

"Not much."

"You know? I'm thinking of joining the choir
and glee club next year. You know why? They've
got a couple of dances next fall. One with St. Cath-
arine's and another with St. Tim's. You wanta try
out with me?"

"I don't know. I can't sing."

"Who's gonna sing?" P.S. grabbed Charlie's arm
and growled, "Baby, I'm no singer. I'm a lover!"

"Lover? Who says you're a lover?"

"Ask me no questions and I'll tell you no lies."

P.S. and Charlie walked up the worn wooden steps of Randolph Hall to the third-floor study hall, where the Latin examination was to be given. They both were in the upper study hall, since they were underclassmen still. P.S.'s desk was in the back corner of the study hall, against the wall. He sat down and brushed the dust off the top of his desk with his palm. Someone had traced a hand into the wood. Others had traced and re-traced the hand and deepened the grooves. They had added fingernails and rings. P.S. had added a Marlboro tattoo. He lifted the desk top and, searching for his pencil sharpener, saw that he had some more Latin translations in his desk. He read them through quickly and decided it was too late to learn anything from them. He pulled out his pencil sharpener and closed his desk. The study hall was filling with boys, who took their places at their desks and called back and forth to each other in their slow Southern voices. It was a long, thin room with high windows on either side, and the walls were painted a dirty yellow. Between the windows were framed engravings of Roman ruins and Southern generals. The large fluorescent lights above the desks buzzed and blinked into life. A dark, curly-haired boy sat down in the desk next to P.S. and began to empty his pockets of pencils and pens.

"Hey, Jumbo," P.S. said. "You gonna kill the exam?"

"I hope so. If I can get a good grade on it, then I don't have to worry so much about my math exam tomorrow."

"Well, if we don't know it now we never will."

"You're right."

Jumbo had played second-string tackle on the varsity this year. He was expected to be first-string next year, and by his final year, the coaches thought, he might become an All-Virginia High School tackle. Jumbo was a sincere, not very bright student who came from a farm in Virginia and wanted to be a farmer when he finished college. P.S. had sat next to Jumbo all year, but they had never become particularly close friends. Jumbo lived in a different dormitory and had a tendency to stick with the other members of the football team. But P.S. liked him, and Jumbo was really the only member of the football team that he knew at all.

P.S. looked up at the engraving of General Robert E. Lee and his horse Traveller. He glanced over at Jumbo. Jumbo was cleaning his fingernails with the tip of his automatic pencil.

"Well, good luck," P.S. said.

"Good luck to you."

"I'll need it."

P.S. stood up and looked for Charlie. "Hey! Hey, Charlie?"

Charlie turned around. "Yeah?"

"Piggo, piggere, squeely, gruntum!"

"For Pete's sake, P.S.!"

"Hey, P.S.?" someone shouted. "You gonna flunk it again this year?"

"No, no, I don't think so," P.S. answered in mock seriousness. "In point of fact, as the good Dr. Fairfax would say — in point of fact, I might just come out with the highest grade in class. After all, I'm such a brain."

The noise in the study hall suddenly stopped; Dr. Fairfax had entered. The Latin instructor walked to the back of the study hall, where P.S. was sitting.

"And what was all that about, Wilkinson?"

"Sir, I was telling the others how I'm the brain in your class."

"Indeed?" Dr. Fairfax asked.

"Yes, sir. But I was only kidding."

"Indeed," the Latin instructor said, and the other students laughed.

Dr. Fairfax was a large man with a lean, aesthetic face, which he tried to hide with a military mustache. He had taught at the Virginia Preparatory School since 1919. P.S.'s father had had Dr. Fairfax for a Latin instructor. When P.S. read *Good-bye, Mr. Chips,* he had kept thinking of Dr. Fairfax. The Latin instructor wore the same suit and vest all winter. They were always immaculate. The first day of spring was marked by Dr. Fairfax's appearance in a white linen suit, which he always wore with a small blue bachelor's-button. Before a study hall last spring, someone had placed an alarm clock set to go off during the middle of study hall in one of the tall wastepaper baskets at the rear of the room. The student had then emptied all of the pencil sharpeners and several ink bottles into the basket and covered all this with crumpled-up pad paper. When the alarm clock went off, Dr. Fairfax strode down the aisle and reached into the wastepaper basket for the clock. When he lifted it out, the sleeve of his white linen jacket was covered with ink and pencil shavings. There was a stunned silence in the study hall as Dr. Fairfax looked at his sleeve. And then Dr. Fairfax began to laugh. The old man sat down on one of the desk tops and laughed and laughed, until finally the students had enough nerve to join him. The next day, he appeared in the same linen suit, but it was absolutely clean. Nobody was given demerits or punished in any manner. Dr. Fairfax was P.S.'s favorite instructor. P.S. watched him separate the examination papers and blue books into neat piles at the proctor's desk. Dr. Fairfax looked up at the electric clock over the study-hall door and then at his thin gold pocket watch. He cleared his throat. "Good morning, gentlemen."

"GOOD MORNING, SIR!" the students shouted.

"Gentlemen, there will be no talking during the examination. In the two hours given you, you will have ample time to complete all of the necessary work. When the bell sounds signifying the end of the examination, you will cease work immediately. In point of fact, anyone found working after the bell will be looked upon most unfavorably. When you receive your examinations, make certain that the print is legible. Make sure that you place your names on each of your blue books. If you have any difficulty reading the examination, hold your hand above your head and you will be given a fresh copy. The tops of your desks should be cleared of all notes, papers, and books. Are there any questions? . . . If not, will Baylor and you, Grandy, and . . . and Merritt . . . will the three of you please pass out the examinations."

P.S. watched Charlie get up and walk over to the desk.

Dr. Fairfax reached into his breast pocket and pulled out a pair of steel-rimmed spectacles. He looked out across the room. "We are nearing the end of the school year," he said. "Examinations always seem to cause students an undue amount of concern. I assure you, I can well remember when I was a student at V.P.S. In point of fact, I was not so very different from some of you — "

The instructor was interrupted by a rasping Bronx cheer. He looked quickly over in the direction of the sound. "Travers, was that you?"

"No, sir."

"Brandon, was that you?"

The student hesitated, then answered, "Yes, sir."

"Brandon, I consider that marked disrespect, and it will cost you ten demerits."

"Aww, sir — "

"Fifteen." Dr. Fairfax cleared his throat again. "Now, if I may continue? . . . Good. There are a few important things to remember when taking an examination. First, do not get upset when you cannot at once answer all of the questions. The examination is designed — "

P.S. stopped listening. Charlie was walking down the aisle toward him.

"Hey, Charlie," he whispered, "give me an easy one."

"There will be no favoritism on my part."

"How does it look?"

"Tough."

"Merritt and Wilkinson?" Dr. Fairfax said. "That last little bit of conversation will cost you each five demerits."

The Latin instructor looked up at the electric clock again. "When you receive your examinations, you may begin. Are there any questions? . . . If not, gentlemen, it might be well for us to remember this ancient Latin proverb: *'Abusus non tollit usum.'*" Dr. Fairfax waited for the laugh. There was none. He cleared his throat again. "Perhaps . . . perhaps we had better ask the class brain what the proverb means. Wilkinson?"

P.S. stood up. "*'Abusus non tollit usum,'* sir?"

"That's right."

"Something like 'Abuse does not tolerate the use,' sir?"

"What does the verb *'tollo, tollere, sustuli, sublatus'* mean?"

"'To take away,' sir."

"That's right. The proverb, then, is 'Abuse does not take away the use,' or, in the context I was referring to, just because you gentlemen cannot do Latin properly does not mean that it should not be done at all."

"Yes, sir," P.S. said, and he sat down.

Dr. Fairfax unfolded his newspaper, and P.S. began to read the examination. He picked up his pencil and printed in large letters on the cover of his blue book:

PHILIP SADLER WILKINSON
LATIN EXAMINATION
LATIN II — DR. FAIRFAX
VIRGINIA PREPARATORY SCHOOL
7 JUNE 1962 — BOOK ONE (1)

Then he put down his pencil, stretched, and began to work.

P.S. read the examination carefully. He saw that he would be able to do very little of it from memory, and felt the first surge of panic moisten his palms. He tried to translate the first Latin-to-English passage. He remembered that it fell on the right-hand side of the page in his Ullman and Henry, opposite the picture of the Roman galley. The picture was a still taken from the silent-movie version of *Ben-Hur*. He recognized some of the verbs, more of the nouns, and finally he began to be able to translate. It was about the Veneti ships, which were more efficient than the Roman galleys because they had prows and flat keels. He translated the entire passage, put down his pencil, and stretched again.

An hour later, P.S. knew he was in trouble. The first translation and the vocabulary section were the only parts of the exam he had been able to do without too much difficulty. He was able to give the rule and examples for the datives of agent and possession. The English-to-Latin sentences were the most difficult. He had been able to do only one of those. For the question "How do you determine the tense of the infinitive in indirect statement?" he wrote, "You can determine the tense by the construction of the sentence and by the word endings," and hoped he might get some credit. The two Latin-to-English passages counted twenty points apiece. If he could only do that second translation, he stood a chance of passing the examination. He recognized the adverb *"inde,"* but he saw that it didn't help him very much. The examination was halfway over. He tried to count how many points he had made so far on the examination. He thought he might have somewhere between fifty and fifty-five. Passing was seventy. If he could just translate that second passage, he would have the points he needed to pass. Dr. Fairfax never scaled the grades. P.S. had heard that one year the Latin instructor flunked everybody but two.

He glanced over at Jumbo. Then he looked back down at his own examination and swore under his breath. Jumbo looked over at him and smiled. P.S. pantomimed that he could not answer the question, and Jumbo smiled again. P.S. slid his glasses off and rubbed his eyes. He fought down the panic, wiped his hands on his pants legs, and looked at the passage again. He couldn't make any sense out of the blur of the words. He squinted, looked at them, put on his glasses again, and knew that he was in trouble.

He leaned over his desk and closed his eyes. *Dear God, please help me on this examination . . . please, God, please . . . I must pass this examination. . . .* He opened his eyes and looked carefully around to see if anyone had seen him praying. The others were all working hard on the examination. P.S. looked up again at the engraving on the wall above his desk. Beneath the portrait was the caption "Soon after the close of the War Between the States, General Robert E. Lee became the head of a school for young men. General Lee made this statement when he met with his students for the first time: 'We have but one rule in this school, and that is that every student must be a gentleman.'" They left out that other rule, P.S. thought. They left out the one that says you have to have Latin to graduate! Or is that part of being a gentleman too?

He read the Latin-to-English passage through twice, then he read it through backwards. He knew he had seen the passage before. He even remembered seeing it recently. But where? He knew that the passage dealt with the difficulties the Romans were having in fortifying their positions, but there were so many technical words in it that he could not get more than five of the twenty points from the translation, and he needed at least fifteen to pass. . . . He was going to flunk. *But I can't flunk! I can't flunk!* I've got to pass!

P.S. knew if he flunked he wouldn't be able to face his father. No matter what excuse P.S. gave, his father would not believe he hadn't loafed all term.

He looked at the passage and tried to remember where he had seen it. And then his mouth went dry. He felt the flush burn into the back of his neck and spread to his cheeks. He swallowed hard. *The translation's in my desk!* . . . *It's in my desk! . . . Oh, Lord! . . . It's the translation on the top of the stack in my desk . . . in my desk!*

All he would have to do would be to slip the

translation out of his desk, copy it, put it away, and he would pass the examination. All of his worries would be over. His father would be happy that he passed the examination. He wouldn't have to go to summer school. He and Charlie could go out to Colorado together to work on that dude ranch. He would be through with Latin forever. The Latin grade would never pull his average down again. Everything would be all right. Everything would be fine. All he would have to do would be to copy that one paragraph. Everyone cheated. Maybe not at V.P.S. But in other schools they bragged about it. . . . Everyone cheated in one way or another. Why should that one passage ruin everything? Who cared what problems the Romans had!

P.S. glanced over at Jumbo. Jumbo was chewing on his pencil eraser as he worked on the examination. Dr. Fairfax was still reading his newspaper. P.S. felt his heart beat faster. It began beating so hard that he was certain Jumbo could hear it. P.S. gently raised his desk top and pretended to feel around for a pencil. He let his blue book slide halfway off his desk so it leaned in his lap. Then he slid the translation under the blue book and slid the blue book and notes back onto his desk. He was certain that everyone had seen him — that everyone knew he was about to cheat. He slowly raised his eyes to look at Dr. Fairfax, who went on reading. P.S. covered part of the notes with his examination and began to copy the rest into his blue book. He could feel the heat in his cheeks, the dryness in his mouth. *Dear God . . . God, please don't let them catch me! . . . Please!*

He changed the smooth translation into a rough one as he copied, so that it would match his other translation.

From these things the army was taught the nature of the place and how the slope of the hill and the necessity of the time demanded more than one plan and order for the art of war. Different legions, some in one part, others in another, fought the enemy. And the view was obstructed by very thick hedges. Sure support could not be placed, nor could it be seen what work would be necessary in which part, nor could all the commands be administered by one man. Therefore, against so much unfairness of things, various consequences ensued.

He put down his pencil and looked around the study hall. No one was watching. P.S. carefully slid the translation back into his desk. He looked to see if the translation gave him any words that might help him on the rest of the examination. His heart was still beating wildly in his chest, and his hands shook. He licked his lips and concentrated on behaving normally. *It's over. . . . It's over. . . . I've cheated, but it's all over and no one said anything!*

He began to relax.

Fifteen minutes later, Dr. Fairfax stood up at his desk, looked at the electric clock, then down at his pocket watch. He cleared his throat and said, "Stop!"

Several student groaned. The rest gathered up their pencils and pens.

"Make certain you have written out the pledge in full and signed it," Dr. Fairfax said.

P.S. felt the physical pain of fear again. He opened his blue book and wrote, "I pledge on my honor as a gentleman that I have neither given nor received unauthorized assistance on this examination." He hesitated; then he signed his name.

"Place your examination inside your blue book," Dr. Fairfax continued. "Make certain that you put your name on your blue book. . . . Baylor? If you and, uh, Ferguson and Showalter will be good enough to pick up the examinations, the rest of you may go. And, um, gentlemen, your grades will be posted on the front door of my office no sooner than forty-eight hours from now. In point of fact, any attempt to solicit your grade any sooner than that will result in bad temper on my part and greater severity in the marking of papers. Are there any questions? . . . If not, gentlemen, dismissed."

The students stood up and stretched. An immediate, excited hum of voices filled the study hall. P.S. looked down at his exam paper. He slid it into his blue book and left it on his desk.

Charlie was waiting at the door of the study hall. "Well, P.S., how'd the brain do?"

"You know it's bad luck to talk about an exam before the grades are posted."

"I know. I'm just asking how you think you did."

"I don't know," P.S. said.

"Well, well, I mean, do you think you passed?"

"I don't know!"

"Whooey!" Charlie whistled. "And you called *me* a grump!"

They walked down the stairs together. At the bottom, Charlie asked P.S. if he was going to go to lunch.

"No, I don't think so," P.S. said. "I'm not feeling so well. I think I'll lie down for a while. I'll see ya."

"Sure," Charlie said. "See ya."

In his cubicle in Memorial Hall, P.S. took off his

lucky exam tie. He put his silver dollar back onto his bookcase. He reached inside the hollow copy of *Gulliver's Travels* for the pack of cigarettes he kept there. Then he walked down the corridor to the bathroom, stepped into one of the stalls and locked the door. He lit the cigarette and leaned his forehead against the cool green marble divider. He was sick with fear and dread. *It's over! It's all over!* he said, trying to calm himself. He did not like the new knowledge he had of himself. He was a cheater. He rolled his forehead back and forth against the stone, pressing his forehead into it, hurting himself. P.S. had broken the Honor Code of the school, and he was scared.

I shouldn't have cheated! What if someone had seen me! I shouldn't have cheated! Maybe somebody did see me. . . . Maybe Dr. Fairfax will know I cheated when he sees my exam. . . . Maybe somebody will check my desk after the exam and find the copy of the translation. . . . I cheated. Damn it, I cheated! Stupid, damned fool. . . . What if somebody finds out! . . . Maybe I should turn myself in. . . . I wonder if they'd kick me out if I turned myself in. . . . It would prove that I really am honest, I just made a mistake, that's all. . . . I'll tell them I couldn't help it. . . . Maybe they'll just give me a reprimand.

But P.S. knew that if he turned himself in, they would tell his parents he had cheated, so what good would that do? His father would be just as angry. Even more so, since Wilkinsons don't cheat, either. P.S. knew how ashamed his father would make him feel. His father would have to tell others that P.S. had cheated. It was a part of the Southern tradition. "My son has disgraced me. It is better that you hear it from me than somebody else." His father would do something like that. And having other people know he had cheated would be too much shame to bear. And even if he did turn himself in, the school would make him take another exam. . . . And he'd flunk that one, too. . . . He knew it. . . . *Oh, God, what am I going to do?*

If he didn't turn himself in and no one had seen him, then who would know? He would never cheat again. If he could just get away with it this one time. Then everything would be okay. Nobody need ever know — except himself. And P.S. knew he would never be able to forget that he had cheated.

Maybe if he turned himself in, it would be better in the long run. *What long run? What ·the heck kind of long run will I have if I turn myself in? Everybody in the school will know I cheated, whether I turn myself in or not. . . . They won't remember me for turning myself in. . . . They'll remember that I cheated in the first place. . . .*

P.S. wanted to cry, but he couldn't. He dropped the cigarette into the toilet and flushed it down. Then he went over to the sink and rinsed his mouth out. He had some chewing gum in his room; that would cover the smell of his smoking. He looked at himself in the mirror. He couldn't see any change since this morning, and yet he felt so different. He looked at his eyes to see if there were lines under them now. *What shall I do?* he asked his reflection. *What the heck shall I do?* He turned on the cold water and rinsed his face. He dried himself on a towel someone had left behind, and walked back down the corridor to his room. He brushed aside the curtain, entered the cubicle, and stopped frozen with fear. Mabrey, the head monitor, was sitting on P.S.'s bed.

"Wilkinson," Mabrey said, "would you mind coming with me? Just outside for a few minutes."

"What about?"

Mabrey got up from the bed. "Come on, P.S."

"What . . . what do you want me for?"

"We want to talk to you."

We! WE! P.S. picked up his jacket and started to put it on.

"You won't need your jacket," Mabrey said, as he walked into the corridor.

"It doesn't matter, I'll wear it anyway."

P.S. followed Mabrey out of the dormitory. *I didn't have a chance to turn myself in,* he thought. *I didn't have a chance to choose. . . .*

"You think you'll make the varsity baseball team next year?" Mabrey asked.

"I don't know," P.S. said. *What is he talking about baseball for?*

The new boy who had wakened P.S. passed them on the walk. He said hello to both Mabrey and P.S. He received no answer and shrugged.

Mabrey and P.S. took the path to the headmaster's office. P.S. could feel the enormous weight of the fear building up inside him again. Mabrey opened the door for P.S. and ushered him into the headmaster's waiting room. Nelson, a pale, fat-faced senior, was sitting there alone. He was the secretary of the Honor Committee. P.S. had always hated him. The other members of the Honor Committee were Mabrey, the vice-president; Linus Hendricks, the president; Mr. Seaton, the headmaster; and Dr. Fairfax, who served as faculty adviser. Mabrey motioned that P.S. was to sit down in the chair facing the others — the only straight-backed wooden chair in the room. Every now and then, Nelson would look up at P.S. and shake his head. The door to the headmaster's office opened and Mr. Seaton came out, followed by Linus Hendricks, Dr. Fairfax, and — *Lord, what is Jumbo*

*doing here! Don't tell me he cheated too! He was
sitting right next to me!* Jumbo walked out of the
room without looking at P.S.

Linus Hendricks waited for the others to seat
themselves, then he sat down himself and faced
P.S. "Well, P.S., I imagine you know why you're
here."

P.S. looked at Hendricks. Hendricks was the captain of the football team. He and Mabrey were
the two most important undergraduates in the
school.

"Well, P.S.?" Hendricks repeated.

"Yes, sir," P.S. said.

He could feel them all staring at him. He
looked down at his hands folded in his lap. He
could see clearly every line in his thumb knuckle.
He could see the dirt caught under the corner of
his fingernail, and the small blue vein running
across the knuckle.

He looked up to Dr. Fairfax. He wanted to tell
him not to worry. He wanted to tell him that he
was sorry, so very sorry.

The headmaster, Mr. Seaton, was a young man.
He had just become the headmaster of V.P.S. this
year. He liked the students, and the students liked
him. He was prematurely bald, and smiled a lot.
He had a very young and pretty wife, and some of
the students were in love with her and fought to sit
at her table in the dining room. Mr. Seaton liked
to play tennis. He would play the students and bet
his dessert that he would win. And most of the
time he would lose, and the students were enor-
mously pleased to see the headmaster of the school
have to get up from the table and pay his bets.
Mr. Seaton would walk very quickly accross the
dining hall, his bald head bent to hide his smile.
He would swoop up to a table, drop the dessert —
and depart, like a bombing airplane. P.S. could

tell that the headmaster was distressed he had cheated.

Linus Hendricks crossed his legs and sank back into the deep leather armchair. Mabrey and Nelson leaned forward as though they were going to charge P.S.

"P.S.," Hendricks said. "You're here this afternoon because the Honor Committee has reason to suspect that you may have cheated on the Latin exam this morning. We must ask you whether or not this is true."

P.S. raised his head and looked at Hendricks. Hendricks was wearing a bright striped tie. P.S. concentrated on the stripes. Thick black, thin white, medium green, thin white, and thick black.

"P.S., did you, or did you not, cheat on the Latin examination?"

P.S. nodded.

"Yes or no, P.S.?" Hendricks asked.

P.S. no longer felt anything. He was numb with misery.

"Yes," he said, in a small, tired voice. "Yes, I cheated on the examination. But I was going to turn myself in. I was going to turn myself in, I swear I was."

"If you were going to turn yourself in, why didn't you?" Nelson asked.

"I couldn't . . . I couldn't yet. . . ." P.S. looked at Dr. Fairfax. "I'm sorry, sir. I'm terribly sorry. . . ." P.S. began to cry. "I'm so ashamed. . . . Oh, God . . ." P.S. tried to stop crying. He couldn't. The tears stung his eyes. One tear slipped into the inside of his glasses and puddled across the bottom of the lens. He reached into his back pocket for a handkerchief, but he had forgotten to bring one. He started to pull out his shirttail, and decided he'd better not. He wiped his face with the side of his hand.

Mr. Seaton walked over to P.S. and gave him his handkerchief. The headmaster rested his hand on P.S.'s shoulder. "Why, P.S.? Why did you cheat?"

P.S. couldn't answer.

"P.S., you were the last boy I expected this of. Why did you feel you had to cheat on this exam?"

"I don't know, sir."

"But P.S., you must have had some reason."

Nelson said, "Answer the headmaster when he's asking you a question, Wilkinson."

P.S. looked up at him with such loathing that Nelson looked away.

Mr. Seaton crouched down next to P.S. "You must have been aware of the penalty for cheating."

P.S. nodded.

"Then why, in heaven's name, did you risk expulsion to pass the examination?"

"Sir — sir, I flunked Latin last year, sir. I knew I'd flunk it this year, too. I — I knew I couldn't pass the Latin exam ever."

"But why did you *cheat?*"

"Because . . . because, sir, I had to pass the exam."

The headmaster ran his hand across his forehead. "P.S., I'm not trying to trick you, I'm only trying to understand why you did this thing. Why did you bring the notes into the exam with you?"

"Sir, Mr. Seaton, I didn't bring the notes in, they were in my desk. If they hadn't been, I wouldn't be here. I didn't want to cheat. I didn't *mean* to cheat. I — it was just the only way I could pass the exam."

Nelson rested his pudgy arms on the sides of his leather armchair and looked at the headmaster and then back to P.S. Then he said, "Wilkinson, you have been in V.P.S. for two years. You must be familiar, I imagine, with the Honor Code.

In fact, in your study hall there is a small wooden plaque above the proctor's desk. On it is carved the four points of the Honor Code: 'I will not lie. I will not steal. I will not cheat. I will report anyone I see doing so.' You are familiar with them, aren't you?"

"Of course I'm familiar with them," P.S. said impatiently.

"Why did you think you were so much better than everyone else that you could ignore it?"

"I don't think I'm better than everyone else, Nelson," P.S. said.

"Well, you sure aren't! The others don't cheat." Nelson sat back again, very satisfied with himself.

Dr. Fairfax came from behind the chairs and stood next to P.S. "Unless you hold your tongue, Nelson — unless you hold your tongue, I shall personally escort you out of here."

"But, sir," Nelson whined. "I'm only trying to — "

"SHUT UP!" Dr. Fairfax roared. He returned to the back of the room.

Mr. Seaton spoke again. "P.S., if you had flunked this exam, you would have been able to take another. Perhaps you would have passed the re-examination. Most boys do."

"I wouldn't have, sir," P.S. said. "I just cannot do Latin. You could have given me fifty examinations, sir. And I don't mean any disrespect, but I would have flunked all fifty of them."

Mabrey asked the headmaster if he could speak. Then he turned to P.S. "P.S., we — all of us have been tempted at some time or another to cheat. All of us have either resisted the temptation or, perhaps, we were lucky enough to get away with it. I think that what we want to know is what *made* you cheat. Just having to pass the exam isn't

enough. I know you, P.S. I may know you better
than anyone in the room, because I've shared
the same floor in the dorm with you for this year.
And we were on the same floor when you were a
toad. You're not the kind who cheats unless he has
a damn good — " Mabrey glanced over at the
headmaster. "Excuse me, sir. I didn't mean to
swear."

The headmaster nodded and indicated that
Mabrey was to continue.

"What I mean is this, P.S. I know you don't care
how high your grade is, just so long as you keep
out of trouble. . . . You're one of the most popular boys in your class. Everybody likes you. Why
would you throw all of this over, just to pass a
Latin exam?"

"I don't know. I don't know. . . . I had to pass
the exam. If I flunked it again, my father would
kill me."

"What do you mean he would 'kill' you?" Mr.
Seaton asked.

"Oh, nothing, sir. I mean — I don't mean he
would hurt me. He would just — Oh, I don't
know how to explain it to you. If I flunked the
exam again, he'd just make me feel so, I
don't know . . . *ashamed* . . . so terrible. I just
couldn't take it again."

There was a moment of silence in the room.
P.S. began to cry again. He could tell the headmaster still didn't understand why he had cheated.
He looked down at his hands again. With his in-
dex finger he traced the veins that crossed the back
of his hand. He looked over at the wooden arm
of his straight-backed chair. He could see the little
drops of moisture where his hand had squeezed
the arm of the chair. He could make out every
grain of wood, every worn spot. He took off his
glasses and rubbed his eyes. He tried taking deep

breaths, but each time his breath would be choked off.

Hendricks cleared his throat and recrossed his legs. "P.S.," he said, "we have your examination here. You signed your name to the pledge at the end of the exam. You swore on your honor that you had not cheated." Hendricks paused. P.S. knew what he was driving at.

"If I hadn't signed my name to the pledge, you would have known I had cheated right away," P.S. explained. "I didn't want to break my honor again. I was going to turn myself in, honest I was."

"You didn't, though," Nelson said.

"I would have!" P.S. said. But he still wasn't sure whether he would have or not. He knew he never would be certain.

"So, we've got you on lying and cheating," Nelson said. "How do we know you haven't stolen too?"

Dr. Fairfax grabbed the lapels of Nelson's jacket, pulled him out of the chair, and pushed him out of the room. The old man closed the door and leaned against it. He wiped his brow and said, "Mr. Seaton, sir, I trust you won't find fault with my actions. That young Nelson has a tendency to bother me. In point of fact, he irritates me intensely."

P.S. looked gratefully at Dr. Fairfax. The old man smiled sadly. Mabrey was talking quietly to Hendricks. Mr. Seaton sat down in Nelson's chair and turned to P.S. "I know this is a difficult question. Would you — would you have turned Jumbo in had you seen him cheating?"

P.S. felt the blood drain from his face. *So Jumbo turned me in! . . . Jumbo saw me! . . . Sitting next to me all year! . . . Jumbo turned me in! Why?*

He looked up at the others. They were all waiting for his answer. He had the most curious feeling of aloofness, of coldness. If he said yes, that he would have turned Jumbo in, it would be a lie, and he knew it. If he answered yes, it would please the headmaster, though. Because it would mean that P.S still had faith in the school system. If he said no, he wouldn't have turned Jumbo in, it would be as good as admitting that he would not obey the fourth part of the Honor Code — "I will report anyone I see doing so." He waited a moment and then answered, "I don't know. I don't know whether I would have turned Jumbo in or not."

"Thank you very much, P.S.," the headmaster said.

P.S. could tell that Mr. Seaton was disappointed in his answer.

"Gentlemen, do you have any further questions you would like to ask Wilkinson?"

"Nothing, sir," Hendricks answered.

The headmaster looked over at Dr. Fairfax, who shook his head. "Well, then, P.S., if you don't mind, we'd like you to sit in my office until we call for you."

P.S. got up and started for the door.

"Have you had any lunch?" Dr. Fairfax asked.

"No, sir. But I'm not very hungry."

"I'll have Mrs. Burdick bring in some milk and cookies."

"Thank you, sir."

The door opened and P.S. stood up as Mr. Seaton walked over to his desk and eased himself into the swivel chair. P.S. had been sitting alone in the headmaster's office for several hours.

"Sit down, please," the headmaster said. He picked up a wooden pencil and began to roll it back and forth between his palms. P.S. could hear the click of the pencil as it rolled across the headmaster's ring. Mr. Seaton laid the pencil aside and rubbed his cheek. His hand moved up the side of his face and began to massage his temples. Then he looked at P.S. and said, "The Honor Committee has decided that you must leave the school. The penalty for cheating at V.P.S. is immediate expulsion. There cannot be any exceptions."

P.S. took a deep breath and pushed himself back into the soft leather seat. Then he dropped his hands into his lap and slumped. He was beyond crying; there was nothing left to cry about.

"Your father is waiting for you in the other room," Mr. Seaton said. "I've asked him to wait outside for a few minutes, because I want to speak to you alone. I want you to understand why the school had to make the decision to expel you. The school — this school — is only as good as its honor system. And the honor system is only as good as the students who live by it."

P.S. cleared his throat and looked down at his fingernails. He wished the headmaster wouldn't talk about it. He knew why the school had to expel him. It was done. It was over with. What good would it do to talk about it?

"The honor system, since it is based on mutual trust and confidence, no doubt makes it easier for some students to cheat," the headmaster said. "I am not so naïve as to believe that there aren't any boys who cheat here. Unfortunately, our honor system makes it easy for them to do so. These boys have not been caught. Perhaps they will never be caught. But I feel that it was far better for you to have been caught right away, P.S., because you are not a cheater. Notice that I said you *are* not a cheater instead of you *were* not a cheater. . . .

Yes, you cheated this one time. I do not need to ask whether you cheated before. I know you haven't. I know also that you will not cheat again. I was frankly stunned when I heard that you had cheated on Dr. Fairfax's examination. You were the last boy I would have expected to cheat. I am still not entirely satisfied by the reasons you gave for cheating. I suppose a person never is. Maybe it is impossible to give reasons for such an act." Mr. Seaton began massaging his temple again. "P.S., the most difficult thing that you must try to understand is that Jumbo did the right thing. Jumbo was correct in turning you in."

P.S. stiffened in the chair. "Yes, sir," he said.

"If no one reported infractions, we would have no Honor Code. The Code would be obeyed only when it was convenient to obey it. It would be given lip service. The whole system would break down. The school would become just another private school, instead of the respected and loved institution it now is. Put yourself in Jumbo's shoes for a moment. You and Jumbo are friends — *believe me,* you are friends. If you had heard what Jumbo said about you in here, and how it hurt him to turn you in, you would know what a good friend Jumbo is. You have been expelled for cheating. You will not be here next fall. But Jumbo will be. Jumbo will stay on at V.P.S., and the other students will know that he was the one who turned you in. When I asked you whether you would have turned Jumbo in, you said that you didn't know. You and I both know from your answer that you wouldn't have turned Jumbo in. Perhaps the schoolboy code is still stronger in you than the Honor Code. Many students feel stronger about the schoolboy code than the Honor Code. No one likes to turn in a friend. A lot of boys who don't know any better, a lot of your friends, will never forgive Jumbo. It will be plenty tough for him. Just as it is tough on anybody who does his duty. I think — I honestly think that Jumbo has done you a favor. I'm not going to suggest that you be grateful to him. Not yet. That would be as ridiculous as my saying something as trite as 'Someday you will be able to look back on this and laugh.' . . . P.S., you will *never* be able to look back on this and laugh. But you may be able to understand." The headmaster looked at his wristwatch and then said, "I'm going to leave you alone with your father for a few minutes; then I suggest you go back to your room and pack. The other students won't be back in the dormitories yet, so you can be alone." He got up from behind the desk. P.S. rose also. He looked down at the milk and cookies Mrs. Burdick had left him. There was a half a glass of milk and three cookies left.

The headmaster looked at P.S. for a moment and then he said, "I'm sorry you have been expelled, P.S. You were a good student here. One of the most popular boys in your class. You will leave behind a great many good friends."

"Thank you, sir," P.S. said.

"I'll see you before you and your father leave."

"Yes, sir."

The headmaster walked into the waiting room. P.S. could hear Dr. Fairfax talking, and then his father. The door closed, and P.S. sat down to wait for his father. He could feel the fear building up inside of him again. He did not know what to say to his father. What could he say? He sipped the last of the milk as the door opened. P.S. put down the glass and stood up.

Stewart Wilkinson closed the door behind him and looked at his son. He wanted to hold the boy and comfort him, but Phil looked so solid, so strong, standing there. Why isn't he crying, he wondered, and then he told himself that he wouldn't have cried, either; that the boy had plenty of time to cry; that he would never cry in front of his father again. He tried to think of something to say. He knew that he often was clumsy in his relations with Phil, and said the wrong thing, and he wondered whether he had been that sensitive at his son's age. He looked down at the plate of cookies and the empty milk glass.

"Where did you get the milk and cookies, son?"

"Mrs. Burdick brought them to me, sir."

He never calls me "Dad" now, Stewart Wilkinson said to himself. Always "sir" . . . My own son calls me "sir." . . .

"Did you thank her?"

"Yes, sir."

Stewart Wilkinson walked over to the couch next to his son and sat down. The boy remained standing.

"Phil, son, sit down, please."

"Yes, sir."

Looking at his son, Stewart Wilkinson could not understand why they had grown apart during the last few years. He had always remained close to his father. Why wasn't it the same between him and the boy who sat so stiff beside him, so still in spite of the horror he must have gone through during the past few hours?

"I'm sorry, sir."

"Yes . . . yes, son, I know you are. . . . I'm terribly sorry myself. Sorry for you . . . Mr. Seaton told me another boy turned you in, is that right?"

P.S. nodded.

"He also told me that he believes you would

have turned yourself in had you been given enough time."

"I don't know whether I would have or not. I never had a chance to find out."

"I think you would have. I think you would have."

He waited for his son to say something; then, realizing there was nothing the boy could say, he spoke again. "I was talking to Dr. Fairfax outside — you knew he was my Latin teacher too?"

"Yes, sir."

"We always used to be able to tell when the first day of spring came, because Dr. Fairfax put on his white linen suit."

"Yes, sir."

"At any rate, that man thinks very highly of you, Phil. He is very upset that you had to be expelled. I hope you will speak to him before we go. He's a good man to have on your side."

"I want to speak to him."

"Phil . . . Phil. . . ." Stewart Wilkinson thought for a minute. He wanted so desperately what he said to be the right thing to say. "Phil, I know that I am partly responsible for what has happened. I must have in some way pressured you into it. I wanted your marks to be high. I wanted you to get the best education that you could. V.P.S. isn't the best school in the country, but it's a damn fine one. It's a school that has meant a lot to our family. But that doesn't matter so much. I mean, that part of it is all over with. I'm sorry that you cheated, because I know you're not the cheating kind. I'm also sorry because you are going to have to face the family and get it over with. This is going to be tough. But they'll understand. I doubt that there is any of us who have never cheated in one way or another. But it will make

them very proud of you if you can go see them and
look them in the eye."

He picked up one of the cookies and began to
bite little pieces out of the edge. Then he shook
his head sadly, in the gesture P.S. knew so well.
"Ah, son, it's so terrible that you have to learn
these lessons when you are young. I know that you
don't want me to feel sorry for you, but I can't
help it. I'm not angry with you. I'm a little disappointed, perhaps, but I can understand it, I think.
I suppose I must appear as an ogre to you at times.
But Phil, I — if I'm tough with you, it's just because I'm trying to help you. Maybe I'm too
tough." Stewart Wilkinson looked over at his son.
He saw that the boy was watching him. He felt a
little embarrassed to have revealed so much of
himself before his son. But he knew they were
alike. He knew that Phil was really his son. They
already spoke alike. Already laughed at the same
sort of things, appreciated the same things. Their
tastes were pretty much the same. He knew that,
if anything, he was too much like the boy to be
able to help him. And also that the problem was
the boy's own, and that he would resent his father's interfering.

"Phil, I'll go speak with Mr. Seaton for a little
while, and then I'll come on over and help you
pack. If you'd like, I'll pack for you and you can
sit in the car."

"No, that's all right, sir. I'll pack. I mean, most
of the stuff is packed up already. I'll meet you over
there."

Stewart Wilkinson rose with his son. Again he
wanted to hold the boy, to show him how much
he loved him.

"I'll be through packing in a few minutes. I'll
meet you in my room," P.S. said.

"Fine, son."

Together they carried the footlocker down the staircase of Memorial Hall. P.S. stopped at the door, balanced the footlocker with one hand, then pulled the heavy door open. The door swung back before they could get through. Stewart Wilkinson stumbled and P.S. said, "I'm sorry."

They carried the footlocker across the small patch of lawn between the front of Memorial Hall and the main drive and slid the footlocker into the back of the station wagon.

"How much more is there, son?"

"A couple of small boxes, some books, and a couple of pictures."

Stewart Wilkinson pulled a silk handkerchief out of his back pocket and wiped his brow. "You think we can get all of them in one more trip?"

"I think so, sir. At least, we can try."

They turned back toward the dormitory. Stewart Wilkinson rested his hand on his son's shoulder as they walked back across the lawn.

"Phil, Mr. Seaton told me that he thinks he might be able to get you into Hotchkiss. How does that sound to you?"

"It's a funny name for a school."

"Hotchkiss, funny? Why?"

"I don't know, it just sounds funny."

"Well, do you think you'd like to go there?"

"Sure, I mean I don't know. I haven't given it much thought."

Stewart Wilkinson laughed. "I guess you haven't."

The boy looked worriedly at his father for a moment. He wondered whether his father was making fun of him. And then he saw the humor in his remark and laughed too.

They brought the last of the boxes down from

the room and slid them into the car and closed the tailgate.

"Did you get a chance to talk to Dr. Fairfax?"

"Yes, sir. He came by the room while I was packing."

"What did he say?"

"I don't know. I mean he was sorry I was going and all that, but he said I'd get along fine anywhere and that it wasn't the end of the world."

"Did he say 'in point of fact'?"

"Yeah," P.S. laughed. "He said, 'Well, boy, you'll do all right. In point of fact, you have nothing to worry about.' I really like old Doc Fairfax."

They went around the side of the car and climbed in.

"Anythi..g you've forgotten? Books out of the library, equipment in the gym? Anybody special you want to see before we go home?"

"No, Dad, thanks, that's all — Hey, wait a minute, could you, Dad?" P.S. got out of the car. "It's Charlie — Charlie Merritt. I'd like to say goodbye to him."

"Sure, son, take your time."

The two boys spoke together for a moment, standing in the road; then they shook hands. Stewart Wilkinson turned off the engine and watched as the boys walked back to the road toward him. As they drew near, he got out of the station wagon.

"Dad, this is Charlie Merritt. . . . Charlie, you remember my father."

"Yes, sir. How are you, sir?"

"Fine, thank you, Charlie."

"Sir, Mr. Wilkinson, I'm sorry about P.S. getting kicked out and all."

Stewart Wilkinson nodded.

"He's just sorry because I won't be around to borrow his toothpaste any more. He likes to lend it to me because I always roll it from the top and lose the cap."

P.S. and Charlie laughed.

"Hey, P.S.?" Charlie said. "Does this mean you're not going to have to work off the five demerits Doc Fairfax gave us this morning?"

"What did you two get five demerits for?" Stewart Wilkinson asked.

"We were talking about the exam," P.S. said.

Father and son looked at each other, and then P.S. turned away. It was clear that he was thinking about the exam and his cheating again. And then the boy took a deep breath and smiled. "You know? It's funny," he said. "I mean, it seems that exam took place so long ago. . . . Well, Charlie," P.S. stuck out his hand and Charlie took it, "well, I guess we'd better get going. I'll see you around. Okay?"

"Sure, P.S.," Charlie said.

The two boys shook hands again solemnly. Then Charlie shook hands with P.S.'s father. P.S. and Stewart Wilkinson got back into the station wagon.

Charlie walked around to P.S.'s window. "Hey, P.S.? Make sure you let me hear from you this summer, okay?"

"Sure, Charlie. Take care of yourself."

They drove around the school drive, by the Wilkinson Memorial Library and the Sadler Gymnasium and then they turned down the slight hill toward the Breastworks, and as they passed through the ornate, wrought-iron gate P.S. began to cry.

19/YOUNG MAN AXELBROD

The cottonwood is a tree of a slovenly and plebeian habit. Its wooly wisps turn gray the lawns and engender neighborhood hostilities about our town. Yet it is a mighty tree, a refuge and an inspiration; the sun flickers in its towering foliage, whence the tattoo of locusts enlivens our dusty summer afternoons. From the wheat country out to the sagebrush plains between the buttes and the Yellowstone, it is the cottonwood that keeps a little grateful shade for sweating homesteaders.

In Joralemon, we called Knute Axelbrod "Old Cottonwood." As a matter of fact, the name was derived not so much from the quality of the man as from the wide grove about his gaunt white house and red barn. He made a comely row of trees on each side of the country road, so that a humble, daily sort of man, driving beneath them in his lumber wagon, might fancy himself lord of a private avenue. And at sixty-five, Knute was like one of his own cottonwoods, his roots deep in the soil, his trunk weathered by rain and blizzard and baking August noons, his crown spread to the wide horizon of day and the enormous sky of a prairie night.

This immigrant was an American even in

speech. Save for a weakness about his j's and w's, he spoke the twangy Yankee English of the land. He was the more American because, in his native Scandinavia, he had dreamed of America as a land of light. Always, through disillusion and weariness, he beheld America as the world's nursery for justice, for broad, fair towns, and eager talk; and always he kept a young soul that dared to desire beauty.

As a lad, Knute Axelbrod had wished to be a famous scholar, to learn the ease of foreign tongues, the romance of history, to unfold in the graciousness of the wise books. When he first came to America he worked in a sawmill all day and studied all evening. He mastered enough book learning to teach district school for two terms; then when he was only eighteen, a great-hearted pity for faded Lena Wesselius moved him to marry her. Gay enough, doubtless, was their hike by prairie schooner to new farm lands, but Knute was promptly caught in a net of poverty and family. From eighteen to fifty-eight he was always snatching children away from death or the farm away from mortgages.

He had to be content — and generously content he was — with the secondhand glory of his children's success and, for himself, with pilfered hours of reading — that reading of big, thick, dismal volumes of history and economics which the lone, mature learner chooses. Without ever losing his desire for strange cities and the dignity of towers, he stuck to his farm. He acquired a half-section, free from debt, fertile, well-stocked, adorned with a cement silo, a chicken-run, a new windmill. He became comfortable, secure, and then he was ready, it seemed, to die; for at sixty-three his work was done, and he was unneeded and alone.

His wife was dead. His sons had scattered afar,

one a dentist in Fargo, another a farmer in the
Golden Valley. He had turned over his farm to his
daughter and son-in-law. They had begged him to
live with them, but Knute refused.

"No," he said, "you must learn to stand on your
own feet. I will not give you the farm. You pay me
four hundred dollars a year rent, and I live on that
and vatch you from my hill."

On a rise beside the lone cottonwood which
he loved best of all his trees, Knute built a tar-
paper shack, and he "bached it": cooked his meals,
made his bed — sometimes sat in the sun, read
many books from the Joralemon library, and began to feel that he was free of the yoke of citizen-
ship which he had borne all his life.

For hours at a time he sat on a backless kitchen
chair before the shack, a wide-shouldered man,
white-bearded, motionless; a seer despite his gro-
tesquely baggy trousers, his collarless shirt. He
looked across the miles of stubble to the steeple
of the Jack-rabbit Forks church and meditated
upon the uses of life. At first he could not break the
rigidity of habit. He rose at five, found work in
cleaning his cabin and cultivating his garden, had
dinner exactly at twelve, and went to bed by after-
glow. But little by little he discovered that he
could be irregular without being arrested. He
stayed abed till seven or even eight. He got a large,
deliberate, tortoise-shell cat, and played games
with it; let it lap milk upon the table, called it the
Princess, and confided to it that he had a "sneak-
ing idee" that men were fools to work so hard.
Around this coatless old man, his stained waistcoat
flapping about a huge torso, in a shanty of rumpled bed and pine table covered with sheets of
daubed newspaper, hovered all the passionate aspiration of youth and the dreams of ancient
beauty.

He began to take long walks by night. In his necessitous life, night had ever been a period of heavy slumber in close rooms. Now he discovered the mystery of the dark; saw the prairies wide-flung and misty beneath the moon; heard the voices of grass and cottonwoods and drowsy birds. He tramped for miles. His toots were dew-soaked, but he did not heed. He stopped upon hillocks, shyly threw wide his arms, and stood worshiping the naked, slumbering land.

These excursions he tried to keep secret, but they were bruited abroad. Neighbors, good, decent fellows with no nonsense about walking in the dew at night, when they were returning late from town, drunk, lashing their horses, and flinging whisky bottles from their racing democrat wagons, saw him, and they spread the tiding that Old Cottonwood was "getting nutty since he give up his farm to that son-in-law of his and retired. Seen the old codger wandering around at midnight. Wish I had his chance to sleep. Wouldn't catch me out in the night air."

Any rural community from Todd Center to Seringapatam is resentful of any person who varies from its standard and is morbidly fascinated by any hint of madness. The countryside began to spy on Knute Axelbrod, to ask him questions, and to stare from the road at his shack. He was sensitively aware of it, and inclined to be surly to inquisitive acquaintances. Doubtless that was the beginning of his great pilgrimage.

As a part of the general wild license of his new life — really, he once roared at that startled cat, the Princess, "By gollies! I ain't going to brush my teeth tonight. All my life I've brushed 'em, and always vanted to skip a time vunce" — Knute took considerable pleasure in degenerating in his taste in scholarship. He wilfully declined to finish *The*

Conquest of Mexico, and began to read light novels borrowed from the Joralemon library. So he
rediscovered the lands of dancing and light wines,
which all his life he had desired. Some economics
and history he did read, but every evening he
would stretch out in his buffalo-horn chair, his feet
on the cot and the Princess in his lap, and invade
Zenda or fall in love with Trilby.

Among the novels, he chanced upon a highly
optimistic story of Yale in which a worthy young
man "earned his way through" college, stroked
the crew, won Phi Beta Kappa, and had the most
entertaining, yet moral, conversations on or adja-
cent to "the dear old fence."

As a result of this chronicle, at about three
o'clock one morning when Knute Axelbrod was
sixty-four years of age, he decided that he would
go to college! All his life he had wanted to. Why
not do it?

When he awoke in the morning he was not so
sure about it as when he had gone to sleep. He
saw himself as ridiculous, a ponderous, oldish
man among clean-limbed youths, like a dusty cottonwood among silver birches. But for months he
wrestled and played with that idea of a great pilgrimage to the Mount of Muses; for he really supposed all college students, except for the wealthy
idlers, burned to acquire learning. He pictured
Harvard and Yale and Princeton as ancient groves
set with marble temples, before which large
groups of Grecian youths talked gently about
astronomy and good government. In his picture
they never cut classes or ate.

With a longing for music and books and graciousness such as the most ambitious boy could
never comprehend, this thick-faced prairie farmer
dedicated himself to beauty, and defied the uncon-
querable power of approaching old age. He sent

for college catalogues and schoolbooks, and diligently began to prepare himself for college.

He found Latin irregular verbs and the whimsicalities of algebra fiendish. They had nothing to do with actual life as he had lived it. But he mastered them; he studied twelve hours a day, as once he plodded through eighteen hours a day in the hayfield. With history and English literature he had comparatively little trouble; already he knew much of them from his recreative reading. From German neighbors he had picked up enough Plattdeutsch to make German easy. The trick of study began to come back to him from his small schoolteacher of forty-five years before. He began to believe that he could really put it through. He kept assuring himself that in college, with rare and sympathetic instructors to help him, there would not be this baffling search, this nervous strain.

But the unreality of the things he studied did disillusion him, and he tired of his new game. He kept it up chiefly because all his life he had kept up onerous labor without any taste for it. Toward the autumn of the second year of his eccentric life he no longer believed that he would ever go to college.

Then a busy little grocer stopped him on the street in Joralemon and quizzed him about his studies, to the delight of the informal club which always loafs at the corner of the hotel.

Knute was silent, but dangerously angry. He remembered just in time how he had once laid wrathful hands upon a hired man, and somehow the man's collarbone had been broken. He turned away and walked home, seven miles, still boiling. He picked up the Princess, and, with her mewing on his shoulder, tramped out again to enjoy the sunset.

He stopped at a reedy slough. He gazed at a hopping plover without seeing it. He plucked at his beard. Suddenly he cried:

"I am going to college. It opens next week. I t'ink that I can pass the examinations."

Two days later he had moved the Princess and his sticks of furniture to his son-in-law's house, had bought a new slouch hat, a celluloid collar, and a solemn suit of black, had wrestled with God in prayer through all of a star-clad night, and had taken the train for Minneapolis, on the way to New Haven.

While he stared out of the car window, Knute was warning himself that the millionaires' sons would make fun of him. Perhaps they would haze him. He bade himself avoid all these sons of Belial and cleave to his own people, those who "earned their way through."

At Chicago he was afraid with a great fear of the lightning flashes that the swift crowds made on his retina, the batteries of ranked motorcars that charged at him. He prayed, and ran for his train to New York. He came at last to New Haven.

Not with gibing rudeness, but with politely quizzical eyebrows, Yale received him, led him through entrance examinations, which, after sweaty plowing with the pen, he barely passed, and found for him a roommate. The roommate was a large-browed, soft, white grub named Ray Gribble, who had been teaching school in New England, and seemed chiefly to desire college training so that he might make more money as a teacher. Ray Gribble was a hustler; he instantly got work tutoring the awkward son of a steel man, and for board he waited on table.

He was Knute's chief acquaintance. Knute tried

to fool himself into thinking he liked the grub, but Ray couldn't keep his damp hands off the old man's soul. He had the skill of a professional exhorter of young men in finding Knute's motives, and when he discovered that Knute had a hidden desire to dabble in gay, polite literature, Ray said in a shocked way:

"Strikes me a man like you, that's getting old, ought to be thinking more about saving your soul than about all these frills. You leave this poetry and stuff to these foreigners and artists, and you stick to Latin and math and the Bible. I tell you, I've taught school, and I've learned by experience."

With Ray Gribble, Knute lived grubbily, an existence of torn comforters and a smelly lamp, of lexicons and logarithm tables. No leisurely loafing by fireplaces was theirs. They roomed in West Divinity, where gather the theologues, the lesser sort of law students, a whimsical genius or two, and a horde of unplaced freshmen and "scrub seniors."

Knute was shockingly disappointed, but he stuck to his room because outside of it he was afraid. He was a grotesque figure, and he knew it, a white-polled giant squeezed into a small seat in a classroom, listening to instructors younger than his own sons. Once he tried to sit on the fence. No one but "ringers" sat on the fence any more, and at the sight of him trying to look athletic and young, two upperclassmen snickered, and he sneaked away.

He came to hate Ray Gribble and his voluble companions of the submerged tenth of the class, the hewers of tutorial wood. It is doubtless safer to mock the flag than to question that best-established tradition of our democracy — that those who "earn their way through" college are

necessarily stronger, braver, and more assured of
success than the weaklings who talk by the fire.
Every college story presents such a moral. But
tremblingly the historian submits that Knute discovered that waiting on table did not make lads
more heroic than did football or happy loafing.
Fine fellows, cheerful and fearless, were many of
the boys who "earned their way," and able to talk
to richer classmates without fawning; but just as
many of them assumed an abject respectablity as
the most convenient pose. They were pickers-up
of unconsidered trifles; they toadied to the classmates whom they tutored; they wriggled before
the faculty committee on scholarships; they looked
pious at Dwight Hall prayer meetings to make an
impression on the serious-minded; and they drank
one glass of beer at Jake's to show the light-
minded that they meant nothing offensive by their
piety. In revenge for cringing to the insolent athletes whom they tutored, they would, when safe
among their own kind, yammer about the "lack
of democracy in colleges today." Not that they
were so indiscreet as to do anything about it. They
lacked the stuff of really rebellious souls. Knute
listened to them and marveled. They sounded like
a young hired man talking behind his barn at
harvest time.

This submerged tenth hated the dilettantes of
the class even more than they hated the bloods.
Against one Gilbert Washburn, a rich esthete with
more manner than any freshman ought to have,
they raged righteously. They spoke of seriousness
and industry till Knute, who might once have desired to know lads like Washburn, felt ashamed of
himself as a wicked, wasteful old man.

With the friends of his roommate began
Knute's series of disillusions. Humbly though he
sought, he found no inspiration and no comrade-

ship. He was the freak of the class, and aside from
the submerged tenth, his classmates were afraid of
being "queered" by being seen with him.

As he was still powerful, one who could take up
a barrel of pork on his knees, he tried to find
friendship among the athletes. He sat at Yale
Field, watching the football tryouts, and tried to
get acquainted with the candidates. They stared
at him and answered his questions grudgingly —
beefy youths who in their simple-hearted way
showed that they considered him plain crazy.

The place itself began to lose the haze of magic
through which he had first seen it. Earth is earth,
whether one sees it in Camelot or Joralemon or
on the Yale campus — or possibly even in the
Harvard yard! The buildings ceased to be temples
to Knute; they became structures of brick or stone,
filled with young men who lounged at windows
and watched him amusedly as he tried to slip by.

The Gargantuan hall of Commons became tri-
daily horror because at the table where he dined
were two youths, who, having uncommonly penetrating minds, discerned that Knute had a beard,
and courageously told the world about it. One of
them, named Atchison, was a superior person,
very industrious and scholarly, glib in mathematics and manners. He despised Knute's lack of
definite purpose in coming to college. The other
was a playboy, a wit and a stealer of street signs,
who had a wonderful sense for a subtle jest; and
his references to Knute's beard shook the table
with jocund mirth three times a day. So these
youths of gentle birth drove the shambling, wistful
old man away from the Commons, and thereafter
he ate at the lunch counter at the Black Cat.

Lacking the stimulus of friendship, it was the
harder for Knute to keep up the strain of studying
the long assignments. What had been a week's

pleasure reading in his shack was now thrown at
him as a day's task. But he would not have minded
the toil if he could have found one as young as
himself. They were all so dreadfully old, the
money earners, the serious laborers at athletics,
the instructors who worried over their life work
of putting marks in a class-record book.

Then, on a sore, bruised day, Knute did meet
one who was young.

Knute had heard that the professor who was the
idol of the college had berated the too-earnest lads
in his Browning class, and insisted that they read
Alice in Wonderland. Knute floundered dustily
about in a secondhand bookshop till he found an
Alice, and he brought it home to read over his
lunch of a hot-dog sandwich. Something in the
grave absurdity of the book appealed to him, and
he was chuckling over it when Ray Gribble came
into the room and glanced at the reader.

"Huh!" said Mr. Gribble.

"That's a fine, funny book," said Knute.

"Huh! *Alice in Wonderland*! I've heard of it.
Silly nonsense. Why don't you read something
really fine, like Shakespeare or *Paradise Lost*?"

"Vell — " said Knute, but that was all he could
find to say.

With Ray Gribble's glassy eye on him, he could
no longer roll and roar with the book. He wondered if indeed he ought not to be reading Milton's pompous anthropological misconceptions.
He went unhappily out to an early history class,
ably conducted by Blevins, Ph.D.

Knute admired Blevins, Ph.D. He was so
tubbed and eyeglassed and terribly right. But most
of Blevins' lambs did not like Blevins. They said
he was a "crank." They read newspapers in the
class and covertly kicked one another.

In the smug, plastered classroom, his arm leaning heavily on the broad table-arm of his chair, Knute tried not to miss one of Blevins' sardonic proofs that the correct date of the second marriage of Themistocles was two years and seven days later than the date assigned by that illiterate ass, Frutari of Padua. Knute admired young Blevins' performance, and he felt virtuous in application to these hard, unnonsensical facts.

He became aware that certain lewd fellows of the lesser sort were playing poker just behind him. His prairie-trained ear caught whispers of "Two to dole," and "Raise you two beans." Knute revolved, and frowned upon these mockers of sound learning. As he turned back he was aware that the offenders were chuckling, and continuing their game. He saw Blevins as merely a boy. He was sorry for him. He would do the boy a good turn.

When the class was over he hung about Blevins' desk till the other students had clattered out. He rumbled:

"Say, Professor, you're a fine fellow. I do something for you. If any of the boys make themselves a nuisance, you yust call on me, and I spank the son of a guns."

Blevins, Ph.D., spoke in a manner of culture and nastiness:

"Thanks so much, Axelbrod, but I don't fancy that will ever be necessary. I am supposed to be a reasonably good disciplinarian. Good day. Oh, one moment. There's something I've been wishing to speak to you about. I do wish you wouldn't try quite so hard to show off whenever I call on you during quizzes. You answer at such needless length, and you smile as though there were something highly amusing about me. I'm quite willing to have you regard me as a humorous figure, privately, but there are certain classroom conventions, you know, certain little conventions."

"Why, Professor!" wailed Knute. "I never make fun of you! I didn't know I smile. If I do, I guess it's yust because I am so glad when my stupid old head gets the lesson good."

"Well, well, that's very gratifying, I'm sure. And if you will be a little more careful — "

Blevins, Ph.D., smiled a toothy, frozen smile, and trotted off to the Graduates' Club, to be witty about old Knute and his way of saying "yust," while in the deserted classroom Knute sat chill, an old man and doomed. Through the windows came the light of Indian summer; clean, boyish cries rose from the campus. But the lover of autumn smoothed his baggy sleeve, stared at the blackboard, and there saw only the gray of October stubble about his distant shack. As he pictured the college watching him, secretly making fun of him and his smile, he was now faint and ashamed, now bull-angry. He was lonely for his cat, his fine chair of buffalo horns, the sunny doorstep of his shack, and the understanding land. He had been in college for about one month.

Before he left the classroom he stepped behind the instructor's desk and looked at an imaginary class.

"I might have stood there as a prof if I could have come earlier," he said softly to himself.

Calmed by the liquid autumn gold that flowed through the streets, he walked out Whitney Avenue toward the buttelike hill of East Rock. He observed the caress of the light upon the scarped rock, heard the delicate music of leaves, breathed in air pregnant with tales of old New England. He exulted:

"I could write poetry now if I yust — if I yust could write poetry!"

He climbed to the top of East Rock, whence he could see the Yale buildings like the towers of Ox-

ford, Long Island Sound, and the white glare of
Long Island itself beyond the water. He marveled
that Knute Axelbrod of the cottonwood country
was looking across an arm of the Atlantic to New
York State.

He noticed a freshman on a bench at the edge
of the rock, and he became irritated. The freshman was Gilbert Washburn, the snob, the dilet-
tante, of whom Ray Gribble had once said: "That
guy is the disgrace of the class. He doesn't go out
for anything, high stand or Dwight Hall or anything else. Thinks he's so doggone much better
than the rest of the fellows that he doesn't associate with anybody. Thinks he's literary, they say,
and yet he doesn't even heel the 'lit,' like the
regular literary fellows! Got no time for a loafing,
moonin' snob like that."

As Knute stared at the unaware Gil, whose pro-
file was fine in outline against the sky, he was
terrifically public-spirited and disapproving and
that sort of moral thing. Though Gil was much
too well-dressed, he seemed moodily discontented.

"What he needs is to work in a thrashing crew
and sleep in the hay," grumbled Knute almost
in the virtuous manner of Gribble. "Then he
would know when he was vell off, and not like he
had the earache. Pff!"

Gil Washburn rose, trailed toward Knute,
glanced at him, hesitated, sat down on Knute's
bench.

"Great view!" he said. His smile was eager.

That smile symbolized to Knute all the art of
life he had come to college to find. He tumbled
out of his moral attitude with ludicrous haste, and
every wrinkle of his weathered face creased deep
as he answered:

"Yes, I t'ink the Acropolis must be like this
here."

"Say, look here, Axelbrod, I've been thinking about you."

"Yas?"

"We ought to know each other. We two are the class scandal. We came here to dream, and these busy little goats like Atchison and Giblets, or whatever your roommate's name is, think we're fools not to go out for marks. You may not agree with me, but I've decided that you and I are precisely alike."

"What makes you t'ink I come here to dream?" bristled Knute.

"Oh, I used to sit near you at Commons and hear you try to quell jolly old Atchison whenever he got busy discussing the reasons for coming to college. That old, moth-eaten topic! I wonder if Cain and Abel didn't discuss it at the Eden Agricultural College. You know, Abel the mark-grabber, very pious and high stand, and Cain wanting to read poetry."

"Yes," said Knute, "and I guess Prof. Adam say, 'Cain, don't you read this poetry, it von't help you in algebry.'"

"Of course. Say, wonder if you'd like to look at this volume of Musset I was sentimental enough to lug up here today. Picked it up when I was abroad last year."

From his pocket Gil drew such a book as Knute had never seen before, a slender volume, in a strange language, bound in hand-tooled, crushed levant, an effeminate bibelot over which the prairie farmer gasped with luxurious pleasure. The book almost vanished in his big hands. With a timid forefinger he stroked the levant, ran through the leaves.

"I can't read it, but that's the kind of book I alvays t'ought there must be some like it," he sighed.

"Let me read you a little. It's French poetry."

Gil read aloud. He made of the alien verses a music which satisfied Knute's sixty-five years of longing for he had never known what.

"That's — that's fine," he said.

"Listen!" cried Gil. "Ysaye is playing up at Hartford tonight. Let's go hear him. We'll trolley up, make it in plenty of time. Tried to get some of the fellows to come, but they thought I was a nut."

What an Ysaye was, Knute Axelbrod had no notion, but "Sure!" he boomed.

When they got to Hartford they found that between them they had just enough money to get dinner, hear Ysaye from gallery seats, and return only as far as Meriden.

At Meriden, Gil suggested:

"Let's walk back to New Haven, then. Can you make it?"

Knute had no knowledge as to whether it was four miles or forty back to the campus, but "Sure!" he said. For the last few months he had been noticing that, despite his bulk, he had to be careful, but tonight he would have flown.

In the music of Ysaye, the first real musician he had ever heard, Knute had found all the incredible things of which he had slowly been reading in William Morris and *Idylls of the King*. Tall knights he had beheld, and slim princesses in white samite, the misty gates of forlorn towns, and the glory of the chivalry that never was.

They did walk, roaring down the road beneath the October moon, stopping to steal apples and to exclaim over silvered fanedog. It was Gil who talked, and Knute who listened, for the most part; but Knute was lured into tales of the pioneer days, of blizzards, of harvesting, and of the first flame of the green wheat. Regarding the Atchisons and the Gribbles of the class, both of them were youthfully bitter and supercilious. They were wandering minstrels, Gilbert the troubadour with his man-at-arms.

They reached the campus at about five in the morning.

Fumbling for words that would express his feeling, Knute stammered:

"Vell, it vas fine. I go to bed now and I dream about — "

"Bed? Rats! Never believe in winding up a party when it's going strong. Too few good parties. Besides, it's only the shank of the evening. Besides, we're hungry. Besides — oh, besides! Wait here a second. I'm going up to my room to get some money, and we'll have some eats. Wait! Please do!"

Knute would have waited all night. He had lived sixty-five years and traveled fifteen hundred miles and endured Ray Gribble to find Gil Washburn.

Policemen wondered to see the celluloid-collared old man and the expensive-looking boy rolling arm in arm down Chapel Street in search of a restaurant suitable to poets. They were all closed.

"The Ghetto will be awake by now," said Gil. "We'll go buy some eats and take 'em up to my room. I've got some tea there."

Knute shouldered through dark streets besides him as naturally as though he had always been a nighthawk, with an aversion to anything as rustic as beds. Down on Oak Street, a place of low shops, smoky lights, and alley mouths, they found the slum already astir. Gil contrived to purchase boxed biscuits, cream cheese, chicken loaf, a bottle of cream. While Gil was chaffering, Knute stared out into the streets milkily lighted by wavering gas and the first feebleness of coming day; he gazed upon Kosher signs and advertisements in Russian letters, shawled women and bearded rabbis; and as he looked he gathered contentment which he could never lose. He had traveled broad tonight.

The room of Gil Washburn was all the useless, pleasant things Knute wanted it to be. There were more of Gil's Paris days in it than of his freshman-hood: cloisonné on the mantlepiece, Persian rugs, a silver tea service, etchings, and books. Knute Axelbrod gazed in satisfaction. Vast-bearded, sunk in an easy chair, he clucked amiably while Gil lighted a fire and spread a wicker table.

Over supper they spoke of great men and heroic ideals. It was good talk, and not unspiced with lively references to Gribble and Atchison and Blevins, all asleep now in their correct beds. Gil read snatches of Stevenson and Anatole France; then at last he read his own poetry.

It does not matter whether that poetry was good or bad. To Knute it was a miracle to find one who actually wrote it.

The talk grew slow and they began to yawn. Knute was sensitive to the lowered key of their Indian-summer madness, and he hastily rose. As he said good-bye he felt as though he had but to sleep a little while and return to this unending night of romance.

But he came out of the dormitory upon day. It was six-thirty in the morning with a still, hard light upon red-brick walls.

"I can go to his room plenty times now; I find my friend," Knute said. He held tight the volume of Musset, which Gil had begged him to take.

As he started to walk the few steps to West Divinity, Knute felt very tired. By daylight the adventure seemed more and more incredible.

As he entered the dormitory he sighed heavily:
"Age and youth, I guess they can't team together long." As he mounted the stairs, he said:
"If I saw the boy again, he vould get tired of me. I
tell him all I got to say." And as he opened his
door, he added: "This is what I come to college
for — for this one night; I live for it sixty-five
years. I go avay before I spoil it."

He wrote a note to Gil, and began to pack his
telescope. He did not even wake Ray Gribble, son-
orously sleeping in the stale air.

At five that afternoon, on the day coach of a
west-bound train, an old man sat smiling. A
lasting content in his eyes, and in his hands, a
small book in French, though the curious fact is
that this man could not read French.

IRWIN SHAW

20/STRAWBERRY ICE CREAM SODA

Eddie Barnes looked at the huge Adirondack hills, browning in the strong summer afternoon sun. He listened to his brother Lawrence practice finger exercises on the piano inside the house, one-twothreefour*five*, onetwothreefour*five*, and longed for New York. He lay on his stomach in the long grass of the front lawn and delicately peeled his sunburned nose. Morosely he regarded a grasshopper, stupid with sun, wavering on a bleached blade of grass in front of his nose. Without interest he put out his hand and captured it.

"Give honey," he said listlessly. "Give honey or I'll kill yuh! . . ."

But the grasshopper crouched unmoving, unresponsive, oblivious to Life or Death. Disgusted, Eddie tossed the grasshopper away. It flew uncertainly, wheeled, darted back to its blade of grass, alighted and hung there dreamily, shaking a little in the breeze in front of Eddie's nose. Eddie turned over on his back and looked at the high blue sky.

The country! Why anybody ever went to the country. . . . What things must be doing in New York now, what rash, beautiful deeds on the steaming, rich streets, what expeditions, what joy,

what daring sweaty adventure among the trucks,
the trolley cars, the baby carriages! What cries,
hoarse and humorous, what light laughter outside
the red-painted shop where lemon ice was sold
at three cents the double scoop, true nourishment
for a man at fifteen.

Eddie looked around him, at the silent, eternal,
granite-streaked hills. Trees and birds, that's all.
He sighed, torn with thoughts of distant pleasure,
stood up, went over to the window behind which
Lawrence seriously hammered at the piano, one-
twothreefour*five*.

"Lawrrrence," Eddie called, the rrr's rolling
with horrible gentility in his nose.

Lawrence didn't even look up. His thirteen-
year-old fingers, still pudgy and babyish, went
onetwothreefour*five*, with unswerving precision.
He was talented and he was dedicated to his talent, and some day they would wheel a huge piano
out on the stage of Carnegie Hall and he would
come out and bow politely to the thunder of applause and sit down, flipping his coattails back,
and play, and men and women would laugh and
cry and remember their first loves as they listened
to him. So now his fingers went up and down, up
and down, taking strength against the great day.

Eddie looked through the window a moment
more, watching his brother, sighed and walked
around to the side of the house, where a crow was
sleepily eating the radish seeds that Eddie had
planted three days ago in a fit of boredom. Eddie
threw a stone at the crow and the crow silently
flew up to the branch of an oak and waited for
Eddie to go away. Eddie threw another stone at
the crow. The crow moved to another branch.
Eddie wound up and threw a curve, but the crow
disdained it. Eddie picked his foot up the way he'd
seen Carl Hubbell do and sizzled one across not

more than three feet from the crow. Without nervousness the crow walked six inches up the branch. In the style now of Dizzy Dean, with terrifying speed, Eddie delivered his fast one. It was wild and the crow didn't even cock his head. You had to expect to be a little wild with such speed. Eddie found a good round stone and rubbed it professionally on his back pocket. He looked over his shoulder to hold the runner close to the bag, watched for the signal. Eddie Hubbell Dean Mungo Feller Ferrell Warnecke Gomez Barnes picked up his foot and let go his high hard one. The crow slowly got off his branch and regretfully sailed away.

Eddie went over, kicked away the loose dirt, and looked at his radish seeds. Nothing was happening to them. They just lay there, baked and inactive, just as he had placed them. No green, no roots, no radishes, no anything. He was sorry he'd ever gone in for farming. The package of seeds had cost him a dime, and the only thing that happened to them was that they were eaten by crows. And now he could use that dime. Tonight he had a date.

"I got a date," he said aloud, savoring the words. He went to the shade of the grape arbor to think about it. He sat down on the bench under the cool flat leaves, and thought about it. He'd never had a date before in his life. He had thirty-five cents. Thirty-five cents ought to be enough for any girl, but if he hadn't bought the radish seeds, he'd have had forty-five cents, really prepared for any eventuality. "Darn crow," he said, thinking of the evil black head feeding on his dime.

Many times he'd wondered how you managed to get a date. Now he knew. It happened all of a sudden. You went up to a girl where she was lying on the raft in a lake and you looked at her, chubby in a blue bathing suit, and she looked seriously at you out of serious blue eyes where you stood dripping with lake water, with no hair on your chest, and suddenly you said, "I don't suppose yuh're not doing anything t'morra night, are yuh?" You didn't know quite what you meant, but she did, and she said, "Why, no, Eddie. Say about eight o'clock?" And you nodded and dived back into the lake and there you were.

Still, those radish seeds, that crow food, that extra dime. . . .

Lawrence came out, flexing his fingers, very neat in clean khaki shorts and a white blouse. He sat down next to Eddie in the grape arbor.

"I would like a strawberry ice cream soda," he said.

"Got any money?" Eddie asked, hopefully.

Lawrence shook his head.

"No strawberry ice cream soda," Eddie said.

Lawrence nodded seriously. "You got any money?" he asked.

"Some," Eddie said carefully. He pulled down a grape leaf and cracked it between his hands, held up the two parts and looked at them critically.

Lawrence didn't say anything, but Eddie sensed a feeling developing in the grape arbor, like a growth. "I gotta save my money," Eddie said harshly. "I got a date. I got thirty-five cents. How do I know she won't want a banana split tonight?"

Lawrence nodded again, indicating that he understood, but sorrow washed up in his face like a high tide.

They sat in silence, uncomfortably, listening to the rustle of the grape leaves.

"All the time I was practicing," Lawrence said,

finally, "I kept thinking, 'I would like a strawberry ice cream soda, I would like a strawberry ice cream soda. . . .'"

Eddie stood up abruptly. "Aaah, let's get outa here. Let's go down to the lake. Maybe something's doing down at the lake."

They walked together over the fields to the lake, not saying anything, Lawrence flexing his fingers mechanically.

"Why don't yuh stop that fer once?" Eddie asked with distaste. "Just fer once?"

"This is good for my fingers. It keeps them loose."

"Yuh give me a pain."

"All right," Lawrence said, "I won't do it now."

They walked on again, Lawrence barely up to Eddie's chin, frailer, cleaner, his hair mahogany dark and smooth on his high, pink, baby brow. Lawrence whistled. Eddie listened with disguised respect.

"That's not so bad," Eddie said. "You don't whistle half bad."

"That's from the Brahms second piano concerto." Lawrence stopped whistling for a moment. "It's easy to whistle."

"Yuh give me a pain," Eddie said, mechanically, "a real pain."

When they got to the lake, there was nobody there. Flat and unruffled it stretched across, like a filled blue cup, to the woods on the other side.

"Nobody here," Eddie said, staring at the raft, unmoving and dry in the still water. "That's good. Too many people here all the time." His eyes roamed the lake, to the furthest corner, to the deepest cove.

"How would yuh like to go rowing in a boat out in that old lake?" Eddie asked.

"We haven't got a boat," Lawrence answered reasonably.

"I didn't ask yuh that. I asked, 'How'd yuh like to go rowing?' "

"I'd like to go rowing if we had a . . ."

"Shut up!" Eddie took Lawrence's arm, led him through tall grass to the water's edge, where a flat-bottomed boat was drawn up, the water just lapping at the stern, high, an old red color, faded by sun and storm. A pair of heavy oars lay along the bottom of the boat.

"Jump in," Eddie said, "when I tell yuh to."

"But it doesn't belong to us."

"Yuh want to go rowing, don't yuh?"

"Yes, but . . ."

"Then jump in when I give yuh the word."

Lawrence neatly took off his shoes and socks while Eddie hauled the boat into the water.

"Jump in!" Eddie called.

Lawrence jumped. The boat glided out across the still lake. Eddie rowed industriously once they got out of the marsh grass.

"This isn't half bad, is it?" He leaned back on his oars for a moment.

"It's nice," Lawrence said. "It's very peaceful."

"Aaah," said Eddie, "yuh even talk like a pianist." And he rowed. After a while he got tired and let the boat go with the wind. He lay back and thought of the night to come, dabbling his fingers in the water, happy. "They oughta see me now, back on a Hunnerd and Seventy-third Street," he said. "They oughta see me handle this old boat."

"Everything would be perfect," Lawrence agreed, picking his feet up out of the puddle that was collecting on the bottom of the boat, "if we only knew that when we got out of this boat, we were going to get a strawberry ice cream soda."

"Why don't yuh think of somethin' else? Always thinkin' of one thing! Don't yuh get tired?"

"No," Lawrence said, after thinking it over.

"Here!" Eddie pushed the oars toward his brother. "Row! That'll give yuh somethin' else t' think about."

Lawrence took the oars gingerly. "This is bad for my hands," he explained as he pulled dutifully on the oars. "It stiffens the fingers."

"Look where yuh're goin'!" Eddie cried impatiently. "In circles! What's the sense in goin' in circles?"

"That's the way the boat goes," Lawrence said, pulling hard. "I can't help it if that's the way the boat goes."

"A pianist. A regular pianist. That's all yuh are. Gimme those oars."

Gratefully Lawrence yielded the oars up.

"It's not my fault if the boat goes in circles. That's the way it's made," he persisted quietly.

"Aaah, shut up!" Eddie pulled savagely on the oars. The boat surged forward, foam at the prow.

"Hey, you there in the boat! Hey!" A man's voice called over the water.

"Eddie," Lawrence said, "there's a man yelling at us."

"Come on in here, before I beat your pants off!" the man called. "Get out of my boat!"

"He wants us to get out of his boat," Lawrence interpreted. "This must be his boat."

"You don't mean it," Eddie snorted with deep sarcasm. He turned around to shout at the man on the shore, who was waving his arms now. "All right," Eddie called. "All right. We'll give yuh yer old boat. Keep your shirt on."

The man jumped up and down. "I'll beat yer heads off," he shouted.

Lawrence wiped his nose nervously. "Eddie,"

he said, "why don't we row over to the other side
and walk home from there?"

Eddie looked at his brother contemptuously.
"What're yuh — afraid?"

"No," Lawrence said, after a pause. "But why
should we get into an argument?"

For answer Eddie pulled all the harder on the
oars. The boat flew through the water. Lawrence
squinted to look at the rapidly nearing figure of
the man on the bank.

"He's a great big man, Eddie," Lawrence reported. "You never saw such a big man. And he
looks awfully sore. Maybe we shouldn't've gone
out in this boat. Maybe he doesn't like people to
go out in this boat. Eddie, are you listening to me?"

With a final heroic pull, Eddie drove the boat
into the shore. It grated with a horrible noise on
the pebbles of the lake bottom.

"That," the man said, "is the end of that boat."

"That doesn't really hurt it, mister," Lawrence
said. "It makes a lot of noise, but it doesn't do any
damage."

The man reached over and grabbed Lawrence
by the back of his neck with one hand and placed
him on solid ground. He was a very big man, with
tough bristles that grew all over his double chin
and farmer's muscles in his arms that were quivering with passion now under a mat of hair. There
was a boy of about thirteen with him, obviously,
from his look, his son, and the son was angry too.

"Hit 'im, Pop," the son kept calling. "Wallop
'im!"

The man shook Lawrence again and again. He
was almost too overcome with anger to speak. "No
damage, eh? Only noise, eh!" he shouted into
Lawrence's paling face. "I'll show you damage. I'll
show you noise."

Eddie spoke up. Eddie was out of the boat now,

an oar gripped in his hand, ready for the worst. "That's not fair," he said. "Look how much bigger yuh are than him. Why'n't yuh pick on somebody yuh size?"

The farmer's boy jumped up and down in passion, exactly as his father had done. "I'll fight him, Pop! I'll fight 'im! I'm his size! Come on, kid, put yer hands up!"

The farmer looked at his son, looked at Lawrence. Slowly he released Lawrence. "Okay," he said. "Show him, Nathan."

Nathan pushed Lawrence. "Come into the woods, kid," he said belligerently. "We c'n settle it there."

"One in the eye," Eddie whispered out of the corner of his mouth. "Give 'im one in the eye, Larry!"

But Lawrence stood with eyes lowered, regarding his hands.

"Well?" the farmer asked.

Lawrence still looked at his hands, opening and closing them slowly.

"He don't wanna fight," Nathan taunted Eddie. "He just want t' row in our boat, he don't wanna fight."

"He wants to fight, all right," Eddie said staunchly, and under his breath, "Come on, Larry, in the kisser, a fast one in the puss. . . ."

But Larry stood still, calmly, seeming to be thinking of Brahms and Beethoven, of distant concert halls.

"He's yella, that's what's the matter with him," Nathan roared. "He's a coward, all city kids're cowards!"

"He's no coward," Eddie insisted, knowing in his deepest heart that his brother was a coward. With his knees he nudged Lawrence. "Bring up yuh left! Please, Larry, bring up yuh left!"

Deaf to all pleas, Lawrence kept his hands at his sides.

"Yella! Yella! Yella!" Nathan screamed loudly.

"Well," the farmer wanted to know, "is he goin' to fight or not?"

"Larry!" Fifteen years of desperation was in Eddie's voice, but it made no mark on Lawrence. Eddie turned slowly toward home. "He's not goin' to fight," he said flatly. And then, as one throws a bone to a neighbor's noisy dog. "Come on, you. . . ."

Slowly Lawrence bent over, picked up his shoes and socks, took a step after his brother.

"Wait a minute, you!" the farmer called. He went after Eddie, turned him around. "I want to talk to ye."

"Yeah?" Eddie said sadly, with little defiance. "What do yuh wanna say?"

"See that house over there?" the farmer asked, pointing.

"Yeah," Eddie said. "What about it?"

"That's my house," the farmer said. "You stay away from it. See?"

"Okay, okay," Eddie said wearily, all pride gone.

"See that boat there?" the farmer asked, pointing at the source of all the trouble.

"I see it," Eddie said.

"That's my boat. Stay away from it or I'll beat the daylights outa ye. See?"

"Yeah, yeah, I see," Eddie said. "I won't touch yer lousy boat." And once more, to Lawrence, "Come on, *you*. . . ."

"Yella! Yella! Yella!" Nathan kept roaring, jumping up and down, until they passed out of earshot, across the pleasant fields, ripe with the soft sweet smell of clover in the late summer afternoon. Eddie walked before Lawrence, his face grimly contracted, his mouth curled in shame and bitterness. He stepped on the clover blossoms fiercely, as though he hated them, wanted to destroy them, the roots under them, the very ground they grew in.

Holding his shoes in his hands, his head bent on his chest, his hair still mahogany smooth and mahogany dark, Lawrence followed ten feet back in the footsteps, plainly marked in the clover, of his brother.

"Yella," Eddie was muttering, loud enough for the villain behind him to hear clearly. "Yella! Yella as a flower. My own brother," he marveled. "If it was me I'da been glad to get killed before I let anybody call me that. I would let 'em cut my heart out first. My own brother. Yella as a flower. Just one in the eye! Just *one*! Just to show 'im. . . . But he stands there, takin' guff from a kid with holes in his pants. A pianist. Lawrrrence! They knew what they were doin' when they called yuh Lawrrrence! Don't talk to me! I don't want yuh ever to talk to me again as long as yuh live! Lawrrrence!"

In sorrow too deep for tears, the two brothers reached home, ten feet, ten million miles apart.

Without looking around, Eddie went to the grape arbor, stretched out on the bench. Lawrence looked after him, his face pale and still, then went into the house.

Face downward on the bench, close to the rich black earth of the arbor, Eddie bit his fingers to keep the tears back. But he could not bite hard enough, and the tears came, a bitter tide, running down his face, dropping on the black soft earth in which the grapes were rooted.

"Eddie!"

Eddie scrambled around, pushing the tears away with iron hands. Lawrence was standing there, carefully pulling on doeskin gloves over his small hands. "Eddie," Lawrence was saying, stonily disregarding the tears. "I want you to come with me."

Silently, but with singing in his heart so deep it called new tears to his wet eyes, Eddie got up, blew his nose, and followed after his brother, caught up with him, walked side by side with him across the field of clover, so lightly that the red and purple blossoms barely bent in their path.

Eddie knocked sternly at the door of the farm house, three knocks, solid, vigorous, the song of trumpets caught in them.

Nathan opened the door. "What do ye want?" he asked suspiciously.

"A little while ago," Eddie said formally, "yuh offered to fight my brother. He's ready now."

Nathan looked at Lawrence, standing there, straight, his head up, his baby lips compressed into a thin tight line, his gloved hands creased in solid fists. He started to close the door. "He had his chance," Nathan said.

Eddie kept the door open firmly. "Yuh offered, remember that," he reminded Nathan politely.

"He shoulda fought then," Nathan said stubbornly. "He had his chance."

"Come on," Eddie almost begged. "Yuh wanted to fight before."

"That was before. Lemme close the door."

"Yuh can't do this!" Eddie was shouting desperately. "Yuh offered!"

Nathan's father, the farmer, appeared in the doorway. He looked bleakly out. "What's goin' on here?" he asked.

"A little while ago," Eddie spoke very fast, "this man here offered to fight this man here." His eloquent hand indicated first Nathan, then Lawrence. "Now we've come to take the offer."

The farmer looked at his son. "Well?"

"He had his chance," Nathan grumbled sullenly.

"Nathan don't want t' fight," the farmer said to Eddie. "Get outa here."

Lawrence stepped up, over to Nathan. He looked Nathan squarely in the eye. "Yella," he said to Nathan.

The farmer pushed his son outside the door. "Go fight him," he ordered.

"We can settle it in the woods," Lawrence said.

"Wipe him up, Larry!" Eddie called as Lawrence and Nathan set out for the woods, abreast, but a polite five yards apart. Eddie watched them disappear behind trees, in silence.

In silence they both looked across the field to the woods that shielded the battlefield. The tops of the trees waved a little in the wind and the afternoon was collecting in deep blue shadows among the thick brown tree trunks where they gripped the ground. A chicken hawk floated lazily over the field, banking and slipping with the wind. The farmer regarded the chicken hawk without malice.

"Some day," the farmer said, "I'm going to get that son of a gun."

"What is it?" Eddie asked.

"Chicken hawk. You're from the city, ain't ye?"

"Yeah."

"Like it in the city?"

"Nothing like it."

The farmer puffed reflectively. "Some day I'm goin' to live in the city. No sense in livin' in the country these days."

"Oh, I don't know," Eddie said. "The country's very nice. There's a lot to be said for the country."

The farmer nodded, weighing the matter in his own mind.

"Say," said the farmer, "do you think your brother'll damage my kid?"

"It's possible," Eddie said. "He's very tough, my
brother. He has dozens a' fights, every month.
Every kid back home's scared stiff a' him. Why,"
said Eddie, sailing full into fancy, "I remember
one day, Larry fought three kids all in a row. In
a half 'n hour. He busted all their noses. In a half
'n hour! He's got a terrific left jab — one, two,
bang! like this — and it gets 'em in the nose."

"Well, he can't do Nathan's nose any harm."
The farmer laughed. "No matter what you did to
a nose like that it'd be a improvement."

"He's got a lot of talent, my brother," Eddie said,
proud of the warrior in the woods. "He plays the
piano. He's a very good piano player. You ought
to hear him."

"A little kid like that," the farmer marveled.
"Nathan can't do nothing."

Off in the distance, in the gloom under the
trees, two figures appeared, close together, walked
slowly out into the sunlight of the field. Eddie and
the farmer stood up. Wearily the two fighters approached together, their arms dangling at their
sides.

Eddie looked first at Nathan. Nathan's mouth
had been bleeding and there was a lump on his
forehead and his ear was red. Eddie smiled with
satisfaction. Nathan had been in a fight. Eddie
walked slowly toward Lawrence. Lawrence approached with head high. But it was a sadly battered head. The hair was tangled, an eye was
closed, the nose was bruised and still bled.
Lawrence sucked in the blood from his nose from
time to time with his tongue. His collar was torn,
his pants covered with forest loam, with his bare
knees skinned and raw. But in the one eye that
still could be seen shone a clear light, honorable,
indomitable.

"Ready to go home now, Eddie?" Lawrence asked.

"Sure." Eddie started to pat Lawrence on the back, pulled his hand back. He turned and waved at the farmer. "So long."

"So long," the farmer called. "Any time you want to use the boat, just step into it."

"Thanks." Eddie waited while Lawrence shook hands gravely with Nathan.

"Good night," Lawrence said. "It was a good fight."

"Yeah," Nathan said.

The two brothers walked away, close together, across the field of clover, fragrant in the long shadows. Half the way they walked in silence, the silence of equals, strong men communicating in a language more eloquent than words, the only sound the thin jingle of the thirty-five cents in Eddie's pocket.

Suddenly Eddie stopped Lawrence. "Let's go this way," he said, pointing off to the right.

"But home's this way, Eddie."

"I know. Let's go into town. Let's get ice cream sodas," Eddie said; "let's get strawberry ice cream sodas."

ABOUT THE AUTHORS

ALBERT HALPER

Albert Halper writes out of his experience and observation of the life and people around him. He was born in Chicago, in 1904, and grew up there in the slum district near the railroad tracks and stockyards. After graduating from high school he worked for seven years at various jobs. He was order-picker in a large mail-order house, jewelry clerk, advance agent for a tobacco company, shipping clerk in an electrotype foundry, and night clerk at the Chicago Central Post Office before he decided to come to New York and write. That was in 1928. He has been writing ever since.

Mr. Halper is the author of nine novels, two plays, and many short stories. His novels include *Union Square*, *The Foundry*, *The Chute*, *Sons of the Fathers*, *The Little People*, *Only an Inch from Glory*, *The Golden Watch*, *Atlantic Avenue*, and *The Fourth Horseman of Miami Beach* which was published in 1966. He is currently writing a new novel.

What Mr. Halper has to say in "Prelude" can be summed up in one sentence of warning, "Look out, America, here comes Fascism!" It's the story of one family in one large American city; but what happens to the Silversteins in Chicago could happen any place in our country unless we all do what we can to stamp out any sign of anti-Semitism whenever or wherever it raises its un-American head. When this story appeared in *Scholastic Magazine,* a high school boy wrote: "I have never read anything else of Albert Halper's, but I think that on the basis of this one short story he should be given the Nobel Prize for Literature at once."

RUTH SUCKOW

When Ruth Suckow was a little girl, her father, who was a Congregational minister, traveled from church to church, from small village to big city, across the broad state of Iowa. His daughter grew up to know and love her native state thoroughly, and eventually to write about it and its people in short stories and novels that show her complete understanding of her subject.

Miss Suckow was born in Hawarden, Iowa, in 1892. After three years at Grinnell College, she obtained a B.A. and M.A. at the University of Denver and taught there for an interval. This, however, left little time for the writing she wanted to do, so she gave up teaching, established the Orchard Apiary back in Earlville, Iowa, and supported herself by selling honey while she was making a fine reputation as an author. She was discovered by H. L. Mencken, who published many of her early stories in *Smart Set* and later in the *American Mercury.* After that she had no trouble getting recognition, and gave up bees for stories.

Among her novels are *Country People, The Odyssey of a Nice Girl, The Bonney Family, Cora, The Kramer Girls, The Folks,* and *New Hope* — all mostly about Iowa. Her short stories were bound into an omnibus volume, under the title *Carry-Over.* In 1952 Rinehart published *Some Others and Myself: Seven Stories and a Memoir,* and in 1959 Viking published another novel, *The John Wood Case.* Ruth Suckow died in 1960.

ELLIOTT MERRICK

Although "Without Words" is a complete short story as it stands, it also appears as a chapter in Elliott Merrick's novel *Frost and Fire*. Mr. Merrick's exciting accounts of life in Labrador are based on personal experience — he taught for more than two years at Indian Harbor, the most northerly station of the famous Grenfell Mission. During that time he took many treks with the fur trappers up Grand River into the interior, where he endured the intense cold and hardship of the Labrador winter — and liked it. Other novels were also inspired by Merrick's life in Labrador: *True North*, *From the Hill Look Down*, and *Northern Nurse*.

Born in 1905, in Montclair, New Jersey, Merrick graduated from Yale University, and then worked as a newspaper reporter and publicity man in New York City. His dislike for the warmth and softness of city life led to his journey to Labrador. After returning from the Far North in 1932, he lived on a farm in Vermont, and combined teaching English (at the University of Vermont), writing, and farming.

From 1942 to 1944 Mr. Merrick wrote for the Office of War Information. In 1947 he wrote a novel, *Passing By*, about crews working on merchant ships during World War II. The following year he completed *Green Mountain Farm*, which is a warm account of the struggles the Merrick family experienced while carving out a satisfactory existence on a Vermont farm.

More recently, Mr. Merrick has taught English at Black Mountain College in North Carolina.

MAUREEN DALY

Maureen Daly was just sixteen years old when her story "Sixteen" won first prize in Scholastic's annual short-story contest. Since its appearance in *Scholastic*

Magazine, "Sixteen" has had a remarkable career. It was published in the *O. Henry Memorial Award Prize Stories of 1938* (the first time a high school student was included in that annual selection of the year's "bests"); it was later reprinted in *Redbook Magazine* and now appears in about a dozen anthologies.

Miss Daly won the first Intercollegiate Literary Fellowship established by Dodd, Mead & Company with her novel *Seventeenth Summer*. It's the story of a boy and girl in love for the first time, and the setting is Maureen Daly's own background — the Wisconsin Lake Country. One of the most popular novels for girls ever written, *Seventeenth Summer* is now in its forty-second printing; it has been translated into thirteen languages and was bought for the movies by Warner Brothers.

Maureen Patricia Daly was born in Castlecanfield, County Tyrone, Ireland, in 1921. When she was two years old her family came to this country and after a short stay in New York moved to Fond du Lac, Wisconsin. Miss Daly was graduated from Rosary College, River Forest, Illinois, where she was interested in dramatics, writing, and sports. She was associate editor of *Ladies' Home Journal* and women's editor of *The Saturday Evening Post*. She has written two short novels, *The Ginger Horse* and *The Small War of Sergeant Donkey*, and several etiquette books, including *The Perfect Hostess* and *What's Your P.Q.?*

During the past few years, she and her husband, writer William McGivern, and their two children have traveled extensively abroad, in countries ranging from Africa to Ireland, and have lived in Spain. Out of these travels Miss Daly wrote *Twelve Around the World, Spanish Roundabout, Moroccan Roundabout, Spain: Wonderland of Contrasts,* and a book co-authored with her husband, *Mention My Name in Mombasa*. She is now living in Hollywood, where she is working on a new novel and writing a screenplay for Universal Studios.

JESSE STUART

Jesse Stuart is a big, husky man who divides his time and energy between running his thousand-acre farm in the Kentucky hills, and singing of those hills in prose and poetry. He is a regional writer, and proud of it.

Mr. Stuart is a native of the Kentucky he loves so much. He was born near Greenup in 1907, rode mule-back or walked to the country school when chores on the home farm permitted, and had to stop school entirely when he was eleven in order to help his family. At fifteen he gave his grammar a sixty-day brush up, then entered high school where, he says, he was like a mule in a new pasture. From there he went to work in the steel mills, and later worked his way through Lincoln Memorial University in three years — the first of his family to attend and finish college.

Mr. Stuart has written thirty-two books. *Man with a Bull-Tongue Plow*, published in 1934, is a volume of poems which almost wrote themselves as the young farmer worked in the barnyard and field. *Taps for Private Tussie* won the Thomas Jefferson Southern Award, was a Book-of-the-Month selection, and has sold over one million copies.

Stuart has also written his personal history, *Thread That Runs So True*. In it he traces his career from the day when he first taught in a one-room rural school in Kentucky, through his years in various teaching positions, to the time nearly twenty years later when he went back to the land. He has combined farming and writing since 1949, and he occasionally conducts creative-writing courses. Mr. Stuart also is in constant demand as a lecturer; he has spoken to thousands of groups of students and educators — both in the U. S. and abroad.

Stuart has written many, many short stories in a wide variety of magazines. "Split Cherry Tree" is typical of these, reflecting as it does his own background and strenuous experience in getting an education. His most recent book *My Land Has a Voice* (1966) is a collection of short stories.

SALLY BENSON

In 1941, when Sally Benson learned that her collection of short stories, *Junior Miss*, had been selected as a Book-of-the-Month and had sold forty thousand copies in advance of publication, she said she felt as if she'd been hit by a truck. But she shouldn't have been that surprised. During the ten years she had been writing stories for the *New Yorker*, Sally Benson had received just one rejection slip — which is probably a record! The one rejection slip was for the story "The Overcoat," which she later sent to the *American Mercury*, from which it was reprinted in Edward J. O'Brien's annual *Best Short Stories* collection.

Mrs. Benson is one of those born writers whose stories apparently flow naturally onto paper, and need no second (or twentieth) revision. Her average time for writing a story is about two hours. *She* says she writes quickly to get it over with — much as other women attack the dinner dishes. Her sister says that she doesn't really write her stories at all — that she gets them from the ouija board. Whatever the explanation, Mrs. Benson's witty and tightly written stories have delighted readers as they have appeared in magazines, and have created a ready audience for her published story collections.

Besides the highly successful *Junior Miss*, Mrs. Benson has two other collections: *People Are Fascinating* and *Emily*. Her book based on her girlhood in Missouri (and her sister's diary) was made into the popular movie *Meet Me in St. Louis*. In 1954 Mrs. Benson wrote a musical comedy, *Seventeen*; she has also collaborated on many movie scripts.

Sara Mahala Redway Smith was born in St. Louis, Missouri, in 1900, and moved to New York when she was ten years old. When she was nineteen she married Reynolds Benson, an administrative officer at Columbia University. The Bensons have one daughter, Barbara. Mrs. Benson does not want Barbara confused with Judy Graves, the lumpy little thirteen-year-old heroine of *Junior Miss*. "Barbara's five feet nine and she's very pretty," she says. "She isn't Judy — at least she hasn't been for a long time."

HARRY SYLVESTER

Harry Sylvester is a past master at writing that particularly difficult kind of tale to come across — the good sports story. Not for him the impossible and sentimental fairy tale of the poor sub, ignored through the season, who goes in during the last two minutes of play to make at least seven touchdowns and win the game for good old ivy-covered Alma Mater. His heroes are made of much better and more human stuff. Sometimes they win, sometimes they lose, but that's incidental. The story itself is a story of character, as you'll see in "Eight-Oared Crew."

Mr. Sylvester was born in Brooklyn, New York, in 1908; he graduated from Notre Dame in 1930. The next year, while he was doing postgraduate work in English at the university, he worked as staff correspondent for the New York *Evening Post* covering football throughout the entire Middle West. Later he was on the staffs of the New York *Herald Tribune* and the Brooklyn *Eagle*. He sold his first short story while he was a senior in college, and since then has published a hundred more in *Collier's*, *Scribner's*, *Story*, *The Commonweal*, *Pictorial Review*, the *American Mercury*. One of his best-known stories, "A Boxer: Old," was reprinted from *Story* magazine in the *O. Henry Memorial Award Prize Stories of 1934*; three of his stories appeared in the O'Brien collection of the year's bests; still others have been reprinted in England and Scandinavia.

Mr. Sylvester is the author of three novels which together constitute a trilogy about the Catholic Church in the United States: *Dearly Beloved*, *Dayspring*, and *Moon Gaffney*. He also had published a collection of short stories, *All Your Idols*, in addition to the novel *A Golden Girl*.

THOMAS E. ADAMS

The bitterness and self-disgust which the boy feels in Thomas Adams' "Sled" is a feeling known to everyone. Who hasn't dreamed up a seemingly perfect plan for revenge, only to find its result is an increase in one's *own* frustration? This story creates a universal experience in many ways: the characters have no names, the setting is not geographically located, the feelings and mood awakened are hauntingly familiar to every reader. But only at the end of the story can we stop to analyze: while reading it, we are gripped by pure suspense.

Mr. Adams was born in Trenton, New Jersey, in 1936. He received a B.A. from LaSalle College in Philadelphia, Pennsylvania, in 1958, and an M.A. from the University of Florida where he studied creative writing under the novelist Andrew Lytle. He is a newcomer to the short story. "Sled" was first published in the *Sewanee Review,* and was included in the *O. Henry Memorial Award Prize Stories of 1962.* It was broadcast over the *Voice of America* in 1963. In 1964 Mr. Adams published another story, "Cloister," in the *Sewanee Review.*

GEORGE MILBURN

George Milburn is the author of the hilarious novel *Catalogue,* and many short stories — some very funny, some, like "A Student in Economics," movingly serious. Milburn was born in 1906, in Coweta, Oklahoma. His career as a writer started when he was sixteen, with a job as correspondent for the Pawhuska *Daily Capitol.* His course at the University of Oklahoma was interrupted by two years of hack writing — mostly joke books — and by a year's traveling with hoboes and tramps in the Midwest, gathering material on their songs. The result of these travels was the "Hoboes' Hornbook," published in 1930.

Back at the university again, Milburn worked part time as a proofreader at the university press. He had been writing stories throughout these years, and when H. L. Mencken, then editor of the *American Mercury*, saw three of the stories (which appeared in the first book printed by the Oklahoma University Press), he promptly bought all the manuscripts Milburn had on hand. After that, stories by George Milburn began to appear regularly in such magazines as *Harper's*, *Scribner's*, the *New Yorker*, and *Story*. His stories were collected in the two volumes *Oklahoma Town* and *No More Trumpets*. Other books by Milburn include *Blackjack Country*, *The Uncommon Man*, and *Flannigan's Folly*.

George Milburn was an author who wrote with honesty and sincerity about life as he saw it in America. Most of his stories have their settings in his native Oklahoma and retain the distinct flavor of that part of our country. Some, however, like "A Student in Economics," could have happened anywhere, as anyone who has worked his way through college knows.

George Milburn died in 1966.

WILLIAM SAROYAN

William Saroyan flashed onto the short-story scene in 1933 with his "The Daring Young Man on the Flying Trapeze," which was published in *Story* magazine. Saroyan was immediately recognized as a talented author, and through the years his mind has continued to be as nimble as a trapeze performer — sometimes indulging in antics, but always swift, alive, and full of grace.

William Saroyan was born in 1908 in the vineyard country near Fresno, California, and grew up there. His flair for writing came quite naturally: his father, a native of Armenia, was himself a writer and a teacher; his grandmother was a storyteller and a source of many of Saroyan's tales. Since the publication of "The Daring Young Man," Saroyan has published enough short stories to put his name in a long, long list of magazines, and to fill more than half a dozen books. Best known of these are probably his collections: *Little Children; Three Times Three; Love, Here Is My Hat; Peace, It's Wonderful;* and *My Name Is Aram.* His five plays produced on Broadway have had much to do with Saroyan's success. Like the readers of his stories, critics either like his plays very much, or not at all. In 1940 his *The Time of Your Life* was awarded the Pulitzer Prize (which Saroyan turned down) as the best play of the year and the Critics' Circle Prize (which he accepted). His best-selling novel *The Human Comedy* was made into a movie.

Saroyan is sometimes condemned as being conceited and aggressive. He once said, "I am so innately great that by comparison others who believe they are great or act as if they are great seem to me to be only pathetic, although occasionally charming." But many who have met him find him only endearingly natural — and something of a character. He has been called a profound humorist; his warm sympathy for people marks all of his work. In "Romance" you will see how this sympathy transforms the most ordinary scene — a journey on a train — into something new and exciting.

Some of Saroyan's most recent books include: *Mama, I Love You; Papa, You're Crazy; The Cave Dwellers* (a play); and *Here Comes, There Goes You Know Who.*

DOROTHY PARKER

Up until the time Dorothy Parker's "Clothe the Naked" appeared, people had been used to thinking of her as a satirist, a deadly wit, and as the national champion of the cutting remark. (She coined, "Men seldom make passes at girls who wear glasses.") She was famous for her stories which exposed hapless characters in an unpleasantly revealing light. It was clear that the author didn't think very highly of the people she wrote about. They were wonderful stories to read, but they didn't leave you with much sympathy for your fellow man. Then along came a most un-Parkerish story, "Clothe the Naked," written with compassion and understanding — one of the best stories Dorothy Parker ever wrote.

Dorothy Rothschild Parker was born in 1893, in West End, New Jersey. Her first job in the literary world was writing fashion captions for *Vogue* at ten dollars a week. A job as drama critic on *Vanity Fair* a few years later was a step up, but ended abruptly when her criticisms of the current theatrical season proved a little too strong for those concerned — but it did a lot toward building up the Parker legend. When, for instance, she did some pinch-hitting for Robert Benchley, then drama critic for the *New Yorker*, her old friend Alexander Woollcott was moved to remark, "It would be her idea of her duty to catch up the torch as it fell from his hand — and burn someone with it."

Mrs. Parker is equally well-known for her stories and poetry. They can be found in the two Modern Library volumes, *Collected Stories* and *Collected Poetry*, and also in *The Portable Dorothy Parker*. Mrs. Parker has often lent her touch for light and witty dialogue to Hollywood script-writing. In 1953 she co-authored the Broadway play *Ladies of the Corridor* with Arnold d'Usseau.

Before her death in 1967, she taught courses on the short story at Los Angeles State College, and reviewed books for *Esquire* magazine.

DOROTHY CANFIELD FISHER

Dorothy Canfield Fisher, whose foreword introduces this collection of the best short stories published in *Scholastic Magazine*, needs no introduction herself. Her name has long been associated with the literature of this country, with education, and with good works in general. She has written many fine novels, short stories, articles, and plays; she was for years one of the judges who made the Book-of-the-Month-Club selections that guide other people to good reading; she was a member of the Vermont State Board of Education; she served as a hard-working and enthusiastic judge in Scholastic's annual Writing Awards.

Anyone who has read her books will know that Mrs. Fisher was an American of New England stock, but he may not realize how far back that heritage goes. Her family came to this country in 1636, and moved to Vermont in 1763. Canfields have owned land there ever since. In fact, Mrs. Fisher often said, "I have lived in Vermont since 1763." From her home in Arlington, Vermont, she looked at the same changeless, yet ever-changing, view of the Green Mountains, their valleys and rivers, that the early Canfields saw over two hundred years ago.

Actually she didn't always live in Vermont. Dorothy Canfield was born in Kansas, in 1879, where her father was president of the State University at Lawrence. She was educated in France and in America, dividing her time from the age of ten between schools in the two countries.

Best known of her books are *The Bent Twig, The Brimming Cup, Rough-hewn, The Deepening Stream, Seasoned Timber* (all novels); her collections of short stories, *Hillsboro People* and *Made-to-Order Stories*; her translation of Giovanni Papini's *Life of Christ*; and *Vermont Tradition: Biography of an Outlook on Life.* She died in 1958.

KATHERINE ANNE PORTER

Katherine Anne Porter is rated by most critics as one of the outstanding stylists among living American writers. She gives us a clue to some of the reasons why in the following autobiographical paragraph:

"As soon as I learned to form letters on paper, at about three years, I began to write stories, and this has been the basic and absorbing occupation, the intact line of my life which directs my actions, determines my point of view, profoundly affects my character and personality, my social beliefs and economic status, and the kind of friendships I form. I did not choose this vocation, and if I had had any sense in the matter, I would not have chosen it. . . . Yet for this vocation I was and am willing to live and die, and I consider very few other things of the slightest importance."

Miss Porter was born in Indian Creek, Texas, in 1894, the great-great-great-granddaughter of Daniel Boone. Even as a child she never stayed in one spot for long. She has lived all over the world — in Chicago, New York, Mexico City, Berlin, Paris, Bermuda, and Italy. Recently, she has been living in Washington, D. C.

After a handful of her early stories had appeared in magazines, they were collected in a limited edition, in 1930, under the title *Flowering Judas* — which promptly became a collector's item. Shortly after, she received a Guggenheim Fellowship and went to Europe where she lived for a number of years. She returned to America in 1935; the same year *Flowering Judas* was reissued with two short and two long stories added. That book brought her a Book-of-the-Month Fellowship and, in 1938, another Guggenheim grant. *Pale Horse, Pale Rider* (a collection of three novelettes), published in 1939, was awarded the gold medal of the Society for the Libraries of New York University, and *The Leaning Tower*, a book of short stories, excited critics. In 1944 Katherine Anne Porter was elected a Fellow of Regional American Literature in the Library of Congress.

Miss Porter's first novel *Ship of Fools* (1962) was on best-seller lists for months, and was made into a popular movie. She spent more than twenty years writing and polishing this novel; it has been called "the crown of her career." Currently, she is busy writing her memoirs, and continuing a historical study of Cotton Mather and the Salem witchcraft trials, which she started in 1928. In addition, she says she is considering writing a medieval mystery story.

STEPHEN VINCENT BENÉT

Most of the stories in this book were chosen because of the picture they present of life in America today. We feel that this story by Stephen Vincent Benét belongs here too, along with the rest, to remind us of the kind of men who did so much to establish the traditions of American democracy. The setting of the story is around 1775, but the truths in it are timeless.

Stephen Vincent Benét, poet, short-story writer, novelist, was born in Bethlehem, Pennsylvania, in 1898, because his Army family happened to be stationed there at the time. Like most military households, they moved about the country from post to post, and the three Benét children grew up in a constantly changing scene — New England, California, and points in between. For generations the Benét men had belonged to the army, first in Spain, then in America. The present generation of Benét sons, however, broke away from that tradition and, with their sister, turned unanimously and successfully to writing. Soon all three, William Rose, Stephen Vincent, and Laura Benét, presented a triple threat on another kind of front — literature.

Stephen Vincent Benét began publishing when he was twelve and kept steadily at it. His first poems won him gold and silver badges from the old *St. Nicholas Magazine*; his later writings have gone on winning him prizes of distinction. In 1929 his book-length poem about our Civil War, *John Brown's Body*, was awarded the Pulitzer Prize; his short story "The Devil and Daniel Webster" was named the best short story of its year. His *Selected Works* came out in 1942. Stephen Vincent Benét died in 1943.

KATHARINE BRUSH

Born in Middletown, Connecticut, in 1902, Katharine Ingham Brush lived in Washington, D. C., and in Baltimore, until her father was made headmaster at a boys' preparatory school in Newbury, Massachusetts. Like so many other authors, her introduction to writing was a newspaper job — mostly drama and movie reviews. Later she tried a bit of poetry, then discovered herself (and alert magazine editors discovered her) in the field of popular fiction. She published some hundred-odd short stories, more than half a dozen books, wrote occasional screen originals (about two a year), and a weekly syndicated newspaper column called *Out of My Mind.* One of her earliest novels was the very popular *Young Man of Manhattan;* the last was *This Man and This Woman.* She also wrote *Boy from Maine* and *You Go Your Way.* The only nonfiction book on her list is her autobiography, *This Is On Me,* which she herself termed hodgepodge, but which critics called a frank stock taking, full of good sense and good humor. Katharine Brush died in 1952.

"Fumble," the story included in this collection, tells of a young man and his inferiority complex. It is one of Miss Brush's earliest stories and one of her best.

MARTHA FOLEY

Martha Foley's fame as a writer and editor has risen steadily, with the result that she now holds one of the very top positions in the short-story field. Miss Foley is the editor of the annual Best Short Stories anthologies which for twenty-six years were edited by the late short-story expert Edward J. O'Brien. Miss Foley has continued to keep up the fine quality of these volumes. She says in her introduction to *The Best American Short Stories of 1953*: "One of the most important services a volume like this can perform is to bring to intelligent readers stories of permanent literary value they otherwise would miss."

Miss Foley was born in Boston, where she went to the Girls' Latin School and later to Boston University. She began her writing career as a reporter and caption writer on the staffs of San Francisco, Los Angeles, and New York newspapers before she went to Europe in

1926. There she worked on the Paris edition of the New York *Herald,* and was sent to the Balkans as foreign correspondent. In Vienna, in 1931, she and Whit Burnett — newspaperman and short-story writer — founded the magazine *Story.* She left *Story* in 1942 to begin editing the short-story annual.

Miss Foley has lectured extensively on the short story at Columbia University, the University of Colorado, and New York University. She has also helped Scholastic judge its annual Writing Awards.

JOHN STEINBECK

When John Steinbeck was writing his first novel he got a job in a fish hatchery at Lake Tahoe, California. He liked that job but when asked why, he could only reply vaguely, "Oh, all the little fishes." That answer explains a lot about John Steinbeck. Little fishes — little people — ordinary lives, are what interest him most; these he writes about with deep understanding. His first successful book, *Tortilla Flat,* was about the Mexican paisanos of Monterey; his next, *Of Mice and Men,* told the story of two migratory farm hands on a California ranch; his most talked-about book, *The Grapes of Wrath* (which won him the Pulitzer Prize in 1940), was an earnest and compelling saga of the westward trek of the small farmers and sharecroppers of our Dust Bowl in search of a self-respecting way of life. Some of his other famous books include *The Moon Is Down, Cannery Row, The Wayward Bus, The Pearl,* and *The Red Pony.* His best-seller *East of Eden* was published in 1952. *Travels With Charley* (a fascinating account of his trailer trip throughout the U.S., accompanied by his poodle) was published in 1963. In it, Steinbeck chats casually with hundreds of "little people" — everyday Americans who sometimes reveal incredible optimism and courage, sometimes weaknesses.

John Ernst Steinbeck was born in 1902 in Salinas, which is located in the heart of the lettuce-growing country of California. Like so many other boys, he worked while he was going to the Salinas High School — running cultivators, doing odd jobs on the surrounding cattle ranches among the people he was to write about later. After attending Stanford University off and on for a number of years, he moved to New York, where he held down a reporter's job until he was fired, then carried bricks to help build Madison Square Garden. He returned to California to write his first novel, *Cup of Gold*, and remained there for many years until he once again became a New Yorker. In 1962 Steinbeck was awarded the Nobel Prize in Literature, principally for his novel *The Winter of Our Discontent*. He was honored for his "realistic and imaginative writings, distinguished by a sympathetic humor and a social perception." He now lives on Long Island.

C. D. B. BRYAN

Born in New York, in 1936, Courtlandt Dixon Barnes Bryan has been a circus roustabout, a jazz guitarist, and a ranch wrangler. He served as a first lieutenant in the U. S. Air Force in Okinawa, in Korea, and during the Berlin crisis of 1961.

"So Much Unfairness of Things" was his first published story; it originally appeared in the *New Yorker* magazine. His other short stories have been published in the *New Yorker*, in *Good Housekeeping*, and *Mademoiselle*.

"I am trying to become as professional and as good a writer as I can," Mr. Bryan has commented. "I take it extremely seriously." Critics have taken his work seriously. His only novel to date, *P. S. Wilkinson*, was awarded the Harper Prize in 1965, and his *Jack and Jackie: A Perfect Day for Honeyfitz* was placed in the Kennedy Library at the Kennedys' request.

A writer-in-residence at Colorado State University, he has also written articles, criticism, movie narration, and political satire.

SINCLAIR LEWIS

Sinclair Lewis, novelist, short-story writer, playwright, and sometime actor, was born in 1885, in Sauk Center, Minnesota, better known to the millions of readers of *Main Street* as Gopher Prairie. The neighbors who saw the lanky red-headed Lewis kid jogging around the country with his doctor father (sometimes holding the horses, sometimes holding the instruments in emergency operations) little suspected then that this young mind was photographing everything it came in contact with for future reference. The boy himself couldn't have suspected that some day he was to write a book that would make Sauk Center famous; that he was to be the first American to receive the Nobel Prize for Literature (in 1930); that he would spurn a Pulitzer Prize; and that, all in all, he would become one of America's best-known writers.

After graduating from Yale, Sinclair Lewis tried out a few new ideas by living in Upton Sinclair's Utopian colony in New Jersey; he went to sea on a cattle boat; he traveled to Panama on a wild goose chase to help dig the canal; and he finally turned up in San Francisco with a job as a reporter. Later he took six months off for serious writing and sold one item — a joke. Then, in 1920, after the publication of five novels which didn't cause a ripple, *Main Street* came out, and the resulting tidal wave of pros and cons was felt around the world.

Sinclair Lewis published a long list of novels, some adding to his stature as a man with a peculiar genius for isolating the germ of American culture, some run-of-the-mill. Best on the list are *Arrowsmith*, in which Lewis created a genuine hero, a doctor, whose complete devotion to science and truth cuts him off from material success and personal relationships; *Babbitt*, which did for the average American businessman what *Main Street* had done for the average American town; *Dodsworth*, a great success as novel, play, and movie; and *It Can't Happen Here*, a book about the threat of Fascism in this country.

More recent were *Prodigal Parents, Bethel Merriday, Gideon Planish, Cass Timberlane,* and *Kingsblood Royal.* Since his death in 1951, Random House has published *Man from Main Street: A Sinclair Lewis Reader, 1903-1950.*

IRWIN SHAW

Irwin Shaw, short-story writer, novelist, movie scenarist, and playwright, was born in 1913 in Brooklyn, New York, where he started his literary career at the age of twelve with a series of essays published in the school paper. At Brooklyn College he divided his extra-curricular time between more writing and four years of varsity football, baseball, and basketball. After leaving school he carried his talent for, and interest in, the theatre to the radio, where he met with great success in writing serial dramatizations of the famous comic strips *Dick Tracy* and *The Gumps.*

In 1936 he was in Hollywood, where his flair for rich and forceful dialogue had inevitably led him, when his one-act play *Bury the Dead* opened in New York. He flew East for the opening. The success of the play and the critics' praise were enough to cheer any young writer's heart — especially a young writer whose first eighteen stories had been turned down. Since then Irwin Shaw has had seven other plays produced. His brilliant novel of World War II, *The Young Lions,* was praised widely. In 1951 his novel about Red witch hunts in the broadcasting business, *The Troubled Air,* was published. His short stories, among them "Strawberry Ice Cream Soda," have been collected in the volume *Mixed Company.* His recent novels include *Two Weeks in Another Town* (1960) and *Voices of a Summer Day* (1965).

Mr. Shaw has lived in Europe since 1951. He is now working on a travel book, a novel, and a play.